WHIRLPOOL

Also by Barry Estabrook

Bahama Heat

Whirlpool

Barry Estabrook

St. Martin's Press
New York

This is a work of fiction and all names, characters, and incidents are entirely imaginary. Any resemblance to actual events or to persons living or dead is coincidental.

WHIRLPOOL. Copyright © 1995 by Barry Estabrook. All rights reserved. Printed in the United States of America. No part of this book may be used or reproduced in any manner whatsoever without written permission except in the case of brief quotations embodied in critical articles or reviews. For information, address St. Martin's Press, 175 Fifth Avenue, New York, N.Y. 10010.

Design by Nancy Resnick

Library of Congress Cataloging-in-Publication Data

Estabrook, Barry.
    Whirlpool / Barry Estabrook.
       p.   cm.
    "A Thomas Dunne book."
    ISBN 0-312-13622-6
    I. Title.
PS3555.S7W48   1995
813'.54—dc20
                                              95-30627
                                                  CIP

First Edition: October 1995

10 9 8 7 6 5 4 3 2 1

WHIRLPOOL

1

Had eleven-year-old Duane Dockwheiller known the first thing about catching trout in Adirondack rivers, there is no telling how long it would have been before anyone discovered what really happened to Barron Quinell IV.

But until that day, a sultry Monday, July 13, Duane's angling had been confined to a stunted population of bullheads in an abandoned quarry beside U.S. 31, just north of Kokomo, Indiana.

The boy had no way of knowing that his father, Dave, had pulled the family's Impala station wagon and attached Prowler trailer off Route 86 up to one of the Ausable River's most over-fished and fished-out pools—recently set aside for catch-and-release angling only. As soon as the car stopped, Duane was out and sprinting toward the water, which, in his imagination, was teeming with the trophy-size browns, rainbows, and brookies of outdoor magazines and Saturday-morning fishing shows.

Coming back to the Prowler at a trot, Duane said to his parents, "Think I'll wet a line."

He went into the trailer and emerged carrying a Zebco rod and reel set. His lure was a plastic imitation minnow measuring eight inches from its clear lip to the fierce gang of treble hooks dangling off its tail.

"Don't think you'll catch anything with that here," said Dave, dipping his chin toward the lure. "Bigger'n most of the trout in these mountain streams. Anyway, nothing's gonna be biting at high noon—and in this heat." He let out a long *"whew"* to emphasize the last point. "Must be ninety."

Duane settled a pair of wraparound Polaroids onto the bridge of his nose. "Never know," he said, his voice carrying a note of authority meant to go with the glasses. "Besides—" He stopped while Dave upended the last dusty bits from a bag of briquets into the family's portable grill. When his dad looked up, Duane said, "Isn't anything else to do around here," and was off again, swinging the rod determinedly in one hand, carrying a plastic tackle box in the other.

"You be back in time for lunch, now, hear," Dave said to the backside of his son.

"And careful around that river. There's currents," said Ma, whose bulk was squeezed into a lawn chair behind a camp table. Her hands were converting the contents of a two-pound pack of Grand Union ground beef into patties.

"Be just like that boy to go and catch himself a lunker," said Dave. He took a swipe at the sweat on his forehead with the back of his arm before uncapping a can of charcoal lighter.

Ma wiped her hands on a paper towel. "Be more like that boy to fall in and get soaked—or worse. That river must have currents, coming out of these mountains." She emitted a quiet "dear" and fished in a cooler, pulling up two cans of Coke. "One for yourself, Pa?" she said.

Dave tossed a match and waited until flames and black smoke were coming off the grill. "Maybe after I've gone and seen what Duane's up to."

Ma smiled sweetly over her Coke can.

Dave found Duane a hundred yards downstream. The boy had worked his way out toward the center of the river over a series of slick-looking stepping-stones the size, shape, and color of the medicine balls kids toss to each other in gym class. Brandishing his rod, Duane balanced on the rock farthest from shore.

"You watch it, son," said Dave.

The current split in front of Duane's rock, making the water a shade lighter there than the deep tea color just a few feet further out. Fifty yards downstream, brownish hues gave way to the white froth of a set of rapids where the Ausable narrowed and drove itself between a half-dozen boulders every bit as big as the trailer attached to the back of the Dockwheillers' car.

Duane did not acknowledge his father. He held his lips in a no-nonsense frown. His Cubs cap sat extra-low over the Polaroids. Once, twice, he false-cast his lure, letting its weight pull the rod tip back and then whip it forward. The third time he let fly. And got off a fairly decent cast. In a low, line-drive trajectory, his lure shot over the water and plopped into a whirlpool just behind the first of the boulders.

He fired a quick glance over his shoulder—just long enough to take in the smile of paternal approval that blossomed upon Dave's face—then snapped his attention back to the river.

"Give her some action, son," counseled Dave, and got one brief, annoyed glare for his efforts. He shrugged and to himself said, "Do it your way."

Duane cranked the reel twice, then gave the rod tip a half-hearted jerk. When that had no effect, he cranked again, and this time ended with a mighty yank that might have sent him backward off the rock, had one of the lure's treble hooks not imbedded itself in something. Duane's rod bent. The reel's drag screeched. "Got a hit!" he cried.

Dave chuckled. "Got yourself a snag there, son, I believe."

Duane pulled, giving forth a deep and manly grunt. His rod bent further. His line whistled. "Don't feel like no snag," he said.

"Well then, you do have yourself a lunker, son," said Dave, trying this time to keep the chuckles to himself. "Like maybe the size of one of them boulders out there. Looks about that energetic, too. Line isn't moving at all."

Duane pulled, released the pressure, and pulled again. Repeated

-3-

that routine three more times. "No," he said. "I felt something move."

"Maybe you're hooked onto a sunken tree branch."

Duane tugged twice. Gave one long heave. His line began to swing downstream. "Ain't no snag, Pa. It's a lunker—makin' a run for it."

Dave watched his son's line take off, picking up speed as it moved toward the rapids. "If that is a fish, son, better try to turn him before he gets to that white water. You'll lose him for sure in that mess."

Duane pulled until his arms quivered. "Can't, Pa. He won't stop." Duane's line was directly downstream.

"A Dockwheiller never uses that 'can't' word, son. Lift your rod."

Duane raised his Zebco overhead and leaned back. Slowly, his line began to rise. "He's gonna break water."

"Just take her easy now, son," said Dave. "Keep him coming just like that. Steady now. You don't want to give him any slack when he jumps. Just keep the tension on, son. See where he's coming up just beside that big rock there. He's gonna give us a look at him. See, son! Now!"

In the instant before the line broke, Duane did get a glimpse of his catch. It was a human hand, hooked in the fleshy part of the palm; Duane's line was wrapped once around the middle finger. From that angle, it almost looked like the hand's owner was flipping the old, familiar one-finger salute to the father and son from Kokomo, Indiana.

As a final earthly gesture, Barron Quinell IV would have loved it.

2

When dispatch phoned, New York State Trooper Garwood Plunkett was alone in his mobile home just outside the village of Wilmington, tying his fourth Ausable Wulff of the morning. It being his day off, Plunkett intended to try the flies on one particular brown trout, an old adversary that lived in a deep hole in the Saranac River. He had already caught and released the fish three times.

Plunkett let his hackle pliers drop and began to paw through the mess on what had once been his wife's dining room table, but now served as a catch-all for the paraphernalia of his fly-tying obsession: a vise, scissors, bottles of glue, clear plastic boxes of hooks, spools of thread (brown, black, silver, red, and orange), tinsel, bucktails, squirrel tails, a menagerie's worth of feathers and fur, and, somewhere, a warbling cordless telephone.

After three attempts, Plunkett uncovered the phone and managed to punch the right button. The trooper on the other end informed Plunkett that some old guy over by the village of Jay had barricaded himself inside his house. His wife was in there with him. Their daughter came to visit, and he fired two shots at her. First trooper on the scene got a one-shot reception and called for assistance.

So much for Plunkett's morning off.

* * *

When Plunkett pulled up fifteen minutes after getting the call, there were three vehicles on the shoulder of the road in front of the old man's house. On the protected side of a marked state police cruiser, the old man's daughter crouched beside Trooper Brenda Jaworski, one of Plunkett's five colleagues in the Wilmington patrol station. Squatting next to Jaworski in a summer-weight, fawn suit, with his Glock nine pointed at a cluster of cones halfway up a nearby white pine, was Sr. Investigator Brian Culley. Take away the Glock and replace it with a handful of apocalyptic literature, and the well-dressed Culley could have passed for a proselytizing Jehovah's Witness—in which case Plunkett wouldn't totally begrudge the old guy a pot shot or two.

Culley began a frantic chopping motion with his free hand as soon as Plunkett stopped his car. Plunkett got out, being careful not to scrape his head on the car's door frame. When Plunkett stood to full height, Culley substituted a downward pushing motion for his chopping.

"He's got a gun," Culley whispered hoarsely, as if the old guy was going to hear a normal speaking voice at that distance. Culley made a series of grimaces to go along with his pushing and chopping. "Get down, for God's sake."

Plunkett settled his Stetson and strode toward Culley, making no effort to get down, figuring that a cop slinking around was more likely to stimulate the old guy's trigger finger than one going about business in a more or less normal fashion.

Plunkett nodded a hello to Trooper Jaworski and addressed the sobbing woman at her side, remembering her name from high school. "Morning, Ila."

Ila stopped sobbing long enough to say, "He's got Mom in there," and burst out crying again.

The shack was a good hundred yards from the road in a grove of white pines whose ancient, drooping boughs would have lent a nursery-rhyme atmosphere to the setting, had it not been for three junked cars, a skeletonized snowmobile frame, one discarded washing machine, and—incongruously—a bright, white satellite dish angled toward the summit of Saddleback Mountain. Where it hadn't peeled and ripped off, reddish Insulbrick sheathed the one-and-one-half-story house from the eaves to a ragged line of unpainted clapboards about three feet off the ground. The two front windows were still partially covered in torn flaps of construction plastic meant to substitute for storm windows. A head appeared behind one of the translucent flaps and ducked back.

"Hector into the whisky again?" Plunkett asked.

Ila got control of her sobs. Breathed deeply. "I'd be surprised if the old fool isn't. Two days I've been callin'. Him refusing to let Mom talk to me. So today I thought I'd drive over and take a look for myself and he—"

She nodded at Jaworski, who said: "Shot at me, too."

"We have back-up personnel coming," Culley said, trying his best to sound authoritative and in command.

Plunkett shook his head. "Christ, Brian," he said, picturing the place swarming with cops—a hostage negotiator, Bureau of Criminal Investigation guys. Hell, he wouldn't have put it past Culley to have called in the Mobile Response Team. Having all those officers around was not only unnecessary, but it pretty well guaranteed someone was going to get shot, either a policeman, the hostage, or an old guy who until that hot summer morning had always gone peaceably enough about his business.

Plunkett muttered, "Back-up personnel," and stepped around the front of the car.

"He's already discharged his weapon three times," warned Culley.

Plunkett cast a bored look over his shoulder. "And missed." For Culley's benefit, Plunkett directed a question to Ila. "When was the last time your father missed three times in a row—drunk or sober?"

Plunkett made it halfway up the rutted dirt driveway before Hector fired. Plunkett flinched—a useless reflex in the face of 180 grains of soft-point lead screaming out of a .303's muzzle at a couple of thousand feet per second. At least Plunkett assumed that was what would be coming toward him. Hector's tool of choice during a six-decade career, sometimes as a guide, sometimes as a poacher, had always been a World War II Lee-Enfield.

The bullet flitted through the leaves of a red maple to Plunkett's immediate right, sending down a few small branches. From the shack, Plunkett heard what sounded like a yowl from a sick calf. He touched the butt of his automatic and took a few more strides.

"*Getoutahere.*"

The black barrel of the Enfield appeared between two of the plastic strips. There was a loud *crack*. This one made the air sizzle somewhere between Plunkett's left earlobe and his shoulder.

"Hector. It's me. Garwood Plunkett. You remember. Woody's boy." Plunkett took off the Stetson and tossed it onto the hard-packed earth of the driveway. "Just want to talk, that's all. Here, look." He put down his Glock beside the hat.

There was silence from the house. Plunkett took a few hesitant steps. "Just want to talk. I'm alone. Unarmed. Okay to come up?"

When no shots came his way, Plunkett increased his walking pace, slowing only when he got to the four rotting two-by-tens laid parallel to the house as a makeshift back stoop.

"I'm coming in, Hector," Plunkett said. He listened. There was no answer, just the muffled sounds of a TV talk show somewhere inside. He opened the door, one of those cheap, unfinished, hollow-core models designed to be easy for weekend carpenters to hang inside the house.

The door opened onto a kitchen. Pots, pans, dishes, bowls, cups, glasses—most sprouting mold—occupied every flat surface except a crescent of pink marbled Formica on the kitchen table just big enough for two over-flowing ashtrays and a fifth of Canadian Club. Houseflies were everywhere, buzzing. Three open green garbage bags took up half the floor space, spilling their contents and explaining the room's smell—the cloying rankness of stale meat.

"One more fucking step and you're dead."

The old man stepped into the doorway at the far end of the kitchen. White spikes of his overgrown flattop protruded at odd angles. Hector's eyes, the palest of blues, were rheumy and rimmed with red. His mouth hung open just wide enough to reveal a single, tobacco-tarnished lower tooth.

Hector rested a shoulder against the door frame for support. He held the heavy old military rifle under one arm, his finger on the trigger guard and the muzzle wobbling in tiny orbits that would have put the bullet a few inches to either side of Plunkett's left nipple, depending on when Hector chose to pull the trigger.

Plunkett took a deep, slow breath, trying to get used to the stench, aware of the syrupy rhythms of Geraldo's voice coming from the next room.

"Don't worry, Hector. Just come to talk, that's all." Plunkett put out his hands, palms open, and risked another shuffling half step.

Hector jerked the rifle upward. The muzzle pointed at Plunkett's forehead. "Leave us be."

Plunkett stopped. Considered Hector's *us*. A good sign. The old girl was still alive. He said, "Hector. We can settle this whole thing."

The rifle returned to its former position and started wobbling again.

"Hector, don't you remember me?" Plunkett spread his arms. "Woody Plunkett's boy."

Hector closed one eye. Now it was Hector that was wobbling, the rifle muzzle staying in place. He closed the other eye and let out a short, high pitched *"Heh-heh."*

Plunkett took another step.

Both eyes opened. Hector smiled the best smile his single-toothed mouth could form. "Woody, old buddy," he said. "It's been ages since I seen you. Why didn't you say it was you all along? You still guidin'? Catchin' any fish lately?"

Plunkett took another step, keeping his eyes on the rifle, letting Hector think he was talking to Woody Plunkett, not Woody's cop kid.

"Don't imagine so." Hector answered his own question. "Not in this goddamn heat we've been having. Water gets any warmer, you're gonna start seeing a die-off like we had back in 'thirty-six. I'm telling you, Woody, it's the fucking *ooze-own* shot all to rat shit.

Goddamn under-arm deodorant they spray. Women's putting it on their pussies now an' everywhere. Ruinin' the *ooze-own* just so they don't smell like a woman no more. No, Woody, things is all screwed up. Good thing you opened that store. Won't be long before all us old guides have to find another way to make a living."

He nodded once, so emphatically Plunkett thought it might send that last surviving tooth flying from his gums. The rifle muzzle dropped. Plunkett took another step. Hector snapped it back in place.

"But hell, Woody, it's good you came by. How them two boys a yours doing? See the one that owns the junkyard outside of Wilmington every so often. Heard the other turned out to be a cop or something. I said, 'No son of Woody Plunkett . . .'" Hector nodded. "No tellin' what kids'll go and do. My daughter . . . ungrateful little . . ." Hector snorted. "What the hell." He shook his head as if to clear it of unpleasant memories and gazed at Plunkett, confused. "But where's my manners?" He hollered over his shoulder, "Mabel, Woody Plunkett's dropped over. Fix us a drink." There was no response. "Mabel!" He twisted his head over his shoulder. Plunkett took another step. "Goddammit, woman!"

Geraldo's studio audience booed.

Hector looked humiliated, the boos might well have been directed at him. "My old woman's no goddamn good no more," he said, man-to-man, gesturing with the rifle muzzle toward the Canadian Club on the kitchen table. "I'll pour you one. She's gotten too goddamn lazy to get off her butt. All she wants to do is sit and watch that TV all day. Worst thing in the world, a woman and a TV. Woulda never got it had I known. But that's what she wanted. Eightieth birthday and she says to me, 'Hector, I want me a color TV before I die.' So I go to that new Sears store there b'side the Northway in Plattsburgh and got her one." Hector swallowed once, his Adam's apple bobbing up and down beneath the turkey-wattled skin of his neck. He said in a choked voice, "An' I think I lost her to it."

He shook his head. "But hell, Woody, go on in. Mabel'd love to see you, anyways. I'll fix us up."

Hector kept the rifle trained on Plunkett and stepped into the kitchen. He waved his hand over the dishes in the sink to flush the flies settled there and then plucked out a jam-jar glass. "Go on in." He gave a gesture with the rifle.

Beyond the door frame was a short hallway with a staircase leading to the second floor on one side and, on the other, the front entry, with fluffy, pink, fiberglass insulation stapled over it. Geraldo's prattle came from the next room.

The curtains were drawn and the only light in that room came from the TV. White-haired and scarecrow-thin, Mabel Hull reclined forty-five degrees in an orange Naugahyde-upholstered La-Z-Boy with a black-and-red-striped trapper blanket folded over her calves, *TV Guide* facedown on her lap, her dark eyes deep in their sockets and staring straight ahead, mesmerized as Geraldo shoved his microphone at some guy in the audience.

"Hello, Mabel," said Plunkett, then louder, "Hello."

Geraldo turned away from the guy, put the mike up to his own mouth, and said something directly into the camera, eyes wide, face contorted into a grossly exaggerated look of indignation. The camera panned to two women—mother and daughter to look at them. Both of their cheeks glistened with tears.

Plunkett came closer. On an aluminum TV table beside the La-Z-Boy was a white-bread sandwich, its edges beginning to turn upwards. A bowl sat there, too, filled with soggy cereal—corn flakes or bran flakes. And there was that same rank meat odor as in the kitchen, only stronger.

"Mabel," said Plunkett, leaning close enough to look into her eyes in the flickering light cast by the TV.

It took a fraction of a second to realize that there was something wrong with the old woman's eyes, then to see what it was: flies. Her eyes were crawling with flies.

Plunkett reeled. He felt a tickle in the back of his throat. Something down there pushing to come back out.

Hector came into the room with the rims of two jam jars pinched between his thumb and index finger, the perfect host, were it not for the .303 tucked under his other arm.

"Won't get a word outta her, Woody, I'm telling you. Not a civil word, not with old Geraldo on. Won't speak. Won't get off her butt. Not even to eat—"

"Hector, Mabel's dead." Plunkett was still swallowing, trying not to inhale through his nostrils or remember the sight of those flies.

The old man snorted. "Bone lazy's more like it."

"Hector," said Plunkett.

The reddened rims tightened around Hector's eyes. He stood swaying and finally put the whiskies on top of a chest of drawers. "You aren't Woody Plunkett," he said, taking the rifle in both hands. "Just who the fuck do you think you are, anyways? Bustin' in here handin' me that sort of bull crap. Been married to that goddamn woman for sixty-three years. You think I wouldn't know—"

"Mabel's dead, Hector. . . . I'm sorry."

Hector swallowed and lowered his cheek to the rifle's stock, aiming. "Shuddup!" he said. "You're no goddamn better than that daughter of mine. Trying to get us locked away so she can sell off this place. You tell them that me and Mabel is getting along just fine on our own. Just fine. Don't need no one meddlin'."

A tear dripped out of his open eye and ran over the bridge of his nose before dropping onto the rifle's stock.

Plunkett reached out. "She's gone, Hector," he said.

The old man sobbed. "Sixty-three goddamn years . . ."

"Just let me have the rifle, Hector." Plunkett took a step toward Hector, waited until another series of sobs wracked his old body and then shot his hand out toward the barrel.

Peering over the top of the cruiser, Jaworski heard the crack of a single rifle shot from inside the shack.

She inhaled one sharp breath. "Shit," she said, feeling her face go cold in the silence that followed the shot.

Culley, still in a half-crouch, said, "Get down, for Christ's sake."

"But Plunkett's . . ." said Jaworski. She twisted and raised herself far enough to see the shack through the car's windows. "If it was one of us—"

"Plunkett broke protocol."

"Plunkett's . . ." Jaworski let her voice trail off. What the hell was *she* supposed to say to Culley, there in his suit: That Plunkett was a good cop? That he would do something if it was one of them in there, shot, maybe lying on the floor of the shack bleeding to death? She sure as hell wasn't about to explain to the likes of Culley that Plunkett also was the only person in Troop B who didn't appear to give a damn one way or another that she happened to be a woman, and how that was more important to her than anything.

To hell with Culley. Jaworski decided to circle around through the trees to the back of the house. Alone and without cover, if she had to. It was better than just doing nothing.

She had taken the first stride in that direction, Culley going "Hey! What the—" when Hector came out all by himself and began to stagger toward them. Culley stood beside Jaworski, taking a two-handed grip on his Glock over the top of the car.

"He's unarmed," said Jaworski.

"That man just shot a state trooper," said Culley, working his fingers more firmly around the pistol, getting into that two-handed stance they taught recruits down at the academy, where you had all the time in the world to line up your target before you shot.

Hector twisted his head back toward the house. He stumbled and went down on one knee, staying there, face craned over his shoulder.

A moment later, the tall, square-built form of Plunkett appeared, casually toting a rifle in one hand the way most guys do after a long and not particularly successful day in the woods.

Plunkett felt more annoyed than relieved when he got back to the cars, guiding old Hector along by a bony elbow, unable to cleanse himself of the stink of that house. "Take him," he said, giving Hector a gentle push toward Culley. "I'm feeling a little shaken-up." He glanced back toward the shack and sighed. "Looks like the old woman passed away a couple of days ago. Heart attack would be my guess. Old man lost it, that's all. That shot just now was accidental—me pulling the rifle away."

Culley twisted the old guy's arms around his back and snapped on a pair of handcuffs.

Plunkett shook his head and went over to Ila.

"Mom?" she whimpered.

"Ila," said Plunkett. For some inexplicable reason he remembered a summer day, hell, probably twenty-five years ago. He was down by Lake Everest with his best friend, Mark James, learning how to inhale L&Ms and watching the girls sunbathe. One of them was perky, flirtatious Ila Hull. Leaning back on the grass, Mark James puffed expertly and, in a voice filled with wisdom and experience, claimed that Ila would never let you go all the way, but she was the easiest feel in the school. All you had to do was buy her a sundae.

"Ila," Plunkett said again, and laid an arm over her shoulders. He didn't even know what had become of Mark James. And since school, he hadn't given two thoughts to Ila Hull, the easiest feel of them all. Now she seemed squat and dull and at least a decade older than she should have been.

"She's gone, isn't she," said Ila.

Plunkett nodded. "Passed away. Your dad didn't—"

Ila buried her face against his chest, sobbed once, and pulled back, nodding matter-of-factly. "Thanks," she said, and walked toward the house, leaving Plunkett standing there beside Jaworski.

"Mind looking after her?" Plunkett said.

Jaworski shook her face, as if awakening. She took a step toward Ila.

"Jaworski," said Plunkett.

She turned.

"Whatever you do, keep her out of that place. In fact, I'd seal it off until the coroner gets here." He tried to swallow away memories of that stink, Geraldo, the flies. "It's pretty bad."

Plunkett was in the car, ignition on, thinking maybe he'd go home and see if one or two of the Gennies he had in the fridge would help wash away images of that place. Culley tapped on the window.

"You still want me to handle things with the old guy?" said Culley.

Plunkett nodded, his mind on those Gennies. A genuine smile replaced the smirk on Culley's face. "Then I guess you won't mind taking a drive over to the other side of Wilmington. Some tourist family called in on their CB. Looks like you might have yourself a floater."

3

Plunkett's right knee started shaking just after he drove through the village of Wilmington. By the time he passed his younger brother's bodyshop/junkyard on the other side of town, it was so bad he had to pull the Caprice to the shoulder of Route 86 and sit there, catching his breath, drumming his thumbs against the steering wheel, thinking, So this is what happens when you stay a road trooper too long: you get cocky, and after you have gotten away with that a few times, you start trusting your instincts, not the procedure manual, and one afternoon the .303 slug doesn't zip through the leaves overhead.

Or you run into one too many sights like poor old Mabel. Her sitting there, flies feasting on her eyes. In twenty years as a trooper, Plunkett had seen his share: highway accidents, drowning victims, guys who couldn't take it anymore, so they swallowed the muzzles of their duck guns and pulled the trigger. But nothing like Mabel. And now a floater. His day.

Plunkett popped the car back into gear.

Just beyond High Falls Gorge, Plunkett saw the trailer. YOU'VE GOT FRIENDS IN KOKOMO, THE DOCKWHEILLER FAMILY announced a yard-long placard. The rest of the rear end of the trailer was covered by bumper stickers—dozens of them—certifying that Plunkett's new Kokomo friends had been ripped off by most of the major tourist traps east of the Mississippi.

He found them huddled together on the far side of the trailer, a grill gone out in front of them, a stack of uncooked hamburgers on a folding table. There was a large bleached blond woman, a lanky gray-haired man, and a fair-haired boy, whose belly suggested he would inherit his mother's build. The man came forward, kid a few paces behind.

"Afternoon, Trooper," said the man, speaking with a slight twang. He stuck out a hand, then, as if realizing the gravity of the situation, pulled it back, shoved it in his pocket. "M' boy here was just down by the river there." He took the hand out of the pocket just long enough to sweep it in the general direction of the 500 feet of sheer rock cliff that shot up from the far side of the river. "Hooked onto something. Can't be sure, sir, but it looked like a body." He nodded, saying, "A human body. Drifted off that way." He directed his pointy chin toward the rapids.

Plunkett lifted his Stetson and wiped his brow. The waterfalls and whirlpools in that narrow stretch of the Ausable were deep enough and powerful enough to suck down a city bus. Finding a corpse—if there was one—wasn't likely to be any fun.

"Rescue is on its way," said Plunkett. "When they come, tell them I've gone down for a look. You folks better stay here."

Plunkett followed a fishermen's path through a grove of aspen saplings growing between the river and Route 86. The path led to a deep, quiet pool at the base of the rapids. Plunkett stood on the bank, looking back up toward the thundering white water. Slowly, he shifted his gaze to the pool at his feet, tea-colored and calm, except for where it was broken by eddies and bubbles sent down from above. Nowhere was there any sign of a corpse.

Plunkett stepped onto some rocks that formed a transition between the earthen banks and the river. He leaned out to see around an alder thicket that overhung the bank twenty yards downstream.

There was a small riffle at the far end of the alders. Something about it didn't look natural. Plunkett scrambled up the bank until he found the path again. It skirted the alders and came back down to a crescent of dark sand not much bigger than a door mat.

The body was lying on its back on the miniature beach, shoulders on the sand, feet in the water. Guy looked so comfortable stretched out there in the sun beside the river he could well have been midway through a pleasant noontime nap.

Rescue showed up five minutes later: two volunteers from Wilmington, one about twenty-one or -two, the other maybe a couple of years older. Plunkett remembered the older one. Coached him in little league, it seemed like a summer or two back. But must have been more like a decade. The clumsy kid Plunkett remembered as an error-prone shortstop was now speaking in a grown man's baritone and acting like a fully responsible paramedic.

He slid down the bank, hugging the jump kit to his lap.

"Hello, trooper," he said cheerfully. "Anything to get in a little fishing, that it? Caught yourself a dandy." He laughed with the forced bonhomie some guys put on when they want to show-off their familiarity with the forces of the law. Plunkett figured no harm was meant. Certainly no disrespect. But it was beginning to make him feel uneasy, these constant reminders that there was a clear line between *we* and *they*, with Plunkett on one side and the rest of his friends and neighbors and even their kids, now, on the other.

"Could have saved yourself the bother of lugging that down here," Plunkett said, indicating the jump kit.

The rescue guy cast his trained eye over the corpse. It was clad in chest waders, the exposed skin of its face and hands grayish and mottled. "Guess we didn't have to break any speed limits for this one," he said.

"May as well leave it right here until the coroner comes," said Plunkett. "Never know . . ."

Plunkett let his voice trail off. For the first time, he noticed what might have been swelling on the left side of the corpse's forehead. There was also a trail of scratches and nicks that trickled across the temple toward the left earlobe.

A snarl of yellow fly line encircled the lower leg sections of the waders. There were a few mummylike wraps holding the shattered remains of a bamboo fly rod to the guy's torso. The fly—a deerhair frog, of all things—was snagged on his collar. Swimming would have been impossible, even without the fast water and that bop on the head.

Plunkett noticed that the rod was an Orvis. It looked like one of their small, lightweight models, specifically designed for taking brookies in the confines of mountain streams with lots of overhanging branches. Plunkett had often promised to get himself just such a rod, like maybe the day after he won the Lotto.

"Guy spends fifteen hundred bucks for a rod and then goes fishing here," Plunkett said. "With that." He gestured with the toe of his shoe to the deerhair frog.

The talkative rescue guy sniggered.

"Looks vaguely familiar," Plunkett went on, "you recognize him—" He paused and tried to recall the rescue guy's name. "Brad?"

"Bart," said the rescue guy. "Bart, trooper. An' you're right, he does look familiar . . . but then, floaters all start looking alike after a while."

His younger partner, whose face was taking on some floaterlike pallor itself, shrugged and shook his head, concentrating on a spot on the ground near his right foot.

Plunkett waded around the body for a better view of the undamaged half of its face. From that angle, and particularly when compared to old Mabel, this corpse was natty, almost debonair. The shirt could have been ordered out of the current Land's End catalog. Even wet, his gray hair had the trim, clipped look of a man who had just emerged from his biweekly visit to the stylist. And beneath the splotches, his face retained an air of patrician dignity and smug superiority. More than anything, the corpse looked mildly put out by the whole misunderstanding.

It was that look that Plunkett recognized. He felt a chill—one that certainly wasn't caused by the outside temperature—and realized he was standing above the body of Barron Quinell. Even though Plunkett had envisioned this scene a thousand times and in a dozen different ways, the shock must have registered on his face.

"You know him?" asked Bart, sounding concerned, all traces of graveyard humor gone.

Plunkett didn't respond. Instead he gazed down into the water of the Ausable. From where he stood, it seemed like the water was motionless and that the uniformly rounded greenish brown rocks on the bottom were moving—rolling upstream against the current. Plunkett was thinking about the night when the girl he loved told him that she was going to marry some rich real estate guy from the city. Funny, but that had been down by the Ausable, too.

Plunkett listened to river gurgling over a riffle below the pool. Heard the riverine breeze rattle the branches of a massive beech on the opposite bank. A swallow skimmed down to pluck an unseen insect from above the water and then soared until its form became lost in the gray rock of the cliff.

Barron Quinell. Dead.

"You okay? You know him or something?" said Bart.

Plunkett splashed back to the other side of the body, the one with the little trail of abrasions. "Not really," he muttered. There was another long pause, Plunkett remembering some old saying of his mother's about how we would often be sorry if our wishes were gratified. "Used to know his wife, though," Plunkett said aloud. He snorted a pathetic little laugh and looked once again at the corpse's forehead before adding, "Thought I knew her."

4

Possessing neither a green card nor a valid driver's license, Lucky Spike felt fortunate to have landed any job and doubly so to have gotten the one he had: driving a truck.

To Lucky, it was the best job in the whole country. Maybe in the world. The fair-haired woman who had hired him was not only the most beautiful white woman Lucky had ever seen, but had given him a pocket full of American twenties. Handed them to him right there on the Lower East Side sidewalk, along with a hand-drawn map and the keys to the truck.

Now, Bob Marley was jamming it out from Lucky's new boom box. And the six survivors from a twelve-pack sat on the seat beside him in a Styrofoam cooler. On that hot Monday, July 13, life was as sweet as it had ever been in Lucky's twenty-three years.

As a bonus, once he pulled the Isuzu delivery truck off the interstate and drove in among the High Peaks, the land reminded him of the home he'd left in St. Thomas parish, Jamaica. Tall, steep mountains everywhere, rugged and eroded, but clad from base to summit in green foliage. For the first time in six weeks, Lucky Spike wasn't homesick. He even enjoyed the heat. To celebrate, he popped beer number seven—and nearly missed the turn off.

He had to stop and consult the fair-haired woman's map. It was supposed to show him exactly where to deliver his cargo. The sign on his truck said High Peaks Lawn and Patio. Sure wasn't lawn furniture he had picked up outside Plattsburgh. Not unless they packed lawn furniture in fifty-five-gallon metal drums in the States. But who was he to ask questions? Just the driver, that's all. Well paid. Happy. Damn lucky.

The new road lacked a center line and guard rails and wound its way in a series of hairpin turns up a steep grade—more reminders of home. Lucky crested the flank of one mountain. Going down was a lot easier. He didn't have to shift as much, so he could let the truck go, steering with one hand, elbow out the window, feeling the wind in his dreadlocks and singing along with Marley. He tossed the empty can on the floor and popped himself another, letting the truck pick up speed.

For laughs, he began taking the turns a little wide. The centrifugal forces felt good. Made him giddy. He got it timed so there was a satisfying rhythm to the turns. The truck handled surprisingly well. Lucky let it have a little more speed. It was fun surrendering to the pull of gravity. Listening to Marley.

He almost lost it on the next turn, sharper than it looked at the bottom of a grade that was steeper than the others. Lucky slowed, felt the beginnings of a skid, and quickly planted his foot back on the accelerator. He slid safely around the corner on the wrong side of the road. Actually, it was the correct side of the road in his country. That thought made him smile. He raised his beer to reward himself.

If only the stupid old lady in the Toyota hadn't come around the bend at that exact moment. But her little white car appeared just as Lucky averted his eyes to slurp the foam off the top of his can. Right in the middle of the road. Lucky dropped the beer on his lap and grabbed the wheel with both hands. Hit the brakes. The dumb woman was frozen at the wheel, eyes wide, heading right toward the Isuzu. She didn't move an inch toward her side of the road.

Lucky twisted the wheel. Saw the little car coming at him, grill getting closer to his truck's heavy front bumper. He braced himself for the crunch of impact.

The Toyota and its wide-eyed pilot scooted past. Lucky moved to correct his steering. As he did, his front tire left the pavement. He felt a bump, then pulling as the tire sunk into the sand of the shoulder. He twisted the wheel harder.

The trucked jumped back onto the pavement and careened toward the far side of the road. Lucky braked, felt the wheels starting to skid, and eased off, willing the truck to correct its course. The same deity that had landed him the job still must have been watching over Lucky. He proceeded for fifty yards past a huge hemlock whose trunk bore the scars of snowplows and drivers not so fortunate as Lucky. Came to a bend that wasn't nearly as sharp as some of the ones on the way up. Easy, now that the truck was getting back under control.

Then the load in the back shifted. Lucky's truck tilted on its springs. There was a thud as the barrels rolled against the sides of the box. The rest was slow motion. Almost dreamlike. The truck spinning sideways. The dark, lichen-covered rock ledge approaching. A surprisingly loud bang. Then nothing at all.

His luck had run out.

Beyond the wreckage, the forest was still, except for the clicks coming from the Isuzu's mangled engine, and a gurgling *chug-a-lug* sound made by a stream of liquid pouring from a gash in the cargo compartment. The same liquid leaked out of six of the eight metal drums that lay crumpled beside two of Lucky's beer cans in the tiny rivulet that bordered the road. An acrid chemical odor, vaguely reminiscent of the smell of agricultural pesticides, overwhelmed all other scents, even the fumes of gasoline.

The rivulet passed under the road through a twenty-inch metal culvert. A mile later, it tumbled into a ravine to join two other spring-fed streams, and together they formed a body of water large enough to merit a local name: Stewart Mountain Brook. It was here that the first fish died—a dace minnow.

In the next mile, Stewart Mountain Brook dropped a thousand feet. Coursing through boulders and between shaggy spruce and hemlock-lined banks, it became a gurgling, bubbling stream of some size, known for the quality of the brook trout that lived in its pockets and holes. Some of those trout came to the surface and began swimming in slow, nervous circles, their bellies flashing in the dappled sunlight.

Finally, Stewart Mountain Brook passed under Route 86 to its confluence with the Ausable near High Falls Gorge and, coincidentally, one hundred yards from the exact spot where the county coroner had just arrived to begin the process of determining how Barron Quinell died.

5

At ten o'clock Tuesday morning, July 14, Percy Quinell sat cross-legged on an old-fashioned porch swing suspended on chains from the rafters of her camp's veranda. Next to Percy, in her husband's former spot, sat Bo Scullin, Barron Quinell's business partner and best friend.

"He was a wonderful, wonderful human being," Bo said for what had to have been the tenth time, blinking a pair of brown eyes large enough to fit a cow, and definitely out of place on Bo's long, angular face, with its dimpled jaw and cap of tight, gray curls.

"Percy," Bo said, scuffing a moccasined heel against the veranda floorboards. "Could we stop . . ." He applied some more heel pressure. ". . . the swinging?" He let Percy bask in the twinkle of those big browns.

Percy stopped the forward and backward pressure that had been keeping the swing moving. She let her gaze wander out across Clear Lake, which was flat calm in the heat of the morning, its smooth surface marred only by the wake of a single swimming loon. Through the haze, she could see the ski-slope-ravaged countenance of Whiteface. As always, Percy felt sorry for the mountain.

"Wonderful, wonderful individual," Bo was going on. If anything, stopping the swing had made him more maudlin. "Best friend a man ever had. . . . Best friend I ever . . ."

Percy gave up the pretense of trying to listen and surrendered her mind to the cobwebby sensations that had been building there ever since she got the call telling her Barron's body had been found. God, it hadn't even been twenty-four hours, though it seemed a lifetime had passed. And, in a way, it had.

If Percy could get rid of Bo, at least she would have time alone to think, something she needed to do badly. But Bo looked perfectly happy to sit there in Barron's seat of twenty-odd summers, batting his too-long lashes, spinning platitude after platitude. He was going on about how devotedly Barron had loved Percy. More now than when they were courting, Bo said. Which was a crock, of course. Bo surely knew that much. And, besides, even if Barron had been the most devoted husband on the Upper East Side, which he definitely wasn't, and which wouldn't have been saying a hell of a lot in any case, was hearing it supposed to make Percy feel any better?

"Thank you, Bo," she said, hoping to cap that line of commentary.

Bo turned his eyes on her and let them fill with tears he made no attempt to wipe away. "Barron always asked me that if—" He stopped himself and seemed to lose track of what he wanted to say. He stayed silent for a merciful instant. "If anything were to hap—" He choked. Swallowed. "Happen to him . . ."

Percy's aged basset hound, Winston, chose that moment to put in his first appearance of the morning. He struggled out of the shadows of the interior of the log camp and sniffed the morning air. Apparently finding neither the heat, humidity, nor company to his liking, he flopped into the shade under a cedar-slab coffee table, issuing one short grunt before falling into what appeared to be a deep and untroubled slumber. Lucky dog.

Bo said softly, "Percy, the business." His tears evaporated. The brown eyes suddenly were not quite so big and much more cunning than any cow's. "I know this isn't a good time." He paused theatrically. "But what is a good time when things like this happen?

I just don't want you to be burdened any longer than necessary. Barron didn't either. Percy, I'll be buying Barron's share—your share, now, technically—of Realty Associates. I have contacted my lawyers and told them to make up a cash offer—all cash—clean and quick. And very fair. Very fair. Percy, rest assured that you will have no financial worries whatsoever. I made that promise to Barron, and I intend to keep it."

The eyes had gone from cowlike to paternal. "Percy," Bo said, letting a fatherly hand come to rest midway between her left knee and where her plain white bathing suit cover-up began. The hand stayed where it was, administering a series of rote pats so devoid of sensuality that not even Winston, who wasn't exactly picky when it came to such matters, would have relished receiving them.

Percy began to wonder if this was what made widows so miserable: having to sit around putting up with crap when all you really wanted was a few hours by yourself to figure out what you were going to do—like for the next four decades or so.

One thing was for certain. She was going to hire the most loathsome firm of lawyers in Manhattan to work over whatever offer Bo made for her shares of Realty Associates. All cash. Since when did Bo have that sort of cash lying around? Very fair. That one was cute.

"Percy," said Bo. His hand stopped its patting but stayed in place. He rotated forty-five degrees to face her. "Percy," he said again, "I just want you to know I'd do anything."

"Anything?" Percy asked, letting her normally husky voice drop into a whisper.

"Anything," he said.

"Then get your hand off my leg," Percy said. She stood and gave the swing a push.

"I was just—"

"Bo, we both know damn well what you were just about to do. And don't bother playing innocent. It becomes you even less than empathetic—or sincere—or whatever you were trying to put across a few minutes ago."

Bo looked like his feelings were hurt. Percy would have wagered her share of Realty Associates that it was the first genuine emotion he had displayed all morning.

"Help me understand something here," Percy said, coming back. "You actually thought that . . . given the circumstances . . . I mean, even if I was interested—which I definitely am not—didn't it dawn on you that maybe, just maybe, I wouldn't exactly be in the mood twenty-four hours after finding out my husband is dead?"

Bo's hurt expression gave way to a smile of victory that shouldn't have been there at all, not unless Percy had badly miscalculated.

"As usual, Percy, you overestimate yourself," Bo said. "Never a very becoming habit for a woman. I didn't give a damn whether you were in the mood, or interested, or anything else. I just figured that under the circumstances, I didn't have a thing to lose. And I was right, wasn't I?"

"I think it would be best if you got off my property."

"My property," Bo said, and let that one settle. "This is my property, technically speaking. Read the deed. It's in the company's name. And I'm going to own the company."

Percy felt something cold growing in her gut. "I guess we'll see about that," she said, but her voice sounded distant, as if it belonged to someone else—someone far more self-confident.

"We'll see all right," said Bo, and went to where his black Mercedes 500 sedan was parked. He got in, slammed the door, and managed to make the monstrous automobile's tires kick up some driveway gravel on the way out.

That left Percy Quinell alone on the veranda of a million-dollar Adirondack camp, widowed at age forty, an old basset hound her sole male companion. Thinking back on twenty years of putting up with being married to Barron Quinell, Percy realized that this was not the way it was supposed to have turned out. Not at all.

6

Plunkett reached down to pick up the discarded cigarette butt, one of those wide Camels every teenage boy in Wilmington seemed to be smoking.

The butt lay on the sandy ground of a picnic area off Route 9N a mile outside the village of Jay. A local service club had put three poured-concrete tables in the shade of some maples growing in the no-man's-land left between the highway and the river after the state completed one of its periodic bursts of road straightening. It was a pleasant, shady spot and offered tourists intrepid enough to think for themselves somewhere other than the Lake Placid McDonald's to stop for lunch. Troopers could also pull their cars beside each other there and—windows down, elbows out—enjoy an on-duty coffee away from public scrutiny.

Now, some enterprising local youths had gone and demolished the tables, carting away the cement-slab benches and throwing them in the river, and using rocks from the river to smash the tabletops, until all that remained were jagged shards of concrete and twisted steel reinforcing rods.

Plunkett surveyed the scene: rocks, cement fragments, a couple of crumpled Camel packs, maybe a dozen Bud tallboy cans. He was angry as hell at the senselessness of the destruction. Pissed off at himself, too, because, at age forty-two, he realized that he had lost all comprehension of the hormonal rush that fuels such teenage acts.

It didn't help Plunkett's mood when his car radio squawked with the news that Culley wanted to see him right away. It being noon, Plunkett suggested they meet in Wilmington for lunch. He was pulling out of the picnic area when a guy, his wife, and about eight little kids drove up in a Buick Skylark. As soon as they saw the vandalism, all faces fell. One of the kids started to bawl.

Plunkett stuck his head out of his car and addressed the father. "Looking for a place to have lunch?"

The couple consulted each other.

"We were," said the man.

"Go up the road a mile until you cross a small bridge. There's an unmarked path to your right. Take it. You'll find a nice clearing there. There's a picnic table set up and a pool in the river where the kids can splash around. Way better than this place. More private, too."

What Plunkett didn't tell the family was that the owner of the property was some big developer from Syracuse. Given the circumstances, he probably wouldn't object—probably didn't even know he owned the property.

And even if the guy did object, what was he going to do about it? Call the cops?

Plunkett knew that someday Culley's superior-sounding voice was going to win him a punch in the nose. No delicate jab, either; it would be one of those full roundhouses preferred by drunken brawlers and directors of B-grade westerns. Plunkett knew this for a fact because he considered himself positively mild-mannered, even docile, by New York State Trooper standards, yet on occasion, he felt the urge to haul off and silence that voice. Which would have been career suicide. Culley's by-the-book sense of discipline and unfettered ambition made it a certainty that before long he would be Troop Commander—Plunkett's boss.

The only element of doubt in that equation was that Plunkett was giving serious consideration to retiring when he got his twenty years in September. Take his half-pay pension and maybe set himself up as a fishing guide. His old man had done it for a half century or more and seemed content enough. Plunkett figured he could tide himself over during the winter as a camp security man. The notion had first dawned on him six months earlier, about the same time Culley arrived at Troop B headquarters in Ray Brook.

Until Culley came, Plunkett had never begrudged a fellow trooper ambition. Hell, if a guy wanted to advance through the bureaucratic ranks, that was fine with Plunkett. Someone had to sit behind those desks, push those pencils, shuffle that paper. Just so long as it wasn't him.

But Culley, tall, skinny, and sporting far more wavy brown hair than any one man needed or deserved, was already acting like Troop Commander, peering condescendingly at Plunkett across the table at the Lumberjack Diner.

Plunkett could feel the perspiration dripping down his spine, but Culley looked cool and comfortable. Externalities such as the weather didn't seem to effect Culley. Nothing about the Troop B region seemed to effect him. Culley viewed the Ray Brook assignment as a mere inconvenience, one of a few such crosses he stoically would have to bear before claiming his rightful position down in Albany as Superintendent.

"Mabel Hull died sometime over the weekend," Culley said from across the table, as if he personally and not the county coroner had arrived at this conclusion. "Myocardial infarction." Culley pronounced the term in a way that suggested he had also picked up a degree in forensic medicine to go along with his John Jay masters in criminology. "Heart attack," he translated for Plunkett's benefit.

"What I guessed," said Plunkett.

For some reason, that seemed to bother Culley. He folded his hands on the tabletop, got an earnest look on his face. "What you did yesterday at the old guy's place," he began, sounding more like the Troop Commander than someone who was finishing junior high when Plunkett was graduating from the State Police Academy. "Went directly against protocol. It was only luck that . . ." Culley stopped talking. He took a moment to look out the picture windows that occupied three of the Lumberjack's walls, offering a fine view of the village's main intersection—it's only real intersection. "Don't see any need for this to go further, officially," Culley said. "Just want it noted."

Plunkett took that in—advice from a guy with less than six years on the force, two of those in a suit. He started thinking again about that roundhouse Culley was going to get and said, "Might not have been one hundred percent by the book, but it saved your ass."

His words had an effect almost as satisfying as the roundhouse of his imagination. Culley immediately improved his posture. His eyes widened with a hurt expression.

Plunkett said, "We'd both be the laughing stock of Troop B if the Mobile Response Team had stormed that place and found nothing other than drunken Hector and poor, old, fly-eaten Mabel. I can just hear the stories."

Culley silently contemplated the ramifications of that.

"Besides," Plunkett said, "I've known old Hector Hull since I was a kid. He and my father were cronies. Both guides. Hector loves to rant and rave—always has. But fundamentally, he's harmless enough. And anyway . . ." Plunkett paused. "Hector is one of the best shots around here. If he had wanted to hit his daughter or Jaworski at that range, he'd have done it. Old fart was bluffing, that's all."

Culley launched an inspection of the wire basket holding the salt, pepper, mustard, ketchup, relish, and napkins. He said, "Yeah, well—" Stopped. Shook his head. "Look. I know you have your problems with the way I do things. I have some with yours. Guess I'm trying to get around to saying I appreciate it. I do."

"What about Barron Quinell?" said Plunkett, figuring the time was right for a change of subject. "I'd be more interested in what the coroner had to say about him than Mabel."

Culley took his eyes off the basket. "Accidental," he said, "A-C-C-I-D-E-N-T-A-L."

"Always wondered how you spelled that word," said Plunkett. "They teach that at John Jay?"

Culley sat there missing the whole point of the taunt. Into the silence, Plunkett said, "So that's it—accidental. You're not going to do anything more about it?"

"No need," Culley said.

Plunkett was tempted to comment that it was too bad Culley skipped classes the day they taught them that rule number one of police investigation is that when a body is found an officer should assume that foul play has occurred unless there is conclusive evidence to the contrary.

But then, rule number one of police politics is that investigators who have a lot of open murders tend not to get promoted as quickly as those without, especially when the victims happen to be influential rich guys. Culley certainly had been in class the day they taught that lesson.

Culley managed to find a bored look that didn't go at all well with his new dove gray three-piece suit. That didn't stop him from wearing the look with pride. "Quinell drowned, pure and simple," he said. "The coroner says it is likely his lungs were functioning flawlessly when he went into the river. They were filled with water, at any rate. Cause of death—suffocation due to drowning. There was some algae under his fingernails, indicating that he struggled in the water—tried to claw his way out before he got tangled in his fishing line. Obviously he was fully conscious, but not feeling a lot of pain. His blood-alcohol level was point-one-eight. That tap on his head caused a little subcutaneous hemorrhaging, but no signs of a concussion. Might have temporarily stunned him—nothing more."

Culley's medical dissertation was cut short when Linda came to their table. A tall, bony woman with a snarl of sandy blond curls and waves on her head, Linda, depending on when you caught her, could be undertaking the duties of cook, hostess, head waitress or sole shareholder of the Lumberjack Diner. She was also the closest thing to a love interest that there was in Plunkett's life. Linda dropped an inch-thick, hand-patted cheeseburger and a haystack of fries in front of Plunkett.

"One Lumberman's Special," she announced with pride and in a voice loud enough for the entire place to hear. Then, sotto voce, she added, "How's the midlife crisis going today, Plunk?" The last bit was delivered with a wink, one of her beguiling smiles, and an ever-so-subtle nod in the direction of Culley, who got a chef's salad—with no fanfare.

When she smiled like that, which was often, there was almost a girlish quality to Linda, even though she was forty-three, a month older than Plunkett. Physically, that smile was the only girlish thing about her, though. At an inch under six feet, she was nearly as tall as Plunkett. And although there wasn't an ounce of fat on her, she had big bones that gave her hard angles in places where most women were soft. Horsey came to mind—but not in a negative sense. Plunkett liked horses. Found them beautiful and admired their grace and muscularity. Besides, the five or ten extra pounds that from time to time affixed themselves to his six-foot-two-inch frame made it difficult for Plunkett to cast the first stone when it came to big-bonedness.

In the ten years since his wife's death, the Lumberjack had supplied Plunkett with at least three-quarters of his caloric intake: a pair of eggs sunny side up with bacon and white toast each morning. A Lumberman's Special for lunch most days. A couple of Gennies and a pork chop with peas and mashed potatoes for dinner—unless Linda was having her meat loaf special, which he never passed up.

Over the years, Linda and he had become friends, not that either would admit to the possibility of a man and woman being friends. They had never gotten around to crossing the line to become lovers. But Plunkett hadn't ruled it out. The way he saw it, there was a lot to be said for a woman who in this day and age still served up an honest burger.

With the Lumberman's Special cantilevered over his plate far enough to allow melting processed cheese and meat juices to drip onto the fries, Plunkett dug in like a man who hadn't had a decent meal in a decade. Culley carefully plucked the rounds of hard-boiled egg out of his salad and banished them to a remote sector of his plate where they were less likely to damage his pampered cardiovascular system. He then began pushing a shred of smoked turkey around as if he wasn't quite sure whether it was edible.

Plunkett chewed through his mouthful and polished his lips with a napkin plucked from the chrome dispenser. He asked, "What about the abrasions on the side of the head? The swelling?"

"Consistent with tripping and striking his head on a rock. Not surprising given the amount of booze he had had. Got tangled in his line, and drowned. Not surprising, either." Culley punctuated his statement with three quick wags of his lower jaw.

There was a moment's silence, broken by the clattering of dishes from Linda's kitchen.

"The rock that made those abrasions had to have a sharp edge on it," said Plunkett. "The rocks in that stretch of the river are round and smooth."

"There are a million rocks in the Ausable," observed Culley. "One of them is bound to be sharp."

"And Barron Quinell chose that one to hit his head on?"

"That's what the evidence suggests."

"Barron Quinell was an experienced fisherman," said Plunkett.

Culley nodded carefully, all senses alert for the logical trap he knew lay ahead.

"That stretch of the Ausable has to be the worst, most overfished piece of water in the county. Why would he fish there? Hell, he owns something like ten thousand acres of land around here. Dotted with trout ponds and crisscrossed with brooks—all better than that place."

Culley shrugged. "He did go there. That much is obvious."

"Or he was brought there."

Culley put down his fork and emitted a surprisingly long and powerful sigh for one so slim and young. "Plunkett, do you think the coroner didn't check for evidence of that during the autopsy? That I wouldn't have gone over all this a hundred times?"

"But his equipment. It was all wrong. Floating line. A deerhair frog, for Chris'sakes. On that tiny rod. Then there's the other matter . . ." Plunkett let his voice trail off.

Culley went back to his chef's salad, poking at a piece of shredded cheddar with one of the tines of his fork, obviously determined not to let his curiosity show. He made two attempts to spear the cheese shred and gave up. "What other matter?" he asked.

"Quinell was a rich man. It goes without saying some people stood to gain by his death—his widow, for instance." When that tidbit of information failed to get a reaction, Plunkett said, "Quite a story, that. She's a local gal. Grew up around here. A good twenty years younger than he is. Swept poor Barron right off his feet. He dumped his first wife for her. There's no secret why she married him: his dough. Now it's all hers."

"Checked out the wife. She was in the city when this happened. There are enough real problems on my plate"—he stopped and looked at his salad—"without your imagination killing off the local rich guys, when all evidence points one way. Besides . . ."

Linda came, holding the pot above them until Plunkett leaned back. She rewarded him with a smile and filled his cup from a height of two feet, her free hand resting on his shoulder. "You?" she said to Culley, still smiling.

He put his hand over his cup and shook his head.

Linda shrugged and was gone.

"Besides what?" Plunkett said.

"Wanted to ask what you made of that truck crash and the fish kill."

"Hadn't given it a whole lot of thought," said Plunkett. "This Quinell thing was on my mind."

Culley shook his wavy locks impatiently. "Well, for better or worse, here's a case right under our noses—right in the middle of your own territory—where we do have a crime. Or rather, several crimes: driving while intoxicated, aggravated unlicensed operation, unauthorized use of a motor vehicle—the truck was probably stolen, not to mention the question of what it was doing up there with a load of metam sodium liquid. That's an agricultural pesticide, which I don't think there's a lot of call for on Stewart Mountain.

We don't have an identity on the driver yet. And there's something else . . ."

Culley stopped talking, making it clear that he was having serious second thoughts about bringing up whatever the something else was. "There's a public-relations issue," he said.

Plunkett knew Culley finally had come to the point of the lunch. Few things in life were more dear to Culley than public relations.

"I got a phone call from the people at Save Adirondack Park—those environmental crazies—"

"—whose executive director happens to be none other than the son of Barron Quinell, by wife number one, and who might also benefit from his death, now that you mention him," Plunkett couldn't help adding.

"The caller said that unless there was a speedy resolution, we'd be—" Culley swallowed and uttered the next word with a note of pain. "Embarrassed."

"Embarrassed?"

"Said the spill was a travesty. A major ecological disaster. He claims that every living aquatic creature in that stretch of the Ausable could die. That we were incompetents letting it happen. And that he'd make sure the entire state knew we weren't doing enough to solve it. I'm not about to give him the pleasure."

He paused and widened his youthful eyes until he looked more like a begging cocker spaniel than an aspiring Troop Commander. "Plunkett, that's where I'd like you to do me a personal favor. A big one," he said.

Culley came from that school of management where requests for favors carried far more weight than do-or-die orders. Plunkett steeled himself.

"The caller was half right," said Culley, all sweetness and reason. "I'm so darn busy I probably won't be able to concentrate on the spill. Lord, I've . . ." He waved a hand in the air. "Well, you know how things are. And then this morning—that hiker they found at the boat access ramp on Lower Saranac Lake. Shot in the chest and pitched in a Dumpster. Christ, it's getting as bad as Flatbush. And guess who the TC has asked to spend all his waking hours on that?"

-37-

He jabbed a thumb into his sternum. "I realize it's irregular, but if you'd be my eyes and ears—"

"I'm just a road trooper. One none too fond of protocol, if I remember."

"Plunkett—a favor. Just one. You know the area. You know the people. You fish, for Christ's sake, that should give you a personal stake. Just look into it for me—if you get a chance, that's all."

"Let me get this straight," said Plunkett. "We got us a dead millionaire that bobs up in the Ausable, and we got us a certain number of dead fish bobbing up in the same river. And you're sitting here telling me to pay attention to the dead fish?"

Culley nodded.

"Then dead fish it is."

A smile of relief swept Culley's boyish face and stayed put until Plunkett added, "Course, I'm sure you won't object if I go up to Clear Lake and see Quinell's widow. Pay my respects."

Linda came over and stood behind the chair Culley had vacated. She whistled softly to herself and plucked a solitary quarter from the paper doily beside his all-but-untouched chef's salad. "Last of the big spenders," she muttered, and for Plunkett's benefit tossed the coin and did a couple of shimmies that made it fall into the front pouch of her apron.

"What caused him to dash out in such a flap—I'm not exactly Julia Child, but my cooking isn't getting that bad. Or is it?"

"Was the company," said Plunkett.

Linda pulled out Culley's chair and dropped into it. She puffed out a breath, and for an instant looked exhausted. But the look was wiped away with the same brisk efficiency she would have used to remove a smear from one of the countertops and was replaced with something that fluttered between canny and friendly without settling for very long on either. "Then what's your excuse?" she said. "You don't look a hell of a lot better than he did."

"Guy gets to me, that's all," said Plunkett.

"That's all," said Linda, and then added a second, "That's all," which was punctuated by a "Men!"

"It's this Barron Quinell thing."

Linda put her elbows on the table and brought her hands together to form a convenient chin support, which she put to use.

"Culley's so damn insistent it's an accident," Plunkett said.

"And . . ." Linda prompted.

"I'm not so sure."

Linda nodded slowly.

"I mean, if it was an accident, I can think of a whole lot of people who might find that very convenient—too convenient."

"You tell Culley?"

"Lot of good it did. He gave me a spelling lesson." Plunkett lowered his voice and spelled, "A-C-C-I-D-E-N-T-A-L," then waited for Linda's response.

"You never did sarcastic very well, Plunk," she said, not bothering to raise her chin from its rest.

"His business partner, for instance," Plunkett said. "Bo Scullin. I suppose he's going to have the company all to himself now. That can't be too much of a tragedy."

"For what it's worth, the Official Lumberjack Rumor Mill says Scullin's tied into the Mafia," said Linda. "Course, so is every other millionaire camp owner around here, according to the same infallible source."

"Quinell's son, who has yet to hold a real job. He'll probably inherit enough to never face that unpleasant prospect."

"Quentin?" asked Linda. When Plunkett nodded, she said, "Doesn't care for my cuisine either. Automatically makes him suspect."

"So there's two people who clearly could benefit," said Plunkett.

"I can think of a third. His wife."

Plunkett took that in silence. He nodded a couple of times slowly. His "Her too," was so soft it could have been a sigh. Aloud he said, "That is what put your recently departed customer off his feed. Me mentioning that I was going to go out and see her, pay my respects."

"That'd put anyone off his feed." Linda shook her head. "What are you going to do about it—Culley's insisting it was an accident?"

"Not a damn thing," Plunkett said. That got Linda's chin up off her palms. Plunkett said, "Just not worth it."

She put the chin back and waited for him to continue.

"You know, I really am thinking about it. Quitting. There has to be more to life than putting up with the likes of Culley after two decades on the job. Or having nightmares about old ladies whose eyes are crawling with flies. The foolishness of me walking up to that shack. Big hero. For Christ's sake. I think it was a sign to get out. I honestly do. Before I really screw one up."

"What you did was the right thing."

"It was a stupid thing. And in this business, you don't get away with stupid too often."

"Not like guiding," Linda said, her attempt at sarcasm no smoother than Plunkett's.

"At least I'd be spending my time doing something I liked. I have to look at my little brother every time I drive past Plunkett Motors. As a kid, all he did was fool around with cars. Only thing he wanted to do. Forever pulling one apart and putting it back together. Impossible to pinpoint where the hobby ended and the real work started. Now, he's got that business. Sons in it with him—and don't think for a minute they're not raking it in. As fulfilled as hell."

Linda pushed herself back and scanned the two other occupied tables in the restaurant. "Well, before you go and quit, keep one thing in mind," she said. "You're a good cop. Damn good. And there's not a person in the whole area who doesn't know that—even Culley."

He looked at her blankly.

"Linda." The voice came from across the room.

"I guess it's time I shifted from being the resident psychiatrist to chief cook and bottle washer," she said.

"I'd still like to talk about this," said Plunkett.

It seemed like she was going to leave, but she said: "Going out to see her." She paused. There was another, louder *Linda*. "You don't have to do that to yourself."

"This the resident psychiatrist talking?" said Plunkett. "In case you haven't noticed, business isn't so fast and furious around here that a restaurant owner can afford to have any more of her customers off their feed."

All in all, it had been one fuck of a twenty-four hours, the worst since Aldon Hewitt got let out of Clinton in the spring, after two whole years' worth of fucked up twenty-four hours.

First, the goddamn trucker doesn't show. That left Aldon alone up there on Stewart Mountain, half-dying for a belt of Jack, knowing damn well that if there was a no-show, then he wouldn't get to do the job, and if he didn't do the job . . . well . . . he wasn't gonna get a plugged nickel, because with these guys, it was all piecework. Simple as that. And just what in hell was he supposed to do waiting there all afternoon? Pick his ass with the hand that he wasn't using to swat deerflies?

To top things off, that stupid little homo in the Yale T-shirt comes nosing around. Saw everything.

And when Aldon asked him, "What the fuck you doing here?" the kid just smiled a smart-ass smile. Said he was awfully sorry, but said it so it came out sounding stuck-up and not in the least bit sorry. Like he had every right to be there in his faggy hiking boots, backpack, and cute little short-shorts that would have looked a whole lot better covering some college girl's butt.

Aldon picked up the 12-gauge Mossberg he kept by the door of the shed and, with the gun pointed at those short-shorts, informed the kid that this was private property. Old Mr. Mossberg got the little homo talking with some respect.

"Look, I'm sorry," he said, backing away, putting his hands out, as if that was going to stop a load of buckshot. "Honest, I was just hiking and I got lost. I came across the trail and just followed it. I didn't know it was private property, sir."

Aldon liked that, the sir part. But the little homo was still full of

-41-

shit. Aldon jammed a thumb toward a yellow placard nailed to a tree. Fifteen feet away, tops. Then toward another one across the clearing. And in case the little homo was slow, a third. "Those signs say, 'No Trespassing.' "

The little homo got that stuck-up look on his face again and was about to say something when Aldon cut in. "Go to Yale?" he said, pointing Mr. Mossberg toward the crotch of the Y on the kid's shirt.

The little homo nodded, taking another step backward, and said, "Law." As if that was supposed to impress Aldon.

"Oughta ask for a refund," Aldon said. The kid looked baffled, so Aldon explained, "Twenty grand a year, they should teach you to read better than that. Lie, too. Now, you gonna tell me what the hell you were really doing up here?"

Instead of answering, the stupid little homo made a run for it. Aldon stood there, trying to figure out what they would have wanted him to do, realizing that the little fag had seen everything. That he would surely report his encounter with the shotgun-toting redneck. Place would be swarming with cops. Fuck everything up. And the guys from the city, the big bosses, Aldon figured they'd sure as hell blame him, which wouldn't do a whole lot in the life-expectancy department. Didn't need no Yale law degree to figure that one out.

The little homo had a good twenty-five yards on Aldon and was heading into a stand of scrub aspens. Aldon started to run after him, but that wasn't doing any good. Fucker was fast, even with the pack. Aldon stopped. Pointed Mr. Mossberg at the base of the kid's skull just above the pack. He fired.

And missed.

It was that type of day.

But the stupid kid stopped. Actually put up his hands and came toward Aldon. "Let's just take this cool," he said, no trace of being stuck-up in his voice now. In fact, it was cracking, like he was gonna bawl or something. Aldon liked that. "I'm sorry," the kid said. "It was a mistake."

"Bad one," said Aldon, and he fired again. This time the load went where he wanted it—right into the crotch of the Y.

Aldon had to spend most of the night cleaning up the mess and hauling the kid over into the next county. He needed to dump him someplace where the body would be found, before someone sent a search party up Stewart Mountain. He had to clean his car's trunk and lie low until morning. And then, when he finally got home, figuring if a man had ever earned himself a belt of Jack, he sure as hell had, Edna started right in on him.

"Where the hell you been?" That was how she greeted him, sitting there with her stringy hair hanging in tendrils, not washed or combed or nothing, and her nightgown hanging all loose off her shoulders. She didn't give a shit what she looked like anymore, never fixing herself up and eating so little she was getting a starved look to her. This bugged the hell out of Aldon, because when he had taken up with her she was kind of good-looking, if you liked them young and skinny, which Aldon did.

"Shuddup," Aldon said, and went right to the fridge and pulled open the freezer compartment. It was as hot as hell, and he wanted a drink. Then he'd think about lunch.

The bourbon he had put in the night before was gone. "Where's my bottle?"

Edna just kept sitting there. Didn't even bother to answer. So Aldon had to grab her by the wrist to get her attention. Squeeze a little until the bones dug into the meat of his hand.

"My whisky," he said.

"Gone," she managed to croak.

Aldon threw her hand back toward her with enough force to cause it to strike her nose, reddening it. "Bitch," he muttered.

She rubbed her nose and wiggled her bony shoulders further into the nightgown. "Yeah, and what am I supposed to do here all night alone while you're off chasing—"

"I'm working my ass off."

"Not your ass you're working off. Your girlfriend called last night looking for you just after you left."

"I told you. One of the bosses. She's a woman."

Edna snorted.

"Twat," Aldon said, and did his best to storm out the door. "Twat, twat, twat," he muttered, once outside, although the only thing within earshot was an old rust-colored hound chained beneath a hemlock. It whined and cowered, tail up around its snout. Aldon went past the dog toward the remains of a matched pair of 1978 Ford LTDs that sat in front of the house, wheel-less, with their hoods removed. He jumped into the third 1978 LTD. It sat low on its suspension with a distinctive yaw to the driver's side. Most of the car was faded turquoise. But its passenger's door was gold, scavenged from one of its immobile buddies.

No goddamned respect. Too fucking dumb to understand that Aldon had learned a few things up in Clinton—and it wasn't just auto mechanics, though he'd learned that, too. Made some new friends. And that they had put him on the fast track. Showed him there were a hell of a lot easier ways to make money than being some asshole's trained grease monkey.

Well, fuck her, thought Aldon, nosing the LTD out onto 9N, lighting a Marlboro. Fuck 'em all. He reached into the glove compartment and felt around until he found his new gold watch—a Seiko. It was two o'clock. He could go on into Wilmington. Buy another bottle. Hell, buy a whole fucking case, that's what he'd do. He'd never owned a case of whisky. Never personally known anyone who had. But he would walk right into the liquor store and buy one. Just like that. Because now that he had money in his pocket, nothing was stopping him.

And after he got to feeling good, maybe he'd just take his case and go out and pay a visit to Quinell's widow. Best-looking widow in the whole county, Aldon'd bet. He could make her the merriest widow in the whole country. He could do that now, if he wanted. No one to stop him. He sucked on the Marlboro.

If he squinted his eyes, he could imagine her. She had the longest legs he had ever seen on a woman. They were muscled and browned. Connected to a tight, perky butt. Good tits, too, not scrawny like Edna's. But it was her hair that really got to Aldon. Long and straight, halfway down to her ass. And the color. Not quite blond. Not gray either. Certainly not gray. Silver came to mind, but that didn't really do it credit. Then it hit Aldon: platinum, the exact color he saw as he squinted into the sun, driving his LTD along 9N. Pure platinum.

Yes, sir. Aldon Hewitt was smarter than they all thought. Because now he had Percy Quinell just where he wanted her. All his. Kind of like a bonus. He'd killed two birds with one stone.

He had to laugh aloud to himself. That was a knee-slapper. One stone.

7

Percy Quinell never imagined pulling off her scheme was going to be easy. But why, she wondered, did everything about dealing with old Ivor Rhys always have to be so confoundedly difficult?

It was even hard to tie her boat—a mahogany Chris Craft inboard—to the old grifter's dock. Or, rather, what passed for a dock on Turnip Island. She couldn't find a cleat or wharf ring anywhere among the jumble of rotted boards and rusty spikes, which barely extended far enough from the shore for Ivor to berth his vessel. His fourteen-foot lapstrake skiff was in no better repair than the dock, but it was Ivor's only link to the outside world.

That the boat was there was a good omen. It meant that Ivor, who also happened to be Percy's godfather, was somewhere on the wooded island. Whether he would go along with Percy's scheme—or even show his aged face—was another matter entirely.

The path that led from the dock to Ivor's camp was steep and rutted with rocks and roots. After a hundred yards, it emptied onto a hillside, barren of trees and dotted with splotchy gray boulders baking in the full glare of the afternoon sun. When she reached the clearing, Percy stopped and blinked her eyes. She flicked a sweat-soaked strand of hair behind her ear.

More than anything, Percy longed for the shade of her own front porch and a tall highball glass, filled with crushed ice, a sprig of fresh mint, and about two ounces of Stoli. In her mind, the glass was dripping with condensation, the vodka clean, cold, and cutting, even on this, the hottest day since 1906, or some such year, according to the radio that morning.

Only the greatest of willpower propelled Percy onward. That and a thorough understanding of the consequences, should her plan fail: no swing, no porch, no Adirondack camp, for that matter—and something a lot less pricy than Stoli in which to drown her sorrows.

Ivor's cabin perched on the highest part of the island, an aerie that afforded a full 360-degree view of Clear Lake and surrounding High Peaks, whose profiles were faded and indistinct in the haze. The cabin's unpainted shingle siding was the same color gray as the island's granite outcrops and supported a complex, diverse and, by all appearances, self-sustaining biological community of lichens identical to that on the surrounding rock.

"Uncle Ivor!" she called. Her voice was absorbed by the noonday humidity. "It's Percy."

She heard nothing except cicadas buzzing, but hadn't really expected much more, even though she knew damn well that Ivor was hiding in the cedars and hemlocks that fringed the clearing.

Ivor Rhys had been Percy's father's best friend—and the most loyal customer in the small tavern her father ran. Before taking early retirement, Ivor had been a highly respected securities broker from Montreal, or at least that's what people thought. What Percy found out for herself years later was that Uncle Ivor had been a ringleader in a band of a dozen or so Canadian stock manipulators who swindled close to $15 million from hundreds of American doctors, dentists, and assorted retirees in the 1960s and 1970s. Not one of the con men served as much as a day in jail, and none of the money was recovered. For as long as she could remember—ever since her mother died when she was two—Ivor acted as the primary consultant in all matters related to Percy's upbringing.

When she reached his cabin, Percy hesitated. She felt a certain trepidation about trespassing upon the sanctum sanctorum of the most private of men. Mingled with that lofty concern was the more basic issue of avoiding a broken ankle. The three wooden steps leading up to the porch were fashioned from what looked to be the same weathered boards down on the dock. Percy picked her route carefully, trying to secure sandal-holds on the few sections that had escaped the ravages of dry rot. She was relieved when she reached the relatively solid terrain of the porch itself.

The only piece of furniture there was an Adirondack chair, pale blue in the places where the fire engine red of a former paint job wasn't peeking through blisters and peels. On its wide, flat arms, the chair held an expensive-looking pair of Leitz binoculars, an Oxford edition of the complete works of Malory, and a crystal tumbler half filled with what had to be single-malt Scotch. The arms of that chair held everything necessary to sustain the old Welshman without his ever having to rise. It was as close to heaven as Ivor was ever likely to get.

Assuming that Ivor was within sight, and that he intended to indulge in a waiting game, Percy decided to make herself comfortable. She sat in the chair and flipped open the Malory. Its pages were soft, dog-eared, and dirtied at the corners from being thumbed. If the card in front was accurate, it was also just shy of two years overdue from Wilmington's Cooper Memorial Library.

As soon as she began to read, the thicket of white cedar shrubs beside the porch shook mightily and a put-out-looking Ivor Rhys strode into the clearing, plucking dried needles, bark peelings, and other forest detritus from a thick shock of pure white hair. Ivor sported a full beard fashioned from hair identical in texture and color to that on his head. And aside from a little arthritis-induced angularity, his frame was lean and wiry, with limbs that looked like they originally had been designed to go on a man seven or eight inches taller.

He stopped midway between the trees and the cabin, apparently having second thoughts about whether he wanted to go through with this encounter. Two pale blue eyes locked onto Percy's. "Mind you don't lose my place."

"Lancelot is just about to select which one of four women he's going to boff. You'll remember your place, Uncle Ivor. And by the way, the book was due back at the library two years ago."

Ivor dipped his chin. "Been meaning to return it, Persephone."

"It's Percy."

Ivor smiled his famous smile, the one that Percy's father called Uncle Ivor's Money Smile. Seductively warm and reassuring, it had loosened investors' purse strings from Bangor to San Diego. He said, "As the only living witness to the day the preacher baptized you forty long years ago—"

"We don't speak of *that*, Ivor."

"—I come honestly by the right to address you by—"

"Percy, Uncle Ivor."

Leaving that matter a stalemate for the moment, Ivor stomped across the clearing. He wore a white, loosely woven cotton shirt and a pair of chino shorts that looked every bit as old, worn, and sun-bleached as their owner. On his feet, he had a pair of olive green Wellington boots that came halfway up to his knobby knees. He shed the boots beside the steps, being careful to align their toes outward, ready to be hopped into immediately should circumstances dictate a hasty dash to the cedars.

Barefoot, Ivor took a single giant stride onto the porch.

"Which reminds me," he said, making a deft and successful snatch for the tumbler. "The same preacher called you Persephone the day I gave you away to that Barron Quinell—an act I have always regretted. But, then, you were never a girl to take advice—certainly not an old man's advice." Ivor punctuated his sentence with a pull from his glass. "However, I'm willing to let bygones be bygones." All merriment left his eyes. "Heard about it belatedly when I went for the paper this morning. My condolences," he whispered.

-49-

"On my marriage or recent bereavement?"

Ivor had to contemplate that. "Would godfatherly decorum prevent me from going for a twofer?"

"Since when did you start letting decorum interfere with your actions?"

Ivor chuckled a private, quiet chuckle that ended with a grunt. "Always concerned me Barron'd dump you—like he did that first wife."

Percy let two beats go by, then said, slowly and clearly lest there be any misunderstanding, "Well, he didn't get the chance, did he?"

That shut Ivor up. But only for an instant. The silence ended when he raised his glass in toast. "This time around, may you find someone more deserving of your considerable charms."

"Ivor!"

"I've grown too old for pretense. You know bloody well what I thought of Barron. I'm not about to change my assessment just because he got drunk and fell into the Ausable."

"It's poor form to speak ill of the dead."

"Normally, I'd agree with you, particularly because it won't be long before I join their ranks. But in this case, I make an exception."

"I didn't come over here to discuss Barron's defects."

Ivor's eyes, which could be so merry and reassuring, contracted into two slits. "No," he said, "I don't suppose you did. But then that begs a question, doesn't it: Why would a beautiful young widow come to see an old man the day after they haul her husband out of the drink? I might add that it's been nearly a year since Turnip Island has been graced—"

"Things have been so busy. Guests every weekend. Back and forth to the city—"

Ivor made a dainty waving motion with his fingers, as if to brush away a tiny unseen insect. "Let's save the dissembling between us for when we really need it."

Percy shrugged a *we'll see.*

"So, out with it," Ivor said. "What do you want of me?" He stood at the railing and put a little twinkle back in his eye; turned the Money Smile to the full "ON" position, but his voice had a businesslike candor that hadn't been there before. "I know you want something."

"Want?" she said innocently.

Ivor hoisted his eyebrows to the white thicket of his hairline. "Out with it."

"I'm an heiress."

His smile instantly went from charming to all-knowing. "Not near so much of an heiress as the world at large might think," said Ivor. "In addition to being a shameless philanderer, Barron Quinell was one of those fools who like to display more wealth than they actually possess, if I'm not mistaken, and I don't believe I am. On either account."

Percy took a moment to assemble her thoughts. "Ever wonder why I didn't leave Barron?"

"Anyone in his right mind would wonder."

"Well for starters, there's that." She gestured toward her camp, a stately log home and the only structure marring the shores of Clear Lake. "Company owns it, so I'd be out on my tush the minute I left Barron. The other reason I stayed has a lot to do with what I've come here to talk to you about—"

"I'd be very interested in hearing that."

"It's simple: Barron wasn't rich enough to dump. Any reasonable divorce settlement would have been too small to—What is it they say? Maintain me in the style to which I had grown accustomed. As it stands, I'm going to inherit a lot less than I thought. In actual cash, Barron leaves behind a measly four hundred and fifty thousand dollars, half of which goes to my stepson, Quentin. You know what his pet name for me is? My stepson's?"

Ivor raised his eyebrows.

"The Cunt."

Ivor gave a single sad shake of his head.

"Turns out nearly every other penny we—I—have is tied up in the company. Mostly brownstones in the city and then this." She swept her arm in an arc that encompassed Clear Lake's eastern shore, Slide Mountain, Kilburn Mountain, Stewart Mountain, and a few of the peaks beyond. "As you'll recall, it was me who found that the land surrounding the camp was for sale. I brought them that deal on a platter. Not that either Barron or his partner, Bo Scullin, would have recognized a deal if it bit them on their—" Percy cleared her throat. "Handled properly, this land alone could keep us all going for decades."

"Ten thousand acres. Purchased for $1.5 million from American Atlantic Paper Company in 1984. Worth, at a guess, ten times that now, more if you develop it," recited Ivor, in the tones of one who had never once in his seven-plus decades forgotten a number—certainly not one preceded by a dollar sign.

"Close," she said. "And now controlled by Bo Scullin—who paid me a rare social call this morning to offer his condolences. Said he would do anything to make things easier for me in my time of great need. Then asked if I wanted to fuck."

"He actually thought that—"

"An hour later his Park Avenue lawyer called. Informed me they intended to force me to sell Barron's shares in the company for what amounts to a joke—a distasteful joke."

Ivor lubricated his tongue with another dram of the amber. "How distasteful is it—Bo's joke?"

"A million."

He made a sour face. "A million," he muttered. "I suppose—"

" 'You could live on a million,' is that what you're about to say?" Percy felt a flush of anger. "Well, believe me, that is one of the many unpleasant possibilities I faced—every time I contemplated leaving Barron. Maybe I could. But what do you think would be left of this particular million after the IRS and the accountants and lawyers pilfer their share?"

Ivor shook his white thatch. "Don't I know, my dear, don't I know. When I retired, I thought I'd put enough away to live like a king. But I went and made the mistake of living too long. Just look at me now. I barely have two dimes to rub together."

Percy closed her eyes, wondering if it was worthwhile trying to make Ivor understand. In the end, she decided he probably wouldn't, but that trying couldn't hurt. "After Dad died, I made myself one promise: No matter what, I would never end up poor."

Ivor stared at her with the sort of callous skepticism most people adopt just after a door-to-door vacuum salesman finishes his canned pitch. He didn't say a word.

Percy cleared her throat. "Then there's the other issue," she said.

Ivor's eyebrows scurried up to their hiding place in his hair.

Percy said, "I'm not about to give Bo the satisfaction of screwing me."

Ivor beamed. "Now we get to the part where poor old Uncle Ivor comes in," he said.

Percy picked up Ivor's binoculars and began to scan the far shore. "About the only sensible business decision Barron ever made was letting his lawyer put a shotgun clause in his partnership agreement with Scullin: If one of the partners makes an offer for the other's shares, then the second partner can turn that offer right around and buy the first one out for the same amount per share."

Ivor nodded. "Shotgun clauses hold a kernel of rough, primal fairness. Personally, I have always avoided them."

"Bo owns three-quarters of the shares. It'd cost me three million to take him out."

"Surely you're not about to hit an old, impoverished Welshman up for a loan?"

"Before he died my father told me two things," said Percy. "One was that he had elicited a promise from you to help me, if I ever needed it."

Ivor shook his head. "At the time, I never dreamed you'd need it."

"The second thing Daddy told me was that in your day you were the smoothest stock promoter ever to grace the shores of North America."

He smiled modestly.

"In business school, they teach that shotgun clauses favor the partner with the most money."

Ivor stuck his lower lip out pensively, either to think, or to make a convenient rest for the rim of his tumbler. "About the only thing they teach at business school I won't quibble with," he said.

"Then it's easy. You're going to have to help make sure it's me who has the most money."

"I don't see how—" He cleared his throat. "Surely you're not proposing . . ." He cast an eye at the Wellingtons so temptingly pointed toward the cedars. "You're not mad enough to suggest that I reenter my former profession."

Percy smiled. "Just a small scam. One time. Say we take a few million off Bo. We have forty-five days until the deal has to close."

"Forget it."

"Daddy told me you kept several inactive numbered companies registered in the Cayman Islands. 'Some retired folks stuff dollar bills in their mattresses for a rainy day. Ivor keeps numbered companies.' That's what he said. It wouldn't take too much effort to activate one. . . ."

"I'm retired, can't you see?" He gestured toward his faded shorts and bare, arthritic feet. "An old man. People think I'm dead."

Percy tried on what she felt was a fair imitation of Uncle Ivor's Money Smile. "Precisely," she said. "And one of the many benefits of my proposition is that if you agree, things will stay that way. Otherwise . . ."

Ivor's eyes darted from side to side, up and down. "Otherwise what?" he said, sounding impatient.

"Daddy always said that Uncle Ivor's greatest fear was that someday somebody at the Securities Exchange Commission would find out the truth about . . . Eureka Mines . . . is that what you called the company?"

She retreated into the larger-than-life world of the binoculars, aimlessly toying with them, working along the shoreline until she came to her own front wharf. There, sitting on one of the deck chairs was a man fanning his square-shaped, somewhat handsome face with a New York State Trooper's gray Stetson. She had hoped that particular policeman would come calling. Half-expected it, but hadn't imagined it would be so soon. She smiled. At least one part of her plan was falling into place.

"You're saying you'd rat on your own godfather . . . who all but raised you . . . gave his—"

Percy put down the binoculars. "Yes," she said, then: "Have to run. A gentleman caller." She handed Ivor the glasses and pointed toward her wharf. He twiddled the focus dial and inhaled once, sharply.

Percy had taken her first step away when Ivor said, "Nice try." She stopped.

Once Ivor had her full attention, he said, "In fact, you made only one error—but a critical error. One of the few benefits of reaching my age is that after a certain point you become too damned old to threaten."

Percy shrugged. "How about pulling down a quick million dollars? That'd be your cut of the take, Uncle Ivor. Too damned old for that?"

She had made it as far as the edge of the clearing before curiosity got the better of her and she turned to see what Ivor was up to. He sat in the Adirondack chair, tumbler in hand, Malory open on his lap, Money Smile radiating full force.

Ivor stayed in his chair, watching as the inboard backed away from Turnip Island. Its engine gave a basso profundo growl, and the boat rose slowly onto a plane, bow high, its skipper sitting on the back of the driver's seat, hair blowing behind her like a silver cape.

Percy certainly had turned out to be a beautiful woman.

What was less certain was whether she had also turned out to be a husband killer. Ivor considered that possibility as the Chris Craft cut a graceful arc toward the Quinell estate, and decided that there was no way he could be sure. And in any case, it wasn't really material.

A million dollars. That was material.

Ivor treated himself to a breath of Scotch and contemplated that million dollars. As he did, it dawned on him that at seventy-two, he was getting old. If one has to grow old, he deduced, rolling the Scotch over his tongue, would it not be better to be old and rich than old and poor? Who could argue with the logic of that? It only stood to reason, then, that it would be better yet to be very rich than just merely rich.

For a man of his experience, figuring out the means to keep every cent of Bo Scullin's money for himself would be relatively simple, and it would make Ivor Rhys very, very rich indeed.

8

Twenty yards away from where Plunkett sat, Percy cut the motor. Her boat slowed. The roar of its inboard became a burble. Its bow settled, cleaving the water in two neat translucent green wavelets.

In an era of fiberglass inboard-outboards driven by beer-bellied louts, there was a lot to be said for a stately, mahogany inboard, idling across a flat-calm mountain lake, chrome and brass polished, a fresh coat of varnish showing off the fine grain in its planking. It almost seemed too much to ask that such a craft be skippered by an elegant and strikingly beautiful woman.

But there she was. Still one of the most attractive women Plunkett had ever seen. Fine and blond when he knew her, Percy's hair had gone uniformly . . . gray came to mind, but it failed to do the hue credit. Silver was better, but not by much.

Whatever the color, she gave her hair a shake and offered him a smile that hadn't changed in two decades of living in the city as some millionaire's wife. The smile was puckish, a few degrees to the right of center, and bisected by a tiny gap between her front teeth. That the gap still existed spoke well of Percy, Plunkett thought. Most other women in her financial position would have paid some fancy Manhattan orthodontist to fix it long ago.

Above the smile sat a small nose, with a dab of red sunburn on its tip, turned up toward a pair of eyes radiating the same calmness and metallic color as the surface of the lake.

"Hi, Plunk," she said, in a voice that was husky and always about an octave deeper than expected. After two decades, that was the sum of it: Hi, Plunk.

She brought the boat parallel to the wharf. Plunkett stood, feeling a little foolish, it becoming clear to him that the real reason he had come out to Percy's camp had nothing to do with wanting to pay respects or even professional curiosity.

She eased the boat into reverse. Its engine made a whining noise. "Going to help tie up?" she asked.

Plunkett took the bow line from her long, thin fingers, thinking, Christ, there was even something sexy about them. He looped the line over a cleat and went back to fend off the stern.

Percy did a little vault out of the boat, quickly spun around, and bent to pick up the stern line. Plunkett observed that time had had no effect whatsoever on Percy's physique—unless it was to make it firmer and more slender.

Yet it was Percy who volunteered the little white lie: "You haven't changed a bit, Plunk." Saying that, standing there beside him in some short-short bathing suit cover-up, her legs long and brown and tight-muscled, the rest of her lean, looking like she hadn't quite grown out of that slightly awkward stage some girls go through in their teens.

She held her ground, grin firmly in place. As always, Percy appeared on the verge of playing some off-the-wall prank—push him in the drink maybe.

What she did was peck him on the cheek. Plunkett felt her lips, moist, lively, and full of promise. Or was that his imagination? He caught a whiff of suntan lotion and some unidentifiable shampoo, the expensive kind that always made him think of a woman's hair salon. She pressed herself against him.

Then it ended.

"Beer?" Percy asked, and without waiting for an answer, started toward a building as large as most midsized Adirondack resort hotels and vaguely Victorian, with its gables and gingerbread trim. It was fashioned from spruce logs of dimensions and straightness that hadn't grown anywhere in the continental United States since the turn of the century, which was when the place had been built as a wedding gift for the youngest daughter of some branch of one of the great robber baron families.

Falling in behind Percy, Plunkett said, "Long time, Percy," before he had a chance to think about it and realize the line was not only not going to get any awards in the originality department, but that it might bring back memories Percy wouldn't care to entertain.

She casually replied, "Twenty-one years, one month and four days."

"You remember," he said.

Percy flashed her slightly gap-toothed smile long enough to thoroughly bewitch him. "A woman rarely forgets that." She tossed her silver hair over her shoulders before adding, "Especially if it's one month to the day before a second man comes along and proposes to her."

The only beer she had was Mexican and came in a clear bottle. Plunkett feared she would serve it to him with a wedge of lime jammed down its neck, an act he had yet to fully comprehend. But in a time-honored Adirondack tradition she apparently had not forgotten, Percy snapped the cap and shoved him the bottle cold and dripping with condensation. He took two swigs. The beer tingled and cut through the heat and dryness.

Percy fished a fifth of Stoli out of the freezer and poured a good two ounces into a glass before filling it with crushed ice. She put her lips to the glass, then thought better of it. "To time," she said, clicking the bottom of her glass to his bottle.

Some vodka slopped over the rim and onto her hand. She slurped the spilled liquor from the webbing between her thumb and index finger. Apparently liking what she tasted, Percy proceeded to drink her glass to the ice dregs.

That task completed, she closed her eyes and let a smile relieve

-59-

her face of all signs of earthly cares. "I was just over at old Ivor Rhys's place," she said. "Ninety degrees. Ninety percent humidity. Not a breath of wind. And all he's got to drink is single-malt Scotch. No ice. No soda. Not a drop of water as far as I could tell. Just Scotch." Percy promptly refilled her glass.

Plunkett watched her. When she capped the bottle, he said, "I thought that old scalawag was dead."

She barked one laugh. "Just what Ivor wants everyone to think. Especially people in your profession."

"With reason," Plunkett said. "But I could have sworn—I mean, it used to be that a week didn't pass without some private investigator or securities guy coming around inquiring about Ivor. It's been . . . a couple of years, anyway. And didn't I read in the paper— Drowned or something?"

"Just goes to show you you can't believe anything you read in the paper." Percy stopped and nodded toward the counter top, where an edition of the Plattsburgh *Chronicle-Herald* lay open. "Get a load of what Gregory Hormel has to say about the passing of my late husband."

She slid the paper in front of her. Lowering her deep voice to a radio-announcerly baritone, she recited: "The North Country lost a longtime friend this week with the passing of millionaire philanthropist—"

Percy interrupted herself to insert: "Philanthropist, my— Well, let's just say that the only charity I ever heard of him giving to was some rabid pro-life outfit—a glorified home for unwed mothers. I'm not kidding you, Plunk. And even then I suspect the mother superior that ran the place had him blackmailed, if you catch my drift."

She went back to her radio announcer's baritone: "and summer resident Barron Quinell. Quinell died with his boots on—his hip boots. He was fishing the gin-clear waters of the Ausable for his beloved quarry, brown trout. If he had his choice, it was the way Barron Quinell would have wanted to—"

All traces of mockery left Percy's voice. She added a feeble "go." Swallowed once.

But when she leveled her gray eyes at Plunkett, there was no mockery or sadness there. They were angry. "Hormel missed the main point, don't you think, Plunk. Barron didn't want to go."

Plunkett followed her out of the kitchen, feeling like he ought to be tiptoeing, just in case he soiled an Oriental rug, scuffed a polished pine floorboard or toppled one of several Eskimo soapstone sculptures.

The large room they entered was designed for one purpose: relaxing, and doing so in grand style. Four Oriental carpets lent their frayed elegance to the pine floors. Plunkett counted three leather sofas and a dozen or so wing chairs, all upholstered from the same forest-green-skinned herd. The room was topped by a cathedral ceiling, held aloft by honey-colored log rafters.

Windows took up three of the room's walls. The fourth was dominated by a massive fieldstone fireplace. Above the fireplace, a taxidermic moose surveyed the room, wearing a wise and worldweary expression. A basset hound slept curled in a tight ball on a bearskin in front of the fireplace. The hound wore the same expression as the moose, and was so motionless that it, too, might have been stuffed.

"Meet Winston," Percy said, indicating the basset. "Currently the only male in my life." She gestured with her glass toward a sofa placed in front of the fireplace.

Plunkett found himself sinking into the most comfortable piece of furniture ever to embrace his backside. Getting up would require tremendous will, particularly with Percy curled up beside him—which she proceeded to do.

"This visit isn't—" Plunkett thought better of saying what he had begun.

"Official?" Percy prompted.

"You may not believe this, but I just wanted to extend my condolences, Percy."

Percy's mouth contorted into a look that could have been quizzical. Or mildly irritated. She swirled her vodka and gazed beyond the sleeping basset into the fireplace. It had been swept as clean as

-61-

most kitchen floors and three birch logs—flawless specimens—were stacked on the andirons for summer ornamentation.

"Condolences," she whispered into the fireplace. She faced him. "Plunk," she began, "it's not condolences I need. Lord, I'm getting more than my share of those. What I need—"

Those calm gray eyes misted over. "Oh who knows what I need. That's the problem." She tossed her hair back. Blinked the moisture out of the eyes. "But tell me one thing, Plunk. When—" She stopped and looked back into the moth-balled fireplace. "I'm sorry, I've forgotten her name—your wife's."

"Martha."

"Martha," Percy said. "When she died, did you feel . . ."

Plunkett sipped from his beer and found himself only half-listening, wondering why the hell anyone would go to so much trouble to make a fireplace look pretty for the summer. The charred remains of the last spring fire lingered in his own Vermont Castings woodstove, with the addition of a few gum wrappers and wadded Kleenex. They would serve as the base upon which he built his first fall fire. "She'd been sick a long time," he said. "That was hard on me. So mostly, I just felt relieved, and because of that, guilty, too."

"I feel that way. Relieved." She swirled her glass introspectively. Her eyes developed a blank, far-away sheen. After what seemed like a long time, she nodded to herself and flashed her smile. "Relieved, but not guilty."

When Percy went into the kitchen fifteen minutes later to replenish their drinks, Plunkett decided to determine whether he was still physically capable of rising from the sofa. To his surprise, he was.

Once standing, he let his curiosity lead him to a corner of the room that served as the camp library. It held as wide a collection as any public library in the county, Plunkett guessed, and what may well have been Upstate New York's most complete set of steamy best-sellers, all with the bent spines and tattered dust jackets that come only from frequent and devoted reading.

A hallway led from the library to a back door. There was a trophy brown trout over the door, an eighteen-incher, preserved in mid-leap with a Royal Coachman fly hanging out of one corner of its mouth. Resting on pegs protruding from one of the hallway's natural log walls was a collection of bamboo fly rods, a few pairs of waders, a wicker creel, and several clear plastic boxes containing an assortment of expertly tied Ausable Wulffs, Usuals, bead-head nymphs and other mayfly patterns. If Quinell or any of his guests was ever overcome by an irresistible urge, they could struggle out of one of those comfortable seats, don gear, select a fly that would match whatever hatch was in progress, and be making casts over the stream out back—all in less time than it would have taken to freshen up in the powder room.

"I caught it." Percy came up behind him carrying her glass and a new bottle for him. "Barron had the thing stuffed." She sipped and swallowed, twitched the sun-reddened tip of her nose and smiled. "I wanted to stuff it, all right, but with scallions, tarragon, and thin-sliced lemons. Grill it over a slow, smoky fire . . . wash it all down with a bottle or two of ice-cold Mersault."

Plunkett shrugged. He sure as hell would have gone with the cooking idea, too, although his tastes would have run toward pan-fried with plenty of butter, and he wasn't too sure what Mersault tasted like, but figured it wasn't exactly Gallo. To be consoling, he said, "At least you got your memories this way."

"I have never in my life forgotten a bottle of Mersault." After a half beat she added, "Either."

Plunkett walked toward the back door, hoping to make it look like he was going for a closer look at Percy's fish. Actually, he was examining the fly collection.

"Barron tie these?" he said.

"I did. Gotta have something to occupy the long evening hours."

"Nice gear," said Plunkett. He fingered the varnished bamboo on one of the rods.

"It was my rod, if that's what you're driving at," Percy said, making no effort to conceal the edge in her voice.

Plunkett could formulate no better response than clearing his throat.

Percy pressed ahead. "The day he died, he'd taken my rod. You're a fly fisherman, Plunk, and an officer of the law. Any justice there? Meeting your end for stealing your wife's favorite fly rod?"

Plunkett shook his head. Two decades. A career. A marriage. And now he found himself standing in a rich man's camp—a dead rich man's camp—with a cold bottle of foreign beer in his mitt and looking at a woman who could still stoke fires that Plunkett thought had been extinguished with his last acne pimple.

"Percy," Plunkett said. "You in any trouble? I can help . . ."

Percy blew a little sniff of air out of her turned-up nose. "And you told me this visit wasn't official."

"It wasn't. Or isn't—" Plunkett stopped and gave serious consideration to apologizing for intruding, then leaving. He took a halfhearted step. But all that did was bring him closer to Percy and her smells of suntan lotion and expensive shampoo. "Percy," he said. "Can you think of anyone—*anyone*—who would benefit from Barron's murder?"

Percy eyed him over the top of her glass. She said, "Present company excluded?"

"Percy, for Christ's sake, let me help. We know each other far too well for this sort of crap."

"Oh do we now," said Percy, treating herself simultaneously to a sip and a long, appraising assessment of Plunkett. Her smile was back in place—the puckish one.

After leaving, Plunkett needed time to think, something he never had been able to do in Percy's presence, not then, not now. He put one big hairpin turn in the driveway between himself and Percy's camp before he stopped, shifted to park, and let the Caprice's air conditioner blow a lukewarm breeze against his sweating forehead and cheeks.

By geological necessity, the Quinell camp's driveway followed the twists and bends of a creek bed. Plunkett stopped near where the creek came around a sharp turn and carved a pool beside a bank with overhanging cedars. Below the pool there was a one-foot waterfall, so neat and square it could have been made from poured concrete; then a series of riffles, interrupted by well-spaced boulders, and finally, a nice run, before the stream disappeared toward the lake. Perfect brookie territory.

He got out of the car and walked to the bank. In the clear water behind one of the boulders, he could see a ten-inch trout, snout pointed into the current, finning lazily with its tail. Some unseen aquatic insect must have floated by. The fish rose, dimpled the surface with its mouth, and settled back to its spot—one of at least a dozen good trout lies Plunkett could see from where he stood.

Then the obvious struck Plunkett: the stream bed was artificial, fashioned not over eons by glaciers, erosion, and the ice floes of spring, but by bulldozers and backhoes belonging to some local landscaper. The whole job was probably done in a week.

Standing there, Plunkett realized he had finally figured out the fundamental difference between the rich and the rest of humanity. A poor man has to hike for miles to find a piece of water as pretty as the one at Plunkett's feet, and even then he'd be likely to encounter some rich guy's No Trespassing sign. A wealthy fellow wants a nice place to fish, he pays someone to custom-build it to his specifications.

Then why the hell bother with the worst, most overfished stretch of river in the area?

Percy's half-mile-long driveway emptied into a secondary road, also dirt-surfaced and looking no more traveled and considerably less maintained than the driveway. Plunkett had just turned onto the road when he was nearly sideswiped by some gawky black-haired guy piloting an ancient Ford LTD.

Flinching and bracing himself for the crunch of fender against fender, Plunkett saw the glint of a square-shaped bottle getting pitched toward the floor on the LTD's passenger's side.

He had to drive another quarter of a mile before he found a place wide enough for a three-point turn, and even then it took five passes, front of the car nosing into some cedars, back wheels teetering on the brink of a deep gully, Plunkett only half-concentrating as he tried to place the face he'd seen behind the LTD's windshield:

long with a jawbone twisted about fifteen degrees off center, black hair hanging straight and wet-looking to the shoulders. A Hewitt, to be sure. But that left Plunkett with no less than a half-dozen lanky, dark-haired choices, and any one of them would have thought cruising the backroads with a fifth of whisky was a fine way to while away a few hours on a hot summer afternoon.

Plunkett figured out which Hewitt he was pursuing at the same time as he saw the rut of freshly carved dirt arching into Percy's driveway. The lopsided jaw belonged to the one they called young Aldon. Except, like everyone else, Aldon wasn't so young anymore. Old enough to have already served a deuce in Clinton for second-degree assault after he kicked some poor kid's head in outside a bar up in Santa Clara. Kid's offense had been to put on a k.d. lang song Aldon didn't like.

Young Aldon, with his piebald, turquoise-gold LTD, was not the sort of gentleman caller you'd expect to come around the Quinell residence.

Percy strode outside for a swim. As usual when no guests were around, she hadn't bothered with a bathing suit. The air against her skin felt soothing and, she had to admit, just a little sensual. Her nipples hardened. Goose bumps tickled her upper arms. She stopped and stood for a moment to relish the coolness and freedom before breaking into a sprint that carried her over a natural staircase of hemlock roots leading down to her wharf.

Not missing a step, she bounded across the wharf and did a perfect front dive, entering the lake with barely a splash. The top few feet of the water was as tepid as the air. But deeper down, it became cool, and—eventually—cold, and biting.

Percy swam in the pellucid green underwater world for as long as she could. When the throbbing at her temples became too much to bear, she burst to the surface, took a deep breath, and did six strong crawl strokes back to the ladder. As usual, Winston, with a whitish X of dog drool across his snout, was there to meet her. She gave the loose and folded skin of his forehead a ruffle and then felt for the bar of biodegradable soap she kept beside the ladder.

On the wharf, Percy lathered herself. Feeling slimy and cool and thoroughly refreshed, she strutted to the end of the diving board, turned to face the camp, and balanced carefully on the balls of her feet with both arms extended toward shore. She took a single mighty breath and prepared to execute the most difficult dive in her repertoire: the one and one-half back flip. While she composed herself, she thought for a moment about Plunkett.

What could she say? That he still seemed to be a genuinely nice guy. And was still smitten. Both traits could be turned to her advantage, should the need arise. And the need probably would.

She'd feel guilty about it. Damn guilty. Which was ironic, given everything else. But the simple fact of the matter was that Percy had no choice. There was a role for Plunkett in her scheme, and he would have to play it—like it or not. And in order for him to do that, he would have to continue buying her story, at least for a while. That part wasn't necessarily going to be easy. Plunkett may have been smitten, but he wasn't stupid. On the contrary: Plunkett's rural mannerisms concealed one of the quickest minds Percy had ever encountered. Of course, there was one way to keep even the wisest of men from using his mind.

From here on in, it was all going to be a matter of a balancing act. A delicate one.

At that instant, she very nearly lost her balance. But as she felt herself falling, Percy threw her arms overhead, sprang, and grabbed her knees, flipping, hitting the water headfirst and once more diving deep into its coolness.

Not far from the spot in Quinell's driveway where Plunkett had paused earlier to contemplate life's economic injustices—and how they applied to brook trout fishing—the old LTD was pulled to the side. Plunkett stopped and hauled himself out of his car. He gasped. The new Caprice had its faults, but its air conditioner functioned well enough to have allowed him to forget the intensity of the afternoon's heat and humidity.

The half-guzzled bottle of Jack Daniel's sat on the passenger seat. It was the only thing in the car, aside from three crumbled Marlboro hardpacks, and—completely out of place—a cellular telephone. Jesus, even the local punks were getting them now.

Faintly and from a distance Plunkett thought he heard *thud-thud-pong*. Sounded like a diving board.

Percy surfaced at the ladder expecting to see Winston's weary, expectant eyes. The eyes that bore into hers were a lot dumber-looking than Winston's and had a vicious glare never seen in the old hound's.

"Help you up," Aldon Hewitt said, his voice emotionless and thick. He stuck out a big hand.

"I thought I told you not to come around here," she said.

Aldon's face kept its stupid look. "Came to pay my respects is all."

At that, he cracked a smile. His too-close-together eyes crossed momentarily before he blinked them back into position.

"My towel," said Percy, trying to keep her voice firm, hoping she could somehow gain control of the situation, which wasn't going to be easy, him up there, her hanging off the ladder, naked.

Aldon stood and picked up her towel, but instead of handing it to her, just stayed there on the wharf, cradling it. His lips started to twitch. He mumbled something Percy didn't understand. Whatever it was made him start breathing deeply. Some of the dumbness left his eyes. He took one step in her direction. She caught a whiff of alcohol mixed with days-old sweat.

"Woman out here all by herself . . . husband dead . . ." he said, his mouth trying its best to work into a full smile while his free hand fiddled with the silver Mack-truck-bulldog belt buckle.

When Plunkett broke into the cleared area immediately behind the wharf, he saw Aldon Hewitt standing there, stoop-shouldered and holding a towel like some ill-groomed manservant. Percy faced him treading water ten yards out.

"Plunk!" she called as soon as she saw him step onto the wharf. The arm she raised to wave allowed Plunkett to see that she was swimming minus the top half of a bathing suit—at least.

Aldon turned. Froze. Obviously not sure whether to bolt, and if so, in which direction.

Percy brought him out of his trance. "Aldon was just dropping by to pay his respects," she said.

Aldon smiled the same belligerent leer Plunkett got from all habitually guilty people who for once find themselves off the hook.

Percy said, "Now, Aldon, my towel, please—and if you two wouldn't mind turning your backs . . ."

An uncomfortable truce was declared as both complied. There was a clumping and thudding on the wharf boards behind them, and eventually Percy's, "There."

Both men executed militarily precise about-faces. She stood dripping on the wharf, swaddled saronglike from armpits to knees in the towel, her hair hand-fashioned into a crude ponytail.

Plunkett decided it was high time he started acting like a police officer. "Passed you on the road, Aldon," he said.

Aldon shoved his thumbs behind his bulldog belt buckle and sneered. His eyes glazed over. Bored.

"Not a good idea to drink and drive," Plunkett said. When all that got was a shrug, he said, "Especially with your record."

Aldon dug his thumbs deeper. "Wasn't drinkin,' " he said.

"Not what I saw."

"Well maybe you oughta get your eyes fixed."

"There's an open bottle in your car."

"Wasn't mine."

"Glad to hear it," said Plunkett, taking a step closer to Aldon—close enough to grab him if he had to. "Because then there's no reason you'd object to coming along and proving that to me by blowing."

A look of hatred as primal as any Plunkett had seen in two decades as a cop grew on Aldon's misshapen face. "Sure," he said. "Sure. Sure."

"Sorry to disturb you like this," Plunkett said, to Percy, tipping his head toward Aldon.

Standing there in that towel, Percy did something with her eyebrows. "Anytime," she said, and quickly added, "In fact . . ."

Plunkett put his fingers on Aldon's elbow and waited for what was going to follow her *in fact*.

Percy squirmed to settle the towel more firmly around her and said, "Anytime."

9

Plunkett's mobile home was a plain white model made distinctive only by a peaked roof he had added over the course of three weekends one summer. It looked like it had fallen off its chassis in the middle of a hay field and been left there because nobody quite got around to moving it. Plunkett and Martha bought the place for fourteen thousand dollars in 1979, twelve acres of quack grass, milkweed, goldenrod, and thistles thrown in for good measure. The real estate guy said it was an ideal starter home. Except nothing ever got started there, nothing other than her tumor.

When somebody started bashing on the screen door just after ten Thursday morning, Plunkett was on the long, flat sofa that took up most of the living room. He lay on his back with a rolled-up copy of *Fly Fisherman* magazine in his right hand, reading some article about trout fishing in Patagonia, which was being described in terms that got him wondering if the Patagonians had any use for forty-two-year-old, retired New York State Troopers.

"C'mon in," said Plunkett, trying to sneak in another paragraph at the same time as he executed a stiff sit-up.

The door squeaked open, then banged closed. "Plunkett?" said Culley's officious voice, dousing all Patagonian fantasies.

Culley came into the room in a two-piece suit—his sporty taupe one. He also had the mildly claustrophobic jitters of someone who had never before entered a trailer, let alone one filled with the clutter of a widower's life. It was obvious he wanted to get out as fast as possible.

"Seat," said Plunkett, showing five days' worth of the *Chronicle-Herald* off an easy chair to expose the same light green paisley upholstery as was on the sofa.

Culley frowned warily and stayed standing. "Just have a minute," he said, keeping an eye on the chair. "Came by to see if there's anything more on that chemical spill."

"Coffee?" said Plunkett. He picked up his empty cup from its perch on the stack of trout-related literature that obscured the top of an end table.

Culley responded with an abrupt head shake.

Plunkett re-balanced the cup. "You didn't get the report?"

"This?" said Culley, producing a folded document from his suit coat's breast pocket.

Plunkett thought maybe he would get himself that coffee after all. Standing, he said, "Looks like a report to me."

Aside from a film of dust, Plunkett's kitchen was neat and spotless—more from disuse than good housekeeping. With its white cabinets, yellow-checked gingham drapes and matching plastic tablecloth, the room came close to being cheery. Except it always depressed Plunkett. Reminded him of Martha. Some mornings, he could still picture her standing at the sink, hands wet, looking through the small bay window at the fields and peaks.

Culley stood a few paces behind Plunkett as he filled a stainless-steel saucepan from the sink and put it on the stove. Plunkett shook Maxwell House instant directly from jar into cup and said, "Sure?" to Culley, who gave his head a single shake.

"Isn't a whole lot," Culley said, snapping the folded report against his palm before slipping it back in his pocket. If he remembered asking Plunkett to look into the chemical spill as a favor, there was no sign of it now. Culley might have already been Troop

Commander, dressing down some rookie who had disobeyed an explicit order.

This pissed Plunkett off more than it should have. He blew one long breath and said: "I found out who the truck belonged to. Furniture store in Dayton, Ohio. Reported stolen a month ago."

Culley deployed his trademark sardonic smirk. "Could have done that much myself in fifteen minutes on the computer in Ray Brook," he said. "You were supposed to be looking around here . . . asking people . . ."

"Have," said Plunkett, taking the pan and upending it over his cup.

"And . . .?"

"And nothing. But I'll keep at it. In fact, I have an appointment to see young Quentin Quinell himself as soon as I come on duty this afternoon. He and that bunch of his at Save Adirondack Park still seem to be taking an extraordinary interest in this spill. Might be able to tell me something."

"SAP," Culley said, spitting out the word like it was something rancid. "You think you'll get any cooperation from those crazies? Good luck. But I should warn you, don't push too hard. Quentin has let it be known that there might be an incident unless the police come up with something soon on the spill. An incident is the last thing we need. Certainly not at this time of year. Not with all the . . ." He let his voice trail off.

"Boys at the Chamber of Commerce on the Troop Commander's back about upsetting the tourists," Plunkett said, meaning for it to sound consoling.

"We're talking about a major public-relations fiasco, Plunkett. People come up here to get away from that sort of stuff. Maybe if you could ID the truck driver," Culley said.

"The only ID he had on him was the business card of a reggae band operating out of some address so low on the East Side that I'm surprised it's on dry land."

"And what did they say? The people who answered when you

called the number on the card?" Culley asked, adding, "You did call?"

"Was a man. West Indian accent of some sort. What he said was, 'We closed,' then hung up as soon as I uttered the word police."

Culley snapped his fingers. "Call Troop NYC then. See if they'll send someone over to the club."

Growing impatient, and making no effort to conceal it, Plunkett said, "Did that all by myself. They delicately implied that they had more pressing things. Said maybe the end of next week sometime."

Culley closed his long-lashed eyes and inhaled. When he spoke next, his voice was soft and oozing meekness. "Plunkett, this is a hell of a thing to ask but—" He stopped and swallowed. "Plunkett, you don't suppose you could go down there and—"

"No way," said Plunkett. "Besides, isn't something like that a little irregular for your tastes?"

Culley folded his hands. "God, don't I know it. But a lot of things are getting irregular around here. That's a fact. This murdered hiker business. I haven't gotten a damn thing on it. Zip. And it's not looking good. I'm going to have one hell of a time closing it." Slowly, he let his eyelids descend. "Troop Commander Fisk is giving me . . ."

Plunkett found himself feeling sympathy for the guy. "Well, there's this appointment with Quentin," he said. "Who knows, maybe something will come of that."

Culley sucked in air. "Just don't piss him off."

"And after that, thought I might talk to the guy who owns most of the land up there on Stewart Mountain where the truck crashed."

Looking happier, Culley said, "Be a start, anyway. He might have noticed something."

Keeping his eyes on Culley's, Plunkett said, "Guy who owns the land—name is Bo Scullin." When that didn't bring a response, Plunkett said, "Barron Quinell's business partner."

At three that afternoon, Plunkett stopped beside a white Toyota pickup truck bearing the forest green SAP logo of the Save Adirondack Park environmental group. The pickup was parked beside Route 86 in the pull off for the Flume. Aside from a flawless honey-brown tan, the attractive young blond woman leaning against the tailgate of the truck wore nothing other than sandals, cut-off jeans, and a bikini top. When Plunkett approached, every inch of him a trooper, from thick black shoes to gray Stetson, she smiled shamelessly and flirtatiously. Held the smile long enough for Plunkett to contemplate the possibility that he really wasn't as far out of action as he thought. Then she unceremoniously upended a plastic pail full of bloated, dead trout.

Plunkett walked toward the smiling woman and looked into the truck bed. Even though he had a pretty good idea of what lay within, he recoiled. The bottom of the bed was about half-covered with swollen, mottled trout corpses.

"There's a lot more where these came from—if you're looking for a late lunch, or anything," she said, demonstrating that she had both arrogance and wit to go along with her flawless tan.

"Quentin here?" Plunkett asked.

She flipped her hair toward the sound of the falls, but gave no clear response, other than a half-dozen bats of her eyelashes.

Plunkett turned to take the path that led in that direction.

"Hey," she said.

He looked back over his shoulder just in time. She threw the empty pail at him. He nabbed it with both hands, basketball-style. "This is a volunteer effort," she said. "Everyone who goes down comes back with a bucket of fish." The shameless smile reappeared. "Quentin's orders."

For someone in his early thirties and who had yet to do an honest day's work, Quentin Quinell boasted an uncommon number of titles. Founder, president, executive director, and sole full-time employee of Save Adirondack Park was just the beginning. He was also the only begotten son of Barron Quinell IV and his first wife. Since reaching the age of majority, Quentin had been hanging around the mountains, deftly skirting institutions of higher education and gainful employment, all the while doing anything he could to keep the title Prodigal Son right up there near the top of his CV.

It was in the latter capacity that Plunkett had encountered him on two occasions: once for criminal mischief when a local lumberman—a decent enough guy trying his best to feed and clothe four kids under the age of eight—had come close to losing his right leg as a result of a spike driven into an old-growth white pine; once for disobeying a lawful order of a police officer when Quentin and two Bennington College dance majors chained themselves together across a logging road that was about to be used for its intended purpose.

With a few wisps of fine-textured blond hair protruding from a SAP cap, Quentin stood on a flat rock beside the pool below the Flume Fall. He was barefoot, bare-bellied, and clad in a nylon Speedo bathing suit. Every rib and tight abdominal muscle showed through a tan that looked like it had been carefully chosen to match the one worn by the debutante back up at the truck.

"Glad to see you brought your bucket, officer," he yelled over the roar of the falls. With a flip of the hula-hoop-sized landing net in his hands, he whipped a dead brown trout into Plunkett's pail. It landed with a soft thud.

Plunkett stepped beside Quentin. The river, which normally exuded a clean, pine-forest-after-a-rain scent, smelled like a down-at-the-heels fish shop. Trout corpses of all sizes swirled and bobbed in the eddies below the falls. In one sweeping glance, Plunkett identified a dozen browns between six and eighteen inches long. There were countless brookies and rainbows and smaller creatures like sculpins, crayfish, and frogs, so numerous that they at first looked like floating bits of leaves.

Quentin netted a foot-long rainbow and held it aloft for inspection. "Metam sodium liquid, trooper, one of the wonders of modern agribusiness. It's supposed to kill weeds, bugs, and fungi in soil." He plopped the trout in Plunkett's pail. "Does a pretty thorough job on fish too. A railroad tank car full of the stuff fell into the Sacramento River a while back. Killed every living aquatic creature in an eleven-mile stretch, not to mention the countless minks, otters, and herons that subsequently starved. We didn't get a railroad car's worth, but we're in for something similar."

"Can we talk?" said Plunkett, anxious to head off the ecological diatribe that he could sense was swelling in Quentin's trim chest.

In one quick swoop, Quentin scooped two of three juvenile brookies circling around a whirlpool in what looked to be a trout's version of tag—only played belly-up and on the surface. He waited for the remaining trout to come full circle and nabbed it. "Cleaning up a river criminal mischief these days, officer? What you going to run me in for—exceeding my daily creel limit?"

A giggle came from behind Plunkett. It was the blond debutante, apparently overwhelmed by her mentor's rakish sense of humor. She put down an empty pail.

"Quentin," said Plunkett. "You and I appear to be on the same side." He let a pause go by, then added emphatically, for the debutante's benefit. "This time."

The oval-shaped hole that replaced her smile indicated she didn't think that last bit was very funny—not at all. And neither did Quentin, judging from the rapidity with which he handed her the net and pointed her toward a nice-looking rainbow that was about to float downstream. "Come on," he muttered to Plunkett, and made a move in the direction of a big hemlock farther up on the bank. He caught himself mid-stride, as if he had overlooked some tiny but crucial detail. Whatever it was that he had forgotten was whispered in the woman's ear, followed by three pats to a buttock whose youthful contours were in no way distorted by her cut-offs.

"Sorry to hear about your father," said Plunkett, thinking that even among rabid environmentalists, a little polite ritual should proceed a police interrogation.

Quentin chuckled. "Thanks, officer, but you can spare your sympathies. Far as I'm concerned, the man who was my father has been dead for twenty years, ever since the day he ditched Mother for that—" Quentin paused to search for the right word. When he found it he smiled to himself and said, "Gold-digger."

Two more college-age women came up the path that paralleled the rapids immediately below the falls. They shared the handle of a bucket.

"Besides," Quentin went on, hiking a thumb over his shoulder—some sort of command to his troops, Plunkett guessed. "Father was never very fond of anyone connected to a political movement that questioned the God-given right of his hired bulldozers to roam at will over this park."

Sensing a harangue, Plunkett changed the subject. "I'm looking into the truck accident that led to—" Plunkett gestured toward the river.

"Saranac Chemicals in Plattsburgh," said Quentin. "Have you talked to them?"

"Should I have?"

Quentin sniffed a single sarcastic sniff. "Should I have," he mimicked.

Plunkett resisted a very real urge to toss Quentin into the river with its fast currents, dangerous whirlpools, and stinking fish. "You have reason to believe what you are saying is true? A reason that's of any use to me, that is. I'd be interested in hearing it."

Quentin laughed aloud. A good, hearty belly laugh. The sound startled all three debutantes, who turned their heads in unison, looking as distraught as they would have if Quentin had just shrieked in pain.

"Of use to you," Quentin said. "I like that." Another laugh. "What if I said I know because Stepmommy told me—" He stopped and got serious. "That any use to you?"

During the silence that followed, it struck Plunkett that all of Quentin's assistants could have come from the very mold that had been used to fashion Percy Quinell two decades before their births. In terms of taste in females, the Quinell apple had fallen very close to the tree.

"That all you wanted to talk to me about—the dead fish," Quentin said.

Plunkett nodded and asked, "Why?"

Quentin shrugged. "When I saw you coming, I thought for sure that you had come to talk about dear old Daddy." He paused, gave another shrug and added: "About his murder."

Plunkett sat down on the bare ground under the hemlock. He nodded for Quentin to do the same. Quentin took in the nod, but instead of sitting, remained where he was, smirking now.

"Your father drowned. No reason to suspect foul play. That's what the coroner says," said Plunkett.

Quentin's smirk transformed itself into a smile of open and genuine mirth. "That just proves what I've suspected all along: the good burghers of this area get no better medical care dead than they do alive." He paused to chuckle appreciatively at his own humor. "Dear old Daddy was having an affair. That little tidbit any good to you?" he said.

"I'll just sit here until you're ready to talk straight," Plunkett said.

There was a silence while Plunkett enjoyed the choreographic spectacle of the debutantes hoisting another net load of fish from the river.

Quentin continued: "Daddy had become smitten by his vice-president of finance. Some vice-president of finance, too," Quentin added. "Was *schtupping* her all summer long down in the city while Stepmommy was up here with her fly rods and Stoli."

"Percy know about this?"

Quentin pondered that question, long and carefully. Finally, he said, "I guess that's pretty obvious."

Bo Scullin greeted Plunkett soaking wet from the swimming pool and wearing nothing other than a hot pink string bathing suit so small it might well have been borrowed for the occasion from the young blond woman Bo left behind in the pool. No doubt it would have fit her. And from what Plunkett could see, she was making do without such a garment, although its absence was not visibly affecting her activities: a series of half-hearted water ballet maneuvers.

Unveiling a set of teeth that were too perfect and too white to have grown there naturally, Scullin fetched himself a towel from a molded plastic deck chair and wiped it twice across his hair. Plunkett could not help noticing that for a man of his years—which must have totaled at least sixty—Scullin was in excellent physical shape.

"You must be Trooper Plunkett," said the radiantly smiling Bo. "I'm Bo. That's my assistant, Bambi-Sue Cline." He swung his dimpled chin toward the pool, where all of Bambi-Sue that was visible was an elegantly sculptured calf and pointed foot sinking into the water in a slow rotation.

Plunkett caught himself wondering if there was anyone on the planet really named Bambi-Sue. He gave up without coming to any conclusion, except that, if there was, she would be very much like the woman in the pool: bleached blond and oblivious to the world around her.

As far as Plunkett could see, it wasn't a bad world at all, if ultramodern ski chalet—about seven thousand square feet of it—was your style, and if your mission in life was to give some big-city architect a chance to exercise all of his self-indulgence on a single project. Scullin's place was three and three-quarter stories tall, a white stucco hybrid of alpine cottage and Southwestern adobe. The whole structure looked to have been erected without recourse to T-square, compass, or level. And no attempt had been made to design a building that was unobtrusive or true to the character of its site. In the background, Whiteface scowled its disapproval.

Bo pointed out a plastic loveseat on the lawn between the chalet and the hemlock forest. Plunkett sat. Bo joined him. The smile widened to unveil two more dimples on either side.

"Sorry to hear about your business partner," said Plunkett, hoping he put enough genuine emotion into his voice to remove the smile.

Maybe he put a bit too much. A look of profound and heartfelt sorrow darkened Bo's face. All three dimples vanished. "Barron was one of those wonderful, wonderful . . ." Bo paused. "Human beings," he said. "Much, much more than a business partner to me, too. Best friend a person could ever have. Best friend I ever had."

Plunkett said, "I'm sorry to intrude at a time like this, but . . ."

"You have a job to do," Bo finished on his behalf.

Bambi-Sue's feet emerged from the shallow end and wobbled as she attempted an underwater handstand.

"You have no reason to suspect foul play, do you?" Plunkett tried to broach Culley's forbidden subject offhandedly, like he was making a casual comment about the weather.

Bambi-Sue's pointed toes came together for an instant of victory, before separating, kicking wildly twice and falling into the water.

Bo watched Bambi-Sue with rapt attention. Just about when Plunkett thought Bo hadn't heard his question, he answered. "Everyone loved Barron. You've never met him, or you'd understand. Just one of those great guys."

"Maybe somebody he did business with . . ." said Plunkett.

Scullin shook his tight gray curls, cropped so short they had already dried. "He was tough, but fair—and honest. Sure he had his share of adversaries. Who in business doesn't. But—" He cut himself off.

"How were he and his wife getting along?" said Plunkett, still trying to sound offhanded.

Bo answered in a quiet monotone. "Devoted to her. Twenty years they've been married, and I honestly think Barron loved that woman with the same intensity he did when they were first courting."

"The son—Quentin."

"Had their differences, like any father and son. But there was a deep, fundamental respect there. Especially since Jennifer, Barron's first, passed—"

Scullin awoke from whatever trance he had been in. His brows came together. "But surely, officer," he stopped and cleared his throat. All cooperativeness vanished. It reminded Plunkett of the sudden weather changes in the Adirondacks. "When you called you said you wanted to talk to me in connection with this terrible chemical spill," Bo said in the same tone he would have used during his annual address to the board of directors.

Plunkett smiled a little too sheepishly. "Just curious. Not official. I mean, when a man of Mr. Quinell's . . ."

Bo nodded.

Plunkett went on: "You own the land where the truck carrying the chemicals crashed."

"The company, officer. The company owns that land, along with ten thousand other acres around here." Bo made a sweep with his hand that took in the chalet, the pool, the adjacent forest, the looming mountains, and even the state trooper next to him.

"Any idea why anyone would be carrying a load of agricultural pesticides over that road?" asked Plunkett.

"Not a clue, officer."

"Notice anything unusual going—"

"Officer, to be perfectly honest, I have never even been up there."

"Was the company doing anything with that land, were there any plans?"

That gave Bo pause. He revealed one quick little frown of irritation before the smile snapped back into place. "Plans, plans, plans. That's all we had, officer. Plans for this, plans for that. But I'm going to put a moratorium on all development plans until such time as a full environmental evaluation can be made as to the best way to maximize the benefits for all concerned—trees, animals . . ." He nodded sagely. ". . . local people, too," he added. "In fact, I have already contracted Save Adirondack Park to conduct a full environmental assessment. That's Quentin Quinell's organization. Until that assessment is complete, the only structures on the land will be the existing ones at Barron's camp over on Clear Lake, which technically belongs to the company."

He allowed Plunkett to bask in the full glory of his smile. "I, for one, think it's entirely fitting that Barron's son should have a direct hand in deciding the future of a tract of land that has meant so much to all of us."

Bambi-Sue began a furious butterfly in the pool. Scullin's white teeth flashed. His dimples deepened. Bambi-Sue's frothy butterfly became suggestive of an entirely different form of exercise, one requiring a partner.

"Any more questions?" Bo stood, simultaneously pumping Plunkett's arm and working his free hand over to Plunkett's shoulder in order to spin him a half turn in the direction from which he had come. "I want you to know officer, that I am glad to help your investigation into this spill in any way, although I can't think—" He drew in a breath. "Anything you need, anytime you need it, just call. Or come on by. I'm here most of the time for the next few weeks . . ."

Plunkett was in the parking area squinting up for one final appraisal of Bo Scullin's architectural monstrosity when a Ford Taurus, a rental, according to its license plate, pulled in. Four middle-aged men Plunkett had never seen before sat inside, all clad in polo shirts of the same design, but differing colors: blue, red, yellow, white. They looked as uncomfortable and out of place in the Taurus as Culley had looked that morning in Plunkett's mobile home.

Bo came around the corner of the chalet, arms open, smiling a dimpled smile of welcome.

Behind Bo, Plunkett saw Bambi-Sue get out of the pool and slip into a bathrobe. She stood on the pool deck, peering at the Taurus. From that distance, it was difficult to pin down the expression on the pretty face that Plunkett had initially categorized as innocent. But one thing was certain. It sure as hell wasn't a smile of welcome.

10

Plunkett tried to avoid Troop B headquarters in Ray Brook. The plain, prefab bungalow that served as home base for the six troopers working out of Wilmington's Patrol Station was plenty cooped-up for Plunkett, who was happiest when he was alone, out in his car.

Headquarters looked like a 1970s junior college dropped into a grove of red pines midway between Lake Placid and Saranac Lake. At eight o'clock Friday morning, July 17, Plunkett pulled into the complex, grumpy because he was there only nine hours after coming off a shift, nervous because Troop Commander Fisk himself had called, ordering him to come. It was shaping up to be a bad day even before he found the sidewalk leading to the troopers' entry blocked by a three-foot-high pile of dead trout.

At least one thing was now clear: There was no doubt why Fisk wanted him in Ray Brook.

A female TV reporter stood beside the pile. Short, dark-haired, and far too zippy given the temperature and stench of dead fish, she looked right into the eye of a Sony Betacam and said, "This is Donna Santoro in Ray Brook for WDNT *News Line Nine."* Her voice was as low and husky as Percy Quinell's.

After she finished, Plunkett took a giant stride, hoping to circumvent both the reporter and the dead fish.

She jabbed her microphone in his face.

"So far, State Police officials have refused to comment," she said.

"Officer—"

She shoved the mike so close that Plunkett would have had no trouble biting its end off—a temptation he found hard to resist. He shook his head and took a step to the side.

She deftly mirrored it, keeping the mike in place. "SAP claims that the police are doing nothing—"

It was the microphone. That and the sad, sorry sight of all those dead trout. "Please," he said, tapping the mike to one side with his index finger.

She pulled the mike back. Thrust again. "Are you categorically refusing—"

Behind the glass doors leading into the building, Plunkett could see four or five of his fellow troopers watching. In front of the pack, wearing a gray suit and a smug simper, stood Culley. Plunkett tried another end run, this one to the fish-pile side of the reporter.

And nearly made it. She had to take three hopping steps backward, still keeping up some prattle about an anonymous caller claiming that some appropriate gesture was required to remind the police that there was an ecological disaster unfolding—right under their noses.

The mike came up right under Plunkett's nose. "Are the police going to do anything?" she said.

Plunkett nudged her hand to one side.

"Watch it," she said. "I—"

She got in his way again, coming back at him with that mike. Thinking to hell with it, Plunkett gripped her gently by the shoulders and rotated her, mike and all, in a slow, ninety-degree arc. The last thing he heard was her too-deep voice saying to the camera man, "You get that, Ernie? All of it?" and Ernie, or whatever his name was, replying, "Yeah, yeah. You were great, Donna."

★ ★ ★

Troop Commander Fisk, it turned out, was too busy with the PR mess resulting from the dead fish to rake Plunkett over the coals. He delegated that task to Culley. It was the sort of assignment Culley tackled with the dedication and self-confident efficiency of someone who had found his true calling.

"I need to see you in my office," Culley said to Plunkett, and then, cutting a rookie trooper from the pack by the front door, added, "You." As they walked down a long corridor that remained faithful to the building's junior-college motif, Culley began bawling out the rookie.

"You," he said, a second time, jabbing his finger toward the young guy's brand new trooper's shield, stopping maybe a quarter inch away. He just let that *You* hang there in the air.

"There were four other people in the building at the time. Why single me out?" said the rookie. "Besides, you should be thanking me. It was me that heard the commotion. From back by your office," he said. "I went to check on it. If I hadn't, they might have dumped the whole load there. Window was broken . . ." He let his voice trail off. "That was when I heard the noise by the door. It was five A.M., exactly. I checked. By then, they had dumped the fish and were turning onto the highway. A small pickup. Light-colored."

"Which fits the description of one of the vehicles Quentin Quinell drives," said Culley.

The young trooper brightened. "Checked on that already. Drew a blank, I'm afraid. Quentin Quinell spent the evening at the camp of John Conoscenti—as in His Honor Judge John Conoscenti of the New York State Supreme Court. There appears to be a relationship with the judge's youngest daughter."

Culley's dainty jaw began to shake. "Surely Quentin can't account for—"

"All evening. He was there all evening. His Honor confirmed it. With pride, I might add. I guess having an environmental activist son-in-law will enhance his chances for a shot at the Senate—"

"Environmental activist." Culley spewed out the words. In the same tone he said, "Plunkett, my office."

Plunkett did as bidden. He settled into a vinyl chair across the desk from Culley, who pulled out his own chair furiously and planted himself with authority that went far beyond his years. "I don't know what the hell you did or said to Quentin. I thought we had matters under control. Well under control."

Still feeling edgy from his encounter with the TV reporter, Plunkett said, "Didn't do a damn thing to Quentin. Should have, though. Like maybe wrung his neck."

"This has caused me tremendous embarrassment. Personal embarrassment," Culley added. "You've given me virtually nothing and now—" He gestured toward the front entrance while he worked his boyish face into as close an approximation of a scowl of paternal disappointment as its fine cheekbones could support. "But that's only the half of it. We would be having this little talk even if this incident hadn't occurred. At Fisk's request," he said ominously.

Culley got up and closed the door to emphasize the gravity of his appointed task.

"Yesterday afternoon Fisk got a fax from Bo Scullin's lawyers. The firm of Banks, Hotchkiss and Goodman—on Park Avenue." He shot Plunkett a look that suggested he should damn well know the significance of that.

Culley consulted a few pieces of fax paper. "They are threatening legal action." He eyed Plunkett. "Harassment,' they say." He began to read: " 'We have been retained by Mr. Robert Scullin . . . blah . . . blah . . . blah.' Here's the interesting part. 'Officer Plunkett did on Thursday, July 16, trespass upon the property of Mr. Scullin without prior warning or without proper warrants—"

"I called in advance."

"Will you let me finish." Culley once again consulted the paper. "And without informing our client that he had a right to have legal counsel present, did proceed to interrogate him for nearly an hour—"

"More like five min—"

"I'm telling you what it says here. These are very"—there was a

-87-

pause—"very high-priced attorneys." He cleared his throat. " 'On matters that—' "

Culley stopped long enough to put on the same scowl of paternal disappointment he had worn a moment earlier. It already looked more at home. " '—appeared to be directly related to the recent and unfortunate accidental death of his late business partner, Barron Quinell IV. Furthermore, the trooper proceeded to interrogate our client on matters related to an accident and resulting chemical spill, the only connection our client having thereto being that his company owns land bordering on a public thoroughfare locally known as Stewart Mountain Road . . .'

"It goes on and on in that vein," Culley said. "It implies that you greatly distressed one of Mr. Scullin's houseguests. That you in fact barged in while she was bathing. It ends by insisting that you cease and desist. Which you are going to do."

"It's all a crock," Plunkett said. "I called and told him I was coming. The meeting was short. Cordial. At the end it was all smiles. He offered to help in any way—"

"Did you ask him about his partner's death?"

Plunkett looked at the toe of his shoe and nodded.

Culley said, "Fisk asked me to inform you that this will all be going into your file—formally. And furthermore—"

Plunkett was spared the lecture that would have followed the *and furthermore* by the receptionist's voice on Culley's speaker phone.

"Mr. Hormel from the *Chronicle-Herald,*" he said.

Culley got out a, "Tell him I'm—" before a timid voice came over the speaker.

"Am I speaking to Investigator Culley?" it asked.

Culley picked up the receiver and said solicitously, "Yes, may I help you." He listened for a full minute. "Yes, that's accurate. . . . At the moment we have no clear idea who dumped the fish. . . . I'm not aware of any note. . . . As I said, I'm not aware of any note, and if SAP is claiming credit, then we'll look into it in the appropriate manner during the due course of our investigation. . . . Yes, I agree, the spill is a very serious matter, and I am treating it as such. All of my available resources are concentrated on bringing the responsible parties to justice and, more important, assuring that a spill like that never occurs here again. . . . My investigating officers have a suspect, yes. . . . I would feel safe in saying that an arrest is imminent, yes, but for obvious reasons, this being an ongoing investigation, I cannot elaborate at this moment. I'm sorry, I have someone here with me, is there anything else?" After a pause, he hung up and leveled an I-told-you-so glare at Plunkett.

"That was stretching it," said Plunkett. "That last bit. About an arrest being imminent."

Culley planted the first full-fledged smirk of the morning on his face and said, "That's your worry, not mine. I suggest you get your butt down to that reggae club and find out the identity of that truck driver."

"Surely you don't expect me—"

"I expect you to do something. Something other than pissing off local rich guys and provoking blatant acts of ecotage."

A full-scale lecture was forestalled by the speaker phone. "It's WDNT on the line," said the receptionist, adding, "the television station."

"Fisk just finished giving their girl a statement," said Culley. "Tell them I'm in a meeting."

Culley turned back to Plunkett. "No more playing Sherlock Holmes. No more imaginary murder investigations. I want you down in the city on Monday."

Sounding exasperated, the receptionist came back on. "Sorry. It's still WDNT. The news director. He insists on speaking with Trooper Plunkett. Something to do with one of their reporters who was just out here." Plunkett could almost hear the gulp that preceded what the receptionist had to say next: "He mentioned . . . brutality."

Plunkett got out of his seat and was on his way to the door.

"Plunkett," Culley said.

Plunkett shook his head. "You're doing fine."

"And what the hell am I supposed to tell them?"

Plunkett shrugged. Over his shoulder he said, "Tell them that I have been ordered to spend one of my precious days off in the city. Punishment."

11

If you factored in his dreadlocks, the black guy was at least six-foot-eight, standing there in the Mango Tree Restaurant saying to Plunkett, "We closed," and pointing a butcher knife toward the door on the off chance there was any misunderstanding.

Plunkett considered a retreat to the safety of Second Avenue, a very relative sort of safety, even at 11:45 on a Monday morning, given the Lower East Side neighborhood. But having imparted his message, the dreadlocked character lost all interest. He turned and disappeared through a door in back. Plunkett heard a few muffled words that were answered by a sing-song female voice.

Figuring that if the guy really had intended to disembowel him, he would have done it already, Plunkett walked toward the voices.

In places where graffitists hadn't donated their talents, the Mango Tree's interior was painted in alternating stripes of hot pink and lime green and decorated with art of vaguely Haitian origins. One wall was taken up by a bar, fringed by a ratty thatch of palm and fronted with cut-in-half steel drums. The place stank of stale beer, citrusy-sweet fruit concoctions, and marijuana smoke.

The latter was accounted for by the three-inch-long spliff that smoldered to one-side of the dreadlocked guy's sausagelike lower lip. He balanced it there while he whacked away at a pile of whole-fryer chickens in the cramped kitchen, reducing them to bite-size pieces, which he scraped with the flat side of the knife toward a slight woman who arranged them on aluminum baking sheets and then brushed them with a greenish brown glop.

The big guy lifted the hoods over his two bloodshot eyes and stared at Plunkett, who, in a yellow polo shirt, pale green cotton slacks and scuffed topsiders, looked like any other tourist who had bumbled into the wrong part of town. Once he had stared long enough to let Plunkett realize the folly of coming into the Mango Tree, he reached to his lip, removed the spliff, and emitted a cloud through both nostrils and his mouth. It should have set off the smoke alarms and sprayer system, had the Mango Tree been the sort of place that paid attention to fire safety.

"We closed," he said, in a slow rumble.

Before Plunkett could say anything, the young woman, whose skin was a light café au lait color in contrast to the man's coal black, wiped her hands and stepped away from the counter. Even though she looked no more than half as tall as her co-worker and weighed about one hundred pounds, she eyed Plunkett with a glare that was every bit as dangerous as the big guy's. More dangerous, once she slid over beside a cash register, careful to keep Plunkett in view and her hands out of sight. Plunkett guessed that was the most likely place to hide something big and nasty and with the sort of stopping power that could maintain peace and order when the Mango Tree was filled with characters like the one with the dreadlocks.

Plunkett got right down to business. He figured there was a better chance the woman wouldn't blast him with her ugly gun once she knew he was a cop. Better, but only marginally.

He flashed his identification shield, introduced himself neither politely nor gruffly, and launched into what he guessed would be a three-minute version of the story about the unknown driver and the smashed Isuzu truck. About a minute and fifteen seconds into his recitation, the slender woman averted her face and picked up two full green garbage bags. She disappeared further into the Mango Tree, clanking bottles.

When Plunkett finished, the hoods over the dreadlocked guy's eyes went up maybe one-eighth of an inch then dropped down until the pupils were obscured. "We closed," he said again.

Plunkett pulled out the business card. "This was in his pocket—the dead man's. Has your address on it. I could pass it along to my associates at the NYPD. They might want to come down here and look into it . . . and a few other things . . ." Plunkett pointed toward the spliff and swung his finger toward a yellowing collection of health department roach control citations that were pinned to the wall where another eatery might have displayed favorable newspaper reviews.

The guy extended two fingers coated in chicken slime. He took the business card and looked at it without expression, unless you counted the slight lowering of the eye hoods. After he handed it back, he merely flipped his dreadlocks toward the cash register. There was a shoe box beside it, about half-filled with business cards from the reggae band.

At least five hundred of them, if Plunkett had to guess.

Manhattan was doing its best that day to live up to all of the evil clichés ascribed to it by out-of-towners. Cloying humidity combined with fawn-colored exhaust from the delivery trucks and taxis gridlocked on Second Avenue rendered the ninety-degree air all but unbreathable—and there were still five or six degrees to go before the forecast high was reached. The skin beneath Plunkett's collar already felt oily.

Among the throngs of pedestrians that barged and bulled along the sidewalks, the only ones displaying anything that would pass for decency, civility, or plain good manners back up in Wilmington were the glassy-eyed homeless.

Plunkett did a little step dance around a deposit of dog manure that clearly bore the partial *Nik-* imprint of a running shoe's sole. Once clear, he stopped to consider whether he would be better off taking his chances with one of the gridlocked cabs or walking to his next appointment—his unofficial appointment, the one Culley would have forbidden him to make. But, after the Mango Tree, he had earned the perk of a little freelance sleuthing into Barron Quinell's professional life. And anyway, who was Culley to dictate that Plunkett couldn't pass a few moments chatting with an accomplished young woman—accomplished and no doubt also beautiful, given Quinell's track record.

Stopping to think was obviously something that was simply not done in that part of town. Two beggars—one northbound, the other south—hit on him simultaneously. Feeling guilty, he fumbled in his pockets and surrendered a quarter to each.

That was when he heard the *hsssst*. It came from behind him. Plunkett assumed fairness might dictate he part with another coin. But the hiss's source was the slight woman who had been in the restaurant. She stood halfway up a steep staircase that rose from between two iron hatches set into the sidewalk.

Once she was sure her hiss had caught Plunkett's attention, she hoisted a green garbage bag that looked like it outweighed her by twenty pounds. "His name was Lucky," she said, and then repeated the name slowly, so even a bumpkin of Plunkett's obvious magnitude would understand: "Lucky Spike." She let the bag drop to the sidewalk and seemed pleased by the clanking of broken glass. "Living in Harlem—West 119th Street—with his aunt. Lezlene Henry." She took a backwards step toward the innards of the Mango Tree.

"Ma'am . . ." said Plunkett, not liking the note of desperation in his voice, but unable to do a thing about it.

The woman stopped with her head a few inches below sidewalk level.

"Can we talk?" Plunkett asked.

She shook her head sadly. "If you find dat bitch, da fair-haired one, you put her away quick b'fore me get to her."

Doors began to close over her like two halves of a badly rusted clam shell.

"What fair-haired—"

She cut him off with her glare. "The one that hire him," she said, as the doors clanged together.

★ ★ ★

The instant he laid eyes on Lisa Perry, Plunkett decided that if what Quentin said about her relationship with Barron Quinell was true, then with Barron's untimely death, the world had marked the passing of one of its greatest philanderers.

The woman who unlatched the three locks on the door of the renovated loft on Bleecker just east of Lafayette wore a pale blue business suit over a white silk camisole. She was in her early twenties and stood somewhere near six feet tall, to judge by the way her blue eyes bore straight ahead into Plunkett's. Her hair was the trademark ultra-blond preferred by Quinell men of all generations, and it had been fashioned into the longest braid Plunkett had ever seen. When she walked, the braid wagged like a tail across the small of her back.

Lisa Perry was so pretty, her looks so refined, that in her presence Plunkett immediately felt uncomfortable: plain, a little unkempt, and in need of a thorough scrub-down.

"You said this visit was unofficial," she said, striking off through the sunny loft. Plunkett assumed he was meant to follow and did. "But I thought it better that we meet here rather than at the office."

When she reached what looked to be a study, or home office, she sat behind her desk—something low, off-white and angular, like every other piece of furniture in the loft. Firing up a cigarette in a way that made it seem like one of the most intelligent acts a human being could perform, she nodded for Plunkett to sit on a rectangular object across from her.

That answered one of the many questions swirling through his mind: Was that particular piece a chair, a stool, a coffee table, or an example of the modern sculpture produced not far from that neighborhood? He sat—or rather squatted—with his knees pressed up against his stomach. The sunlight was so intense he had to squint to see Lisa Perry as anything other than a backlighted silhouette.

Once he was in place, she went on, keeping her eyes affixed to Plunkett's, now a few inches below hers. "Although, to be perfectly frank with you, I'm surprised that there would be anything unofficial about questions related to Barron's—" She paused and set her jaw. It was as thin, angular, and well-sculpted as the loft's furnishings.

Plunkett cleared his throat. "Officially," he said, "Mr. Quinell's death is being treated as accidental. He fell in the river, struck his head on a rock, got tangled in his fishing line, and drowned."

The beautiful face showed not a trace of reaction but there was no doubt that the mind behind it absorbed what Plunkett said, broke it down into its logical components, sorted them out, and then, only once everything was perfectly clear, spoke. "Then why are you here—unofficially?"

"Because I'm not convinced the official version is correct."

She nodded at him, thoughtfully nibbling her lower lip.

"That's strictly a personal opinion," Plunkett said.

She responded by dipping the point of her chin an inch.

Taking that as assent, Plunkett said, "I was hoping to talk to someone from the business side of his life. Ask if maybe there might be anybody who would obviously benefit from his death."

Once again, she went through her mental calculations. "Enough to kill him?" She puffed out a cloud of smoke every bit as formidable as the dreadlocked guy's back at the Mango Tree. "Doubt it. But you should know . . . he and Quent—"

"The son," Plunkett coached gently.

"Yes," she said, with exasperation. "I mean no. Quentin doesn't have it in him to do that. Forgetting all other possibilities, the bottom line is that Quentin's too lazy. But they did have an argument a couple of weeks ago. Quentin was dead set against a plan I have to develop the company's Adirondack lands. Barron," she said the name reverentially, "was all in favor."

"Any threats?"

"Not unless you count a lot of whining on Quentin's part. That seemed to be his preferred tone of voice whenever addressing his father."

Plunkett let a little therapeutic silence settle over the renovated loft, hoping that it might jog her memory. She merely looked at him expectantly with those blue eyes until he said, "If that's all . . ."

When she spoke, it was with a note of defiance. "Barron had problems with his marriage," she began. "His wife is—" She paused to search for the word. Some of the defiance left. "She's . . . They have grown apart over the years. Her background was . . . was different."

There was obviously nothing different about Lisa Perry's background.

"Barron appreciated my mind. My business sense," she said. "You don't know how rare that is when you're as—" She stopped. "It's a rare thing in the corporate world. Barron and I were going to reshape Realty Associates. I had formulated a business plan that would have poised the company for geometric growth with only a modest infusion of investment capital. Barron said it was the finest business plan he had ever seen. He told me . . ."

The corners of her fine, thin lips twitched downward; the blue eyes misted with the first dewiness of tears.

"We were lovers," she confessed, then quickly corrected herself, "More than lovers. Barron proposed to me." She had to stop to wage a battle with a series of sobs.

Feeling like one of the world's biggest boors, Plunkett found a piece of Realty Associates letterhead on the desk and scrawled his name and telephone numbers for her.

"Sorry," he stammered. "I had no— I've left you my phone numbers . . . in case."

Lisa leveled those blue eyes at him and, without a trace of sobbing, said, "He was going to tell her, you know."

12

It took only forty-five minutes for Ivor to officially rechristen 107804 Cayman Ltd. as Biocural Laboratories Incorporated. *"Bio* for biotechnology. *Cur* for cure. And *al* for all," explained Ivor, after Percy observed that the name did not exactly trip off the tongue.

The transformation took place just after lunch on Monday, July 20, in Cayman Trustco Ltd.'s managing director's office, a ten-by-ten-foot space overlooking an alley in downtown Georgetown, Grand Cayman.

Biocural became the three hundred and eighty-sixth active company headquartered in that cramped office. The other three hundred and eighty-five were represented by business-card-sized brass plaques that all but obscured the white plaster wall behind Willard P. Bodden, Jr., Q.C., managing director of Cayman Trustco, if the nameplate on his desk was to be believed.

Bodden was a slight man, an inch or two taller than Percy when he stood to administer a brisk handshake and run his eyes over her black-on-white polka-dotted dress. He was well-groomed—bordering on too well-groomed, for Percy's tastes—in his late thirties, and flaunted enough gold jewelry to make his pirate ancestors swoon. Three heavy chains hung from his neck exactly where the tie to go with his olive-colored silk suit should have been. One wrist supported an inch-wide gold bracelet; the other a gold Rolex. His cuff links were fashioned from authentic doubloons. Bodden even had gold caps on his incisors, which he displayed at every opportunity.

Sitting low in a chair opposite Bodden, Ivor, the newly installed chairman of Biocural Laboratories, wore an ancient powder blue seersucker suit over a white shirt, whose collar flaps arched up and outward like a pair of albatross wings. In silence, he scrutinized Bodden long enough to do a full professional appraisal of the young man's trinkets and made no effort to conceal his distaste.

"I have been a client of this institution for nearly three decades," he said sternly.

Bodden gave him a glimmer of gold incisor along with a timid nod.

"Used to deal with your father," said Ivor.

Both the glimmer and nod became more pronounced.

"Your father?" repeated Ivor.

"Retired three years ago," said Bodden, his words carried along on the softened West Indian lilt of Caymanians. After a pause he pointed to a photograph of a graying version of himself on the far wall and added, "To a beach house on the north coast of Little Cayman. He is now one of two dozen permanent residents on the island. Spends all of his time bone fishing."

"Bone fishing?" said Ivor. "Always thought it would be interesting to try my hand. Must get over and see him sometime."

"He'd be delighted, I'm sure," said Bodden, dully. "But I'm handling matters here now, and you can rest assured the—" Bodden searched the acoustic panels on ceiling for a word. Apparently unable to find one that was satisfactory, he tossed out "principles" with a shrug, saying, "upon which this bank was founded remain intact. Especially for old and valued clients, such as yourself. My father, Mr. Rhys, has told me a great deal about you. He said there was no one better."

It was Ivor's turn to smile. "Did your father ever tell you about Fyndemoor Golds?"

"Nineteen sixty-eight. Vancouver Stock Exchange. Netted you and your associates six hundred and ninety-six thousand, after commissions and fees to this bank of approximately seventy thousand dollars," recited young Bodden.

Ivor *harrumphed*. "Closer to one hundred thousand to this bank. Your father..."

Ivor brought himself up short, but young Bodden's eyes looked at the photograph with admiration that made it evident he had figured out what his father had done—and was proud of it.

"And you say the principles haven't changed under your tenure?" said Ivor.

"Fees have gone up—principles remain intact," said Bodden, treating Ivor and Percy to a glint of incisor.

Ivor *harrumphed* again. "To what extent have the fees gone up?" he said.

"That," said Bodden, "depends upon the nature of the services you will be requiring of Cayman Trustco, Mr. Rhys."

Ivor shifted in his seat until he gave up on the idea of getting comfortable and struggled upright, perching his wiry frame on the edge of his chair, planting his palms on his knees, elbows out. "Your father tell you about Eureka Mines by any chance?"

Young Bodden twisted one of his doubloon cuff links. "That wasn't the little Ponzi scheme you ran back in the early seventies?"

"Little Ponzi scheme," Ivor sniffed. "That, young man, is like calling Mozart's Symphony Number 29 a pleasant ditty. We worked off the finest mooch list in North America. Had beautifully produced tip sheets and prospectuses. Our share certificates were printed at the British Banknote Company and elaborately enough embossed to make IBM's look fly-by-night. We operated out of a full suite of Bay Street offices in Toronto, with a boiler room staffed by the best telephone men in the business... real pros."

"And you intend to repeat it?" said Bodden, sitting forward an inch or two himself.

Ivor formed a pout and nodded. "With some modifications.

We're substituting biotechnology for gold mining and our ambitions are somewhat more modest in scope, but the proceeds should be substantial."

Bodden's eyebrows came together and in unison rose.

Ivor held up five arthritis-gnarled fingers.

"Five large?" said Bodden.

Ivor dipped his chin.

Stroking his lips with a gold Cross pen, Bodden asked, "And what services do you require of Cayman Trustco. Specifically?"

"A numbered account," said Ivor.

"Done." Bodden's pen stayed in place. His eyebrows were still raised expectantly.

"And then—" Ivor stopped himself long enough to make sure he had Bodden's full attention. "At the right moment—" He took in the slight nod from Bodden. "A large sum of money will be transferred here, probably into another account. You will make sure it ends up in ours—through a banking error."

"Such errors have been known to happen in this age of computers and microcircuitry, but they can be very costly, Mr. Rhys."

"How costly?" said Ivor.

"About five hundred thousand dollars, I should expect," said young Bodden.

Outside the Cayman Trustco building, Percy and Ivor stood together and blinked in sunshine made painfully bright by the stark white bank buildings that lined the streets: Barclays, The Royal Bank of Canada, Scotiabank, and at least a dozen others, all within eyeshot.

"That," said Ivor, rubbing his palms together as if to wipe them free of dirt, "was a good morning's work. With our banking arrangements in place, Bo Scullin is one step closer to being destitute. We still have a long way to go, but I think we can call it a day. I'm going back to the hotel. There was a young woman sunning herself there in a coral-colored bikini this morning. . . ." He let his voice trail off wistfully. "We don't get a lot of coral bikinis on Turnip Island. Care to come along?"

"To ogle a young woman? I think not, Uncle Ivor. I'll duck into that jewelry store down the street."

"I'll walk that far with you," said Ivor, taking her arm in his and strutting off through the throngs of tourists disgorged that morning from a cruise ship. They took up every square inch of sidewalk space, racing from shop to shop in a manner that suggested the Cayman Tourist Board had offered a free vacation to the couple who spent the most in the least amount of time.

"This place was a sleepy little backwater in the 1960s," said Ivor. "People called it the island time forgot. That was when I first discovered its charms."

"Charms?" said Percy, dodging a well-fed couple in matching white T-shirts emblazoned with orange hibiscus blossoms.

"Banking charms," said Ivor. "Our transactions will be as safe with young Bodden as with the most discreet gnome in all Zurich. And, frankly, I find the climate here more to my liking than Zurich's."

"And young Bodden isn't exactly a gnome," said Percy.

They arrived in front of the jewelry store. "Here we are then," said Ivor. "I'll be leaving you. But mind you don't spend all your money. You may be needing it." For the first time since boarding the plane at La Guardia the previous afternoon, Ivor flashed the Smile.

The store was as clogged inside with shoppers as the sidewalk was outside. An uncanny number of them also wore hibiscus-emblazoned T-shirts. It took a full ten minutes before Percy could get the attention of a clerk, buy what she had come for, and leave the store, poorer by twelve hundred and ninety-seven Caymanian dollars.

She put the purchase in her handbag and hurried back to a café directly across the street from the building housing Cayman Trustco. There, she found a window table and ordered a double vodka on the rocks, which she immediately reduced to a single. Knowing Ivor, she figured she wouldn't have long to wait.

Precisely eight minutes later—just when the first of Percy's ice cubes surfaced—she saw Ivor, a sedate patch of powder blue bobbing upstream against the garishly clad cruise ship passengers. In front of Cayman Trustco he stopped, looked long and hard in both directions, gave a quick nod of his white-thatched head and disappeared inside.

Percy finished the rest of her drink. Before leaving the table, she opened her purse and took out the emerald-studded gold tie bar she had just purchased and would be parting with as soon as Ivor left the Cayman Trustco building. Admiring it, she mused that old Ivor was right on one count: It had indeed been a good morning's work.

"Mr. Rhys!" said young Bodden, flashing way too much gold tooth for Ivor's liking. The smile stayed where it was until it became apparent that Ivor had returned alone—without Percy—whereupon it was replaced by something very near a sulk.

"There was one other transaction I wanted to discuss," Ivor said. "A personal one."

In one deft flip-flop Bodden's sulk became shrewd and wary.

"As I recollect, I maintain a personal account with this bank," Ivor said.

Bodden spread his hands. "Inactive, I'm afraid." He lowered his voice and said sadly, "Insufficient balance."

"Precisely the situation I came to rectify," said Ivor, taking an alligator wallet from his suit coat pocket and withdrawing a check. "Certified," said Ivor. "For the sum of ten thousand dollars."

Bodden took the check and perused it carefully, as if looking for a flaw he knew was hidden there—somewhere. His clever brown eyes scanned it from top to bottom, then retraced their journey until they peered at Ivor over the top, apparently finding everything in order. "This is not made out to anyone in particular," said Bodden.

"Well, that's because I have two alternatives."

Young Bodden nodded.

"I could make it out to Ivor Rhys, and deposit it in my account here. Or . . ."

Another nod.

"... I could make it out to Willard P. Bodden, Jr., in consideration of services to be rendered."

"And the precise nature of those services would be . . .?"

"That's the easy part," said Ivor. "Really nothing you won't be doing anyway. When the five million comes, instead of slipping it into the Biocural account, deposit it into my personal account."

The gold teeth gleamed. This time, it didn't bother Ivor in the least. Young Bodden shared a knowing smile with the photograph of his father. He chuckled and spoke. " 'Should Ivor Rhys ever darken the doors of this bank again,' my father told me, 'don't, whatever you do, underestimate him,' " Bodden said. "As usual, he was right. But Mr. Rhys"—Bodden once again consulted the portrait of his father—"to do this to such a beautiful woman—it doesn't seem right."

13

Quentin Quinell's offices occupied a frame building located in the section of Saranac Lake that came as close to being a bad part of town as things got in that well-scrubbed village. A damn sight better than the Lower East Side, but given his choice of company, Plunkett might still have gone with the dreadlocked character. A big Rasta, wielding a butcher knife—fellow knew where he stood. Not so with a spoiled rich kid whose main weapons were a sarcastic tongue and the sort of arrogance that comes only from being absolutely certain that most other human beings rank well below oneself on the evolutionary ladder.

SAP's boxy headquarters leaned a good ten degrees into the hillside upon which it had been erected. Where the paint hadn't chipped and peeled, it was a dull yellow, every bit as pale and dreary as the sunshine trying to struggle through the haze that afternoon, Tuesday. The only indication that the place hadn't been abandoned was a crude dot-matrix computer printout taped to the door that said SAP. A ballpoint-drawn arrow pointed heavenward.

Entering and taking two flights of stairs, Plunkett found himself in a cramped vestibule whose main purpose obviously was to let visitors know they were about to enter the presence of a Great

Man. The walls were festooned with newspaper clippings and glossy photographs, all with one feature in common: Quentin Quinell. Quentin shaking hands with former Governor Cuomo; Quentin standing, arms crossed and looking defiant, in front of a bulldozer; Quentin and the two young women being hauled away to a police car. Out of focus and in the background of that one, Plunkett saw a younger, more earnest-looking version of himself.

The prevalent motif inside SAP's offices was stacks of paper, enough computer printouts, press releases, official memos, newspapers, and magazines to reforest a good portion of the park the organization was supposedly trying to save. SAP being an environmentally aware organization, there wasn't an air conditioner on premises. And the three government-surplus window fans didn't seem to be doing anything other than providing an annoying racket to augment the heat.

Looking calm, comfortable, and too much at home for a man who was about to undergo a police interrogation, Quentin emerged from the clutter wearing Birkenstock sandals, a Speedo bathing suit, and a SAP T-shirt. He scanned Plunkett like someone who had never before seen a person clad in a polo shirt or topsiders, and then offered a throwaway handshake, which upon release doubled as a gesture toward a lumpy sofa, circa 1950. Plunkett sat and found himself enveloped in a miniature dust storm.

"Why the civilian duds?" Quentin asked.

"Day off," said Plunkett.

"Thought maybe you'd come looking for work," said Quentin, pulling up a folding metal chair for himself and sprawling, arms hooked over the back, legs spread in front. He explained: "Saw you on the evening news—When was it? Friday? Manhandling that poor, defenseless Donna Santoro. Donna the Piranha, that's what her male colleagues call her, I'm told." Quentin snickered. "About as defenseless as her namesake, that one. Heard there was going to be some sort of reprimand." He kicked off both Birkenstocks and began wiggling his liberated toes.

The truth was that there was not going to be a reprimand. There would be nothing other than a routine Personnel Complaint investigation, overseen by Culley. It would drag on long enough for the public to forget about the film clip of the cop struggling with the television reporter, then Plunkett would be absolved of any wrongdoing, provided—and this was supposed to be Culley's idea of a catch—provided he give up his investigative delusions, at least insofar as they related to the recent unfortunate passing of Barron Quinell.

When it became apparent that Plunkett wasn't going to say anything about Donna Santoro, Quentin gathered his limbs and stood. He went over to one of the desks and came back with a can of Coke. Settling back into his sprawl, he swigged from the can, but made no effort to offer Plunkett a drink.

"Uncle Bo is none too pleased with you either," Quentin said. "In fact, I would go so far as to say that your visit made the poor man distraught." Quentin drew his feet back toward the chair legs and jacked himself up an inch or two. "And those lawyers of his . . ."

Plunkett figured that the only way to handle a guy who liked to hear himself talk as much as Quentin was not to show a trace of reaction. With luck, Quentin would eventually blow himself out. Then Plunkett might be able to work in a question or two.

"You sleuths wouldn't by chance have found who was responsible for dumping the load of fish at the cop shop?" Quentin said, spreading the sarcasm thick enough to elicit a delicate female giggle from somewhere behind a mound of paper in the far corner of the room.

"Maybe we should talk about that," Plunkett said.

Quentin stiffened. "If you're here about that, then I want my lawyer present. I've been through it already. I was a houseguest—"

"Make you feel proud—college kids doing your dirty work. What if we'd caught the girl?"

Quentin sat upright. "Maybe I had better call my lawyer."

"Fine with me," said Plunkett, and waited until Quentin pawed the receiver off a telephone on the nearest desk before he added, "or you and I could get serious with each other for maybe ten minutes and see if we can't make some headway on this chemical spill. If you give a damn, that is."

"Saranac Chemicals, let's start there," Plunkett said, once Quentin was back in his sprawl.

"They did it," said Quentin. "No question."

"So you claim."

"So I know."

"Evidence?" said Plunkett. "Something maybe a police officer could use?"

"The company's going bust. How's that?"

"I'd be more interested in how you came to know that little fact—if it is a fact."

Quentin chuckled. "It's a fact, all right," he said. "And it's like I said the other day down by the river. My stepmother told me." He let that morsel of information settle and added, "Indirectly, of course. We don't communicate any other way, Stepmommy and I. Overheard her and Daddy talking—arguing, actually. A tiff, which was about the only way they communicated. She was going on saying that Saranac was headed down the tubes and that it was good riddance as far as she was concerned. Daddy was saying, 'Fine, fine, fine, fine . . .' I got the impression Daddy had made some sort of investment—a bad one, which would not have been out of character."

Plunkett nodded and said, "Lot of companies going broke these days."

"How many of them sell chemicals?"

Plunkett realized that for once Quentin had a valid point.

"Besides—" Quentin stopped. "Besides, SAP received an anonymous tip just after the spill. Old woman called and said there were trucks coming and going from Saranac Chemicals at all hours of the day and night—three, four in the morning, times like that. She'd never seen it so busy."

"So, they're doing overtime."

"They don't have enough business to keep a full day shift on," said Quentin. "Drive by their parking lot. See for yourself."

★ ★ ★

Plunkett got out of his pickup truck. He took five steps toward the low metal-clad building that housed Saranac Chemicals before hearing what sounded like the thudding of a horse's hooves.

He turned in time to see a rottweiler coming from the building at full gallop. The dog, which had the weight, speed, and muscle tone of a young stallion, launched itself toward Plunkett. Its trajectory would have planted its stubby jaws just above Plunkett's larynx, had the dog not first smashed into a Cyclone fence.

Even then, the fence provided dubious protection. Its posts wobbled with the impact and continued to wobble more vigorously as the dog braced itself against the chain links with its front paws to bark and snap.

Given the appearance of Saranac Chemicals, the guard dog seemed a clear case of overkill, or perhaps a survivor from a more prosperous era. In addition to Plunkett's gray Dodge Ram pickup, seven cars occupied a parking lot that could have handled thirty. Six were rusting North American clunkers: an Impala, an Electra, an Olds 98, two LTDs and one New Yorker. They sat at odd angles on their shocks, settling into the gravel. If Plunkett overlooked the thin cellular telephone antennae on three, he would have sworn the clunkers last rolled sometime back during the Carter administration. The seventh car was a showroom-fresh BMW 750ii sedan.

Two plain, gray-painted metal doors faced the parking lot. Neither bore a sign, and both appeared equally uninviting so Plunkett walked to the closest and tried it, surprised to find that the thing actually swung freely on its hinges.

The receptionist he confronted on the other side could have moonlighted as a bouncer in a bikers' bar. Her gray hair was clipped to an even one inch all around. At a guess, she would have weighed in at somewhere around 190, most of that bone, sinew, and gristle.

"Ain't hirin'," she grunted, keeping her eyes on the copy of the *National Enquirer* in front of her.

Plunkett introduced himself and asked if he could speak to the manager.

That, at least, got her to stop reading the paper. "Don't look like no cop," she said.

Plunkett showed her his shield.

Police officer; prospective employee—it didn't have an iota of effect on her demeanor. She ordered him to "siddown" while she went back to see if "Blevins" would see him.

She returned and glowered in such a way that Plunkett was sure Blevins had commanded her to haul out a shiv and lay the cop open from sternum to scrotum. Instead, she jabbed a thumb over her shoulder.

Blevins's office was air-conditioned—chilled to a meat locker temperature—by a noisy, vibrating machine crammed into one of its two small windows.

Blevins himself was chubby, crew-cut, and sporting a too-small powder blue blazer over black slacks, no belt. He wore a solid navy blue tie that came just below his breastbone. When he saw Plunkett, Blevins burst out in a crinkly-eyed smile, flashing a set of teeth that would have been a lot more becoming had they been in the mouth of a mule.

Without standing, he crushed Plunkett's fingers in his right hand. "Blevins," he said loudly enough to be heard above the air conditioner. He punctuated his sentence by hoisting his upper lip to provide Plunkett with an unobstructed view of his mule's teeth.

Plunkett introduced himself as quickly as possible and retrieved his hand. He shoved it in his pocket.

The news that Plunkett worked out of Wilmington seemed to make Blevins the happiest man in the world. "Love it up there. Just love it," he said, losing all control of his smile. "Business associates of mine have camps up there."

Plunkett waited for him to finish. "Business associates? Who? Probably know them," Plunkett said.

Blevins looked like he had misplaced his smile and was damned if he could remember where. "Oh, just business associates," he said. "But how can I help you, officer?"

Plunkett glanced at the two straight-backed chairs across the desk from Blevins's thronelike, leather executive chair, so far the only sign of prosperity inside Saranac Chemicals. Blevins gestured toward one of the guest chairs, but did so in a way that suggested it went against his better judgment.

Plunkett sat. "You've heard about the chemical spill," he said. Blevins looked at him dumbly.

"Killing all the fish in the Ausable," Plunkett said. "It's been on the news."

"Yeah, yeah, yeah," said Blevins. "That cute little dark-haired number. The one who— Say, you . . ." Blevins pointed a finger skyward. "Now I remember . . . knew I'd seen you somewhere . . . the news the other night. Terrible." He added hastily, "That business about the spill, I mean."

"Mind if I ask you a few questions?" said Plunkett.

"Me? Not at all. Love to answer anything I can." Blevins let his teeth reveal the depth and sincerity of his desire to cooperate, only to sheath them in a frown of regret. "But, I'm just the hired help around here. Answer to a board of directors, and unfortunately there is a company policy that I am not allowed to speak to anybody without the board's written consent. You understand. The chemical business can get touchy at times, what with the media and all these environmental crazies nowadays, even for a company like ours that has a spotless record. But what I can do for you, officer, is I'll happily bring this up before the next meeting of the board. I'm sure Saranac Chemicals will be glad to help you in any way—" He stood, smiling again.

Plunkett tried to match him smile for smile, but gave up. "What do you make here? What sort of chemicals?" Plunkett said.

Blevins came out from behind his desk and walked toward the door to his office. "Oh just chemicals," he said. "Industrial chemicals. Cleaning solvents and the like. Unless you're an engineer, they'd just be scientific-sounding names." Blevins stopped talking. He stood beside the door, smiling. His arm made the faintest shooing gesture.

"Metam sodium?" said Plunkett. "That one of the chemicals?"

The big mule smile stayed in place. May have even widened by another half inch on either side. "That's an agricultural chemical, officer," he said. "I told you, we specialize in cleaning solvents. Now—" He made the shooing gesture again.

The receptionist was on the phone bawling out some caller. Plunkett was about to tiptoe past her, when he noticed a gray metal door at the opposite end of the hall. It was clearly marked EMPLOYEES ONLY and emblazoned with warning decals detailing the ills that would befall anyone foolhardy enough to cross that threshold: skulls and crossbones, skeletal hands, eye-wash instructions, hard-hat admonitions. About the only one they had overlooked was Beware of Dog. The one that mattered, if the door led where Plunkett hoped.

Plunkett tried the handle. It turned. He looked over his shoulder. Saw that Blevins's door was closed. The receptionist-bouncer was still ranting into her phone. Something along the lines of that if whoever was on the other end wanted a check, he could goddamn well . . .

He cracked the door. Listened. Peered through the slit. Just as he lifted his foot to take a step, he heard the receptionist say, "Lose your way?" She held both hands over the mouthpiece. "That's the way out." The thumb was jerked toward the door Plunkett had used to enter. Her smallish, bloodshot eyes traced his progress down the hall, across the reception area and were still on him as he stepped outside, hearing "I could care goddamn less what your terms are. Our terms are that we pay in ninety days. Not a second sooner. If you don't like—"

Plunkett found himself back in the parking lot, thinking he would have loved one quick peek at what was on the other side of that warning-covered door, and that another visit to Saranac Chemicals was definitely in order—well after the normal working hours.

Plunkett was sitting in his truck ready to crank the starter when an employee clad in jeans and a white T-shirt came out of the second of the two doors opening onto the parking lot—the one Plunkett had not used. The employee nudged a hunk of cinder-block against the base of the door with the toe of his workboot. He took a cigarette out of a pack he produced from the sleeve of his T-shirt, lit it, inhaled and exhaled a few times and then, fiddling with the zipper on his jeans, strode stiffly around the end of the building. Plunkett was out of his truck. He walked briskly to the door and slipped inside.

He found himself in a warehouse crammed from floor to ceiling with crudely stacked skids of chemical drums, some dented, rusted metal; their more modern counterparts blue plastic. From the far side of the drums, Plunkett heard the muffled sounds of a lift truck's engine. What he should have done, Plunkett knew, was to turn around, go back through that door, get in his truck, and go home until he could convince Culley to get the paperwork done for a proper search of Saranac Chemicals. An unlikely prospect, given the lack of evidence. But if Plunkett innocently took a wrong turn and saw something . . .

He selected a route between two rows of drums and walked in the direction of the lift truck's rumble.

Plunkett quickly concluded that whoever had stacked the drums either didn't know what he was doing, or had been drinking on the job, perhaps both. They were too high, in some cases leaning against each other, and it seemed as if the smallest vibration—the footfalls of a passing state trooper, for instance—would topple them.

The air was hot, hard to breathe, and had an astringent, vaporous smell: gasoline, engine grease, and the propane stink of the lift truck's exhaust.

In the distance, someone barked a command and got a mumbled one-syllable reply. Plunkett pressed his back into the space between two drums and listened. Whatever was said got drowned out by the lift truck being gunned. Keeping to the side, Plunkett made his way to the end of the passage. There, drums were stacked to within inches of the exterior wall. The lift truck was operating only a few feet away, but to get there Plunkett had to double back. Halfway along the row, he found a gap between two skids. It looked as if it would accommodate Plunkett as long as he held his breath and didn't think about the three tiers of sloppily stacked chemical drums above him.

He was in the gap, half-crouched and squirming through the narrowest portion, when he heard footsteps approaching across the cement floor. He froze, squeezed between a green drum leaking a gummy substance and a red drum with one of those skeletal hands waving its macabre greeting a few inches away from his cheek.

The steps got closer. Looking out, Plunkett caught a flash of powder blue. Blevins. He went past. Stopped. There was a shuffling sound. Plunkett pressed himself against the green barrel. He heard Blevins's steps returning. A quiet *"huh,"* came from only a few feet away. There was a pause, some more shuffling, then a loud, "You boys get a move on. We gotta get that thing loaded this afternoon."

"What's it look like we're doing."

"Looks like you're standing around staring at the barrels you're supposed to be getting on that goddamn truck. Now, move it. I want all of that stuff outa here. Every last drop. Supposed to have been gone last week."

"Then someone should of told me about those four skids out in the yard. Ain't a fucking mind reader."

"Sure aren't," said Blevins.

The lift truck started.

Plunkett stayed there not moving until the lift truck's sounds faded. Carefully, he wiggled out from behind the drums, his shoulder picking up a coating of the gummy stuff in the process. He crept to the end of the passage and looked toward where he had heard the voices. There was a truck parked there. A livestock truck.

He listened. The only thing he heard was the muffled noises of the lift truck moving around outside in the yard. He walked toward the livestock truck.

The ramp was down and still had dried dung on its rungs from when the vehicle was last used for its intended purpose. Plunkett stepped onto the ramp and peered inside. The truck's box was half-filled with drums. Mixed with a faint, barnyard aroma, Plunkett detected a tart scent, one he associated with garden supply stores.

Three of the drums, Plunkett could see, had black rectangles crudely spray painted on their sides. He went over to the nearest and touched the paint. The tips of his fingers came away black. He looked around, thinking there might be a scrap of paper or a rag to wipe off enough of the still-wet paint to see what was underneath. About the time he decided he might have to sacrifice a perfectly good polo shirt, he heard the lift truck approaching.

Plunkett stepped away from the drums and went back down the ramp. The sound of the lift truck got louder, coming from the direction of an open overhead door. He walked smartly toward a passage between two rows of drums and made it there just before the lift truck entered.

He didn't see Blevins standing there beside some guy wearing a security guard's uniform until Blevins said, "What the—"

Plunkett gave what he hoped was an innocent shrug.

Blevins treated him to a brief flash of teeth then wrestled his lips into a frown one side at a time and said, "You shouldn't be back here."

"Took a wrong turn coming out of your office," Plunkett said.

Blevins's lips broke away from their frown long enough to show the squared tips of his teeth. "Better come with me." He set off.

Plunkett turned to follow Blevins. From behind him, the security guard said, "Have a good day."

Plunkett hadn't recognized him because of the uniform. But the dull, dead voice—Aldon Hewitt's voice—*that* he would have known anywhere.

Blevins escorted him as far as the reception area, stopped and pointed a stubby finger toward the door. "That way," he said.

Humid, ninety-degree-plus July air had never felt so fresh or invigorating. Outside, Plunkett paused to breathe deeply, exchanging the rank stuff of the warehouse for something free from the stench of exhaust and chemicals. After filling his lungs to capacity and emptying them four times, he started across the parking lot, noticing that Aldon Hewitt's LTD was there among the clunkers. The lift truck-operator and the receptionist accounted for two of the other jalopies. He had Blevins pegged for the BMW. That left three cars whose owners were unaccounted for. Either they were working elsewhere on premises, or Plunkett's guess that the cars were abandoned derelicts was correct.

In the middle of the parking lot, Plunkett heard the thudding footsteps again and turned nonchalantly. It was the rottweiler, galloping toward him. Only this time there was no Cyclone fence between them.

Plunkett took a half-dozen giant strides toward his truck. He got as far as the tailgate. The dog kept coming, paws scratching the gravel, rounded ears flat against its bear's head, scruff on its broad back raised. It stopped a few feet away from Plunkett, gave a low, quiet growl and raised its upper lip to show thick teeth. Mouth opened, it lunged toward the meaty part of Plunkett's thigh.

Someone yelled, "Down, Tor!" The dog stopped itself in midlunge. It hit the gravel, and lay down, keeping two hateful, beady eyes on Plunkett.

Blevins came trotting across the parking lot, huffing and red-faced. He looped a finger through the dog's choke-chain collar and skidded the snarling animal back a foot or so, giving Plunkett just enough room to peel himself off the pickup's tailgate. Blevins didn't say anything as Plunkett went around and got in.

Holding Tor, or whatever the thing's name was, Blevins came to the window. Between huffs, he said, "I think it would be a good idea, the next time you come around here, if you have a warrant, maybe be in uniform, too, and driving a cruiser—just so there's no mistaking your intentions."

Plunkett popped the pickup into reverse. Over his shoulder, he saw Aldon Hewitt on the other side of the fence beside the gate.

"I think maybe you're right," Plunkett said to Blevins.

Of the two women more or less in Plunkett's life—three counting Percy—Beverly Laney was in many ways the most beautiful. She was also the shrewdest and the oldest—by four decades.

After his departure from Saranac Chemicals, Plunkett found Mrs. Laney at her usual post inside the Cooper Memorial Library, a small Greek revival structure beside the river in Wilmington. She sat behind a big, oaken schoolteacher's desk, said to be the very desk she used for the thirty-eight years that she had attempted to drill the fundamentals of high school English into the skulls of the region's adolescents.

"*Gar*-wood," she said, looking sternly over half-moon spectacles at the oily stain on his shirt. She pronounced the first syllable of his given name with a long, flattened *a* sound Plunkett associated with Boston Brahmins, even though he knew she originally came from some village outside Manchester, New Hampshire, that made Wilmington seem downright cosmopolitan. After pronouncing his name, she said, "What can I do for you?"

"Perhaps this is just a social visit."

That didn't begin to fool Mrs. Laney. Her blue eyes twinkled, spraying dozens of crow's-foot creases out toward the center-parted gray hair that framed her face. "In my experience, police officers rarely visit eighty-three-year-old widows—unless they need something. You least of all, *Gar*-wood. Our little library hasn't been blessed with your presence since June, when you checked out *A River Runs Through It,* now two weeks overdue. But I'm willing to offer amnesty"—she tossed her hair —"in exchange for one hug."

Plunkett complied, squeezing her frame lightly for fear he might break something. She grabbed his shoulders viciously and dug her head into his chest. After the hug she said, "Amnesty, provided you get the book back to me by next week, that is. Tuesday. Around dinner time. At my house. There's a cockerel in my coop who has recently begun crowing—and not very well, I'm afraid. High time I roasted him. Now," she said. "What can I do for you?"

He looked around for a seat. The only one within reach was one of four grade-school-dimension chairs arrayed in a semicircle to the right of her desk. He took it and had to half-sit, half-squat. "I've been having some problems—" he began, and stopped. "Work," he said.

"I watch the evening news, *Gar*-wood. Don't like it, but watch it. Someone really ought to take that Donna Santoro woman aside and impart some of the basics of English usage. Journalistic ethics, too, if such things still exist." Looking directly at him she said, "Some tea?"

Tea was not what he wanted, not on a ninety-degree-plus July afternoon. But without waiting for his answer, Mrs. Laney found two china cups and matching saucers in a side drawer. "Tea," she said, again. "Yes, I thought I had a little bottle of tea. Somewhere." From the same drawer, she produced a fifth of Harvey's Shooting Sherry and poured liberally into each cup. "What's this I hear about a Personnel Complaint?" she said, and composed herself to listen, cup in midair, pinky extended.

"Formality," said Plunkett. "Bunch of—" He stopped himself. "Bunch of nonsense, but I don't really care. Fact is, I've been thinking of retiring. Taking my half-pay and opening my own business . . ."

Her look was the same disapproving one she dealt out those many years ago whenever she encountered a disagreeing subject and verb. She scrunched her lips, forming five vertical furrows in the skin just above her chin. "We're the both of us too old to chase romantic daydreams," she said. "Keep your job." Her face softened. All furrows and crow's feet vanished, replaced by skin as smooth as a toddler's. "The irony is that I never felt you were tempermentally suited for a police officer's work. Too gentle. And, dare I say it, a little too intelligent. But now . . . now you've gone nearly twenty years. It's too late. And believe me, I know all about too late."

"Too late," Plunkett mumbled to himself, then said aloud, "But in the meantime, I'm still a cop, and there's a favor I want to ask of you."

"You have colleagues . . . surely . . ."

"My colleagues are conducting a Personnel Complaint investigation. Besides you'll do a better job, more quickly. Could you look a few things up for me on your—" He gestured with his cup toward the computer terminal on her desk, Mrs. Laney's hardwired connection to the outside world, a tool she deployed with ruthless efficiency. "A company called Saranac Chemicals. Anything you can find: newspaper reports, financial statements if they are available, lawsuits, any accusations of them doing environmental damage and—this is the one I'm really interested in—the identity of any shareholders, directors, and owners."

She took a few quick notes. "Does an old woman get to inquire why she is being asked to perform this service?"

"Because she's good at it?"

"Flattery, flattery, my boy." She reached over and gave him a little pat on the hand.

"Might be connected to the chemical spill," Plunkett said.

"Very well," said Mrs. Laney. "I'll see what my smart friend here"—she patted the top of the terminal with the same affection she had shown Plunkett's hand—"can locate."

Plunkett thanked her for the "tea" and got up. On his way to the door he said, "I'd be especially interested if Barron Quinell or his partner, Bo Scullin, turn up in your search." As an afterthought he added quietly, "Or Quinell's wife."

Mrs. Laney scowled. He thought that he was going to have to depart without fully understanding the cause of the scowl, but she said, "Shame on you, *Gar*-wood, for not telling me the reason you came to me instead of your professional associates—the real reason."

Plunkett opened his mouth to speak, but she put out her palm for silence.

"Don't trouble yourself," she said. "I can imagine. And at my age, that's sufficient. Quite sufficient."

"I know this isn't going to be a real date or anything we're going on tonight, but do you have any idea how long it's been since a man has taken me to the movies?" said Linda, as soon as Plunkett walked into the Lumberjack. "I mean, I think it was *Love Story* or something." She looked at him, did a double take, and said, "Yuck. What is that on your shirt?"

There was no one in the restaurant other than the high school girl Linda had helping for the summer, so without being asked, Linda proceeded to snap a Genny and put it on the counter. Plunkett drank right from the bottle and felt the cold, clean bite of the beer—maybe the best beer he had ever had.

Maybe the last beer he would ever have, given that he had totally forgotten about his suggestion that they go into Plattsburgh that night and see what was playing at the theater.

"I heard *Forrest Gump* is supposed to be good," Linda said, smiling a smile that was one notch too giddy to be worn by a mature, large-boned woman. When she saw Plunkett's face, she stopped being giddy and added, "but if you want, we could see . . ." She picked up a folded section of the *Chronicle-Herald* from behind the counter.

"Would you mind if we made it another night?" Plunkett said.

Linda and the high school girl used their eyebrows to exchange some secret female semaphore to which Plunkett was not party.

"Work," Plunkett said. His tone suggested that should have been explanation enough to make Linda jump in the air with glee.

Instead, she picked up a rag and began to swab the spotless counter. "Nother night'd be fine," she said, to the counter top, working the rag toward Plunkett's beer in vigorous circles.

"Was wondering too . . ."

"Yes," she said, swiping within a half inch of his bottle.

"If I could borrow your car."

"My car?" Linda said, stopping mid-wipe.

"Surveillance work. My truck's kind of obvious. Thought something nondescript . . ."

"A 1982 Subaru wagon—that's nondescript, all right," said Linda and began wiping again, sucking in one big breath for each stroke. "Can I come along?" she asked.

"It's just going to be surveillance work—boring, really. Sitting out beside some road all night, mostly trying to stay awake." Plunkett took a hit from the beer and put the bottle back on the counter.

"Maybe I could help—in the staying awake department." She worked her brows up and down in a flirtatious code that even Plunkett understood. Understood, but didn't take too seriously, noncommittal flirting being as much a basis for their friendship as her coffee and cheeseburgers. "And then if anyone did see us, it'd be the perfect cover. They'd just think we were some kooky old middle-aged couple out having an affair, or something."

"In a 1982 Subaru wagon?" he said.

Linda motioned with her cloth for him to raise his bottle off the counter. As she swiped underneath, she said, "Stranger things have been known to happen."

14

The livestock truck left Saranac Chemicals at 2:38 Wednesday morning, roughly five hours after Plunkett and Linda had taken up their post at an out-of-business gas station beside Route 3, a quarter of a mile west of the company's building.

The truck turned onto the highway and headed directly toward the parked Subaru in which Plunkett and Linda sat with Styrofoam cups of the Lumberjack's notoriously potent coffee. He had backed the little car tightly against the cinder-block side of the building, close enough to get back onto the highway quickly should circumstances warrant, but far enough off the road to go unnoticed—or that was the idea.

The truck's headlights hit Plunkett's eyes. He averted them. With a tremendous grinding of overburdened gears, the truck jolted forward, and crept down Route 3 toward Saranac Lake. If there had been cattle inside, they would have found the pace equal to a comfortable trot. Except, of course, there were no cattle inside.

Plunkett blinked his eyes to restore his night vision.

There were still two cars in the parking lot of Saranac Chemicals. He was wondering whether they would leave now, and if they did leave, whether it would be worthwhile to take a peek around the premises, rottweilers or no rottweilers.

"What are we waiting for?" said Linda.

Plunkett thought he could see someone moving beside one of the cars, but wasn't certain.

"After all this sitting around, we don't even get to follow the truck?" she said.

"I think I've gotten what I came for."

There was a moment's silence from Linda. Then a little snort. "You came all the way out here for some of my overbrewed coffee and career counseling—or was it to count cars on Route 3?"

"I tell you that when I was in Saranac Chemicals yesterday I ran into Aldon Hewitt."

"Thought he was in jail."

"Released."

"Doesn't reflect well on our system of justice."

"You see why I'm reluctant to follow. But I think I've got enough now to go back to Culley. Get warrants."

"The truck went that way." Linda pointed a finger. "That also happens to be the shortest route to Wilmington. If you stayed well back—"

A dim light shone inside one of the clunkers in the Saranac lot and went off. There was another flicker, perhaps from a lighter. Headlights came on and swept the parking lot as the driver turned around. The car pulled out on Route 3 and with a roar of mufflerless freedom, sped away from them toward Plattsburgh.

Plunkett could make out the dark figure of a man in the parking lot. He stood for a few minutes, then got in the remaining car.

Instead of going toward Plattsburgh, that car turned toward them. It accelerated quickly on the highway, but slowed as it approached the abandoned gas station. Headlights lit the Subaru's interior. Without thinking, Plunkett wrapped Linda in an embrace, turning the back of his head toward the car's lights. The scene was illuminated long enough for the embrace to become awkward.

-123-

Plunkett leaned closer to Linda, easing her down below the level of the dashboard.

The headlights swung away, vanishing along Route 3.

"See what I mean," Linda said, still in his arms. "Stranger things have been known to happen."

There was sign of neither the truck nor the car on Route 3, even after Plunkett had driven for ten minutes. Whoever was behind the wheel of the truck had either found some gear that would permit the vehicle to travel at normal highway speeds, or had turned off on any of the dozens of lesser roads and lanes that snaked down from the surrounding hills and mountainsides.

Not that Linda's Subaru would have made an ideal pursuit vehicle, even under the best of circumstances. On downhill stretches, Plunkett could coax it up to sixty miles per hour, but uphill it resolutely refused to struggle along at anything greater than thirty-seven.

Plunkett turned off when they came to the junction with the road that led to Hawkeye, Black Brook, and eventually over to Wilmington—or if one were inclined—to a nondescript side road going up the flank of Stewart Mountain.

Linda's car got plenty of opportunity to exercise its fast-downhill, sedate-uphill philosophy for the next fifteen minutes as they scooted past Silver Lake, gleaming a dull pewter in the faint light of a quarter moon. They saw no other cars on the road until they rounded a curve at the bottom of a long uphill grade. Maybe a half mile distant, a pair of dim red flickers appeared and then disappeared as the vehicle to which they were attached crested the next rise.

"You see that?" Plunkett said. "The truck?"

"Could have been anything," said Linda.

Plunkett jammed the pedal to the floor mat. The little station wagon responded with a pinging, whining noise. A shimmy developed somewhere up in the front end. But the car showed no discernible increase in momentum.

Halfway up the hill, Plunkett dropped back into third. That kept the Subaru happy for a hundred yards or so, before its engine slowed dramatically. Plunkett had to surrender another gear. He was wondering whether he was going to have to jettison Linda, or at very least ask her to get out and push, when the wagon crested the hill and slowly picked up speed.

Below them, at the bottom of a valley that led up another half-mile long grade, were the taillights. They were dim, low to the ground, and close together—a truck's.

A half hour later, the same taillights pulled onto the narrow road that led up Stewart Mountain. Plunkett followed, driving slowly with his head part way out the open window so he could hear the growling of the truck's engine and the grinding of its gears as it labored through the hairpin turns above. In that way, he managed fairly well, until the big car came up from behind, its widely spaced headlights bearing down on the Subaru's rear bumper.

At the next place where the road had anything that resembled a shoulder, Plunkett pulled off to let the car pass. Instead, it slowed. Once Plunkett was off the road, it pulled even.

Plunkett mashed the accelerator.

"Jesus Christ!" Linda cried.

The Subaru shot back onto the road, just as the big car veered to cut it off. There was a crunch of metal as something clipped the Subaru's rear end.

They lurched, first to the left, then to the right. Finally, Plunkett got control of the car, which had now developed a vibrating shake in back to go along with the shimmy in front.

Still, it was faster than the clunker. They took the next bend without a pair of headlights on their tail, and the one after that. Plunkett toyed with the possibility that they had lost the big car, but when they came to a straight stretch, the truck was just ahead, creeping up an incline and straddling the center of the road. To Plunkett's immediate left, a cliff fell off into the darkness. Only occasionally, and apparently at random, had the road department provided guard rails.

The big car came up on their tail. Its lights moved to the right, then quickly back to the left. There was a jolt that sent the Subaru scuttling toward the cliff. Its tires hit the gravel verge.

Plunkett pulled back onto the pavement. The truck, immediately in front, was slowing, coming to a stop, but still determinedly in the middle of the road. There was another impact, this one from the left. The Subaru was sent toward the sheer granite wall on that side. They veered back only to be confronted with the rear bumper of the truck, at face level. Plunkett swung to the left—the cliff side. He twisted the wheel. Too late. His front tires went over the lip.

A nudge from the big car pushed them forward a few feet, just enough so that the dented and wounded bumper of the Subaru tapped a guard-rail post. The station wagon bounced back onto the road, around the truck, and over the top of the Stewart Mountain Pass.

The Subaru seemed positively lighthearted as it picked up speed. For the first mile, the big car was still right behind them, gaining a few yards on each straightaway, but surrendering that and more each time the Subaru banked into a turn.

Even after they could no longer see the other car's headlights, Plunkett kept pushing the Subaru as hard as he dared. He let himself become positively cowboylike as they hit the final S curve before the road ended at Route 86. They careened around one turn.

"Hey, Mario, this ain't exactly a Lotus," said Linda.

Plunkett sped up.

It was on the second curve that they rammed into the rear end of the big, black Mercedes 500 sedan in which Bo Scullin sat with Bambi-Sue Cline.

15

"You got to be able to do it for less than four thousand five hundred and eighty-three dollars," Plunkett said.

It was nine o'clock in the morning, Wednesday, July 22, six hours after Plunkett and Linda's midnight ride.

"Dunno, dunno," said Darwin Plunkett, two years younger than his big brother, fifteen pounds heftier, and with about one-third as much of the light-brown hair meted out sparingly to all male members of the Plunkett clan.

Darwin traced a semicircle in the sandy gravel of the back lot of Plunkett Motors. He wiped a rivulet of early morning sweat from his temple, squinted at the sun and said, "Wow," leaving it to Plunkett to determine whether he was passing judgment on the scorching heat or his own repair prices.

"Damn Subaru's not worth half of that," said Plunkett, tracing his own semicircle.

Darwin put on a blue cap that advertised the Naples, Florida, Fertilizer and Garden Center. Doffing and donning that cap was his main form of exercise, an act undertaken five or six times each minute of every waking hour. More than one wag had suggested the habit, not genes, was responsible for the sparsity of his hair.

Darwin adjusted the cap for balance and angle. "You smashed the hell outta that little car. That'd be what it'd take to fix her . . . right."

Darwin gave a nod to the vehicle in question, still attached to the tow truck, its mangled grill glinting in the sunlight.

"How about *not* right. How much would it cost to fix it that way? I'm your brother, for Christ's sake."

"Dunno, dunno," said Darwin, starting a second concentric semicircle. He nodded once at his own artistic accomplishments. "Always wondered what one of them little cars'd look like if it smashed into a Mercedes," he said. "Bad, but not so bad as you might think. Not a whole lot worse than the Mercedes." That vehicle was beside the corrugated metal fence surrounding the junkyard. It looked like some mechanical *Tyrannosaurus rex* had ripped a half-moon bite out of the Mercedes's rear flank. "I suppose, if a fella wanted—" Darwin stopped to remove the hat, mop his brow, and replace the hat. In the process, his face got a blank look.

"You were saying . . ." said Plunkett.

His younger brother smiled. "Well, seeing as you are my brother, and that you were considerate enough to steer so much business our way . . ." He started to chuckle at his own joke.

"Darwin?" said Plunkett.

"S'pose I *could* have one of the boys go at it for an hour or two with a rubber mallet and a crow bar. Pull any parts we need off that little Subaru way in the back, the engine blew up two years ago. Wouldn't be right. That car's blue. This one's . . ." He made a face of disgust at Linda's hobbled vehicle, which was a dingy mustard color, proof positive, Plunkett thought, that for all their other attributes, Japanese car designers didn't change babies' diapers.

"How much we talking?"

"Dunno, dunno," Darwin said, taking the hat off and using it to slap his palm rhythmically once for each *dunno*. "Give me two fifty. How's that?"

Plunkett shifted from foot to foot. "Good. Was thinking of going over to the Saranac today to see if I could find a few trout," he said, now that the business portion of the morning was over. "Care to come along?"

"Got to work. Don't you?"

"Day off."

Darwin pawed the sand, avoiding his brother's eyes. "Seen you on TV. Heard there was some sort of—"

He was cut off by a bell clanging inside the shop. It sounded like a fire alarm.

"Phone," said Darwin. "Just a minute."

He sprinted over to the shop, which, when it came to architecture and state of repair, had much in common with the head offices of Saranac Chemicals. Except the Plunkett Motors building housed a thriving enterprise, providing employment for Darwin and his twin twenty-year-old sons, throwing off enough cash for a condo on Marco Island in Florida—all the gone-wild result of Darwin's teenage hobby of tinkering with old junkers in the backyard while his big brother was down by the river fishing.

Darwin came out, slapping the cap against his thigh with each step. "Linda called," he said halfway across the lot. When he got closer he said, "Said she was done with your truck, if you needed it. Also said a guy named Culley or something's at the restaurant looking for you. I said we were done here." Darwin put the cap on. "He's waiting."

Plunkett stayed long enough to put the finishing touches on his semicircle. "Was gonna ask you some advice—you being in business for yourself and all," Plunkett said.

Darwin got that blank look again. Plunkett went ahead and gave the three-minute version of his thoughts about leaving the police force in the fall, taking his half-pay pension and setting up as a fishing guide and camp security man.

"And you really want your little brother's advice?" Darwin said, when Plunkett finished.

Plunkett nodded.

Darwin took the cap off and wiped his forehead. "Dunno," he said.

* * *

It was about two hundred sweaty, puffy, uphill yards from Plunkett Motors to the Lumberjack along an incline that went unnoticed in a vehicle, but on foot became as formidable as Whiteface's north face. Plunkett had covered about half the distance when he was overtaken by Beverly Laney, striding along under a haversack bulging with books. With her gray, flipped-under hair bouncing, she looked fresh and relaxed. Could have been out for a stroll on a dewy May morning.

"*Gar*-wood, I tried to call you last night, and then again this morning," she said, with a note of disapproval. "I have a preschoolers' story hour, so I don't have time to talk, but I want you to know that I looked into Saranac Chemicals just after you left yesterday afternoon. I'll keep searching, but I did find a few facts that might be useful."

Her jaunty clip carried her past Plunkett. He took two trotting steps to catch up.

"It was when I checked into the board of directors of the company," she said. "Hoodlums." She bobbed her head. "Or at least one of them. I recognized the name from the papers. One of those men from Brooklyn who were charged a few years ago in connection with that waste disposal racket—putting medical waste in some landfill in Vermont. No other name was familiar. I did, however, notice that this character had been a recent appointment. So I looked back to see if anyone had resigned."

It was getting difficult to keep up, but Plunkett did his best, which required a sideways, crablike scuttle. "Yes?" he said, and immediately regretted sacrificing breath that would have been better put toward supplying his leg muscles with oxygen.

"It turned out that there was indeed a recent resignation from the board," Mrs. Laney said, effortlessly pulling ahead, forcing Plunkett to choose between breaking into a full, shambling trot, or abandoning pursuit. He gave up.

Over her shoulder she said, "The name Percy Quinell ring a bell?"

* * *

Culley sat at the counter in the Lumberjack doing his very best to ignore the mug of coffee in front of him. His youthful face was drawn and there were gray splotches under his eyes. It looked like he, not Plunkett, had been up all night.

Linda put another mug on the counter beside Culley and without making eye contact with Plunkett disappeared into the kitchen. A great clattering of pots and pans rang forth. Culley winced. Plunkett straddled the stool one down from Culley and hooked his index finger through the mug's handle.

"I don't believe this."

Plunkett said, "You mean you don't believe that Bo Scullin would be out in the middle of the night trying to get his jollies in the front seat of a Mercedes 500."

Culley inhaled. "You wouldn't find it so humorous if you had to talk to those damn lawyers of his first thing this morning."

"At least Bo has a legitimate reason to call in the lawyers—now that he's been charged with—"

'The charge will be dropped."

"What? The man was parked on a traveled road—lights out, engine off, at three . . ."

Linda's clattering and clanging intensified. It sounded like every pot and pan in the Lumberjack's kitchen had just fallen to the floor.

Into the dead silence that followed, Culley said, "In exchange, his lawyers will prevail upon their aggrieved client not to go ahead with the suit he instructed them to file."

"And you agreed?"

"Felt very fortunate to have been given a choice, frankly." He filled his trim chest with air. "I wondered if, under the circumstances, you would be willing to provide me with a little bit of an explanation?"

"All in the accident report."

"Will you kindly cut the crap for once," Culley said, without the quaver.

Plunkett shrugged. "There're some loose ends, but I think I got that chemical spill pretty well figured out."

That piqued Culley's interest. What almost passed for normal skin tones spread across his face. He took a sip of coffee.

"Quentin Quinell got a tip about a company outside Plattsburgh called Saranac Chemicals," said Plunkett. "I went there yesterday. Some things struck me as strange, so I borrowed a car that looked anonymous—"

Culley rolled his eyes.

"Well it was," Plunkett said, and then filled Culley in on the rest of the previous evening's events, ending with a judiciously censored description of the furious Bambi-Sue Cline wiggling back into her bra on the passenger's side of Bo Scullin's Mercedes. "The big question is what was Scullin doing out there," said Plunkett.

"His attorney informed me that Mr. Scullin was merely trying to enjoy a few moments of hard-earned privacy with Ms. Cline."

"Don't tell me they couldn't find any privacy in that mansion of his."

"Houseguests, according to the lawyer, and Ms. Cline is . . . Ms. Cline is not exactly . . ." Culley cleared his throat. "The guests were under the impression that Ms. Cline is a cleaning lady."

"I think Scullin has something to do with all this," said Plunkett. "Out there as paymaster, or guarding that end of the road. Maybe he was just there to make sure the job was done right . . . this time. Which, unfortunately, it was—if what I suspect was in that cattle truck was really there."

The lines reappeared on Culley's face. "Be careful with that man," he said. "Very, very careful. He's litigious as hell."

"I thought you wanted me to wrap up this chemical spill."

"I do," said Culley, his voice quavering again. "More than ever. The damned *New York Times* called yesterday. It's just—" He choked on whatever word was to have come next. "Be careful," he said, exhaling all of the air in his chest.

"I got something else," Plunkett said.

Culley winced so visibly he might just have been slapped across the face.

"Percy Quinell, Barron's widow, was on the board of directors of Saranac Chemicals," Plunkett said. "We have the dead man's wife and his business partner linked to—"

"We don't have a damn thing on Scullin," Culley said.

Plunkett ignored him. "The aunt of the Jamaican truck driver that got killed, she said he told her he was hired by a white woman—a white woman with long, fair hair."

"Forget this whole Quinell angle," said Culley.

Plunkett stood and rooted in his pockets for a trio of quarters, which he tossed on the counter. "My day off. Thought I might go wet a line," he said. "There's a hole on the Ausable not far from here I've been meaning to try—now that Barron Quinell's not using it anymore."

Culley sat dumbstruck for a full minute after Plunkett left. The horsey looking blond woman who owned the restaurant came over brandishing a Pyrex coffee pot. Unbidden, she filled Culley's cup with one hand while she scooped up Plunkett's quarters with the other and deposited them in her apron's pouch.

"Get you anything else?" she said.

Culley didn't bother answering. He was thinking about how Plunkett, with his Sherlockian delusions, was becoming a very loose cannon—one that was going to be tied down, one way or another.

The horsey woman didn't seem to be in any mood to go away. She stood there with a stupid look on her face, her elbow on her hip, coffee pot angled to one side. After a while, she smiled. For a fleeting instant, the damnedest thing happened: she actually looked pretty—not beautiful, but a solid, well-earned pretty.

"He really is," she said to Culley, "going fishing."

Aldon had a Marlboro in one corner of his mouth and was lying on his back in the pit dug into his front yard expressly for the purpose of fixing cars. It was about the size and depth of a shallow grave, and when a fellow was working in it, he might as well have been dead, buried, and halfway down to hell. Specially on a day like today. No breeze. Hot as blazes. Aldon feeling all the more miserable because he hadn't slept a wink last night after smashing up his car up there on Stewart Mountain. Chasing off some snoopy homo

-133-

in a Jap station wagon who sure as hell wasn't gonna come back again, at least that much was certain.

Aldon was prying away at the mangled remains of the passenger's-side fender when Edna called him from the doorway.

He didn't answer. Him lying on his back in the goddamn heat and her being too bone lazy to walk the ten steps to tell him what she wanted.

She called again, sounding naggy. He hated that worse than anything. But she kept at it until he inch-wormed his way out into the hazy daylight. Just as he was pulling himself up his fingers lost their purchase and he scraped his knuckles on the jagged edge of the fender.

"Fuck," he yelled, and when he saw the blood he added "Bitch." He swung the crow bar around and smashed it against the hood. It left an inch-deep dent but didn't make Aldon feel any better. Not one bit.

"Phone," said Edna.

"Well can't you see I'm busy. Tell 'em that." To drive home his point, he brandished the crow bar. Felt like whacking her one just for the hell of it. She sure as hell deserved a whacking.

Edna stood there in some sort of faded gray-colored dress, her boney shoulders and knobby arms sticking out. Starved looking, like those pictures from Africa. She took a deep breath and said, "It's her again."

It being his day off, Plunkett honestly intended to go fishing—in due course. He went directly from the restaurant to his place. From the living room, he grabbed a fly rod and a plastic box filled with nymphs, which he thought he might try to drift through some deep, cool holes. He was almost out the door when he remembered two Gennies inhabited his fridge along with a stub of Italian salami and a wedge of sharp cheddar that had been petrifying there since the last game of the Stanley Cup finals. He took one of the Gennies and guzzled it in a half-dozen quick, cold, head-cleaning swallows. The day promptly took a turn for the better.

Ten minutes later, Plunkett arrived at the pull-off from Route

86 near where Barron Quinell's body had been found. Culley was already there, standing beside his car, with the very same pained face he had worn when Plunkett left him at the Lumberjack.

"Care to wet a line," said Plunkett. He opened the cap of his pickup, removed a pair of chest waders, and sat on the tailgate to haul them on.

"I was hoping we could talk...."

Plunkett stuck his head inside the cap and came back out with his eight-and-one-half-foot graphite rod equipped with sink-tip line on the remote chance there really were trout left in that stretch of water.

"Didn't think you'd come for angling pointers," said Plunkett, setting off toward the river, past where the Dockwheiller family had parked their travel trailer, to the very rocks upon which young Duane had planted his pump-up basketball shoes eleven days earlier. Culley, breathing fast, followed.

"The father said the boy cast toward those boulders," said Plunkett, pointing his rod tip in that general direction. But instead of casting, he took a stride off the rocks and waded, retracing the approximate course Duane's plug would have taken.

Plunkett felt the chilly, wet sensation of the water coming up around his thighs and groin. He was in mid-river, and his legs had a buoyant feeling, a sign he should wade no further, not unless he fancied a little swim—hard enough with a pair of waders, virtually impossible if your feet were wound in fly line. And if someone had conked you on the head first . . .

For five minutes Plunkett stared down into the whirlpool that might have been Barron Quinell's final resting place, had it not been for young Duane. Satisfied that the swirling water had no secrets left to impart—and held no trout—Plunkett retraced his route. When he got close enough for the frustrated-looking Culley to hear, he merely said, "You see any sharp rocks?"

It took a few seconds for Culley to get his bureaucratic mind around the meaning of what Plunkett said. Once his mind was around the subject, all Culley was capable of sputtering was, "Doesn't mean a damn thing."

-135-

Plunkett didn't respond. He was at the bank and had bent over to examine a few filaments of yellow-dyed deer hair dangling from an alder bush. He was baffled. For the life of him, Plunkett didn't understand how he—how anyone—could have missed it eleven days ago. But there it was, hanging above the water. At first, Plunkett thought it was just a fishing fly—a Mickey Finn streamer. A second look revealed that it wasn't a fishing fly, after all. It was an earring. He slipped his hand inside a Baggie that was in one of his waders' pouches and reached out, plucking the fly/earring from the alder and palming it so Culley couldn't see.

Plunkett recognized the handiwork. It had been tied by Elwood "Woody" Plunkett, legendary fly-tier, Adirondack guide, and estranged father of Garwood Plunkett.

Old Woody had gotten it into his head the previous winter that he would make his fortune tying ornamental flies to earring posts. Gifts for guilty fishing husbands to take home to their neglected wives.

Wasn't a bad idea, except it hadn't worked. He only sold a handful. So few that there was a good chance he could identify most of his customers—or at the very least he'd remember if one of them was Percy Quinell.

Plunkett's father's fly shop was something of a local landmark, or embarrassment, depending on your point of view. Its presence beside Route 86 was announced by a life-size illustration of a 1950s blond in complete fly-fishing regalia, who had just hooked the back of her skirt, raising it to reveal a pair of white panties.

When Plunkett entered, two fishermen were in the store. From their felt-soled wading boots to their fly-festooned hats, they looked like they were on their way to an audition for the front cover of the next issue of *Fly Fisherman* magazine. They listened reverently as Woody Plunkett said, "Don't you believe a single word of what them gov'mint assholes is saying." Woody punctuated his sentence with a feinted punch from a fist that clutched a pint of Jim Beam. The punch thrown, he treated himself to a swig and nodded, never once giving any sign that he was aware his son had just entered the store.

Like most Plunkett males, Woody had gone from a lean boyhood to husky middle years, then just at the point where he would have crossed over the line to obesity, the fat began to melt away, leaving behind something knobby and deflated-looking. Beneath a bald pate, his face had frozen into a permanent pugnacious scowl that dared onlookers just to try to take on its owner. The bumpy, off-center nose suggested that at least one had accepted the challenge.

"Ain't no chemical killing these fish, I tell you," Woody said. "Or if it did, just a few little brookies up Stewart Mountain. I'm tellin' you, it's this damn heat. Same thing happened summer of thirty-six. Trout bellied up all over. Only person caught trout that summer was me. Fishin' these little stone fly nymphs here—" He tapped the base of the whisky bottle on a glass-topped display case filled with flies. "Tossed them upstream and let them drift slow and deep through the biggest holes." He took another nip and said, "I'm letting them go for three bucks each—the nymphs."

The fishermen said they would take a few of those, too, and accepted them from him with the worshipful eyes of two parish priests receiving the sacrament directly from the fingers of the Pope.

Over the years, Woody Plunkett had become famous as a guide and fly fisherman. A stop at his cluttered, gear-crammed little shop perched on the shoulder of the highway a few miles outside of Wilmington was considered de rigueur by serious anglers. The irony was that Woody hated to fish. Never went anymore, unless a national television crew or writer for a major outdoors magazine was passing through. Instead, he spent his days perched on a tall stool behind his store's counter, slurping bourbon, dispensing lies and wisdom, and at every opportunity, bad-mouthing his son—the one that turned out to be a cop, a profession close to the bottom of Woody Plunkett's caste system, one rung above the lowest of the low: conservation officers.

It didn't help that one of Plunkett's early moves as a rookie state trooper was to pull over a 1968 Ford half-ton doing sixty in a thirty-mile zone and then go on to charge the driver of the borrowed vehicle—one Elwood Plunkett—with Driving While Intoxicated. The old man had never forgiven him.

The first thing Woody said to his son that afternoon was, "So what have I done wrong now, trooper?" The last word was uttered like a vile obscenity. For the benefit of the two fishermen, he held his two hands out, wrists together. "Got your cuffs with you, boy?"

The two customers probably would have sprung to the defense of their mentor had Woody not added in normal speaking tones, "This here's my son, the cop. The tough cop. You might have seen him beating up that cute little TV girl last week. Now, I hear he's thinking about quitting and setting up as a fishing guide." Woody emitted two sardonic chuckles. "Fishing guide, my ass," he said, tapping that part of his anatomy with the Jim Beam bottle.

The two fishermen left the store.

After the screen door screeched and banged closed, Woody said, "So, what do you want? Other than to drive away paying customers."

"Still selling those women's earrings that look like flies?"

"Don't tell me—he's gone and found himself some woman," said his father, fortifying himself with a swig.

Plunkett shoved his hand in his pants pocket and removed the Baggie containing the earring he had found beside the river. "This is one of yours, isn't it?"

Woody poked the bag once with an index finger that reminded Plunkett of the sausage stub back in his fridge. "Might be," he said.

"Did Barron Quinell ever buy one from you?"

The pugnacious look got more pronounced. "Nope," Woody said.

"How about Percy . . . his wife?"

Woody treated himself to a smile. "The one that had you pussy-whipped so bad you—"

"She buy one?"

Thinking that question over demanded another trip to the bourbon bottle. It was only after he swallowed that Woody said, "What's it to you?"

After the door slammed, Woody polished off the pint and rooted around behind the counter until he found a fresh bottle. He cracked the seal and drank to wash away the anger he always felt whenever his goddamn older son came around. Self-righteous little twerp. Cocky. Superior. Better than everybody else—even his own father.

Smarter, too. Or carried on like he was. Well, to hell with him. Let him go of thinking he knew everything now that he'd found out Percy Quinell had bought a pair of the trout fly earrings. So self-satisfied he didn't even ask the important question: When did she buy them?

His Honor Judge John Conoscenti was not in residence at his Lake Placid camp that evening. Quentin Quinell, however, seemed to be doing a fine job in his role as stand-in Lord of the Manor, a title he was destined to assume someday as husband of the judge's only daughter. Quentin padded barefooted around the glass-fronted living room in cut-offs and SAP T-shirt.

"We're out front," he said, sounding like the perfect host.

Plunkett followed him through a sliding glass door to a deck positioned about halfway up the trunks of a stand of white pines. Branches had been carefully pruned from the trees to provide a perfect frame for the lake, its large, well-centered islands and the peaks beyond, each a slightly different hue of purple in the fading light.

Quentin guided Plunkett to a wicker love seat that was far too expensive and well-upholstered to be outdoor furniture—at least Plunkett's idea of outdoor furniture. He settled into its cushions.

Quentin took a wicker easy chair beside the love seat. "You said you wanted to run a few things by me about Saranac Chemicals," he said.

The last shaft of sun reddened the dark belly of a cumulonimbus cloud that might or might not have been bringing a thunderstorm.

-139-

Watching that shaft fade, along with the prospects of an air-cleansing storm, Plunkett went through what he had seen the previous evening.

At the end, Quentin snickered. "Uncle Bo up to his old tricks—guy must be sixty-five, sixty-six . . ."

"That wasn't what I was asking about," said Plunkett. "What do you make of the goings on—at Saranac Chemicals?"

"I'd say it's pretty obvious, isn't it?"

Plunkett allowed himself a little smile. "Would it make it any more obvious if I told you that your stepmother once sat on the board of directors of Saranac Chemicals?"

Quentin laughed happily. "Stepmommy, Uncle Bo, who'd of thought—"

Plunkett waited a minute for Quentin to elaborate. But he apparently intended to spend the rest of the evening mute, shaking his head and wearing a small, private smile.

"You going to let me in on your little secret now that I've told you what I know?" Plunkett asked.

The smile stayed where it was. "Let you in, officer? Why sure, I'll let you in. At my press conference."

16

Percy entered Ivor's minisuite in The Plaza at two o'clock Monday afternoon. She was hot, tired and waging a one-woman war against what may well have been the vilest headache loosed that summer upon any resident of Manhattan. It did not help knowing that Ivor's room was costing her $385 a night. Percy slung the jacket portion of her off-white silk suit over the bed.

Ivor sat comparing two photocopied pages at the writing desk. He didn't bother looking up, so Percy went over to an antique mahogany hutch where there was a full ice bucket, an uncracked fifth of Stoli, and two-thirds of a bottle of Lagavulin. "Could have funded this entire venture if we'd picked up a few shares of stock in Lagavulin's parent company," she said.

Ivor looked up from his photocopies, squinting over the top of a pair of wire-rimmed half-glasses, the only pair Percy could remember any living human being wearing openly and unabashedly. "Never invest in stocks—at least not in legitimate ones—it's far too risky," he admonished sternly. "Thought I drilled that into your head when you were a girl."

For a few seconds, he went back to his cross-referencing, but gave up. "You going to do the honors, or does an old man have to?"

Percy fixed herself a vodka and poured Ivor three fingers of single malt, which she held at arm's length, the same treatment she would have given a hunk of ripe Stilton on that hot afternoon. Even so, her headache worsened.

Someone knocked on the door.

"It's probably old Vinny Zanini." When Percy's eyes widened, he added, "My New York tailor. He's expensive. But good." Ivor scampered out of sight down the short hallway that led to the door.

She heard Ivor sputter a couple of expletives, which were followed by a grumbling "very well then," and finally the muffled flapping sound of a great deal of loose skin.

Winston padded into the room, his head held at a much more elevated position than the normal nose-to-ground posture of a basset hound. Looking as if he was quite accustomed to passing hot summer afternoons in climate-controlled minisuites at the Plaza, he crossed the carpet to the sofa, hopped up, and promptly fell asleep.

Ivor came in after him, holding a silver leash. "How on earth did you get the bellman to usher that creature up here?" he asked.

Percy swirled her vodka. It was drink number one of the day. Overdue, given the temperature outside—ninety-six. Justifiable in view of the number of accountants and lawyers she had seen since coming back from Cayman the previous Wednesday—also ninety-six, it seemed. They were all so self-important and serious they made the mortician who handled Barron's cremation arrangements seem charming and companionable.

"A lap dog is a perfectly acceptable accessory for a New York woman these days. You only have to watch the comings and goings at Bergdorf's. . . ." She looked at Ivor's attire, the oldest and most faded fawn suit she had ever seen, worn with a red and white polka-dot tie wide enough to be a bib. "Of course, you obviously haven't . . ."

"That," Ivor jabbed an index finger at the sleeping Winston, "is no lap dog."

"He's deeply affected by Barron's absence. Plus my going down to the Caymans. I'm trying to keep him with me as much as possible this week."

Ivor *harrumphed*. "Still don't understand how you got them to bring him up here."

"A ten-dollar bill to the doorman."

Ivor raised his eyebrows skeptically.

"Well, it certainly wasn't by grace of my feminine wiles alone." She flashed her best flirtatious smile at Ivor and batted her eyes four times in rapid succession.

Ivor fielded the smile and eye-batting with equanimity. "Talk to me first the next time. Save yourself ten bucks." He paused, then went on: "You might need it when you find out how much your little scheme is going to cost."

Zanini and his two boys showed up five minutes later. Vinny Zanini, tailor to Wall Street gentlemen since 1939, breezed into the suite first. The boys who lumbered in his wake were huge, strapping lunks encumbered by a dozen or more bolts of cloth. Zanini himself was elfin, maybe five-foot-two, and somewhere between a hundred and a hundred and ten pounds, tops. He looked to be about six or seven years older than Ivor—somewhere around eighty, Percy guessed.

"Ivor, it's been what—twenty, thirty years since I make a nice suit for you. I hear all over you dead. Dead, they say. Dead. Dead. Dead. Like all the other good ones—the real pros, eh. Not like this rabble we got nowadays. And now"—he embraced Ivor, then held him out for a thorough inspection—"here I see you. Alive! And you know—just to look at you, I bet you your size has not changed. Not one inch. Ah, maybe we have to do something about the arm length, and take a tiny bit in off the shoulders, eh? Just like me." He did a little wiggling routine with his bony, birdlike shoulders. "The years weigh heavily on that part of the anatomy. But not others, eh." He cast an analytic leer at Percy, and she didn't think it was primarily to determine her dress size, although that, too, was no doubt figured in there somewhere.

"So I brought material for five nice suits for you. Boys!" he hollered. "Unfortunately, Ivor, unlike your suit size, my prices they have—" Zanini paused to select a diplomatic adjective. "Enlarged somewhat since the last time." He frowned and scampered around behind Ivor with the tape. "Two thousand dollars per suit. Much has changed since 1964," he said quickly, a hint of relief in his voice to have finally broached the subject of cost.

"Tell it to the lady. She's paying," said Ivor.

A smile of relief swept Zanini's crinkled face. He said, "At least some things, Ivor, they do not change, eh."

Ivor finally got down to business a half hour later, after Zanini and his boys left, taking with them one of Percy's personal checks for the sum of ten thousand dollars.

"How much you end up with?" Ivor said, tapping Percy's still-open checkbook with the bottom edge of his Lagavulin tumbler.

She tucked the checkbook in her purse. "Two hundred eighty thousand, give or take. Be lucky to walk with an even two and a half by the time the lawyers and accountants get done taking their pound of flesh."

Ivor shook his shock of white hair. "It's going to be tight. Damned tight. And we haven't even taken the factor of time into consideration. The question of time is truly worrying. It's not too late to walk away—"

"No!" Percy went over to the hutch and fixed herself another drink. "I won't walk away."

Ivor buried his snout in the whisky glass and muttered something. Raising his face, he said aloud: "Very well, I'll give you a progress report, and then your marching orders."

He gestured grandly toward the photocopies on the desk. "These are copies of Bo Scullin's Rolodex cards and of pages from his appointment calendar."

"How did you get those?"

Ivor smiled gently. "On occasion things will happen that it is best you don't fully understand. This is one. Let's say it just involves an enterprising young man from Hell's Kitchen who specializes in entering buildings through skylights.

"The important thing," Ivor said, "is that I have cross-referenced the Rolodex and date book, and have developed a primary mooch list." He stopped and eyed Percy over the wire rims. "The man is vain. Vain with a capital V." He read off the list: "We have his manicurist, his hairdresser, his tanning salon operator, his personal trainer, his masseuse, his tailor, his therapist, his chiropractor, his orthodontist, his plastic surgeon, his dietician—and, critical to keeping an older gent in peak form, his girlfriend."

Percy raised her eyebrows. "What's her name, the girlfriend?"

"That's the very best part. Bambi-Sue Cline. There's actually some poor woman out there struggling through life with that handle. Though judging from the number of times each week she dines with our man at Café des Artistes, the struggle is bearable."

"I feel a certain sisterly affection for her—with the name I have," said Percy.

Ivor sulked, an act which would not have become him, even if it were genuine—which it clearly wasn't. "Don't feel too sorry, not yet. If all goes well, she may be one of the lucky ones."

Ivor hurried on: "The idea is simple. We'll paper the entire list of Bo Scullin's personal service professionals. Papering is perfectly legal. So-called legitimate telemarketers have even stolen the technique from us. It means that Bo's associates will receive my newsletter." He held up a well-designed document and read its title aloud: *"Investing for the Future,"* he said. "Current issue has a long article about the huge profits that are sure to be reaped by the biotechnology industry.

"Very nicely written piece, and filled with perfectly sound investment advice," he added. "Wrote it myself." He tapped his temple with the paper. "The newsletter will be followed by some press clippings about Biocural. Here are two—*The Wall Street Journal* and *Business Week*. Wrote them, too.

"After the list has been papered thoroughly, my boiler-room boys will take to the phones. They're pros—can sell anything by phone: Florida real estate, aluminum siding, and of course, nonexistent stocks—their specialty. The intention is to get one or two of Bo's people to buy. Then make sure that they double—even triple—their investment overnight. We'll make sure of that because the funds will be coming right out of your account.

"Then one day, old Bo is getting a rubdown or getting his rocks off—doesn't much matter which—and he hears about how the person administering said service has just made all this profit on a little flyer in biotech and—*BINGO*—that's when our twin allies vanity and greed kick in. Bo comes to us. That's the beauty of it. He makes the initial approach."

Percy nodded and took a sip. "It sounds too simple."

"It is simple," said Ivor. "I ran a scam almost identical to this in 1958. Got a hold of mineral rights to an old, worked-out iron operation, on that property your ex-husband's company owns up there behind your camp—"

Percy interrupted, "A mine?"

Ivor chuckled. "Stick with me for the next little while and you will learn one lesson, that I guarantee: There is a big difference between a mine and a hole bored into a mountainside. That's just a hole. A very deep one—"

"Where?"

Ivor made a waving motion with his hand. "Oh what do I know? Somewhere on top of some mountain. It doesn't really matter."

The hell it doesn't, thought Percy, but before she could ask for more details, Ivor had warmed to his lecture. "Hard rock mining is passé. So is microchip technology. Today, it's biotech. Instead of a mine, we're substituting a lab. I've made arrangements with a facility in New Brunswick, New Jersey, that will do fine as a Biocural lab. The senior researcher there is truly seeking a biotechnological panacea and has run short of funds between grants. He has agreed to help us—in exchange for ten thousand dollars. You might take some comfort knowing that, ultimately, your money will be going to a good cause.

"Then there is the matter of your new company car," Ivor went on. "The Porsche . . . Carrera model. Hope you don't mind red, it was the only color I could lease on short notice. Besides, I thought it would go well with your hair."

"Ivor, I have always prided myself in not needing to wrap myself in seventy thousand dollars worth of plastic and metal in order to impress people I neither like nor respect. I don't think I'm going to start now that I'm a destitute widow."

Ivor puffed his cheeks. "But Bo Scullin is precisely the sort of fool to let himself be impressed by seventy thousand dollars of metal and plastic. And it's him I want impressed. You see, he's going to think that you, too, are a major Biocural investor. That you are making a killing and stand to earn enough not only to buy a Porsche, but to buy his share of the company. That's the kicker to my little plan. With it in place, we'll have all our bases covered: vanity, greed—and pride."

He allowed his cheeks to deflate and lowered his voice. "Time, however, remains a problem. I wish we weren't in such an almighty rush. What do we have—a month, tops? He's going to have to fall for our scam in his own good time. The minute he senses any pressure, he'll back off."

Percy gave a smile of encouragement. "He's pretty stupid," she said.

"Time," said Ivor, growing wistful. "That is our enemy. It would help speed things along if I could generate some real interest in the press, but I've drawn a blank. Back in my heyday, financial journalists fell into two broad categories, both useful: stupid and greedy. Now . . ." Ivor picked up a black, leather-covered book about the size and shape of the New Testaments the Gideons used to pass out to schoolchildren. "I've called them all—"

He ruffled the black book's pages. "All my reporter contacts. They're gone. Four of them vanished without a trace after they got indicted for various securities violations. Two dead of heart attacks. One a PR flack for a Republican senator."

Percy was only half-listening to his lament. What she was really considering was whether another vodka on the rocks—just a child's portion—would add to the blissful drifting sensations she was beginning to feel where there had been nothing but discomfort and throbbing pain moments before. It sounded like it was someone else's voice, someone much more attentive, that said, "Ivor, I think I know a reporter. A stupid one. Quite possibly real stupid. He referred to my late husband as a philanthropist."

Ivor sputtered into his Scotch.

"But he works for the Plattsburgh *Chronicle-Herald,* and that isn't exactly *The Wall Street Journal.*"

Ivor cleared his throat. "Actually, it might suit our purposes. Scullin's date book indicates that he will be at his Adirondack chalet most of the month. He'll certainly see a copy of the local paper. And if there's an article about how rich you are getting off this little investment . . ."

"I'm heading up tomorrow."

Ivor smiled. "Very well, it's settled. And don't worry, I'll handle things from this end. I've got a line on some office space downtown, and will begin interviewing prospective employees shortly. Things are going to be just fine." Ivor hoisted his eyebrows into his white thicket of hair, flashed the Smile and said, "Trust me."

17

Just before sunset on Wednesday, July 29, Percy found herself on the back steps of her camp's main building wondering if Plunkett had actually stood her up.

She was wearing a wide-necked white T-shirt and a pair of baggy khaki shorts that had entered her life the same summer as Barron and had now out lasted him. On her feet were felt-soled wading boots. Her left hand massaged the loose skin on the nape of Winston's neck. In return, he allowed his back to serve as a comfortable arm rest. Her right hand held a highball glass filled with vodka, crushed ice, and a sprig of ginger mint from her garden. The drink was there to fortify her. If all went well, she was about to do the nastiest thing of her life.

Or rather, the second nastiest.

Winston groaned and arched his neck so her fingers could reach under his chin. Percy complied, then rewarded herself with a nip of vodka. She immediately began to feel better, so much better she administered another dose.

A few ounces of vodka, an hour or so of trout fishing, and then dinner with her former lover. If that didn't chase away the blues

. . . well, they didn't make widows dress in black anymore, did they?

Must be some reason.

Plunkett arrived ten minutes late, just in time to spare Percy from having to make a decision about fixing herself a second drink. His arrival was heralded with so much creaking and rumbling and clanging that she at first wondered if he had come in convoy with a dozen or so fellow members of the local chapter of Trout Unlimited.

What ultimately rounded the final turn in her driveway, however, was a solitary oversized Dodge pickup truck, with Plunk's pleasantly handsome mug staring through the windshield. He parked beside her leased Porsche. Stepping out of the truck, he circumvented the Porsche, keeping his eyes glued to it warily and maybe disapprovingly—the same way Percy still viewed the contraption. After clearing the Porsche, he came toward her, looking exactly like a man should: tallish, squarely built, with a tiny smile that indicated its owner was simultaneously pleased with himself and a little shy.

"See that," Percy said, pointing to a mayfly laid out dead on the bent cedar bough that served as the stairs' railing.

"A Siphlonurus," he said.

"This time of year, and with this heat, that creature should not be here," Percy said. "But it is. As are several of its kind down by the brook. A bonafide hatch on the twenty-ninth of July. Can you explain it?"

He revealed as disarming a grin as Percy had ever seen. "Simple," he said. "It's my birthday."

The creek was about a quarter-mile behind the camp, down a trail packed with wood chip mulch and bordered by the occasional rustic cedar-log bench so that even the elderly and infirm could make the journey to Barron Quinell's architecturally designed trout stream. The path led to a pool below a horseshoe bend. At the far side, fish were dimpling the water.

"Your dinner," Percy pronounced, nodding toward the concentric, overlapping circles left by the rising trout.

Getting to where she could reach the trout with a cast was going to require wading the one part of the brook Barron's landscape architects had been unable to alter. It was at the tail of the pool where the water channeled through a narrow gorge between two rock cliffs. Below that point, the creek frothed, swirled, and boiled.

Without looking back, Percy splashed into the brook. Even at that time of year, its spring-fed water was cold enough to send a jab of pure, sharp pain from her calves to her groin. After a moment of shock, a welcome numbness replaced the pain.

Percy waded deeper, holding her fly rod outstretched in front with both hands like a high wire artist, feeling her way along the slimy backs of boulders with her felt-soled boots, listening to the roar of the water to her immediate left.

The creek came up to her knees then her thighs and waist. Current tugged at her hips, gently nudging her toward the chute. Her feet—lightened now—had to scramble against the slick rocks.

Putting her trust in faith, and two decades of experience, she took a giant stride, shooting her numb, weightless right foot toward the far bank. For an instant, it was impossible to tell whether she was wading, or treading water. She drifted downstream.

Then her foot brushed the top of a big, flat boulder. She added some weight to it. Kicked with her back leg. And was standing again, the water just above her knees, the rising trout forty feet upstream.

Plunkett was still on the bank in his waders. His expression waffled between admiration and utter amazement before finally settling on the latter.

Percy fed out a little line and did a half-hearted false cast, still looking back toward Plunkett.

He plunged into the stream and churned steadily in her direction. When he reached her side he said, "Show me how it's done."

Percy eyed him and said, "My intention exactly."

In three easy back and forth motions, Percy worked out fifty feet of line. Her fly touched the water just upstream of where a trout had risen. Instantly, there was a splash. Percy raised the tip of her rod. She felt the nervous jerking of a brookie. The fish broke water showing its silver and reddish flanks. Percy kept the tension on, gaining line slowly with her reel, letting the fish do most of the work, tiring itself until she got it in close enough to net. It was a ten-incher. Perfect dinner fish.

"One to nothing," she said.

"Cradle robber," Plunkett muttered, and fed out line, bringing it back in a graceful parabolic loop that smoothly uncoiled upon itself, sending it forward in a mirror image of the backward loop. After the third false cast, he let the tip of his rod follow the line forward. His fly touched the water, then his monofilament leader, and finally the rest of his line.

The fly drifted back toward him, bobbing and twisting with the current. No takers.

"Just don't have the touch," Percy said.

"To catch a tame brookie?" Plunkett asked, and did another series of three false casts.

The instant his fly touched the water, even before the leader and the line had a chance to come down, a trout's head bobbed above the surface. Plunkett raised the tip of his rod, shot a so-there look at Percy, and proceeded to bring the fish to net—all nine inches of it.

"Cradle robber?" said Percy, beginning her own cast.

Whatever combination of water temperature, time of day and barometric pressure had coaxed those thousands of Siphlonurus larvae to shed their exoskeletons and leave the safety of the streambed for the risks and dangers of a life on the wing stopped twenty minutes later. The surface of the pool became flat. The flies so temptingly presented by Plunkett and Percy were ignored. By that time, the score was two to two.

"I won," said Percy.

"Seems more like a draw to me."

"Based on weight and total inches caught, I beat you hands down."

"I don't recall that being anywhere in the rules," said Plunkett.

"My creek; my rules."

Plunkett made a halfhearted effort at splashing her—a mere flick of the wrist, sending a few droplets skittering across the creek's surface, two of which landed on the dry fabric of her T-shirt. She examined the two water splotches, shaking her head sadly. "You know what they say, Plunk," she said. "Don't get mad, get . . ." Percy dug her hand—all of it—into the water. As she shoveled it forward, Plunkett dodged a half step to his left.

It was a bad mistake. He slipped backwards off the submerged boulder, spread-eagled, one hand holding his rod, the other clawing the water. His feet bobbed to the top. At that same time, his head and shoulders disappeared. When they resurfaced, he was coughing and spitting water. He began an awkward backstroke, churning the surface with both arms while maintaining his grip on the rod.

Plunkett and Percy reached the bank at the same time, her dry from the waist up, him dripping. He ran a hand through his hair and made a show of shaking the water off it. One-sixteenth of an inch at a time, a smile forced its way onto what had started out as a passably stern face.

Percy fingered one of the water spots on her T-shirt. "We even?" she said.

Twenty minutes later, Percy was in the kitchen barefoot and wearing ultra-short shorts and a white halter top. Plunkett came in. He was towel-dried and wearing a borrowed T-shirt that proclaimed Keene, New York, to be Home of the High Peaks. He also had on a pair of teal-colored hiking shorts Percy had bought for Barron two summers earlier.

She thought the shorts would nicely complement the contours of Barron's butt. Except Barron refused to wear the shorts. Now, seeing them modeled for the first time, Percy realized she indeed had been right—about the butt part.

Having Plunkett standing beside her in the pants her ex-husband refused to wear made her feel melancholy and a bit rotten. But then, no one said pulling this off was going to be easy. If it was, every woman in her right mind would be doing it.

The four trout stared at her accusingly from the counter, bellies slit, gills removed. Percy salted them, ground some fresh pepper on each, then, one by one, rolled them in flour. Into an ancient, cast-iron frying pan that had been handed down from her grandfather, she put a stick of butter and a liberal dollop of olive oil—the dark, heavy-tasting kind. The air filled with rich, olive-scented fumes. When the oil and butter began to foam, she lay the trout in the pan beside each other, head to tail.

That done, she turned her attentions to an avocado that had been sitting on the windowsill for the past week. She circumscribed it in two deft strokes and popped out the stone. A little lemon juice, mustard, and olive oil went into the resulting halves.

"Beer?" she said to Plunkett. "Something stronger?"

Plunkett said a beer would be fine. She got a Corona out of the fridge, then took her half-empty fifth from the freezer. "Glass?" she said, taking one for herself and pouring a jolt into it.

"Bottle's fine, thanks," said Plunkett.

Percy handed him the bottle and said, "Opener's in the drawer, somewhere under all the junk."

While Plunkett pawed through the contents of the drawer, Percy quartered a lemon and chopped up a handful of fresh parsley, wondering what the hell was taking him so long.

"This yours," Plunkett finally said, his voice sounding far away.

Percy put down her knife.

Plunkett was holding an earring patterned after a Mickey Finn streamer.

"Never seen it before," Percy said.

The trout were ready ten minutes later. Percy laid two on each plate beside lemon wedges, sprinkled them with the parsley, tossed another stick of butter in the pan and when it had melted poured the pan scrapings on the trout.

"*Voilà!*" she proclaimed. "Bring thou, those teal pants and that jug of wine and follow me."

The *jug* was a bottle of 1987 Bourgogne Aligoté that had been cooling in a silver ice bucket. Plunkett took it out of the bucket and padded along behind her as dutifully as Winston.

Glancing back over her shoulder, Percy noticed that both the males in her entourage wore the same looks on their faces. Only one of them had legitimate claim to hangdog—at least for the present.

That didn't stop her from heartily tucking into what turned out to be one of the top ten meals of that year, the fish fresh and buttery, the avocado pungent and ripe, the wine ice cold and biting. As they dined, the sultry summer day went quietly about the business of transforming itself into a cool mountain evening.

Across the table, Plunkett poked a fork at the side of one of his fish. He barely touched his wine—a situation that did not fit in at all well with Percy's original plan, which had called for one pleasantly intoxicated state trooper.

"Percy," Plunkett said.

She made an effort to raise her eyebrows.

"There's this case I'm working on . . ."

Her eyebrows went up another inch—this time with no effort.

"The chemical spill. The one that's killing all the fish."

Still operating on their own, Percy's eyebrows came together.

Plunkett cleared his throat. "I have reason to believe that Saranac Chemicals might be involved."

He stopped and let that information hang there without further elaboration or explanation.

"Name ring a bell? Saranac Chemicals?" he said again.

Percy shrugged and took a swallow of Aligoté. She was beginning to get a pleasant buzz and hoped whatever Plunkett was about to say wasn't going to spoil it.

"You were on the board of directors," Plunkett said.

"Last count, I sat on something like nine boards of directors," she said calmly. "Most are just numbered companies—corporate shells set up by the shysters that work for my ex-husband and his partner. Ways to get around the tax man. To protect assets from the banks. Once a year I go to the lawyers' offices and sign a sheaf of papers that make the Manhattan telephone book look like a pamphlet. I don't even get a chance to look at them while I sign. No time. That's the extent of my directorial duties. So, yeah, I suppose I could have been on Saranac's board."

"I'm told it was losing a bunch of money, or something," Plunkett said.

Percy barked a laugh. "That hardly distinguishes it, not from most of my late husband's forays into the world of commerce."

Plunkett nodded to himself.

She reached a hand across the table and put it on top of his. "Plunk," she said, looking directly at him. "That's all there is to it—honestly."

He returned her gaze, keeping his gentle, handsome eyes affixed to hers far longer than necessary. When he spoke, he said, "Had to check."

"But Plunk—" she began, and stopped.

He dipped his chin, eyes still affixed to hers.

"It's strange, you're the second person to ask me about Saranac Chemicals since I got back up here yesterday." She fortified herself with the wine that remained in her glass. "Quentin, the dear boy, harangued me about it over the phone for fifteen minutes last night."

"And . . ."

"I told him the same thing I just told you."

They finished the meal to the reds and oranges and purples of a sun that seemed more reluctant than usual to disappear behind the distant peaks, but finally did, leaving in its wake Venus, a handful of evening stars and the serenading calls of the loons.

Percy and Plunkett went back inside only when driven there by an attack by mosquitoes that seemed every bit as big and energetic as the hatching Siphlonurus. He walked directly into the kitchen and proceeded to rinse his plate and wine glass, then took hers.

"I don't believe I've ever seen a man do that," Percy said. "Not of his own free will. Not unless he wanted something. Really wanted something."

Poor Plunkett looked so sheepish he would probably have re-soiled the dishes, had there been a way. "Habit, I guess," he muttered, more to the sink than Percy.

"After dinner drink?"

"Better not . . . the drive and all," said Plunkett.

"Coffee? Decaf?"

"Thanks, Percy, but no. I—" He made a movement that suggested he was truly serious about walking out the kitchen door and getting into that truck.

"Not so fast," Percy said.

He gazed back at her quizzically.

"You don't have to leave," she said, tossing in a weak, "that's all."

"It'd be best."

"Best," Percy said. "That about sums you up, doesn't it, Plunk? Always doing what's best—best for everyone except maybe you."

"Maybe going's best for me, too. I am a cop, you know. Working on a case. There could be a conflict—"

"Balls!" said Percy. When he looked at her wide-eyed she said, "Balls!" in case he missed the point the first time and added, "Please spare me. Just drop Barron's clothes off when you're done with them."

"Damn it Percy."

There was a silence. Plunkett stood his ground, moving neither toward the door nor closer to her. At the point where the standoff threatened to become downright silly, she took a half step toward him and did exactly what she had done that night twenty years earlier: She kissed him.

But his response was coy, almost dismissive, no more than she would expect from any male guest after a moderately successful dinner party.

She hugged him tightly. Pressed herself against his chest and let out a *"M-n-n-n-n."*

He pushed his mouth down hard, parting her lips.

Until that night, Percy had felt nothing other than sympathy for the black bear, shot by her paternal grandfather in November, 1917.

But that evening, while she and Plunkett lay on the bear's skin, Percy decided that if there was in fact a great hereafter where the spirits of *Ursus americanus* sniff and root through all eternity, then there would have been one very smug and proud old Adirondack bear up there. No hide could have been put to better use.

For the first fifty minutes, they simply kissed on the bearskin like they used to as inexperienced teenagers: fully clothed, extracting the most from every hug and timid caress, wary of the uncharted terrain that lay ahead, but moving inexorably in that direction anyway.

He kissed her lips, meeting the tip of her tongue with his, stroking her hair, whispering over and over that she—Percy Quinell, age forty, widow—was beautiful, nibbling at her neck and ears and the soft flesh above her collar bones. For long periods he would do nothing. Just hold her tight, one hand gently stroking her hair, the other on the base of her spine.

Outside, across the lake, a pair of loons began a duet that was at first mournful, but rose steadily until it became a crazy symphony, echoing off the surrounding High Peaks.

He slid her top off one of her shoulders. But no more. Acted like the ultimate sexual act was kissing and nipping a woman's throat, maybe occasionally coming up to whisper how pretty she was.

She held onto him tightly, pressing against his thick body until she could stand it no longer. She broke away—two inches away. His eyes were closed, but his comfortable-looking face wore a smile. She slid her hands up his back, removing the borrowed shirt.

He took his own sweet time with her. His fingers played lingeringly with the elastic on the top of her shorts, sliding beneath it, retreating, exploring the regions under her shirt. Finally, with the tips of his index fingers, he eased both her shorts and panties to her ankles and began kissing the insides of her thighs.

Percy sat, pulling him up. She kicked free of the shorts and took off her top.

He gripped her by the shoulders and guided her down until she lay on top of him. His skin felt moist. He held her close. She felt his nipples against hers. Felt him hot and hard against her thigh. All it required was the smallest rotation of her hips and he was inside her. They made love slowly. It seemed like he was perfectly prepared to go on forever, that comfortable pace, his hand tracing and retracing the same route from the base of her spine to the nape of her neck. Occasionally, he stopped altogether, still inside. Sometimes just to look at her. Sometimes to tell her she was beautiful. Sometimes for a long, sweet kiss.

Gradually, his pace picked up. He began to emit a series of little moans as the thrusts that had been so gentle became forceful. He rolled on top, and holding her tightly, began a frenzied rotation, grinding his hips.

His thrusting became deeper, more powerful. He arched his back, let out a yell, and, quivering, held on as if she was the last thing in the world—which is exactly what Percy felt like.

Plunkett stayed there a long time afterwards, lying beside her on that old bear hide letting the night breezes cool them. Percy found a very pleasant place to nuzzle under his chin, so pleasant she could have spent the rest of her life right there.

The rest of her life. That was the rub. If there was to be a rest of her life, at least one she cared to contemplate, Plunkett was going to have to stay badly deceived for as long as possible. And if he found out?

Or, rather, when he found out?

That was the true irony. If Percy's plan went well, she would soon fulfill her lifelong dream: having money and freedom, enough of both to finally be with the type of man she had always wanted—a man much like the one who at that moment held her in his well-muscled arms, his chest rising and falling so gently he might have been asleep.

"Hey, Plunk, happy birthday," she whispered.

"Percy," he said quietly. "You know what I'm thinking."

Out on the lake, a loon called its two-note wail.

Plunkett went on: "That other night we— Before . . . before you and Barron . . ."

Another loon answered the first.

"I was remembering how grateful I was then," Plunkett said.

"Still am. And I remember wondering, why would she do this? Then realizing it was for me. Your way of . . ."

"*Shush,*" she said, wiggling from under his arm and propping herself on one elbow so she could see him. She ran a hand down his belly. "Plunk . . . that night . . . I did it for me." She slid her hand lower and touched him. "And tonight, too."

On the drive home all of Plunkett's senses were given over to cataloging and assessing what had transpired back on the bearskin. At some later date, he might come to understand. For the present, he was left with a pastiche of fast-fading images and memories: Percy's deep voice, the beauty-parlor scent of her shampoo, the softness of her skin against his chest.

Percy had just given him back part of his life that he had thought was lost forever. He wanted to keep it. And that would be easy. It just meant doing one thing he usually found repugnant: doing exactly what Culley asked, no more, no less—at least as far as investigating the death of Barron Quinell was concerned.

Musing over the ramifications of that, Plunkett arrived at the foot of his driveway feeling light and drifting and emptied of something vital. Still smelling Percy's wonderful smells. Envisioning Percy—her hair, her breasts, that silly little gap between her front teeth.

The first sign that something was amiss was the Subaru wagon parked in Plunkett's driveway. The second was that someone had spruced up the inside of his place. His table was cleared of fly-tying gear and set with a red-and-white-checked cloth, silverware, white plates, and wine glasses. A red candle had been shoved in a wicker-basket Chianti bottle. The air was thick with the onion, bacon, and tomato sauce aroma of meat loaf. A chocolate cake was on the coffee table, bristling with so many candles it looked like a blue-spined porcupine. And on the couch, asleep when he came in, curled up and looking girlish, was Linda.

She rolled over and mewed, rubbing her eyes. When she became aware that Plunkett was in the room, she gave a shy smile and said, "Surprise."

18

At ten o'clock the next morning, Percy was in the smallest of her half-dozen bikinis—the black one, her favorite. She lay on the wharf, on her stomach, feeling the sun tingle the backs of her thighs and shoulders and was making commendable headway through the old Judith Krantz novel in front of her. The heroine and her daughter were in the middle of a terrifically juicy argument when a man's shadow crossed the page.

Percy half-rolled, holding the book in front of her eyes as a sun visor. Before her was the silhouette of Plunkett in full trooper regalia, from clunky black shoes to gray Stetson. His face bore the self-important frown of all on-duty law enforcement officers and, for that matter, any man who is about to say something accusatory or—worse, given the previous evening—apologize.

"Sorry, Percy . . . to disturb you," Plunkett said, scuffing the wharf boards with his shoe. The only reminder that there ever had been a previous evening was that he replaced the self-important frown with a hangdog mug identical to the ones he and Winston had on just before dinner.

"I've been giving a lot of thought to . . ." He did a little more board scuffing and did not finish his sentence.

Which was just as well. In Percy's experience, the words "I've been giving a lot of thought to" usually served as preamble to some of the most dangerous utterances to come out of men's mouths.

Figuring that someone had to do it, she got up and gave him a hug. Plunkett responded with the minimum acceptable amount of pressure and broke off, stepping back.

"Why do I get the feeling that something's wrong?" said Percy. There was an unplanned-for edge to her voice, which was fine. Plunkett was beginning to get her mad. She stomped over to the end of the wharf and sat. Plunkett eased himself onto the side of the diving board and began to examine a nearby wharf ring. The hangdog look had been overshadowed by one of genuine and well-earned fatigue. Plunkett obviously hadn't gotten anymore sleep than she.

"I gotta ask you," he said, not to her but to the wharf ring. He huffed and shrugged in a way that left open any number of possibilities, none of them particularly enticing. "Aldon Hewitt," Plunkett said.

Percy concentrated on making a pair of perfect circles in opposite directions with her toes in the water.

"He was around here the other day. He in your employ?" asked Plunkett. Her lover of the previous evening actually used those words: He in your employ?

"No," Percy said, too fast for her liking, so she added, "Used to do odd jobs for Barron and his partner. Keep people off the company's land, guard construction projects."

"Humph," Plunkett said, to the wharf ring, then *humphed* again, this time at Turnip Island, whose outlines were blurred in the shimmering haze. "He works for Saranac Chemicals now," Plunkett said. "Pretty sure he chased me up Stewart Mountain Road the other night."

Having imparted that information, Plunkett stood, slapped both thighs simultaneously and said, "Thanks for your time—" He stopped and consulted the wharf ring again. "And for last night," he added.

He made it as far as the big over-hanging cedar at the edge of the wharf in whose shade Winston dozed. There, he stopped and administered a half-dozen ritual strokes to the sleeping hound's head. The affection went unacknowledged. Plunkett turned back to Percy.

"Lisa Perry," he said with a pained look on his face.

Percy nodded.

"She was having an affair with Barron," he said, and if Percy hadn't known better, she would have sworn he was trying to be cruel. Except he wasn't. What he was trying to be was in many ways worse.

"He proposed to her." Plunkett pointed an accusing index finger at Percy and demanded in a heartless, once-and-for-all tone: "Did you know?"

Percy had to suck in her breath and fight to stop her face from showing what she felt. She looked Plunkett in the eyes and held his gaze. She said, with more resignation than anger, "Now that you mention it . . ."

Ultimately, it was the light that made living in the Bleecker Street loft worthwhile to Lisa Perry. In the winter, the sun's slanting rays coming through the floor-to-ceiling windows warmed the apartment. Early spring mornings Lisa liked to stand and brush her hair in the sunlight—hair and sunlight the same color. Even on hot summer afternoons, Lisa Perry still loved the light, particularly now, the way it made Bo Scullin's body glisten as he lay on her bed.

For a man of his years—for a man of half his years—Bo was in tremendous shape. Age had sculpted his dimpled face, clearly delineating his cheeks, jaw line, and brow. His belly was square-muscled, tight-skinned, and bronzed from his three-week retreat to the chalet. As an added bonus, Bo was remarkably well-endowed, even afterwards. She reached down and gripped him gently. Her bonus. The very least she deserved for sleeping with her boss.

Both her bosses.

During their ritual shower together afterward, Lisa steeled herself for the confrontation. Bo had been acting skittish, almost paranoid, since coming back. In less than one month, Bo would own the company outright. The new investors would be pouring in huge amounts of fresh capital. With success so near, the last thing Lisa wanted was a partner who was losing his composure. Their romp in bed had provided only temporary relief.

He was toweling himself in front of one of her floor-to-ceiling windows when she said, "While you were gone I had a visit from one of our investors. Right here. He made it clear he was upset. Wanted to know what went wrong up there."

She put on her smart pale blue dress with the six big white buttons running from collar to hem.

Bo dropped the towel on the floor and picked up her hair dryer and a brush, trying to appear nonchalant, but his hand was shaking. He went back into the bathroom and stood before the mirror. She leaned against the door frame.

"Stupid kid drove the truck off the road," Bo said. He flicked on the dryer.

Lisa spoke loud enough to be heard over the noise. "You see the *Times* article? Christ, they gave the fish kill a half page. Our investor made it very clear he doesn't like publicity. Said you assured him there wouldn't be any."

Bo worked on the jaunty curls that rose from his forehead, twirling the brush, pausing now and then to pat an errant hair into place. "It's blowing over," he said.

Lisa wasn't sure whether his reference was to the fish kill or his hair. "A cop came to see me," she said.

He hadn't heard her. Or if he had, he clearly had other more important things on his mind.

She yanked the dryer's cord. "I said, 'A cop came to see me.' "

Bo gave her his full attention.

She proceeded slowly, spelling it all out, as one often had to do with Bo. "The cop who came thinks Barron might have been murdered." Lisa swallowed hard. "Bo," she said, "there was never anything like that supposed to happen. And if it did . . ." She paused and made sure he was still listening, that, indeed, something was getting through his thick, albeit well-coiffed, skull. "Bo, if I find out that it did, don't think for one minute I'm going to take the fall. I'll go and cop a plea so fast—"

"Accidental," Bo said. "That's what they say—officially."

"The cop who came to see me sure didn't seem to think it was accidental."

"What did you tell him?"

"The truth," she said, and watched as Bo's handsome features crumpled in shock. He mouthed a silent *why?* She went on, "Or at least the half of the truth I figured he'd be able to find out for himself if he has a functioning brain, which he appeared to have."

Bo let out an exasperated groan. "Six-one or two? Solid build? Brownish hair?"

"You just described three-quarters of the cops in North America."

"Should have called," he said. "After the cop came." He turned his head. "Mind plugging me in?"

She began to whirl the cord in slow, little circles, but made no attempt to plug it in. "I did call you. Immediately afterward. I was scared. Some woman answered."

The effects of three weeks' worth of ultraviolet rays seeped from Bo's handsome face.

Lisa said, "You told me you were going up there alone."

Bo cleared his throat. "Must have been the cleaning woman. Have a local woman come in a few days a week."

"Local. Why lord bless, I never done did hear tell they spoke like that way up there in little old Lake Placid," she said in a half-assed imitation of Southern belle.

"She's from Alabama, or someplace like that. Married a guy. Just moved into the area."

"Fine," Lisa said sharply. "One favor, though."

"Anything."

"Try to do a better job of lying when the cops ever come asking you the questions."

19

KRANTZ'S HEROINE AND her daughter were still on as bad terms as ever when the second masculine shadow of the morning crossed Percy's page. She did a half-roll, already rehearsing her muted response to a well-earned "I'm sorry," from Plunkett.

But it was Quentin standing above her, just Quentin and his smirk, with enough patrician handsomeness showing through the boyish good looks to remind Percy of Barron. She felt a jab of remorse.

"Quentin, I'm sorry," she said, and meant it. When there was no change in the smirk, she said, "Your father . . ."

"Spare me," said Quentin, taking up Plunkett's former perch on the diving board and saying, "Why don't you and I cut the crap, for once? The only real question is which of us is gladder to see the old bastard gone. Funny, we finally find something we have in common, after all these years."

"He had some stuff of yours. I put it in a box. It's on his bed," said Percy.

Quentin gave a mean-sounding laugh and shook his head. "You think I came around to collect mementos of my dysfunctional childhood, that it?"

"Didn't think you dropped over to extend your condolences."

"How observant." Quentin looked across the lake. "Been thinking about Saranac Chemicals," he said.

She rolled and pivoted so her feet were in front of her, pointing toward Quentin. Beneath the cedar on the far side of the wharf, Winston shook himself and came out of the shade to sit protectively at her side. Percy stroked the smooth hair on top of his head.

Quentin continued to study the contours of Turnip Island.

"Seems to have been on your mind a great deal lately," said Percy.

"Yours too, no doubt," he said.

"Never heard of it, as a matter of fact—not until you came by the other night."

Quentin spun to face her. "Like I said, 'Let's cut the crap for once.' SAP has called a press conference for tomorrow afternoon where I will blow the lid off this whole Saranac mess. While we still have a chance to talk, I thought maybe you'd have something to tell me. Something that might be of use to me, but also might serve your long-term self-interests, of course. Very long-term, if my hunch is correct."

Winston lifted his muzzle skyward to allow Percy to scratch beneath his chin. "What on earth made you think a thing like that?" she said.

Quentin stood and did little limbering motions with his arms. "Just don't say I didn't give you a chance—more than you deserve."

Percy raised her eyebrows a quarter of an inch. She shrugged.

"I'm going to take a little walk this afternoon . . . on Stewart Mountain. There's an abandoned mine up there. I suspect it might be interesting. Care to come along?"

"Mines—abandoned or active—have never really held very much attraction for me."

"That so," said Quentin. "Not what I would have thought—" He stopped himself. "What about the press conference. We'll see you there, no doubt."

"I plan to be back in the city."

"How prudent." Quentin gave her three little pats on the bare shoulder. "Had a pleasant telephone conversation with Lisa Perry this morning. Sounds like she's an enterprising young woman, one who keeps her own long-term interests in mind. Maybe you ought to look her up when you're in town. You have a lot in common."

Percy twisted away. "The whole subject of Lisa Perry is beginning to bore me," she said.

"What she said to me about the ownership structure of Saranac Chemicals wasn't boring at all. Love to tell you all about it, but that will have to wait until the press conference. Mustn't steal one's own thunder."

"Want some advice?" said Percy.

"From you?"

"Yeah, from me. Before you waste an afternoon up on Stewart Mountain, go see your Uncle Bo. He just may have something interesting to say."

"That," said Quentin, "will be the day."

Quentin almost ran over the guy's feet. He was sitting there, back against a rock, legs half on, half off the driveway, not one hundred yards from the main building of the camp. His face was tilted toward the sun and he cradled a bottle of whisky whose label was the same color black as his hair.

The crunching of gravel under the SAP pickup's tires caused him to open a pair of watery, dull-looking eyes, then nonchalantly retract his legs, one at a time, as if he wasn't sure whether the effort was worthwhile. Quentin slowed and drew up beside the guy, who he now vaguely recognized, but couldn't place precisely: some local.

The fellow just sat there, staring at Quentin, nodding slightly to himself.

"Morning," said Quentin.

The guy got up and put both his hands on the window frame of the truck. He scanned the interior, still nodding to himself, holding his mouth half-opened in a way that suggested his jaw muscles were too tuckered out to bother keeping it closed. He smelled of liquor and tobacco smoke. With one final nod, he sat again. After settling himself, he looked up, seemed surprised to see Quentin still there. All he said was, "Bye-bye, homo."

Alone again, except for Winston, Percy gave up on her book for the morning. Quentin had her worried. For all his faults, he did possess a terrierlike determination when it came to the pursuit of perceived environmental wrongdoers. That, and his own personal aggrandizement. Here was an opportunity for him to do both.

And where would that leave Percy?

She felt a chill, despite the heat.

Things were definitely spiraling out of hand, going way too fast and getting way more complicated than Percy planned. And the worst thing was that she didn't have a clue about what she should do. If only Barron hadn't—

Winston let out a single, deep *who-o-o-o-f*. There was a thud of a heavy sole hitting a wharf board. Standing beside the overhanging cedar, with his mouth half-open, cuddling a fifth of Jack Daniel's like it was a new pet kitten, was Aldon Hewitt.

That gave Percy an idea. Not a great one. But an idea.

20

Gregory Hormel sat in his tiny office, bedecked in a nut brown Sears suit, so complacent you'd think the news editorship of the Plattsburgh *Chronicle-Herald* was the second, or at very least, the third most prominent post in American journalism. Percy was relieved. Despite everything, she still thought of herself as basically an honest person—given half a chance. Hormel's smug comportment was going to make lying to him a lot easier.

It was just after lunch on Friday—the last day of what was now officially the hottest month on record for Franklin, Clinton, and Essex counties. Hormel's office was Percy's last stop before taking the USAir shuttle back to Newark, a trip she would normally have dreaded. But with Quentin's news conference still scheduled for later that afternoon, being 15,000 feet somewhere above Lake Champlain seemed like a good idea.

"Wonderful, wonderful human being, your late husband. A fine man," Hormel said, standing, extending one of his chubby hands, and in the process putting so much strain on his vest that Percy was forced to reassess her previous doubts about the quality of Sears' tailors, or at least those whose job it is to affix buttons.

The act of standing and speaking at the same time caused Hormel's face to go red. He slumped back into his chair, breathing loudly and allowing the uppermost of his two chins to recline on its pal. "An all-around great guy," he added, between breaths.

"You knew Barron?" Percy said.

She might as well have hauled off and slapped poor, plump Hormel. He winced, cleared his throat, flapped his eyelids. "Not personally," he blurted. "But, you know—Darn near everyone around here—I mean we all . . . Wonderful man." He nodded proudly, as if that should put to rest any question about his close personal association with Barron.

"Well, Barron always had great respect for you—as a journalist," Percy said, amazed how glibly that one rolled off her tongue.

Hormel beamed. "He really . . ."

"Always said the *Chronicle-Herald* was the finest local paper in the country," Percy said. "And thought your stuff was some of the best in the paper."

"I do what I can," said Hormel.

"And then that beautiful obituary," Percy said. "I hope you don't mind. I had it copied and have given it to Barron's friends. So much more meaningful than the impersonal drivel the *Times* ran."

Hormel averted his eyes.

"And because what I have to tell you today is going to be very important—locally—I wanted the *Chronicle-Herald* to be the first with the story. Barron would have wanted it this way."

Hormel selected a pen from among the four in his shirt pocket. He flipped open a notebook, one hundred percent business now.

"It's all in here," Percy said, taking one of Ivor's press releases out of the burnished leather and brass briefcase Ivor had forced upon her, along with the keys—and the lease agreement—for the Porsche. "There are some other background clippings." She handed Hormel the rest of Ivor's media packet in a slick folder embossed with the Biocural corporate emblem; Percy had yet to figure out whether it was a heavily stylized physicians' caduceus or a somewhat mangled dollar sign.

"In short," Percy went on, and had to stop herself. Hormel had actually taken notes on her *In short*. She inhaled. "In short—" His pen wagged again. "In short," she said a third time, and continued, "one of Barron's last investments was in a small company called Biocural Laboratories. The company has been working on a way to genetically replicate a drug that is useful for patients on chemotherapy. There has recently been a breakthrough. Now, with the help of an unannounced major corporate partner, the company will be building a new laboratory and research center. The Barron Quinell Research Center, to be exact."

Hormel's pen scratched furiously to keep up. When he stopped scribbling, she added, "Here. Just outside Plattsburgh."

His breath came in short, shallow gasps.

"Three hundred jobs," Percy said.

"Three hundred," Hormel whispered in reply, as if saying it too loud might cause all those jobs to vanish. Very slowly, very carefully, he wrote the number out.

"Permanent," Percy added, and he dutifully wrote down that word, too.

His task complete, Hormel mopped his brow and said, "Wonderful, wonderful man." He checked his watch, a black plastic gadget, probably from the same retail outlet as his suit. "Big news day," he said. Checked the watch again. "This story—" He indicated his notes. "Real page one stuff, Mrs. Quinell. I'll run it either tomorrow or on the front of our Business Monday section. All depends what comes out of the news conference in Ray Brook this afternoon. But of course I imagine you know. . . ."

He let his voice drift off and flashed a knowing smile so out of place on his chubby face that he had to have plagiarized it from some journalist far more seasoned and worldly than himself. "The press conference your stepson, Quentin, called. Out in front of the state office complex. Word is he's gotten to the bottom of this terrible chemical spill. Gigantic cover-up. Cops involved. Big business guys. Mafia. You name it. Say . . ." He let the knowing smile slip down into the conspiratorial range, also obviously plagiarized. "You couldn't fill me in on what's going to happen?" He put out a hand and added hastily, "Strictly off the record. Deep background only."

"I . . . Really I—" Percy stammered.

"Wouldn't be right," he said, quickly, all traces of conspiracy gone.

"No," she said, relieved to be telling the absolute truth again. "Wouldn't be right at all."

He nodded his assent and kept nodding as Percy stood. That action apparently jogged his memory. His head stopped bouncing up and down and he said, "This Biocural outfit—can a fella invest in it?"

Quentin's news conference had been called for four o'clock. By 4:15, a crowd of at least two hundred had gathered amid the red pines on the front lawn of the New York State Police Troop B post: Donna the Piranha and her cameraman front and center; Gregory Hormel beside her, note pad and ball point at the ready; a dozen or so SAP volunteers, all young, pretty, and female; and in the back beside Culley, Trooper Garwood Plunkett, who looked and felt like he was a captive audience for a public execution—his own.

About the only person of note not there was Quentin himself.

But everything had been readied for his arrival. A temporary dais was erected on sawhorses and plywood. It was backed by an eight-foot, forest-green-on-white SAP banner. There was also a podium and microphone. Every minute or so the same SAP volunteer who had tossed Plunkett the empty fish bucket got up, tapped the microphone, blew into it, nodded to her associates, checked her watch, tapped the microphone again.

"Just like him," Culley whispered. "Not showing up on time for his own press conference."

One of the SAP volunteers broke ranks and sprinted over to the building and went inside.

"Build suspense. Dramatic tension. Whatever you call it," said Plunkett.

"Grandstanding. That's what I call it," said Culley. "Or maybe obstructing." Culley smiled, actually looked happy, for once.

"You gonna be the one that charges him with it?" Plunkett said, nodding toward Donna the Piranha and her cameraman.

Culley became happier. "No," he said. "You are."

Twenty minutes later, when Quentin still hadn't arrived, the first of his would-be audience started to leave in ones and twos. That led to a general exodus. Donna the Piranha and her cameraman came over to where Culley and Plunkett stood. Hormel tagged along.

Donna shoved her microphone at Culley, thrusting out and upward, exactly the way they taught recruits to jab with their batons down at the police academy. "Any comment," she said.

Culley smiled at her politely. "I'm as surprised as anyone," he said, sounding sincere.

"Rumor had it that Mr. Quinell had resolved the chemical spill case. That today's conference was going to be an embarrassment to the police." She poked the microphone closer to Culley's white teeth. The only visible effect was that his smile grew more polite. The WDNT viewing audience might mistakenly have believed getting a metal thing shoved in his face was about the most pleasant diversion imaginable for the youthful investigator on a hot Friday afternoon.

"We have made very satisfactory progress in our investigations into the chemical spill. If Mr. Quinell—or any other concerned citizen—feels they have information that may further our efforts, they should get in touch with us," he said, finding more of the smile.

Donna the Piranha looked crestfallen. She pulled the microphone back and rolled her eyes at the camera guy. He shrugged.

"That blond one over there." He pointed a finger toward the SAP volunteer who was coming back from the building. "She's his girlfriend. Conoscenti's kid."

Donna set off at a full run, cameraman following, Hormel a distant third, and falling farther behind with each step.

Off camera, Culley's polite smile was promptly replaced by a smug one.

"Quinell found out he didn't know as much as he thought.

That's why he didn't show. Embarrassed. Or maybe he discovered he was wrong," Culley said.

Plunkett was looking at the blond woman—the judge's daughter. She was speaking fast into Donna's microphone. Gesticulating hysterically.

Plunkett turned to Culley and said, "Hope you're right."

By 9:00 that same evening, Plunkett had seamlessly undergone his daily transformation from loyal Lumberjack patron to unpaid employee. He sat on a stool at the counter, trying to pour salt into the dozen shakers ranked in front of him. Only half of the salt ended up on the counter. That made it a better than average night.

"What are you thinking about?" said Linda, and when he didn't answer she said, louder, "You there, O Silent One."

What Plunkett was thinking about was Percy Quinell. Or more specifically, her metallic gray eyes. Lately, when he thought about Percy, he found he had to take one part at a time. Contemplating the whole was beyond the scope of his finite human imagination. The silver hair was what he usually thought of first, blowing in the wind as she skippered her inboard. Then he visualized her long, tan legs. Or her turned-up nose with its permanent dab of sunburn—just enough to be endearing. Sometimes, if he was lucky, he could drag back images from that night. But he was surprised how fast those memories were fading. They already needed replenishing.

"Cat got your tongue," said Linda. Without waiting for an answer, she put a Genny beside him and went about the business of pulling down the front blinds. She came back and started wiping the counter, beginning at the end farthest from Plunkett, who hadn't moved toward his beer.

He was trying to make some sense of the money-crazed, mixed-up world Percy's ambition had sucked her into: a dead husband who was unfaithful to her; a spoiled, sarcastic, self-proclaimed protector of the environment as a stepson, who had just vanished; her husband's business partner, a retirement-aged guy who acted like a hormonally overcharged twenty-year-old; Blevins; Aldon Hewitt;

a river full of dying fish. All of them swirling around Percy somehow. A whirlpool.

"H-m-m-m-m?" said Linda, working toward him in a series of wet, sudsy circles.

Plunkett shook himself out of his deep thinking and came back to reality—the soapy-handed vision of femininity across the counter from him, one of those women who simply always had been there. He suddenly became aware of the new, sweating Genny and took a swig.

"Linda, you're a good, commonsensical woman," Plunkett said, and meant it.

Linda clutched her wet hands to her bosom. "Gee, Plunk, you sure know how to sweet talk a gal. Just hearing that, I go all squishy inside. 'A good, commonsensical woman.' " She grabbed his beer and took the type of swig you might expect of a good, commonsensical woman.

"It's Percy Quinell," Plunkett said.

Linda snorted and turned her back to him as she went about opening cellophane bags of ground coffee and emptying the contents into filters for the morning rush. "Always been Percy," she said.

"That's not true," said Plunkett, defensively.

Linda ran a hand through her dirty blond curls. She snorted again. "Plunk," she said. "You and I have known each other too long for any of that b.s. So do me a favor."

"Can we talk . . . confidentially?"

Linda cut him off with a scowl. "That's why God put us good, commonsensical women on earth," she said.

Plunkett swigged, swallowed, swigged again, and consulted the counter top. "What would you say if I told you that there's a possibility Percy Quinell killed her husband," Plunkett said. "I mean, may have. Or rather had someone—There's no proof or . . ."

"You just keep up your rationalizing and qualifying while I fill these," Linda gestured to a row of stainless-steel creamers on the shelf behind the counter. "When you want to really talk, I'll still be here—probably."

Plunkett cleared his throat. "I think someone bashed Barron Quinell on the head and dumped his body in the Ausable. Did a piss-poor job of trying to make it look like an accident. Percy stood to inherit Barron's money—and there must be a fair bit. And I found out Barron was having a little fling with a woman about twenty years younger than Percy—and better looking, if you can believe it."

Linda responded with a scowl that suggested only a tremendous amount of self-discipline on her part had saved Plunkett from a face full of half-and-half.

"I found an earring that could have been one of Percy's down near where the kid hooked Quinell's body. Percy's fishing rod was there. And Aldon Hewitt has been hanging around Percy's lately."

Linda frowned. "She's lowered her standards, then. Even I don't let him darken the doors of this place. And as you see, I ain't too selective about my clientele." She went back to her pouring.

"So that's my problem," Plunkett said. "That's what I need to talk to you about."

"Doesn't sound to me like what you have is a problem so much as it is an opportunity—to get in that cruiser at your earliest convenience and go out there and haul in Percy Quinell for Murder One, or whatever you guys really call it. Obviously she had Aldon do the dirty deed on her behalf. And if you are soliciting my good, commonsensical advice on this matter, it'd be arrest her sooner rather than later."

"It's not so simple."

"I bet," said Linda.

"It's not simple because for some reason Cully has blocked all efforts to initiate a proper investigation. And there's something else. . . ."

"I was waiting for that. The something else part," said Linda, who was leaning close, elbows on the counter.

"I mean, for the life of me, I can't envision Percy doing a thing like that. I know her."

"We all know her," she said. "Since we were kids. And I figure Percy'd be capable of damn near anything. Always has been, as far as I'm concerned. Look how fast she dumped you when Barron came sniffing around."

"You blame her for that?" Plunkett spread his hands to display himself for comparison's purpose.

Linda examined the merchandise, top to bottom and back again before saying, "Yeah, I do."

"Tell me. Can you imagine Percy living in some mobile home with a cop? Raising two or three brats on my wages? Getting middle-aged and worn-looking before her time?"

"Like all the rest of us mere mortals," Linda said.

"Or"—Plunkett looked hard at Linda—"marrying young to some guy who turns out to be a no-good drunk and having to raise a kid all alone and run some roadside restaurant sixteen hours a day, seven days a week?"

"That's a low blow, Plunk," Linda said.

Plunkett softened his voice. "I don't know, but somehow I have always been able to forgive Percy for that, for wanting more."

"Well," said Linda. "Percy sure wanted more. And I don't think she would stop at anything to get it—and more to the current point—keep it. What do you think she's going to do when she finds out her life's meal ticket is about to take off with some bimbo? Call up her friendly, local real estate agent and start pricing mobile homes?"

Plunkett stared at his beer bottle. "There are still a few loose ends," he said, and went back to his study of the bottle.

For a long while afterward, neither he nor Linda spoke. They stayed on their opposite sides of the Formica counter, listening to the nighttime whirring and rattling of the fans of the appliances in the empty restaurant.

Linda consulted the Coca-Cola clock and menu board behind the counter and groaned. She gave Plunkett a light punch on the shoulder, and then stood there looking at him as if he represented one of those nagging little closing-time chores that could either be gotten out of the way at this late hour or be held over for another day, maybe when she had more energy.

He finished his beer. "Suppose I'd better get along," he said.

"Do you, now," Linda said, widening her eyes and letting one corner of her mouth rise. She got two more Gennies from the cooler and put them on the counter. "Upstairs. Second door on the right," she said. When Plunkett just sat there, she leaned over the counter until her face was only inches from his, and said, "My bedroom."

The way the sun shone through the windows may have been the big advantage to the Bleecker Street loft. The big disadvantage was coming home after dark. Lisa Perry hated that part.

At ten o'clock Friday night Lisa strode briskly in from Lafayette, with her eyes directed toward an imaginary point five feet off the ground directly in front of her. Her keys were clutched on her right hand, with the one that opened her apartment building's entrance pinched between the thumb and index finger and held in front of her, like a knife, ready to be plunged into the lock or, if need be, any would-be mugger or molester's eye socket.

Her senses were alert for subtle changes in the street. She cataloged, then dismissed the heaps of newspapers and angle-parked grocery carts that marked the nocturnal roosts of the homeless. With a nod, Lisa acknowledged the thirty-year-old securities lawyer from upstairs as he jogged past on the other side, cocooned in Spandex and the music of his Walkman. But when the lanky figure detached itself from where it had been leaning against the building at the corner of Bowery and began to walk toward her, all of her survival instincts went on full alert.

He came in her direction, shuffling, turning his head from side to side, obviously timing it to bring them both together in front of her building.

She probably would have run or screamed, but the guy passed under a street light. He was wearing a uniform. A blue policeman's uniform. She relaxed. Proceeded to her door. Inserted the key. Fumbled with the first lock until the bolt *clunked* open. The second lock always wanted two or three twists of the key before relenting—especially if she was in a hurry. Tonight, mercifully, it sprang on the first turn.

-179-

It was too late: It was only after she had the door open wide enough for the guy to wedge in his foot and flash her a sick-looking smile that Lisa Perry realized what bothered her about his uniform. It wasn't a policeman's.

21

Plunkett saw the headline as soon as he entered the cubicle he used when work brought him to Ray Brook: LIFE AFTER DEATH FOR BARRON QUINELL.

At times you had to love the *Chronicle-Herald*.

The story took up the better part of the Business Monday section. It told how some company called Biocural Laboratories was going to open a research center near Plattsburgh. Hundreds of new jobs were going to be created. The name of a prominent local financial backer of the firm was also mentioned: Mrs. Barron Quinell.

Plunkett punched a number on his telephone. Beverly Laney answered midway through the first ring.

"Does that computer of yours work this early Monday morning," he said.

There was silence. Two of Mrs. Laney's dry chuckles. "It's ten A.M., *Gar*-wood. I've been expecting your call. I had hoped for a personal visit. But . . ." She let her voice trail off.

"There's a company, Biocural Laboratories. I'd like some information."

Two more of Mrs. Laney's dry chuckles. "I presume you are

referring to that article in this morning's newspaper. If so, I've got a bit of a head start on you. When I saw Percy Quinell's name there, I assumed that it fell within the bounds of my previous assignment. I'm already looking into it."

"You missed your calling," said Plunkett.

There was a pause. "It wasn't me who missed my calling."

Five minutes later, Culley stuck his blown-dried head over the partition. For a brief, blissful instant, he looked like a hunter's trophy, bagged, stuffed, and attractively wall-mounted, lacking only a brass plaque indicating the date and place of his demise. Until that moment, Plunkett had never fully understood the allure of taxidermy.

"Come into my office," Culley said, and promptly pulled back his head.

When Plunkett got to Culley's office, Cully was pacing, rubbing his palms together in agitated half rotations. "For once," he said, freeing one of his hands and forming it into a gunlike shape, which he proceeded to aim at Plunkett's heart. "I'd like to know what the hell is going on around here."

Culley made the finger gun into a fist and slammed that into his other palm.

Plunkett could think of at least a half-dozen replies, any one of which would earn for his nose the same treatment Culley's palm had just received. So he didn't respond. He took a seat and sprawled to get a safe vantage point from which to observe what looked like was shaping up to be Culley's first on-the-job tantrum.

"You've no doubt heard," Culley said, moving behind his own desk and sitting. As always, he seemed out of place and uncomfortable, like a child caught playing in his father's office.

Plunkett was wondering what, specifically, he was expected to have heard when Culley said, "Lisa Perry."

At first the name meant nothing. Then Plunkett said, "Barron Quinell's . . ." Not knowing how to finish that sentence.

"Exactly," said Culley. "Exactly!"

"What about her?" said Plunkett. "Exactly."

"She's dead. That's what about her."

Culley sat on the other side of the desk, smug now that he had imparted his news. He held up a sheet of fax paper. "All right here. Fascinating reading. She was beaten half to death. Then brutally raped. When the guy had finished with her, he smacked her on the head with a piece of the modern sculpture she liked to collect. But of course you probably know all about that."

Plunkett cleared his throat, buying a bit of time to think of a response.

Culley saved him the trouble. "The investigators down there found a piece of paper in the apartment with your name and phone numbers on it."

"I was there when I was in the city—what was it?—week before last. Talked to her in connection with Barron Quinell's . . ." He stopped.

Culley had rediscovered his superior smirk and wore it in a way that suggested he never intended to part with it again. "They have a witness, some neighbor out jogging, says he saw a guy go in with her at approximately ten o'clock Friday night. Guy was wearing a police uniform."

"Plunkett," Culley said. "It might save a lot of headaches if you have an alibi for Friday night. Something ironclad."

Judge John Conoscenti and his daughter Ashley came into Culley's office before Plunkett could respond, the judge well groomed and white-haired, already looking the part of the senator he hoped to become. Ashley appeared frightened and a good decade younger than her two dozen years. The judge walked right over to Plunkett and extended a hand, as if practicing for the upcoming campaigns. "Investigator Culley," he said.

Not wishing to offend, Plunkett took the hand, but nodded toward Culley, who was still at his desk. "That's Investigator Culley, Your Honor," he said.

The judge looked slightly taken aback, but managed a recovery that suggested he very definitely had a promising career ahead as a politician. Plunkett's hand was dropped, Culley's gripped over the desk, vigorously shaken three times and released. Throughout the ritual, Judge Conoscenti cast about for a chair that would be acceptable for his daughter. He gestured to the one next to Plunkett. The young woman collapsed into it.

"I'm afraid we have a missing person," the judge said. Ashley burst into sobs, her head bowed, her shoulders shaking. The judge put out a hand to steady her.

"My daughter's fiancé," he said, and seemed disappointed when that didn't elicit an immediate response from the police officers. Reluctantly he said, "Quentin Quinell."

Culley sat erect behind his desk. Picked up a pen.

"Come on, Ashley, dear," said Conoscenti.

She raised her head and inhaled four times, shallowly and in rapid succession. "It was Thursday morning. At the office. He got a call. Afterwards he said he had to go see somebody. Something to do with the press conference . . . Took a camera . . ."

She started to sob again.

Despite his run-in with Conoscenti, Plunkett wasn't thinking about the missing Quentin Quinell as he walked outside to his patrol car and the freedom it represented. He was thinking about Lisa Perry and Percy Quinell.

When he thought about Lisa Perry, he remembered the golden braid running halfway down her back and the bright sun streaming through the windows of her apartment.

Percy, he remembered sitting on her dock, making circles in the water with her toes, hearing word of her husband's infidelity, the ripples expanding across the lake.

None of it added up yet, but the way Plunkett figured it, there was a good chance that before long some cop or another was going to arrest Percy. After all that had happened, the very least Plunkett could do was make sure that cop was him.

22

Percy dropped by Ivor's new offices at eleven that same Monday morning. She decided to do so unannounced, just to see what the old rascal was up to.

Fifty Wall Street was a modern marble-fronted skyscraper sporting four mock-doric columns, an attempt to make it look as permanent and secure as the surrounding edifices that housed respectable brokerages and banks. The space Ivor had taken was formerly the retail division of a small, specialized investment firm, now defunct, whose managing partner would not be requiring the space for two years less a day on account of some shenanigans connected to a recent insider trading scandal.

Ivor's offices were fitted with all the trappings of a successful brokerage: a smattering of modern art and sculpture with no discernible pedigree, plenty of walnut, thick blue-gray pile carpet, the odd fake Persian rug, even a stock ticker running the length of one wall with six-inch-tall symbols and numbers scurrying across the screen to give the place an added air of legitimacy.

The only things Ivor had found it necessary to add were four well-tailored salesmen, all recently let go by major brokerages, all with young families and high six-figure mortgages. Percy felt underdressed in her dove gray Calvin Klein suit as she strode in with Winston panting at her heels. Not one of the young men acknowledged her. They were models of efficiency and professionalism, scrutinizing their computer terminals, speaking animatedly into head sets.

"Ivor here?" said Percy.

One of the well-turned-out fellows gestured over his shoulder to a hallway guarded by a very stern and efficient-looking young African American woman. She sat with finishing-school posture behind a small desk, smartly tapping the keyboard of her word processor.

"Come on, then," Percy said to Winston.

The efficient young woman shot a who-do-you-think-you-are glare at Percy and her dog. "Mr. Rhys is in a meeting," she said.

"I bet," said Percy, proceeding toward a set of double doors at the end of the hall.

She opened one. Winston bounded directly over to a leather sofa, where he promptly made a bed out of the softest, most comfortable-looking object in the room, a crumpled ball of masculine clothing that Percy picked out as a Zanini original: a spiffy olive green two-piecer. Poplin, she guessed.

The suit's owner lay spread-eagled on the mahogany conference table wearing nothing other than a white face cloth, and that was folded over his eyes.

Above him, sat a slim scarlet-haired woman in black jeans and a matching sleeveless T-shirt, holding a bottle of mineral oil.

Ivor groped for his glasses. "How good of you to drop by." He shot the smile of a delighted host. "This is Dr. Erline Birdsell . . . my . . . chiropractor," he said. "I read an article in *Fortune* about how Robert Mondavi has a therapeutic massage every day. Seeing as how he and I are contemporaries—and both still active in business—thought I'd follow his example. The mind-body relationship is an amazing thing."

"I bet," said Percy.

Erline capped the mineral oil. She grabbed her shoulder bag and was about to exit when Ivor swung his legs off the table.

"One minute," he said. He slipped into a thick terry-cloth robe, liberated from the Plaza to judge by the emblem it bore. From one of the pockets, he produced an alligator-skin wallet and removed two bills, at least one of which was a fifty. "Same time tomorrow," he said. "We can work on this darn third cervical vertebrae."

"Certainly, Mr. Rhys," said Erline. "And maybe your neck, too."

Once Erline left, and some of the flush vanished from Ivor's face, Percy got down to business.

"You've seen this?" she asked, holding up an edition of the *Post*. The two-inch tall headline read, KILLER COP!

Ivor nodded sagely, looking in control and businesslike even though he was wearing only a terry-cloth robe. "Bit of bad luck. Might have to take things more slowly. With Bo losing his partner and his VP of Finance so close together, he might not think this is the most propitious time for investing."

"What it means is we have to move faster than ever," Percy said. "You see the other newspaper piece, the one I had faxed down— about me."

Ivor brightened. "See it. It was perfect. Absolutely perfect. A journalistic coup. Doesn't get any sweeter than that. I've had several dozen reprints made to be distributed to our mooch list. We're already receiving unsolicited phone calls." He paused for a breath, which he drew in while shaking his head. "How did you get them to believe such a—" He sought the right word but failed to find it.

"My upbringing," Percy said.

Ivor bestowed a paternal smile. He turned his back to Percy and shifted Winston off his suit by administering a tap to the old hound's rump.

"Hey!" said Percy.

Ivor pulled on his shorts and trousers under the purloined Plaza robe. Shedding the robe and hauling on his fawn shirt, he chuckled and muttered, 'Life After Death for Barron Quinell.' I'll have to remember that one." He walked over to a bar established in one corner of the office and, unbidden, poured drinks for himself and Percy.

I have some good news," Ivor said. He handed Percy her glass and then bent to put on socks and Gucci loafers. Straightening, he looped his necktie into a perfectly crafted double Windsor.

"Biocural may well have its first key investor," Ivor said. "Dear, sweet Bambi-Sue Cline has fallen for my pitch." Ivor swirled his Scotch as he admired its amber coloration through the florescent light. "Poor woman is dumb—dumb, dumb, dumb. So dumb it's almost too good to be true. But there you have it."

There was a light tap on the door. One of the well-attired young men from the boiler room came in. "Pardon me," he whispered to the room at large. "But, Mr. Rhys, you asked to be interrupted if any serious investment inquiries came in."

"Well?" said Ivor.

"I think we might have someone."

"The amount?"

"Five thousand."

"You handle it."

Once the young man was gone Percy said, "If there's any truth to Mendel's law, generations yet unborn had better hope that Bambi-Sue and Bo are practicing family planning. Otherwise there could be a whole new race of dummies—very vain dummies."

Ivor picked up his suit jacket and shook it free of wrinkles and basset hairs. "She's due here later on this morning," he said. "Wanted to bring the check by personally. A check for one hundred thousand dollars."

"Sounds too easy."

"Don't worry, I still intend to handle the situation with my usual kid gloves. Besides, she's destined to be one of the fortunate ones. At the right moment, she will be told that the value of her stock has increased dramatically—which will be one of the very few opportunities I will have to speak the truth over the next couple of weeks." Ivor eyed Percy over the rim of his tumbler. "You will be supplying the necessary funds, of course."

Percy opened her mouth and managed to get out a "Wha—" before being cut off by the clanging of a fire bell. She was prepared to walk smartly toward the nearest exit sign. Ivor, however, merely ambled over to his desk and removed a horn from from one of the drawers. He began to toot it.

A moment later, the well-attired young men burst through the double doors pushing one of their number ahead.

"Well, let's hear it," said Ivor.

"Ten thousand," said the young man modestly. "But it's really Ms. Quinell we should be toasting. The investor came to us as a result of her efforts. Editor at the Plattsburgh paper."

That called for a round of drinks—vodka and single malt for Percy and Ivor, Perriers all around for the natty boiler-room crew. The merriment continued unabated for fifteen minutes, with the younger men telling and retelling the story of how their colleague nursed the editor from five thousand to six then to seven-point-five before finally closing at ten. Just after Ivor suggested they all treat themselves to another round, the secretary came in.

"There's a woman to see you, Mr. Rhys," she said, letting the note of disapproval in her voice show that she thought no more of the newcomer than she had of Percy, or for that matter the recently departed Erline. "Says her name is—" She paused and swallowed hard, once. "Bambi-Sue Cline."

The young men quickly removed all signs of the recent revelries. One of them even tucked Ivor's robe and the bottle of mineral oil in a drawer. Ivor himself placed a hand gently upon the base of Percy's spine. He gave her a nudge. "Would you and that animal mind stepping out the back way?" he whispered.

"There's actually a back way?" asked Percy, feeling the pressure on her spine increase.

A young man slid aside one of the walnut wall panels to reveal a gray metal door.

"Do you think for a minute I would have taken these premises without one?" Ivor said.

-189-

23

The walnut panel had barely closed behind Winston's hindquarters when Bambi-Sue Cline strode in, blond curls bouncing, wearing a cute floral dress that stopped abruptly one-third of the way down to her knees. But it wasn't her hair or her tanned thighs or even her enormous blue eyes that put the leer on Ivor's face. Bambi-Sue had her checkbook in hand.

"I am just so sorry to intrude like this," she said, shamelessly deploying the sort of twangy drawl rarely heard nowadays outside Nashville recording studios. That Bambi-Sue sounded even dumber in the flesh than she had on the phone made Ivor's leer grow. "I know you must be terribly busy, but this is all the money I have, and before I invested it, I wanted to meet you face-to-face."

Ivor did a little bow and waited until the last of his boiler-room boys left the office before saying, "Miss Cline—"

"Bambi-Sue," she said. "Just call me Bambi-Sue, most everyone does."

"Bambi-Sue," said Ivor, having trouble uttering such a name. "Let me assure you that we view our investors as part of a big, extended family. You are welcome to drop by these offices at any time."

She smiled and giggled. "That just makes me feel so much better about handing over this." Bambi-Sue sat down on one of the leather chairs and scribbled out a check, hand trembling.

Carefully, Ivor put out his fingers to take it. She eased it back.

"This is going to sound silly, but I never wrote a check for this much. It's my college savings. You promise to take good care of my money. I'd just die if I lost it," she said.

Ivor extended his fingers further, this time securing purchase on the piece of paper. She still held her end. "Bambi-Sue, I can assure you we will treat your money as if it were ours," Ivor said. "A major multinational corporation has approached Biocural. A buy-out is imminent. Your shares will double. I guarantee it. Double. Trust me."

He tugged. The check came away, easily. More easily than Ivor would have liked.

Bambi-Sue gazed at it wistfully.

But when Ivor had squirreled it in his desk drawer, she snorted—once, loudly and derisively. "Well, slap my grandma," she said, her twangy accent replaced with something still Southern, but much harder, huskier and streetwise, what you'd expect from the mouth of a seasoned New Orleans hooker. "Given that your papering was pretty good and your telephone pitch as smooth as they come, I'd honestly hoped for something a little more impressive." She snorted again—this time for her own benefit. "What you running, gramps?" she said. "Has the trappings of your basic Ponzi scheme?"

Ivor cleared his throat. He cast a worried look in the direction of the hidden door and took a step over toward the walnut panel that concealed it. "Er—I—"

"While you put yourself to all the trouble of trying to figure out that lie I ain't gonna believe anyways, why not do something useful, like fix me a Jack Daniel's, straight up," Bambi-Sue said. She sat, crossed her legs, and took a Virginia Slim from her handbag. Glad for a diversion—*any* diversion—Ivor produced a gold lighter, which was flickering by the time it reached the end of her cigarette. "I believe I have a balance of eighty-seven bucks in that account."

Bambi-Sue puffed a cloud of smoke toward Ivor's desk drawer. She waited until the smoke dissipated before adding, "It's my other one, the Colonial tax-free municipal bond one, that's got a hundred grand in it. And it's gonna have a whole lot more soon, specially now that it looks like we're partners."

Ivor was still working on getting his throat cleared, and having little success. He delivered a drink to Bambi-Sue. "Can we talk frankly?" he asked, settling onto the sofa and having a restorative pull from his glass. "Or is it your intention to continue the cryptic banter for a while? Not that that, too, wouldn't be pleasant—given its source."

"My intention is to come away from here with a deal from you, or to blow the lid off this entire shabby little operation. Your call. And I won't put up with any crap out of you. That frank enough?"

In a deft, one-two movement, she took a pair of quarter-inch hits, the first off her Virginia Slim, the second from her glass. "I've been working on dear, sweet Bo for nearly a year now," she went on. "I've raised the heifer, to draw upon a figure of speech my dear departed daddy might have used, and now I'll be damned if I'm about to let someone else milk her. Bo is not going to lose all his money, not to anyone other than me, that is."

A look of revelation lit Ivor's wrinkled features. "You're a grifter."

"Then you'll understand my position," said Bambi-Sue. "Believe me, I have searched, and Bo Scullin has to be one of the stupidest millionaires in the land—and I met a lot of stupid millionaires in my former profession." She batted her eyes in a way that left no doubt about the precise nature of said profession.

"So where do I come in," said Ivor.

"From the minute your phony newsletters started coming, I figured that some sort of con was afoot. First, I was just gonna blow the lid off your little scam, then when I saw that some of your stuff was really pretty smooth, it dawned on me that maybe you knew what you were doing, that we might just have the basis for a deal. I mean, I can nickel-and-dime Bo for a long time—my monthly allowance, the usual jewels and furs. But it's a long, slow process, and believe me, Bo Scullin's company is no fun. Especially since his partner died. He's going bonkers. And now that woman."

She nodded toward the *Post*. "Worked for him. Gave him blow jobs on the side." Bambi-Sue waited to see if that information sparked any interest. When it didn't, she said. "Bo's acting weird, I tell you. Real weird. Like he's gonna lose it soon. Keeping things together is getting to be too much like work. And that, gramps, is something I have scrupulously avoided since leaving Muscle Shoals, Alabama, when I was sixteen." She polished off the rest of her Jack Daniel's and held her glass out for a refill.

Ivor sprang to his feet. "Not so very long ago, I'd venture," he said.

Bambi-Sue snorted. "Cute," she said to Ivor. "Real cute. You always like this?"

"Only in the presence of a beautiful and intelligent young woman," said Ivor.

Bambi-Sue choked on her Virginia Slim. "Oh, my Gawd," she said. She grew serious. "How much you planning to clip him for?"

"Whatever we can get. Hundred thousand. Maybe two, I'd hope," said Ivor.

Bambi-Sue eyed him coolly. "For a guy who has survived as long as you have in this business, you're a piss-poor liar. Wanna try one more time. And if you don't tell the truth, I'm history. And so is your little scam. Must be someone at the SEC who'd pay a few bucks to know you're back in business. You understand me, old man? We're either partners, or your scam is dead meat. Either way I win. The minute I get even a tiny feeling that you're fucking me over . . ."

Ivor handed her the refilled glass. He took one look at those hard blue eyes and said, "Excuse my initial lack of candor. It's habitual, I'm afraid. Utterly impossible to break at my age. The truth is that I am aiming for between five and six million dollars."

Bambi-Sue whistled softly.

"That's the good news," Ivor went on. "The bad news is that I have certain expenses"—He swept the room with his arm—"and a partner . . . a very greedy partner."

"What's he in for?" asked Bambi-Sue.

"She. My partner is a she. And she is in for three million. I get a paltry million for my services."

Bambi-Sue whistled again. Then she shook her head authoritatively. "You mean five hundred thousand. That's what one million comes to—one million divided by two: half for me, half for you. Not a whole hell of a lot."

Ivor nodded sadly as he mentally ran the numbers for himself. "Put that way, it certainly isn't," he said.

"So it looks like you are just going to have to find a way to cut your other partner out of the deal."

From behind his desk, Ivor deadpanned, "Already have."

Ivor waited until he heard the solid *click* of the door to his office closing behind Bambi-Sue before he stood up, clapped his hands together and treated himself to a long, sibilant. "Yeeeee-e-s-s-s!"

The cheer winded him, so he promptly sat back down.

That had been a close one. Too close. But the irony was that with Bambi-Sue on his side, Ivor was now willing to give his half-baked scheme a better than even chance of succeeding, with a few modifications, of course.

Ivor hand-wrote a memo to his boiler-room staff and Doris, the receptionist, saying that they should all be ready for contact from Bo Scullin—by telephone or face-to-face—and that in either case he should be referred directly to Ivor.

One thing bothered him, however. That bit Bambi-Sue had said about Bo acting strange. Ivor picked up the copy of the *Post* with the KILLER COP! headline. His old body cringed, wracked by the sudden jolt of some emotion Ivor couldn't immediately identify. When he did, he cringed again, recognizing the emotion as fear. In her front-page picture, Lisa Perry seemed very much alive—and beautiful, every bit as beautiful as Percy Quinell.

Sitting there looking at the picture of the dead woman, Ivor made a mental note to be very careful. He had already made one potentially grave error in his approach to Bambi-Sue: underestimating the capabilities of a beautiful woman. It could get very costly if he did it again.

24

On Thursday, August 6, Plunkett pulled his truck into Percy's camp—the fifth time since Monday. This time she was there, or at least her Porsche was. And someone was grilling dinner, to judge by the aroma of garlic, fresh basil, and seared meat.

Plunkett got out of his truck hoping that Percy might somehow make his job easy. Or as easy as such things can be. But when he saw her standing beside the back stairs of her camp with the evening sun on her silver-blond hair, the flames of the grill leaping in front of her, she wearing a pair of white, cuffed, jean shorts and a peach-colored tank top, all Plunkett could think about was having Percy beside him on the bearskin. Things were going to be anything but easy.

Fifteen feet away, he cleared his throat.

Without looking up she said, "Medium-rare?" and flipped one of the four lamb chops on the grill.

"You're expecting a dinner guest?" said Plunkett, feeling awkward, self-conscious and guilt-ridden—painfully aware of the purpose of his visit.

Percy looked at him perplexedly, then back down to the lamb chops. "You get used to doing everything for two," she said. Another chop got flipped. "Winston and I have each put on three pounds since Barron died. That's not good. Not at our age."

At the mention of his name, Winston looked up. His sad eyes could have been begging either for compassion, sympathy, or a medium-rare chop.

"There's a bottle of red Hermitage on the kitchen counter," Percy said. "Pour us each a glass. Join me and Winston for dinner."

Plunkett already had a dinner engagement. With Linda. But that was for nine—closing time. His appetite would rebound. Besides . . .

He put that thought out of his mind and went in to pour the wine. Before he could go back outside with the filled glasses, Percy came in carrying a plate and three of the chops, looking good in her tight shorts and flimsy top. Winston was at her heels. The charred end of the fourth chop protruded from his muzzle.

"It's cooler in the living room," she said. "I thought we could eat there."

All Plunkett could think of was that the living room was where the bearskin was.

After a dinner of chops, baby red potatoes with rosemary, a simple salad, and the wine, Plunkett snuck a look at his watch.

"Eating and running this time?" Percy said, her deep voice sounding full of promise.

"I came over here for a reason," said Plunkett.

"Obviously not the reason I had hoped," Percy said.

Plunkett had to look away, anywhere other than those gray eyes that were peering so steadily at his.

"Percy," he said, and stopped. Tried to figure out the best way to say what he wanted. But as always with Percy, the thoughts tumbled out ahead of him, rolled just beyond his grasp and vanished. "Percy," he said. "You've got to let me help you."

Plunkett figured it was safe to hazard a glance in her direction. The metallic eyes looked back coolly. The only sign of encouragement was the slightest dip of her chin.

"Goddamn it, Percy!"

Winston let out a *whoof,* tumbled off the sofa in front of the fireplace and took up position at his mistress's side. He *whoofed* again.

"Percy," Plunkett said. "Your husband is dead."

Her eyes remained impassive.

"Lisa Perry—his lover—was murdered."

There was a slight tightening in the corners of Percy's eyes, but it quickly dissipated.

"Now Quentin . . . disappeared."

Percy's eyes widened, but by no more than one-sixteenth of an inch.

Plunkett fortified himself with a sip of the wine, which was far too dry for his liking, especially in the heat. A beer, that's what the occasion called for. An entire six-pack. "Percy," he said. "You have motive in all of those cases. Then there's this business about Saranac Chemicals and the spill. Again you're connected. I haven't figured out how, but you're connected. And now, this new laboratory. A punk like Aldon Hewitt hanging around here all the time. . . . Percy, I think you can see what all this is adding up to. I want to help. As your friend. As . . ." He stopped to swallow something. It wasn't Hermitage. "Dammit, Percy, do you have any idea how much I—" After a one-beat pause, he shrugged and added a very quiet, "Do you have any . . ."

Her eyes stayed cool. "I need a drink," she said huskily, and then, glancing down at her own half-full wine glass, she explained, "a real one."

Plunkett followed her to the kitchen. "Mind if I have a beer?" he said.

Without replying, she nodded in the direction of the fridge and fixed herself an eight-ounce highball glass filled with ice cubes and vodka from a bottle stashed in the freezer. Standing there she took three swallows, draining half the glass, then topped it back up before closing the door.

Those gray eyes were still expressionless when she turned back to Plunkett. "You mean what you just said?"

"Isn't that obvious?"

"No, as a matter of fact it isn't." Percy inhaled and expelled the breath. "Would you believe me if I told you I will give you your answers? All in good time. If I swore it to you?"

"Guess I don't have a choice, do I?"

Percy's eyes flickered. "No, you don't."

Plunkett was in his truck, engine on, gearshift in reverse, already fifteen minutes late for his dinner date with Linda, when Percy tapped on the driver's door and leaned in the window. "One other thing," she said.

He turned off the ignition and lifted his foot from the clutch.

When she had his full attention, she said, "There's one other thing you should know about. The last time Quentin came around here he was asking me about some old abandoned mine on the land Barron's company owns. Evidently it's somewhere up Stewart Mountain. He said if I wouldn't tell him what was going on, he'd have to go up to that mine and find out himself."

"And did you?" said Plunkett. "Tell him?"

"I told him to go ask his Uncle Bo."

At that moment, Bo Scullin and Bambi-Sue Cline lay on the plush, off-white wall-to-wall carpet of the West 81st Street apartment Bo leased in her name. He was on top, looking down at the glistening skin of his own pectoral and abdominal muscles, running smooth and taut to where he disappeared into the triangle between Bambi-Sue's legs.

Bo liked nothing better than to watch himself at work. Liked the way he drove Bambi-Sue nuts. The way she writhed and bucked. Moaned. Cried that she couldn't take it anymore. Dug her nails into the tight muscles of his ass. And finally lay there whimpering. It was then that he usually came.

But he couldn't. He was too nervous and jittery. He thrust. Ground his hips against her. Bambi-Sue crying, "Oh, oh, oh!" Bo still not coming. He withdrew and rolled onto his back. Bambi-Sue bent down and took him in her mouth.

Even that was no good. After a while Bo felt himself going soft.

He pushed her off and went to the kitchenette for the whisky she always liked afterward and a Chardonnay for himself, but decided he needed a gin instead—a good two ounces, neat.

"This evening was perfect," she said when he came back, her missing the whole goddamned point, as usual.

She cuddled beside him. He handed her the drink and pushed himself away, not liking the feel of her sweaty skin now, needing space. "I tell you, honey, I'm gonna make me a whole pile of money," she said.

"Buy a lottery ticket?" Bo said, wishing she wouldn't be so damn talkative. It was her hillbilly accent that bothered him. Bugged the hell out of him. And he didn't need that. Not now.

"No, you silly," she said, sounding silly herself. "I bought shares in a biotechnology partnership. A hundred thousand dollars worth."

"A hundred thou—" said Bo, and cut himself short, thinking that the very last thing he needed in his life at the moment was Bambi-Sue having some sort of financial crisis. "Bambi-Sue, are you sure that was smart?" he said, sounding moneywise and worldly, which was exactly the way he felt around Bambi-Sue. "I mean, risking all that money."

"No risk at all," chirped Bambi-Sue. "That's what the man who sold it to me guaranteed. As a matter of fact, he promised me it would double. Double. Isn't that just wonderful, honey?"

"Christ, Bambi-Sue," Bo said. "How could you be so—" He caught himself. Took a deep breath. "That was illegal—what he told you. It's illegal for a securities salesman to make promises about a stock's performance." He stopped and looked her directly in the eyes, wanting to make sure she understood, but doubting it. "You could lose everything."

Bambi-Sue emitted a series of little *peeps*. She battled her eyes, then bravely threw her naked shoulders back. "It was through you that I found out about the company," she said. "There was some information in those papers you had sent up to the chalet last week. I read all about it one afternoon when you left me all alone to have that meeting with those four yucky men. Biotechnology is the wave of the future. What microchips were to the eighties, it will be to the nineties. That's what it said."

Bo muttered *"shit."* He stood and paced twice across her small living room, letting his second pass take him into the kitchenette for another gin. "Bambi-Sue," he said coming back in to the living room, where she still sat naked on the floor. "That was just a piece of junk mail. I get them all the time. You've been taken for a ride."

Bambi-Sue took that news silently. Then she started to sob. "I just wanted enough to put myself through college. That's all. Better myself, maybe."

"First fucking thing tomorrow—" Bo said, wheeling and jabbing an index finger at her. "Before our flight up to the country, we're going to see them. Have a face-to-face. Sometimes if they are threatened by someone they know they can't bullshit, they'll pay back the money, just to avoid trouble and publicity."

"You think you could?" she whimpered.

The way she looked up at him from the floor, naked, wide-eyed, and vulnerable, took the edge off Bo's temper. He even felt himself getting hard again.

25

"Do you have an appointment?" the black receptionist demanded.

It was just after nine Friday morning. Bo was feeling ragged-edged from the previous evening's gin, and her tone made him angry. The way Bo saw it, equality was one thing, but he wasn't about to have them talking down to him, not with Bambi-Sue standing there looking helpless and innocent in her white summer-weight suit worn *sans* blouse with its top unbuttoned almost to her navel. Bo drew himself up. "I want to see Mr. Rhys."

"Mr. Rhys is out at the research center today," said the secretary. Her voice was as smooth and polished as any cum laude Barnard grad's. That bothered Bo, too. Jive, drawl—he figured the African American larynx was genetically designed for those. Anything else was affectation, pure and simple. He felt the jitters coming back. "I need to see him," Bo said.

"Out of the question, sir," said Ms. Barnard Grad, or whoever the hell she thought she was. "Mr. Rhys never allows interruptions of his sessions with our director of research and development. It's critical in a cutting-edge company like Bio—"

Bo slapped a business card on her desk. "He's either going to see me immediately—" Bo didn't like the slight warble in his voice, so he swallowed and went on a few notes lower. "Or see my lawyers later."

One of two wooden doors directly behind the receptionist swung open. A young fellow wearing an immaculate suit of banker's navy pinstripes and carrying what looked to be a $500 leather and brass briefcase strode out. At first he didn't appear to notice them. Bo straightened his spine and inhaled, preparing to speak.

But the handsome young man beat him to it. "Bambi-Sue!" he said jovially, not even acknowledging the presence of Bo, which made Bo more angry than the black receptionist's uppityness. "No doubt you've heard about your investment. Congratulations. Love to talk, but I have to take an important phone call—"

He cut himself off and scurried toward the outer room.

Bo made a move to follow, then decided against it. He took one giant stride toward the office.

"I told you—" said the secretary.

To Bo's extreme satisfaction, those words were carried on a faint drawl. He shot a bored look over his shoulder.

"I told you, Mr. Rhys is out at the laboratory. If you want, I could call there." She fingered Bo's business card and hoisted her painted-on eyebrows.

"What I want is some satisfaction. And I want it damn soon."

She punched some buttons on her phone and after a moment said, "Hi, Leslie, this is Doris from head office—Mr. Rhys get out there. . . . I know but there's a"—she consulted Bo's card—"a Mr. Scullin here. Insists—" She listened, nodding into the handset. "I told him that." Another series of nods. She looked at Bo and said, "May I ask what it concerns?"

"One hundred thousand dollars is what it concerns," said Bo. "One hundred thousand dollars that Mr. Rhys took from Ms. Cline." He shot an index finger toward Bambi-Sue, who stood against the wall gazing intently at her dainty white pumps.

"He would like to inquire about the Cline account," said the receptionist. After a long silence, she said. "Very well, I'll send him out." To Bo, she said, "You ever been to beautiful downtown New Brunswick, New Jersey?"

Bo shook his head.

"Then you're in for a rare treat, sir," she said, without a trace of drawl or jive.

Sitting in his own office not ten yards from Bo and Bambi-Sue, Ivor hung up the phone and took a moment to straighten his tie and congratulate himself on his hiring skills. "He would like to inquire about the Cline account. . . ." Doris had performed admirably under fire. He suspected she did indeed have a fine career to look forward to once she had finished studies in her chosen field: acting. Now, through the doors, he could hear her giving long, overly elaborate instructions on how to get out to the New Brunswick lab. Satisfied that all was well, Ivor slid aside the walnut panel and—as they say—stepped out the back way.

One of his young associates was waiting for him in the hallway, holding the elevator. "Good luck, sir," he said, settling Ivor's suit coat with a little tug and giving his tie a pinch. "I've made arrangements for a limo to be waiting for you out front. We'll keep all the elevators tied up as long as we can. Hopefully, that will give you enough of a head start."

One and one-half hours later, Bo and Bambi-Sue found themselves outfitted in white lab coats, plastic hats and slippers, and latex gloves. A similarly attired young woman pushed open a door clearly marked BIOHAZARD DO NOT ENTER and with a casual sweep of her arm, bade them to do what the sign explicitly prohibited.

Feeling awkward, Bo complied, with the wide-eyed Bambi-Sue trailing behind.

The place certainly looked like a legitimate laboratory—which was more than you could say from the outside, where it was just another door in a long strip of small warehouse-related businesses facing onto Route 18. Someone had at least gone to the trouble of painting the Biocural logo on the door, but so recently that Bo was tempted to touch it to see if his fingers came away with enamel on their tips.

Inside, the cramped space was filled with microscopes, test tubes, Bunsen burners, beakers, centrifuges, microwaves, computers, reams of print-outs, and all of the other trappings of a laboratory, right down to three nerdish-looking researchers dressed similarly to Bo and Bambi-Sue.

At the far end of the room, the young woman tapped on a door. It was opened by a middle-aged man in a lab coat. His gray hair shot straight upward in a wild, electroshocked version of a pompadour. From behind a pair of black horned rim glasses, his magnified eyes had a crazed, panicky look.

"What?" he said, eyes darting from Bambi-Sue to Bo to the young woman, then retracing their route.

"Mr. Rhys's visitors are here," said the young woman.

That information did nothing to change the guy's demeanor. He squinted at Bo, sticking his lower lip out in a pout, which might have stayed there for the rest of the day, had a wiry old man, also wearing a lab coat, not come up and rested a hand on the crazed one's shoulder.

"Bambi-Sue, a delight," said the old guy, gripping a few of her fingers with his. "And you must be Mr. Scullin. A pleasure, indeed. I am Ivor Rhys. This is Doctor Bernard Schwartz, our research director. We were just finishing." He gave Schwartz a gentle shove back into the lab.

Schwartz darted off like a fish returned to water. He plopped down behind a computer and started to whack away at the keys, the crazed look replaced with one that could have either been concentration or relief, or maybe a little of both.

"Please sit down," said Ivor, gesturing toward a small, plastic-topped folding table that was sagging in its middle due to a load of computer printouts and used paper coffee cups. "And kindly excuse our Spartan surroundings—a situation that will soon be rectified. We're building a wonderful new facility in upstate New York. Remind me to show you the architect's plans, Bambi-Sue."

-205-

Bo pulled out a molded plastic chair and then paused before sitting, overcome by an urge to seize a wet paper towel and administer a thorough wipe-down.

"Appearances aside, our investors are always welcome to drop by," Ivor said to Bambi-Sue, then to Bo, "In a few weeks, Schwartz will become one of only a handful of researchers in the world to have developed recombinant biopharmaceuticals, which are ready for human trials. We call his product Hemotropin. Essentially, it helps patents by stimulating the production of white blood cells to fight infections. Obvious applications in chemotherapy—perhaps even in the battle against AIDS-related illnesses. Marvelous profit potential, and—"

A telephone pinged somewhere over on a metal office desk supporting a burden identical to the one on the table. "Pardon me a moment," said Ivor, going behind the desk, finding the receiver and immediately saying, "Leslie, I told you not to disturb us under—" He sucked in a shallow breath. "Very well, then, I'll take that one." Two pale blue eyes looked up. "Do excuse me," he said.

Into the phone he said, "Ivor Rhys speaking." There was a pause. Shrugging his scrawny shoulders, he said, "Do as you wish, but frankly I think selling now would be a grave mistake. . . . It could double, you know. Very likely will. . . . My recommendation is that you hold—for just a few more days. . . . Don't you trust me? . . . Why not think about it over the weekend? . . . Trust me on this—a few more days."

He hung up.

"Another sucker," said Bo.

Ivor looked startled but managed a dextrous recovery. "Can I get you coffee?" He shot a gnarled hand toward the corner of his office where a coffeemaker sat atop a two-drawer file cabinet.

"You can get this girl her money back is what you can get," said Bo, pleased at the no-nonsense tone in his words, all traces of jitters and nervousness gone now that he was in the thick of action. It was good to know that he could still depend on himself—when it really mattered. He laid it right on the line: "The whole hundred thousand."

Ivor gazed directly at Bo. Didn't even flinch. Then, one by one, crinkles sprouted in the corner of his aged eyes. The most beguiling little smile chased the crinkles over his temples until they vanished into his thick, white hair. "A hundred thousand, you say. Be my pleasure." He let that little smile play on his aged face. "Course, I'd be doing Bambi-Sue out of—" He tapped the keys on a computer that occupied a little table of its very own to the right of his desk. A moment later he nodded. "Thirty-nine thousand two hundred forty-six dollars."

That caught Bo off guard. But only long enough for him to decide to call the old guy's bluff. It was Bo's turn to try on a beguiling smile. "Very well, then, let's have a check for the whole amount. Now. Or I call the cops."

To give him credit, Ivor managed to summon enough gall to look insulted. "Very well," he said. "Have it your way." He punched two buttons on the phone. "Leslie, have a check cut for Ms. Cline. One hundred thirty nine thousand two hundred forty-six—less the usual commissions." He dropped the receiver. "It will only take a moment," he said. "But Bambi-Sue, I beg you, stay with us. I fully expect your stock's value to double—minimum. Very soon." He lowered his voice to a conspiratorial whisper, which he shared with Bo. "A major player is discussing a buyout. If you're interested . . ."

"That's the same crock you handed the sucker on the phone," said Bo.

Two minutes later, the woman named Leslie came in carrying a check. Ivor scribbled his name on it with no more ceremony than if he had been paying his monthly phone bill. "There you are," he said, extending the check to Bambi-Sue.

Bo snatched it. "I thought you said something about one hundred and thirty-nine. This is only for one thirty one—"

"Commission," said Ivor. "We take twenty percent."

Bo felt the anger coming back. "Twenty percent—that's highway robbery."

Ivor put up an arthritic index finger. "Only on our client's profits. Twenty percent of what you make. If you lose, we don't take a cent."

"That's as crooked as—"

"It is perfectly legal—if somewhat unique. We are a private investment consortium, seeking out special situations for a select list of clients with funds to invest. We find solid little companies in temporary need of bridge financing, and bring the two groups together. The profit potential is enormous, so, yes, we do take our share. With no compunction, I might add. It's all in the agreement. Ms. Cline signed it."

Bo sniggered. "So that's the scam." He turned and presented the check to Bambi-Sue. "Told you it was crooked," he said. "Let's get out of here, while you still have something."

The telephone pinged. Ivor punched a button and Leslie's voice came over the speaker. "There's a Mr. Olmstead. Says he's the chairman of Genentech. He wants to talk about—"

Ivor turned off the speaker phone.

He looked at Bo coldly. "I have an important call coming in. If you have gotten what you came for, Leslie will show you out."

When they were halfway to the door he added, "And Bambi-Sue, you are going to be a very sorry young woman."

"I don't think so," she said, looking fondly at the check.

After Bo and Bambi-Sue left, Schwartz came back in, his hair brushed neatly to one side, the horn rims replaced by stylish wire rims. For the crazy look, he had substituted one of mild annoyance.

"How'd we do," he said, pouring himself a cup of coffee and coming over to where Ivor sat behind the desk. "Outta my seat, Ivor. Wouldn't want you getting too comfortable," he said.

Ivor hopped up and spun the chair toward Schwartz. "You do a flawless mad scientist. Should you ever decide to abandon research, there would always be a place for you in my organization."

Schwartz smiled. "You're something else, Ivor. But I have no plans of retiring—not now."

Ivor's features shaped themselves into a quizzical look that would have appeared innocent on any other face. On his, it came off cagey.

"Not now that I'm ten thousand dollars richer," said Schwartz.

Nursing a tumbler of Lagavulin in the back seat of the rented limo on his way back to the city, Ivor called the Plattsburgh *Chronicle-Herald* on the car phone. He asked to speak to Gregory Hormel, who came on the line quickly with a breathless "What is it?"

Poor guy sounded winded.

Calmly, Ivor said, "Very good news, Mr. Hormel," and got a long, audible sigh for his efforts. He went on, "Your investment is doing very well—a little over double the value of your purchase price."

"Double," Hormel croaked.

"Currently worth twenty-one thousand six hundred and forty dollars. Congratulations."

"What's going to happen to it now?"

"To be honest, I think it's had its big run-up. There is still some possible upside potential, mind you, but . . ."

"Should I sell?"

"It might be prudent to take some profit now—say your original ten thousand investment—and leave the rest in case we have some more good news."

"Could you do that?"

"No problem whatsoever. I shall Fed Ex your check today, Mr. Hormel. Oh—I should mention that this information will be going out over the Dow wire this evening, but if you want it for your business pages tomorrow . . ."

"Sounds great. And thank you, Mr. Rhys. I mean that. From the bottom of my heart—fella like me, with a family, saving for my own home. You have done me a big favor, Mr. Rhys."

"My pleasure," said Ivor. After Ivor turned off the phone, he settled further into his seat and treated himself to a well-earned dram of the old amber. Life had suddenly become sweet indeed. A boiler room up and running. Good lads, too, every one of them, damn good. It was as smooth and slick an operation as he had ever overseen, right down to his daily massage. Schwartz's lab and act were perfectly convincing. Hormel at the paper was now firmly in his back pocket. As for Bambi-Sue, she was nothing short of a marvelous—in all ways. Almost overnight, it seemed, the downward spiral of Ivor's fortunes had been reversed. But, he mused, wasn't that exactly what made this business so beautiful?

There was only one cloud on Ivor's introspective horizon as he sat there behind tinted glass in the backseat of that big car on the New Jersey Turnpike. And she, too, was beautiful.

26

A⊤ 10:52 A.M. on Saturday, August 8, Plunkett's Dodge pickup was one of two dozen vehicles caught behind a convoy of Winnebago motor homes creeping along the winding section of Route 86 between Wilmington and Lake Placid. The lead Winnebago had set a stately pace of 37 miles per hour, too slow to generate much of a breeze through the pickup's open windows, but adequate to allow in plenty of exhaust. Plunkett exhaled and ran his hand over his sweat-slickened hair. He drummed his fingers on the steering wheel, veered just over the center line and craned his neck to see around the motor home in front of him.

What he saw was yet another motor home, this one with Florida plates, careening around a bend toward his front bumper. It was piloted by a frightened-looking old man, who until that week probably had never driven anything more challenging than a Lincoln Town Car on the flat boulevards of his home state. Only at the last possible instant did he manage to get back on his side of the road.

Chastened, Plunkett edged his truck closer to the safety of the shoulder and abandoned any thoughts of getting to Bo Scullin's in time for their scheduled meeting.

* * *

When Plunkett did arrive, no one answered his first volley of knocks. He stood waiting, examining a massive oak door that looked to have been pried off a medieval monastery and temporarily hung on Scullin's ultra-modern chalet until the designer could find something more in keeping.

Following his second volley of knocks, Plunkett heard a girlish squeal coming from behind the building. He strolled in that direction, taking in the three stories of white stucco, noticing that the Mercedes in the driveway was now as dent-free as it was the day it rolled off its German assembly line. The job had probably added a new VCR or some other state-of-the-art gizmo to his little brother's vast collection of electronic equipment.

The squeal came from the same blond woman Plunkett had seen during his previous visit to Scullin's. Then, she had been in the pool alone performing nude water ballet. This time, Bo was with her; and she was wearing a string bikini. She saw Plunkett first, and took Bo's chin in her hands to point his eyes in Plunkett's direction.

Bo executed two nearly perfect Australian crawl strokes to pool edge and hauled himself out on the third. Water poured off the ridges of his chest and belly muscles and ran down the front of a yellow bathing suit that looked like a flimsily manufactured jock strap.

"I expected you earlier," he said, going over to a table that held two folded towels and a tall glass filled with clear liquid, lime wedge floating on top. He reached for one of the towels, thought better of it, and treated himself to a third of whatever it was in the glass. Only after he had issued a quiet, private sigh did he take the towel and administer a vigorous and thorough rubdown to himself.

"Traffic," said Plunkett. "Every summer there seems to be more. . . ."

He extended a hand to be shaken. Bo cast him a look of near-total disinterest, but finally reached out and gave an uncertain squeeze. "I've had second thoughts—" Bo began, then corrected himself: "When I agreed to talk to you last night I had been traveling. I was tired." He slung the towel around his shoulders and sat at

-212-

the table, crossing his legs. "My lawyers have since advised me to be circumspect."

"Quentin Quinell is missing," Plunkett said. "Officially."

Bo kept his mask of disinterest firmly in place. "Quentin is a grown man."

The woman in the pool got out and stood on the deck twenty feet away. She put out a hand. Bo tossed her the remaining towel, which she caught. With it clutched against her chest, she scampered to a chaise lounge on the other side of the pool, sat, and began to paw sections of a newspaper.

"There's reason for concern," said Plunkett, and when Bo cast him a look of befuddlement, he added, "Concern about Quentin. I thought perhaps you'd be interested in helping us out, but . . ."

"Let's go inside," said Bo, nodding in the woman's direction and then getting up and heading toward the chalet.

Plunkett followed Bo into what he suspected the architect would have labeled the great room. It was an open, informal space, stretching from the picture windows in front with their unobstructed views of Skyward Trail on Whiteface to the French doors in back, which offered an equally good view of the pretty woman curled up reading her paper. The whole place was furnished in showroom-fresh modern pieces, and the only area that looked at all used or lived-in was the wet bar along the nearest wall, where there were two Boodles bottles, tonic, an ice tray, and the hacked-away remains of a lime. It was to that spot that Bo went.

Turning away from the bar, he said, "You're disrupting my weekend."

"I just thought—"

"I don't know a damn thing about Quentin Quinell," said Bo. "And frankly . . ." He let that trail off. "I suggest you leave."

Plunkett walked to the French doors.

"Not that way," Bo said, pointing to the oaken portal upon which Plunkett had rapped earlier.

Plunkett obediently hiked across the sterile expanse of the great room. When he got to the door, he raised his voice and said, "I'll be back with the necessary paperwork. Judge Conoscenti is very interested in this case, so there shouldn't be any trouble."

That stilled Bo's hand midway through pouring himself a gin. "What is it you want?" he said, barely loud enough to be heard across the room.

Plunkett stayed by the door. "I want to know what you and Quentin talked about last Thursday."

"Haven't spoken to him in weeks," said Bo. "Not since—Not since the memorial service for Barron."

"Ever hear of a company called Saranac Chemicals?" said Plunkett.

Bo shook his tight gray curls.

"Interesting," Plunkett said. "Your ex-business partner's wife sits on the board of directors. She seems to think it's one of the many investments you and Barron Quinell were involved in together."

"Barron might have been—separately," said Bo. "We weren't exactly joined at the hip or anything. I suggest you talk to Percy. Besides, what does this have to do with Quentin?"

"He thought Saranac was involved in the chemical spill."

Bo shrugged.

"You know anything about an abandoned mine up on your Stewart Mountain property?" said Plunkett.

"I know there are nearly as many abandoned mines in these mountains as there are hemlock trees," Bo said.

"There's one specific one up there, I'm told. I'd like to take a look up there later today. You mind?"

"Could care less."

"Well, thanks," Plunkett said. He nodded twice to himself and added, "Must be tough . . ."

Plunkett had taken a half step toward the door when he heard Bo's weak, "What? What must be tough?"

With his back to Bo, Plunkett said, "First Barron, then Lisa Perry—must be tough, being the last surviving executive at Realty Associates."

There was no answer.

-214-

Plunkett turned to face Bo and said, "Was wondering about one other matter."

Bo dipped his dimple-bisected chin, looking as wary as a man with a couple of late morning gin and tonics under his belt can.

"You fish?" said Plunkett.

When Bo came back outside, Bambi-Sue had undergone the worst sort of transformation—from being kittenish to pure wildcat: mean, vicious, hard-eyed. And worse, she had done something she rarely did in the country—put on clothes.

"You!" she hissed, as soon as Bo stepped through the French doors. "You!"

"Sorry I took so long, honey," said Bo. "I got rid of—"

Bambi-Sue turned her back. Her shoulders began to heave. Bo reached out and placed a hand on one. She pulled away.

"I want my Biocural stock back. Now," she said, smoothly executing the transition from angry hiss to a three-year-old's whine. "Look." She shoved him the paper. "Says right here. The value of the stock has gone and doubled, just like Mr. Rhys said it would yesterday morning when—" She stopped herself long enough to look directly at Bo, her big, blue eyes overflowing with tears. "You made me sell them," she said, then broke into a full-blown wail.

Bo tried to touch her.

"Get your hands off of me!" she said. She took several deep breaths, those beautiful breasts heaving up and down. "You just got jealous. You just couldn't abide the fact that I did something smart all on my own. That I made some of my own money."

Her piece said, she lost control again, well before Bo could fashion a response. Tears flowed. She pounded a dainty fist into the chaise.

"Look," said Bo, in what he hoped would pass for soothing tones. "I'll give you the money."

"I don't want your filthy money." She glared, lip quivering, suddenly not crying. "I want my shares back."

"But I'll—"

"You heard me."

"First thing Monday, when we get back to town, we'll see what we can do about it," said Bo.

Her eyes, normally so round and so blue, fashioned themselves into two mean slits. "We'll see, all right," she said.

On those rare occasions when Aldon was both at home and more or less sober, he usually spent all his time down in the front yard pit, tinkering with his car and drinking whisky. Which was fine with Edna. Kept him off her.

But for the last week, ever since he unexpectedly had come cruising up to the house in that black 1988 Trans Am, the routine had changed. He now spent all his time drinking whisky and washing the new car. It looked sleek and wet out there in the sun of their barren front yard. The old LTD had joined its two cronies beside the house. It was impossible to tell which were the wrecks and which was still operative.

The new car had made all the difference in the world in Aldon. Made him more like he was when they were courting, if that's what you'd call the two-week interlude between when he met Edna at the bar in Au Sable Forks and the night he first fucked her in the backseat of the original LTD, her skirt hoisted up to the middle of her belly, his jeans unzipped and dropped just below his ass.

Telephone calls normally got him all pissed off. But after the call came in Saturday, he was happy—giddy almost. He kept punching the air and going, "Yes! Yes! Yes!"

And then he even asked her along for a ride in the new car. It had bucket seats and smelled like pine needles inside, thanks to a little cardboard tree that Aldon had hung from the rearview mirror. They went along 9N at a hundred miles an hour—only it felt like you were maybe doing thirty, tops. The Trans Am was that smooth. Somewhere near Keene, they turned off the highway and took a road over Stewart Mountain. That was nice, too, feeling the car slither around those hairpin turns. At the top of the mountain, they passed a Dodge pickup pulled off the road.

Aldon stopped the Trans Am. Fumbled under his seat until he found a tire iron, which he smacked once into the palm of his hand. He got out, serious and mean, more like his old self, now, slapping the tire iron into his palm, one, two, three, four times as he went around to the trunk and opened it. Edna suddenly felt a chill of fear, wondered what was going to happen to her way up there.

He came back dressed in the old green coveralls he always wore for really dirty work. He had his 12-gauge Mossberg pump-action shot gun.

Aldon tossed the car keys on the driver's seat, said he had to do something—something about work—told her someone else would give him a lift home. She knew better than to ask what it was he had to do or who the hell it might be who'd be driving him home. The stiffness on the left side of her jaw reminded her of what could happen, and that was just with his fist.

27

PLUNKETT THOUGHT HE heard a car.

He listened, trying to make out the road sounds over the swishing of the trees. There was a *thunk*. An engine rumbled.

According to the topo map he left on the dashboard of his truck, he was supposed to be on an access road leading to the abandoned mine. Which just went to show how little the state's cartographers knew. Logic and all of Plunkett's senses told him he was not on any sort of road, but rather in a stand of young, vigorously growing mixed hardwoods. To judge by the stoutness of the maples in the flattened indention on the forest floor, two decades had passed since anything much larger than a red squirrel had traveled the "road." It had taken Plunkett five minutes of thrashing and lunging to gain twenty five yards in the tangle. Giving up that hard-earned ground to go back to the truck was not a task he relished.

On the other hand, Plunkett wasn't in the mood for unexpected companions either. If there was somebody back there, it would be nice to know who he was. Or for that matter who she was.

Plunkett returned to Stewart Mountain Road. He arrived panting, sweating, picking scratchy twigs from under his collar and feeling stupid because, of course, the road was empty.

After a minute spent verifying the obvious, he turned to face the solid green wall, wondering how after two of his less-than-graceful passages there was still no evidence of a trail having been cleared.

Fucking cop was no Daniel Boone, that was for sure. It was all Aldon could do to keep from busting out laughing as he watched from behind a hemlock on the other side of the road. The cop out there in the sun, dressed in civvy clothes, sweating like a pig. Huffing and puffing. Gawking around. What did he expect? A welcoming committee?

Well Aldon had that—a welcoming committee of one. Two if you counted old Mr. Mossberg. For the fun of it, really intending just to get an idea of what it was going to feel like, Aldon brought Mr. Mossberg down and sighted along the barrel until the bead steadied itself right in the middle of the cop's stupid-looking face.

A little wiggle of Aldon's index finger, maybe one-eighth of an inch, and the cop's head would pop like an overripe melon. Splat. Cop brains and cop blood all over the roadside.

It would be the simplest thing in the world to do it right now. Get it over with. One eighth of an inch.

Summoning his resolve to see the damn thing through now that he had sacrificed a perfectly good day off to drive all the way up Stewart Mountain, Plunkett charged back into the forest, head ducked, arms in front to shield his eyes from leaves and twigs.

It took him just as long to gain back those twenty-five yards as it had the first time. When he arrived at the turnaround point, he stopped, tried to wipe a spider web from his mouth and eyes. Had no luck. His hands were too sweaty; his face, too sticky. The entire mission began to look even more senseless.

But then, Quentin had been convinced that some critically important bit of information was to be found at the abandoned mine at the end of the overgrown road. Or he had if you chose to believe Percy Quinell.

★ ★ ★

Aldon was left standing there with a gun that was pointed at nothing other than maple leaves.

He kept the gun in place anyway, thinking only one thought: just how goddamn easy it would have been. But his orders had been to make it look like an accident, if he could. That was the part Aldon always liked with these assholes. They always threw in that—the "if he could" bit.

While he was thinking, Aldon heard the stupid homo of a cop thrashing around in there. Let him waste his strength. That'd only make Aldon's job all the more easy. Not quite as much fun, but a lot easier.

Aldon lowered the gun and put it against the tree. He felt the tire iron tucked beneath his belt and slid it upwards so he could sit at the base of the tree and have a smoke without its sharp end jamming him in the ass. At the rate the cop was going, Aldon'd easily have time for a smoke, maybe two.

And after he finished his second, he'd stroll along the shortcut and catch up to the cop. It was that simple. You just had to know what you were doing. And by now, Aldon figured, it was safe to say that much: When it came to this business, he knew what he was doing.

Plunkett tripped, falling with his palms outstretched, bashing a knee against the sharp edge of a football-sized hunk of quartz. The fall disoriented him. He got up and had to stand still for a minute to try to get his bearings. In the tangle, there was now no way to tell where the logging road was. Along with the burning from his hurt knee, he felt a tingle of primal panic.

He charged ahead, oblivious now to the branches scraping his face and the limbs and vines wrapping around his ankles. He threw his elbows and shoulders into each stride, lifting his feet high, kicking outward—too bad about the pain in his knee. He was startled when one of his lunges carried him into the middle of a clear and well-groomed woodland trail.

Someone had removed the young trees and piled their dried

remains on either side of the trail. The square, knobby tire tracks of an all-terrain vehicle showed clearly on the bare ground. Ten feet from where Plunkett stood, the tire tracks veered off the trail and into the rocky bed of a dried-up stream that led back in the direction of the road.

Plunkett squatted and looked down the stream bed. Compared to the forest, it was a clear, wide-open thoroughfare offering easy access to the road. He closed his eyes and thought, trying to envision the route the stream might take. It came back to him in fragments: Lucky Spike's truck, the crushed fifty-five gallon drums. A stream bed paralleled the road at that point.

Plunkett stood and began to walk briskly along the tracks left by the all-terrain vehicle. The route was clear. A merciful breeze cooled his face.

A chipmunk squeaked at his feet, then scurried off through the forest litter, making far more noise than its small size merited. Plunkett was listening to the departing rustle, when he heard a branch snap.

That sound made him freeze. He stood listening. There was nothing other than the *whishing* of the big hemlock branches high above and the flapping of the deciduous leaves closer to the ground. The chipmunk, thought Plunkett, resuming his amble.

Another branch snapped. Plunkett wheeled.

Aldon muttered, "Oh shit," to himself.

Cop must have heard him. Now he was squatting and peering right at the spot where Aldon crouched. Aldon tightened his grip on the shotgun. Clicked off the safety.

No more than fifty feet away, the cop was tilting his head from side to side. Shifting his weight from one foot to another. He took a step toward Aldon, leaving the traveled part of the road.

The pile of brush Aldon had stacked there early in the summer stopped the cop. He stood with his hands on his hips. Aldon could tell he wasn't in the mood to go into the forest.

But he took another step. Right into the center of the brush pile. Coming directly toward Aldon now. Aldon eased his finger onto the trigger and remembered, one-eighth of an inch.

There was another snap of a dead branch as the cop came closer. It was followed by the squeak of a startled chipmunk that scurried away through the leaf litter to the cop's right. The cop stopped.

Fucking chipmunk. Probably saved the cop's life. And made Aldon realize that he would have to be a little more careful. But what the hell. There was no rush. Now that there was no doubt where the cop was heading, Aldon figured he had the whole afternoon. Might just as well enjoy himself.

Plunkett had to laugh. A chippy. He was obviously getting nervous. Overreacting. He returned to the road and continued, confident now, following the depressions of the ATV tracks. He walked for thirty minutes, maintaining a relatively brisk clip given the heat and uphill grade.

The trail made a gentle circle around the shoulder of the mountain, gradually climbing higher. The hemlocks began to thin and get shorter, and were replaced by lower-growing, stunted-looking birches and spruce. In places, the forest opened to offer sweeping views out across the Wilmington Valley toward Lake Placid and the peaks on the other side. Plunkett stopped to take in the view and at the same time treat himself to a rest. He was breathing fast. Sweat soaked his shirt.

Ahead, the road dipped and disappeared around a hairpin turn. When he started walking again, the downhill stretch spurred Plunkett along. He let gravity pull him forward, lengthening his strides, putting some extra hip motion into each step. At that jaunty pace, Plunkett rounded the turn.

He found himself in a bowllike depression the size of a football field. Shoulder-high birches and aspens grew in what had been a clearing at one time—a clearing that was littered with hunks of cracked and broken rock. Mine tailings, Plunkett guessed.

There were a couple of old outbuildings beside the road. The corrugated tin on their sides had rusted and curled up at the edges. On one, the roof had caved in, coming to rest on the body of a pickup truck with Model-T-like lines. The glass had been smashed out of its windshield, and a dozen or so of the rock shards littered the area around the truck.

Plunkett went over to the second building. It looked much like the first, except for the roof, which had yet to cave in, and it still bore a few strips of tar paper over bleached, skeletal boards. It also had a pair of doors. They were held closed by a padlock and a length of chain—a bright, new padlock and a gleaming length of chain.

He parted the doors as far as the chain would allow. That enabled him to peer inside with one eye. At first all he saw was a chrome handlebar. As his eye adjusted, he made out the rest of the ATV.

Someone was still using the mine. Someone who didn't want that information broadcast to the world, to judge by the way the entrance to the access road was left concealed. He wondered what Percy and Bo would say about that.

The mine itself was sealed by two ancient wooden doors built into the gray rock of the cliff face. They, too, were held closed by a new padlock and a length of chain.

In the sand, Plunkett could see ATV tracks leading to the mine entrance. He followed the tire trail up to the doors and gave a tug. With a screech of ancient, tired hinges, the doors parted enough for him to squeeze through.

He looked back the way he had come. Nothing. Just the rhythmic *swish* of wind. At the best of times, Plunkett was mildly claustrophobic. Instinct told him to go back and confront Percy and Bo with the fact that someone was working the old mine. See what they had to say about that.

Talk about your All-American sitting duck. Aldon couldn't have asked for a better setup. If only the cop would go inside.

He watched the cop part the doors and stick his head in. Come on cop—get in there, Aldon silently coached. And, sure enough, the cop went and wedged himself between the doors. Began squirming and wiggling, trying to squeeze through. Getting stuck halfway. Having to push the doors as far apart as he could. Quite a show.

On the fourth or fifth wiggle, the cop popped through. Behind him, the doors *clunked* closed.

Aldon stayed there for a while, just thinking. He wanted to get this right. One thing for sure, Aldon could just wait and take the cop as he came out of the mine. Or he could go in there where he knew every turn and passage like his own goddamn house and have himself some fun. On top of that, it was the perfect place for a little accident.

He transferred Mr. Mossberg to one hand and with the other drew the tire iron out of his belt. Walking toward the mine, Aldon was thinking that the thing about working for these assholes was that there was no sense doing it unless you got in some fun. Business and pleasure.

That got him daydreaming about Percy Quinell, stark naked and coming up the ladder out of the water like some goddess, all just for him—until that cop came along. Well, that wouldn't happen again, Aldon promised himself, wondering who the hell the dumb fuck was that said business and pleasure didn't mix.

Inside, the air had a heavy chemical smell to it. Oily, gaseous, a little acidic, like a refinery, or a very old and poorly maintained service station. It was vaguely familiar. Plunkett couldn't place it at first, then he remembered: Saranac Chemicals.

Aside from the astringent air, the rest of the place lived up to most of the images of what a mine was supposed to be—mainly dark and cramped. The space he was in didn't seem much bigger than the average one-car garage. At the far end, the slit of light from the doors struck a wooden structure, an A-shaped support for what looked like a locomotive wheel. It took a moment before Plunkett figured it was a pulley, probably for some sort of crude elevator used by the men who once toiled in the mine. Poor devils.

He carefully made his way toward the wheel, sliding one foot forward at a time across the gritty floor, feeling in front of his face with his hands, smelling the heavy petroleum smells, listening to his own heart's *thump-thump-thump.*

His knee hit something big and metallic. He felt for it. His fingers told him it was an engine, probably a car or truck engine judging by its size. A taut cable ran from it to the pulley wheel.

Plunkett held onto the cable and crept forward until his belly brushed against a wooden railing. He leapt back. Then slowly, with his heart thumping, he inched forward again until he felt the railing. Peering below, he could see a rectangle of total blackness. Deep, profound, and devoid of shadow and light. Reason told him to get his butt in gear and clear out of that place. Come back with a flashlight—and some backup. Or at the very least his Glock, which was back in the truck's glove compartment.

That's when everything suddenly went darker.

But only for an instant. When the dim light returned, Plunkett took a jaunty step toward the two doors.

A shadow crossed the slit of daylight again.

Plunkett heard shuffling. Feet. Someone was in there with him. "Who's there?" he said, getting back his own faint, echoed *there*.

Thinking that maybe his claustrophobic mind was playing tricks, Plunkett took a bearing on the slit of light and walked directly toward it. He managed two successful steps before his legs tangled in a piece of cable. He fell.

Now there definitely was the sound of feet shuffling in the dust, sand, and pebbles on the mine floor—shuffling toward Plunkett. He rolled to one side and lay still, listening, trying to peer through the darkness. The noise came to where he had fallen and stopped.

In darkness, Plunkett spoke, "My name is Garwood Plunkett. I'm a New York State Trooper—"

The shuffling turned ninety degrees—toward him. It was now accompanied by heavy, sibilant breathing.

Plunkett dove for the slit of light. He managed to get off one good, solid stride. Two more like it would carry him to the doors. On his second stride he ran into something big and fleshy—a body. All fleshiness vanished as an arm, as hard as an old hunk of elm, came in under his chin and began to crush his Adam's apple.

"Hi, homo," said a dull, monotonous voice.

Yellow specks began to dance upon Plunkett's retinas. He felt his legs going numb. He tried to strike the guy with his fists and elbows, but whoever had him, knew something about fighting. He kept his body close to Plunkett's, never giving him any room for a clear swipe. After four or five futile blows, Plunkett stopped and focused on keeping conscious long enough to think of something.

With the last reserves of his strength, he swung his shoulders to the right. Whoever had him was forced to take a rotating step backwards. As he did, Plunkett dug his heels into the floor, got as much purchase as he could, and threw all his weight into a backward lunge.

The guy tightened his grip, but had to take two dancing steps in the direction Plunkett had lunged. He had just begun his third step when the cable caught him. He fell backwards, with Plunkett on top and now able to twist around and break free of the choke hold. Suck in one half-decent breath.

The guy caught him on the side of the head with what must have been a fist, but felt like a hunk of granite. Those clichéd stars, which Plunkett reminded himself are anything but clichés when they really appear, began dancing for Plunkett.

He brought his fist around. Felt gratifying contact with the bridge of an invisible nose. Heard the guy grunt. Plunkett rolled free.

He lay panting in the dark. His attacker couldn't have been more than a few feet away, but there was no sign of him. Plunkett tried to still his own breathing long enough to listen. He couldn't. So he just lay there, filling his lungs, watching the last of the stars disappear, trying to find enough strength to crawl for the slit of light across the underground room.

Maybe the guy was knocked out—a one-punch miracle. If so, Plunkett figured he had better get moving. He rolled over, trying to make as little noise as possible. He began to half-crawl, half-drag himself toward the light.

The blow caught him just as his fingers touched one of the doors.

It whistled past his left ear and smashed into his collarbone. A whack from something heavy and hard, like iron. Instinctively, Plunkett raised an arm in the darkness. His fingers hit something.

The guy's wrist. Plunkett yanked downward with all his strength. The move pulled him to his feet and sent his attacker sprawling.

Not wasting any time, Plunkett bolted for the doors. Got there and shoved himself between them, getting stuck again, having to pry and squirm, hearing the guy inside coming at him.

He caught a glimpse of what looked like a tire iron coming out of the darkness toward his head. He ducked and raised his shoulder to take the blow, which came down with a hollow *thud* and caused so much pain that it took a second for Plunkett to realize he was outside. Blinded now by too much light, he began a shambling trot toward the forest's edge.

"Hold it right there," said whoever it was behind him.

Plunkett didn't stop. Didn't even look in the guy's direction as he acknowledged to himself that "Hold it right there" was supposed to be one of his lines.

He had taken maybe ten steps when the shotgun roared.

Good, old Mr. Mossberg dug into Aldon's shoulder with a solid kick, sending the slug on its little errand. He watched the fucking cop actually manage another two waddling strides. Pathetic bastard.

Aldon was thinking maybe he'd have to let loose another slug when the cop stopped. He found himself a little disappointed. The second slug wasn't gonna be aimed over the cop's head.

The look of recognition, then shock, then genuine fear on the stupid cop's face came close to making it all worthwhile. Aldon walked toward him, Aldon calm, putting what he figured was a sort of sly, cool half-smile on his face. Not paying any attention to the trickle of blood coming out of his right nostril. Saying, "On your belly, homo," and watching the cop squat and roll over just like a fucking trick dog.

Now, the fun was gonna begin.

Aldon walked up to the cop and put Mr. Mossberg's muzzle right at the point where the first roll of neck meat ran up against the base of his skull, jammed it in and gave it a little half twist to make the cop squirm.

Aldon said, "Hi there, homo. Snooping around up here where

you don't belong. Curiosity killed the cat, didn't you know?" Aldon chuckled a flat sounding *Ha-ha*. "Killed quite a few cats."

Silently, Plunkett counted to three, breathing deeply on each count, comforting himself with one thought: He had nothing to lose. No way was Aldon going to let him get away alive. At the end of the third breath he rolled violently to the side, reaching a hand out for the shotgun's barrel.

He was surprised not to hear a roar, was wondering why he was still alive. Then he saw the tire iron in Aldon's right hand. Saw it begin the downward swing.

The blow from the tire iron sent Plunkett into a netherworld of fragmentary visions and nightmares.

He lay on the ground, drifting in and out of consciousness, but unable to move. Slowly, he became aware of the rope that bound his wrists to his ankles. The racket of a small engine came and went. Doors closed. Then it seemed like a long time passed. The light grew dim.

Somewhere out in the darkness, the engine started again. There was a period of jostling and bouncing. Then a more familiar lulling sound—the drone of his own truck. Plunkett lying on his back, smelling the faint exhaust smells, feeling the curves of the road on the side of his face pressed against the pickup's cargo bed.

He passed out again. The next thing he was aware of was being half-kicked, half-dragged into his own place. Dumped on the sofa, still hog-tied. Through the doorway he could see Aldon standing in the kitchen, making a phone call.

Plunkett started to come to his senses while Aldon put a pan on the stove, rummaged until he found the cooking oil, filled the pan, and then went outside. He came back carrying a two-gallon red plastic gasoline container—the type you'd use to fill an ATV. He put the gas can on the stove top a few inches away from the oil-filled pan, then turned on the stove, pausing long enough to make sure the pilot light caught. That job completed to his full satisfaction, he came over to Plunkett, bringing along a bottle of Jack Daniel's.

Aldon treated himself to a slug of the whisky. Let out an exaggerated sigh. Licked his lips and offered the bottle. Plunkett shook his head no. Aldon's twisted face came as close as it could to looking hurt. He planted a gasoline-smelling hand over Plunkett's nose.

When Plunkett parted his lips to breathe, Aldon shoved in the neck of the bottle, all the way down until Plunkett gagged, swallowed a big mouthful of whisky, and spewed the rest. Aldon offered the bottle again. "My way or your way," he said.

Plunkett opened his mouth, accepted the bottle baby-style, and had a sip.

"Take your medicine like a man, homo," said Aldon, holding the bottle to Plunkett's lips.

He complied, taking down enough to cause his gorge to rise, the liquor burning all the way to his gut.

Aldon took back the bottle. Treated himself to another belt and then poured the remainder over Plunkett's head and shoulders, causing the whole place to fill with the perfumed aroma of Jack Daniel's. He laid the empty bottle carefully on its side beside the magazines on Plunkett's coffee table.

"Shouldn't drink so much. Accidents can happen. Bad ones," Aldon said, then added a *"Ha-ha."*

From his hip pocket Aldon withdrew a five-inch buck knife and opened its blade. Moved it slowly toward Plunkett's face, stopping a half inch from his left eye. He let out two little *ha-has* and placed the blade of the knife against Plunkett's cheekbone. Applied pressure.

Plunkett felt a burning pain as the point broke his skin.

Aldon removed the knife and said, "No such luck, homo. You're gonna fry. Fried homo." That got him *ha-ha-ing* again.

He grabbed the rope that ran from Plunkett's hands to his feet and sliced it through with one swipe of the knife. "Move a fucking inch and I cut your balls off," he said, pulling the rope away and shoving it half in, half out of his hip pocket.

The hand that performed that task came back holding the tire iron. Aldon smacked his open palm once, testing the heft of the iron. He smiled a smile that hovered on the edge of gentleness. "Sweet dreams, homo," he said.

28

A<small>LDON SLIPPED A</small> smoke from his pack and leaned against the rock outcrop to watch the little fireworks show he personally had arranged. *Whoooosh. Bang.* That's what he envisioned. *Whoooosh. Bang.* Then the fireball. Afterwards, one roast pig.

It was a good spot to watch everything, across the road and a couple of hundred yards away from the cop's trailer house—close enough to see, but not so close that Aldon would have a hard time sneaking away undetected when the show was over. He lit the cigarette, drew on it, and wished he'd saved a hit of that Jack.

His little show would be beginning any minute. He was glad he had called and arranged for there to be an audience. An appreciative audience.

He stubbed out the first smoke on the rocky ledge. Fished out another and lit it. Nothing happening down at the trailer. He checked his watch. Fifteen minutes had passed. Probably twenty or more since he had made his telephone call.

Three drags into that cigarette he heard a high-pitched whine coming along the highway. He hoped it wasn't her arriving early. Then he saw the low bug-eyes of that Porsche Percy'd been driving.

It stopped. The interior lights came on. Aldon caught a glimpse of that hair. Her silhouette began to walk toward the cop's trailer. Aldon said, "Fuck" to himself, ditched the cigarette, picked up Mr. Mossberg, and started back to the trailer. The very last thing he wanted was to have Percy Quinell dead. At least not yet.

Popcorn. That was the first coherent thought that struggled into Plunkett's consciousness. He could smell popcorn. The movies with some girl whose name he couldn't even remember. The fair in Elizabethtown. The time he and his brother had tried to make popcorn at home without their mother's permission and let the oil get too hot.

That was the smell his memory fastened upon.

Plunkett vividly recalled the oil in the pan had caught fire. A frightened ten-year-old Plunkett had taken the flaming pan out the backdoor and dropped it onto the grass. Inside, his brother was crying and the kitchen was filled with black smoke. Plunkett could smell that smoke again. Could hear Darwin's mewing little cries there in the kitchen.

Then his mind started to play tricks on him. Someone was slapping his face. That hadn't happened back then. The slapping stopped and the person began to shake him violently by the shoulders, saying, "Plunk! Plunk! Wake up, Plunk!"

The popcorn smells went away and were replaced by gasoline vapors. Now whoever it was pulled his hair. He fell to the floor. The person grabbed his armpits and tugged at him.

He tried to make his eyes focus. It was impossible. The light in the room was too bright. Flickering. When he looked up, he saw the blurry face of Percy Quinell, which had no place in his dream. Plunkett closed his eyes. He heard a voice, Percy's, saying, "Plunk, please!"

He felt himself trying to haul his body off the floor. The pulling at his shoulders was still there. He heard, "Please, Plunk. It's not far."

Plunkett was vaguely aware of putting a little weight on his feet and falling. Being pulled again toward the door. He stood. Felt something coming around under his arm. When he looked down he could see Percy's silver hair.

That was the last thing he saw before the explosion and its searing, engulfing heat.

It was like the place vaporized. Aldon was on the other side of the road, coming toward the cop's trailer when there was the *whoooosh*. Just like he had imagined. After the *whoooosh*, glass flew out of all the windows, followed by flames that began to crackle and send sparks up into the night sky. No *bang*, though.

Impossible anyone could still be alive in there. Aldon felt the heat on his cheeks and forehead all the way across the road. He wasn't sure what he was going to do now.

Except get his sweet ass out of there, and fast.

If God possessed a wry but poorly timed sense of humor, as Plunkett often suspected He did, then Plunkett might already have been in heaven: Eternity with his head nestled in the lap of a beautiful woman who had soot on her face and tear streaks glistening on her cheeks in the flickering orange light.

After a few minutes Plunkett got to thinking that maybe it wasn't heaven at all, but hell. The heat was bad. Across the road he saw a man standing in the orange light. A man who looked a lot like the devil—a lot like Aldon Hewitt, too.

As soon as the man appeared, Percy pushed Plunkett's head aside and bolted toward her car. Aldon, if that was who it was, ran in the same direction. He arrived at the car just after Percy. There was a tug-of-war with the door. The car inched away, the man running alongside, still pulling at the door.

When the car was gone, Plunkett realized he was in neither heaven nor hell but behind a boulder in the weedy hay field that served as his own front yard.

Plunkett was still dazed and in the same place when the Wilmington Volunteer Fire Department arrived to attack the embers that were by then all that was left of his home.

Red lights pulsed. Sirens wailed. Hoses were connected to the two trucks and snaked across the yard. Three, four, five zealous volunteers manned each nozzle. Water was trained on the coals from all quarters, and a great, melodramatic cloud of steam rose into the night.

The little matter of Plunkett himself, lying semiconscious behind the boulder, seemed to have been overlooked until a light shone in his eyes.

"Look there," said a male voice from behind the light.

"He dead?" said the deep female voice beside him.

The lights came closer and got lower to the ground. Plunkett tried to block out their brightness with a hand. All he could get it to do was move to one side and wag back and forth two times.

"Not yet," said the man, without bothering to hide the depth of his disappointment.

"Get a shot of him anyway," said the woman. "Then we'll go back over to where the firemen are, and I'll do a quick stand-up there. Make the eleven o'clock news."

"Anything you say, Donna," said the man, putting the lights right up to Plunkett's face.

"What's going on over here," said another male voice, which after a moment's thought, Plunkett realized could belong to only one person.

Culley appeared in the light. He knelt in front of Plunkett. "Plunkett," he said, and administered a slap to Plunkett's right cheek that packed far more sting than was necessary. Culley sniffed and more quietly said, "Plunkett, you've been drinking—" He caught himself and turned to the TV crew. "Would you mind?" he said.

There was nothing but silence.

"Nice shot," Donna finally said. "Now let's do that stand-up and get out of here."

Culley came close again. "Plunkett? You okay?"

Plunkett managed a nod.

"Good, good, good," Culley said. He breathed in, glancing around the scene. "What happened?" he said.

Plunkett squirmed upright, his back propped against the rock. The squirming helped clear his head enough for him to realize that he should be asking himself precisely that question: What happened?

To Culley he said, "Terrible accident. Trooper comes home after a tough day. Has a couple of belts. Puts some cooking oil on the stove. Lies down for just a minute to read while it heats up. . . . Terrible accident. Just like Barron Quinell falling into the Ausable. Just discovered the cause—of both accidents. The hard way." He gestured toward the smoldering ruins.

"Chemical spill, too, which may really have been an accident, ironically. In fact, there's only one thing I haven't figured out: Percy Quinell's role in all this. But I'll find the answer to that before long."

Culley nodded for him to go on, so he did. "She promised she'd tell me. 'All in good time,' those were her exact words."

"And you believed her?"

"What if I told you it was Percy who'd pulled me out of there."

Culley's fine features were impassive in the orange light. After what seemed like a long time, he said, "I guess I'd owe you an apology."

29

P̲LUNKETT CAME TO at 11:29 Sunday morning. At least that's what the fuzzy green numerals on the digital clock a few inches away from his eyes said. He sat upright, momentarily disoriented: head aching, vision wavy and blurred, stomach churning. He had no idea of where he was, except that he was in someone's bed, in a darkened room smelling of coffee, toast, eggs, and bacon.

Thinking back, he caught only dreamlike fragments of the previous day. The Winnebago convoy. Bo's front door. The fight in the mine. The fire. Being hauled out of his trailer. Lying behind the rock. Culley. His brother, Darwin's, face smudged with soot beneath the helmet of a Wilmington Volunteer Fireman.

That was it. After the fire, he had gone home with Darwin. He was now in his brother's guest room.

Plunkett swung his legs to the floor and had to sit there, sucking in breaths while the room stopped seesawing. He swallowed, got a taste of something bitter, then stumbled the two paces over to the window and had to reach out for the ledge to keep from falling. Supporting himself, he went through the deep breathing routine again. Opened the drapes and had to avert his eyes.

On the dresser, someone had left a stack of Darwin's clothes: socks, jockey shorts, jeans, and a Plunkett Motors T-shirt. Just like Darwin to try to get in a little free advertising for the family firm. No doubt about it, everybody in the area would want to get a good long look at the cop who got drunk and let his place burn down.

Well, thought Plunkett, charting an unsteady course to the bathroom, let them. He intended to do some looking of his own.

Margo, Darwin's wife, was up on a step stool putting newly cleaned curtains back on their rods when Plunkett came into the kitchen, a vast space, done from maple floor to wagon-wheel light fixtures in natural wood—a rustic ranch-house effect, if you could look past all the state-of-the-art appliances and gadgets.

"Hi there, sleepy head," Margo said, stepping down. Darwin's wife of twenty-one years was a buxom woman who always went around with a friendly round-faced smile.

"Men went off to the shop an hour ago," Margo said. "Work, work, work, that's all they seem to do. But boys like their toys, and it keeps them happy—and out of my hair. I've got a plate warm." Margo wrapped her hand in a dish towel that matched her clean drapes and opened the oven door. She took a plate from inside heaped with all the things Plunkett had woken up smelling. "Go ahead, Garwood, sit down. Food'll do you good."

Plunkett sat, breathed a few times through his mouth, and then braved a peek at the plate. His stomach tightened. He pushed himself back and swallowed.

"You okay?" said Margo.

"Must of bumped my head. Feel a bit queasy, that's all. Teach me for drinking hard liquor."

Margo put a hand on his forehead. Looked him in his eyes. "You sure you don't have a concussion? Why don't you let me drive you into Emergency? They'd—"

"It's nothing," said Plunkett. "Besides, there's a lot I have to do today."

Margo smiled. Said, "Men."

★ ★ ★

Margo insisted on driving him back to his place, or rather what was left of his place: an oblong scorched area in the hay field with only a few blackened sheets of aluminum, their curled ends protruding here and there to remind passersby that someone had spent the better part of his adult life on the site.

"Oh, Garwood," said Margo, stopping her car, a pink Cadillac she had won by selling cosmetics.

"Least I still have my truck," said Plunkett.

Shiny and unblemished beside the garage, the vehicle looked as out of place as Margo's pink Caddy.

"Thanks for everything," he said.

"You sure you shouldn't go to Emergency? Just let them look at you quickly."

"Feel fine, now, really."

Margo hesitated. "I just hate . . . hate leaving you like this."

Plunkett got out and, holding the door open, said, "I'm fine."

He closed the door and the pink Cadillac hissed away. Averting his eyes from the remains of the trailer, Plunkett walked to his truck. He had to hold on to the door handle and blink away yellow spots in front of his eyes. When those left, he opened the door.

Aldon Hewitt had left the keys in the ignition. Damn decent of him. Plunkett opened the glove compartment. The Glock automatic that was always there—Aldon had had the decency to leave that behind too.

When Plunkett arrived, Edna Hewitt stood outside her home, a converted deer camp painted some hideous hot turquoise hue that had been springing up here and there in the North Country, probably dumped onto the local market at deep discount. She was pulling the last of a very small load of laundry off the line—jeans, T-shirt, coveralls—when Plunkett stopped on the bare sandy patch between the forest and 9N. It was as close as things got to a front yard at the Hewitt residence. From the shade under a hemlock, a starved-looking hound *whoofed* a token warning and then stood whining at the end of its chain.

"Aldon here?" said Plunkett, going toward her, pulling down the Plunkett Motors T-shirt to conceal the Glock shoved in the small of his back.

Edna looked at him with eyes that bulged from their sockets, the eyes of a starving person or terrified wild animal. There was a faint half-moon bruise under one. Elsewhere, her skin had a gray pallor. Blue veins crisscrossed under its surface. She was shivering, even though it was in the eighties.

Getting closer, Plunkett repeated, "Aldon here?"

She cast those terrified eyes over her shoulder and quickly brought them back, hugging her small stack of laundry to stop the shivering. Plunkett followed her gaze. He saw nothing. Just the forest, the trees' branches hanging limp, as if they were sagging under the weight of the humid air. He brushed his finger tips over the Glock.

Edna gave a gesture that might have been a shake of her head. She swallowed—croaked, "Ain't here." Shivered again.

Plunkett looked toward the trees. "His car is," he said, nodding toward one of three ancient LTDs in the clearing—the faded turquoise one with the gold door.

Edna's eyes bulged farther. A blue vein on her temple throbbed. "Got charged," she said. "Ain't driving no more. Took that car off the road. Pulled the plates an' everything."

Plunkett saw that the plates were indeed gone. It wouldn't be long before the recently mobile LTD was indistinguishable from the wrecks.

"He come home last night?" Plunkett said, dipping his chin toward Edna's load of laundry.

"Ain't seen him, not in three days."

Plunkett nodded. Tried to sweep the place one final time with his eyes: the hound, the LTDs, the forest, the hot turquoise of the cabin, an old woodshed half hidden in the trees, the quaking woman in front of him. Damn headache pounding so hard he couldn't concentrate on anything other than the pain.

"Edna," he said. "I can help. Things don't have to be like this for you."

-239-

She stood mute.

"Well, think about it," he said.

The terrified eyes softened. She swallowed and said, "Ain't seen him."

As soon as Plunkett's truck disappeared on 9N, Aldon struggled out from the repair pit under the turquoise and gold LTD. "I don't fucking believe it," he said.

"Gas smell came out pretty good," Edna said.

Aldon yanked the pile of clothes from her arms and used it to wipe the sweat from his face. "That was Plunkett, wasn't it?"

"So what if it was? You gonna tell me why the cops are coming around here?"

"None of your goddamn business." Aldon took a step away.

"He was lookin' for you," Edna said.

Aldon stopped. "For his sake, he better hope he doesn't find me," he said.

Taking the laundry with him, Aldon went over to the woodshed. The Trans Am's engine rumbled, and Aldon drove out, burning rubber when his tires hit 9N, leaving Edna standing there alone looking up and down the empty highway: one direction the way her husband went; the other, the cop.

And Edna thought about it. Just like the cop said she should. She thought for a long time. What she thought was how things didn't look very good for her—not in either direction.

Plunkett saw the deer standing on the shoulder just in time. He hit the brakes. But by then the deer had become a boulder covered in tan-colored lichens. He blinked. Was overcome by a yawn.

A beeping noise came from behind him. There was a car on his tail. The driver was flashing his lights. Hitting the horn. Pulled right out and passed, double line be damned. Crazy asshole, Plunkett thought, and checked his own speed. Fifteen miles per hour.

He shook his head. Rolled down the window and breathed deeply. Felt his eyelids closing. Batted them open. Saw some kids playing beside the road. They became a clump of scrub birches. He realized he was over the center line and pulled back.

In that manner, Plunkett made his way back to Darwin's place and pulled into the driveway in the spot normally occupied by Margo's Caddy. An hour later, when Darwin and his two sons came back from the shop, that's where they found him, slumped over the wheel, sound asleep.

30

Ivor took Percy's telephone call at 8:56 Monday morning, August 10, which, coincidentally, marked four weeks to the day since Duane Dockwheiller fished Barron Quinell's corpse out of the Ausable. Ivor hoisted the receiver into position, simultaneously issuing a cheery, "Good morning."

His hearty greeting was met with a flat-sounding, "Where in hell have you been?" When he didn't immediately answer, she elaborated: "I've been trying to call you since Saturday night. Left three messages."

Ivor lubricated his vocal chords with a sip of coffee, his own blend ground fresh daily at Dean & Deluca. "Was away for much of the weekend," he said.

"Great. Great," she said. "Disappear for two days without telling me."

"I do not remember it being part of our bargain that I tell you my whereabouts twenty-four hours a day. Besides . . ." He let his voice trail off.

"Besides what?"

"Besides," he said, "it was not until my new acquaintance and I were three-quarters of the way through our second bottle of Château de Beaucastel 'eighty-six Saturday night that I had the foggiest inkling I might be away for the rest of the weekend. At my age you'd have to be a fool to pass up such opportunities."

He was somewhat surprised when his explanation mollified Percy. She muttered, "Not that it matters."

"Problem?"

"How's Grand Cayman this time of year?" she asked.

"Cayman? You saw it for yourself."

"I was thinking long term."

"Like any tropical island, it can get rather dull. But why are you asking?"

"Deal's off," she said. "Things are going to hell up here in the worst way. I think we should hightail it—while we still have tails."

Ivor felt the need for another splash of coffee. "It's not the—" He swallowed and half-whispered, half-croaked, "Police."

"I said in the worst way."

"Very well," said Ivor, feeling not very well at all. "But listen—" He paused to compose something soothing. "We're very, very close at this end. Bo has an appointment to see me in one half hour. Today might be the day. Is there no way, after all this time and invest—"

"Bo's in town? You're certain?" Percy said.

"Just talked to the man on the telephone."

The pause that followed went on so long Ivor began to fear the connection had been broken. He was ready to hang up when Percy, still in her deadpan mode, said: "Three this afternoon, I'm on my way south."

"Three," Ivor repeated. He sipped from his cup. "Will you be safe . . . where you are?"

After all the deadpan it was a relief to hear her pleasantly deep voice give forth a series of chuckles. "Wasn't it you who taught me to always make sure I occupy a thoroughly defensible position?"

"Let's have a telephone number, then. I'll ring as soon as there are any developments."

Ivor wrote as she dictated. It wasn't until he had scribbled the last digit that he realized why the number seemed so familiar. It belonged to the phone at his camp.

Bo finally stormed into Ivor's office at 9:50, twenty minutes late and looking badly hungover. He refused Ivor's offer of coffee and instead reached into the breast pocket of his gray double-breasted suit coat—Brooks Brothers was Ivor's guess. "Here's a check for one hundred thirty-one thousand and ninety-seven dollars," Bo said.

Ivor did his best to muster more disinterest than anyone had the right to expect in the presence of a six-figure financial instrument. He raised a single eyebrow.

"Ms. Cline wants to buy her investment unit back," said Bo, coming close enough to Ivor to give him a bitter blast of day-old alcohol.

"Can't do," said Ivor.

Bo's jaw began to quiver. "What the hell do you mean, can't do?" he said.

For the very first time in his long and fulfilling career, Ivor worried he may have overplayed a hand. True, the plan had called for Bo Scullin to get agitated. With luck, even unreasonable. But not this bad this quickly. Ivor swallowed once and tried to hide behind a frown of concern and sympathy.

Bo was too furious to notice. "What do you mean I can't buy another investment unit?"

Ivor sighed and tried to look into Bo's eyes. To no avail. They darted here and there about the room, from the bookshelves to the broadloom, to the ceiling, to Ivor and then started the circuit over again.

"What I mean," said Ivor, "is that there are no units to buy. They are all subscribed to. And any that come on the market are spoken for by—" Here, Ivor paused and did his best to make it look like he was waging an internal battle with conflicting ethical principles: Half of him wanting dearly to tell Bo everything, but duty and a deeply ingrained sense of professional confidentiality dictating otherwise.

Having never felt the weight of any ethical burdens in real life, Ivor was winging it. But it seemed to be working, so he went on: "The shareholders' agreement gives our principal investors the right to purchase any units that come for sale. And since the rumors about Gene—" Ivor prudently stopped talking. He sighed. "Let's just say that one of our shareholders has left me with standing orders to purchase any units that come up. That's what happened to Ms. Cline's."

"One hundred and fifty. I'll go that high," said Bo.

Ivor allowed himself a smile. He took a half step backward and tapped four keys on his computer. Following each tap, he ratcheted his smile down a notch until it was transformed into a pensive frown. Ivor nodded sagely. "One hundred ninety-six thousand," he said. "That was the last trade."

Bo threw the check toward Ivor's desk. It made it about one third of the way there. Bo didn't notice. He was busily rooting around inside his suit coat. His hand came back out with a pen and checkbook.

"But as I said," Ivor went on, "the units are all spoken for, so in this case, price is moot."

Bo paid that statement no heed whatsoever. He fumbled with the pages of the checkbook and began to scribble. "Two hundred thousand. Here," he said. He ripped out a check and threw it, too, in the direction of Ivor's desk. Check number two made it a foot farther than the first one, but still fell onto the blue-gray broadloom.

Ivor retrieved the two checks. He went around his desk and sat, tapping the edges of the pieces of paper until they were perfectly aligned. After allowing Bo to bask in the radiance of his most beguiling smile, Ivor ripped in one quick motion, and began his tapping routine with what were now four pastel green pieces.

"Mind you," Ivor said. "We do represent several other young, growth-oriented biotechnology firms. I could have Doris gather together the prospectuses—"

"Two-twenty-five," said Bo.

Ivor smiled, benevolently this time, and in a way that made it clear that although he personally would dearly love to help, his gnarled old hands were tied by powers far greater than his own. Tied or not, Ivor's hands were still capable of ripping the four-pieces of paper, which he demonstrated.

"Surely—" Bo sputtered. Some of his tanned skin tones faded, replaced by a gray only a shade lighter than the carpet. "The unit was sold by mistake. I thought—" He brought himself up short, but his jaw wagged on silently for a few syllables. He clamped it shut and took a sharp breath through his nose. "How much?" he asked with a note of finality. When that drew no reaction, he raised his voice and said, "How fucking much?"

Ivor shook his head. "If anything comes up—but, as I said . . ." He tossed his hands skyward, sending a blizzard of green paper down upon his desktop.

The phone pinged and Doris's voice came over the speaker. "It's the lawyer from Genentech again. 'Urgent,' he said."

Ivor looked sadly at Bo. "I'm sorry, Mr. Scullin. I have to take this call."

He listened to the dial tone until the door closed behind Bo.

Thirty seconds later, precisely on cue, Ivor emerged from the back entrance of his office to intercept a still-sputtering Bo in the elevator vestibule.

"Mr. Scullin, I always feel uncomfortable talking candidly in that office," Ivor said. "You never know . . ."

Bo grunted in a way that made it clear that he knew. The elevator bell dinged. Its doors opened. "What's that supposed to mean, 'You never know'?" Bo said, stepping inside.

The doors began to close.

Ivor looked nervously over his shoulder. "There were some things I couldn't say . . ."

Bo reached between the moving doors and jabbed a finger into

Ivor's chest. His lips curled up in a fair imitation of a dog's snarl.

"I—"

Ivor managed to pop the doors back open with his hip. They immediately and determinedly started to close again. "Look, to be frank, I do not want to talk here." Ivor absorbed another blow from the persistent doors. "Would you be so kind as to meet with me, off premises, as it were. Do you know the Oak Room? At The Plaza?"

Bo stopped his snarling long enough to nod.

"There then," Ivor said. "Noonish, say."

The elevator doors closed on the mean little grin that was spreading over Bo Scullin's face.

Ivor secured a window table looking onto Central Park South. It was windy outside, and pedestrians scurried to escape the first splats of rain. A waiter came across the dark wood-paneled room, took Bo's order for a gin martini—very dry, thank you, with a twist—and then inquired if Mr. Rhys would be having his usual beverage. The waiter returned about thirty seconds later bringing the martini and a tumbler full of Scotch.

"I'll come right down to business," Ivor said. "At Biocural I am more or less a figurehead carrying out instructions from a small group of controlling shareholders. Call me a front man if you will. Or the fall guy. Whatever the case, for some time now there have been irregularities in the sales of our units. Frankly, I have been explicitly ordered to favor one of the shareholders of Biocural at the expense of all others."

Bo held the already empty martini glass over his head in a decidedly un-Oak-Room-like gesture until the waiter saw it. "How does this effect me?" he said, shifting in his chair.

"According to the official agreement, an existing investor has the right of first refusal for any units that come onto the market. But— And this is a very operative *but* in this instance. If a third party comes forward with a higher offer, the unit goes to that person. You follow?"

Bo sighed impatiently and began to search the room for the waiter.

"A-a-a-a-a-a-nd," Ivor proceeded floridly. "There was a unit available today."

The waiter came. Bo grabbed the new martini off the tray and slurped an ounce of it en route to the table. Another ounce slopped over his hand and wrist and disappeared down the sleeve of his suit coat. "And . . . ?"

"And it's really rather simple," said Ivor. "If I receive a higher bid from you, I am obligated to accept it—legally. Full stop." Ivor dipped his chin to his chest. "But you see my bind. If I did, I would lose my job. All units that come available are reserved for—"

Ivor put a cautionary hand out. "Kindly forget what I just said. I'll rephrase it. A major shareholder, who shall remain unidentified, has a standing order out for units to add to those she already has. Naturally, she wants to pick them as cheaply as possible. I believe she has a certain financial goal in mind: To walk away from Biocural with three million dollars in her pocket. Looks like the controlling shareholders are willing to sidestep legalities in order to assure that she gets those units at her price."

Bo rose a good six inches off his seat, an act that may well never have been performed in that, the most subdued of watering holes. "Percy Quinell," he said.

Ivor chuckled. "Now it's me who's committing corporate indiscretions. But I can't see what it would hurt. Not now. I mean. It is public record."

He bent over and fished in his briefcase. "Ah, here it is," he said, coming back with a folded section of the Plattsburgh *Chronicle-Herald,* which Bo promptly snatched away.

Bo got no further than the first few paragraphs and threw aside the paper. "Barron Quinell Research Center," he sputtered.

"He was partially responsible for assembling the investors' group behind Biocural. Passed away recently," said Ivor, letting his tone grow somber. "Shortly after his death, she came to the controlling shareholders and convinced them she desperately needed three million dollars, and needed it as soon as possible. Out of kindness toward her and respect for her late husband—not to mention the fact that they all stand to make a pot of money on this deal—they are playing along. If she can lay her hands on a few more units for the right price, she'll jolly well have her three million by next week. That's when the Genentech buyout will be announced."

Ivor nodded to himself and chuckled once. He brightened. "But fear not. You'll be able to get your unit soon enough. I was contacted by one of our investors just this morning. He is cautious and would like to take some profit before the announcement, so it looks like a major block is coming up for sale. Twenty-five units. I suspect the controlling shareholders will let Ms. Quinell get the few units she needs to meet her investment goals, then the others will be sold on the open market. Just give me your card—"

"No!" Bo blurted, loudly enough so that the three blue-rinsed heads at the next table were forced to turn from their inspection of a string of cultured pearls that still lay coffined in its original Tiffany's box.

"A problem?" Ivor said.

"No!" Bo said, again. This time his hollering did have the beneficial effect of bringing over the waiter with a fresh martini. Thus armed, Bo was able to add, "I want them all. Do you understand? All of them," he said, downshifting to a low, menacing voice.

Ivor chuckled nervously. "I don't—I mean, I'll have to talk to—" He hoisted his rear end clear of the chair and was swinging it toward the pathway between the tables. "I'm just the front man. I've probably said too much as it—"

Bo's hand clamped Ivor's wrist. "Sit back down," he hissed. "How much?" When an answer failed to leap from Ivor's lips, he hissed again: "How fucking much do you want?"

The blue-rinsed table went silent.

"Two hundred a unit should do it, I should—"

"You!" Bo shouted the word. Every waiter in the place heard and turned toward their table. "How much do *you* want?" He poked his index finger up to its second knuckle in Ivor's belly and whispered, "To personally make sure that I get that block and every other Biocural share that comes on the market."

Ivor started his nervous chuckling routine again—a routine that suddenly placed no demands whatsoever upon his acting abilities. "Me? Well, normally I ask one percent of any transaction for special personal services, but—"

Bo pulled out his checkbook, opened it, and calmly wrote a check for fifty thousand dollars. "There," he said, pushing it over. "Think of it as a retainer."

It required all his willpower, but Ivor put his index finger on the check and slid it back toward Bo. "Totally irregular, I'm afraid. Improper." He raised himself again.

"You get to keep it even if the deal falls through," Bo said.

That was enough to allow Ivor to slowly lower his buttocks back to the Oak Room's upholstery.

"Perhaps if you openly bid for all the units as a block . . . and did so quickly, before . . ." Ivor let his voice trail off. "But that would require something in the order of five million dollars."

Mention of that figure caused a hush to fall over the table.

"Doable," Bo finally said. He sounded far more canny and businesslike than anyone with a couple of drinks under his well-cut suit coat had a right to. "Circumstances have left me 'cash-rich,' as they say. Of course," he added, "before handing you that sort of money I would have to investigate."

Ivor let Bo's countenance go from canny to sage before he said, "I would never dream of asking you to commit that sort of money to us directly." He chuckled. "That's not the way we operate at all. If it was, we wouldn't have many investors. All financial arrangements are handled through our corporate bankers, Cayman Trustco," he explained. "You purchase a fully secured certificate of deposit from them, they retain it as secondary collateral against an internal loan they then issue to Biocural, which is, in turn, secured by your investment units. In that way, your money never really leaves your possession. And, there are distinct tax advantages to routing the transaction through the Caymans. Many of our investors find themselves more or less permanently in what you just referred to as a 'cash-rich' situation. The Caymanian banking system has thrived by accommodating such situations—discreetly. Willard Bodden, the managing director at Cayman Trustco, would be more than pleased to explain."

Ivor could almost see the wheels begin to turn beneath that well-coiffed hair. There was a glimmer of understanding in the eyes. To Ivor he said: "When does this buyout come down?"

"Late next week, early the week after. Depending."

Bo thought for a moment. "This Bodden guy," he said. "Maybe I should give him a call." He stopped and shot a mean glare at Ivor and corrected himself, "Maybe we should give him a call."

Right there in the Oak Room, Bo's mean glare transformed itself into a tiny private smile of satisfaction. Could have been caused by vanity. Could have been caused by greed. Or both.

Doris looked up from her perusal of the latest issue of *Variety* a fraction of a second too late. Ivor was already past her and had his hand on his office's doorknob. "You have—" was all she was able to blurt before he had the door fully opened.

Bambi-Sue sat behind his big desk, looking far too at home and comfortable there with her whisky.

"Back so soon," she said, adding, "Well . . . ?"

Ivor raised the edges of his lips to form a naughty smile. The smile was followed by a series of quiet laughs.

"Mind sharing your little joke?"

"A joke? I'm not sure one should refer to it as a joke. And as for it being little . . ." Ivor formed a fist, then one-by-one raised his fingers until all five were showing.

"Five?" she asked.

Still smiling, Ivor nodded. "Five million one hundred twelve thousand net of commissions, management fees, and other miscellaneous charges for professional services rendered on our behalf by one Mr. Willard Bodden, Q.C. Wired to Cayman Trustco this afternoon, and due to one of those unfortunate banking glitches that crop up now and then in this electronic global village, deposited into my personal account."

Bambi-Sue pouted.

-251-

"Do I detect moroseness?" Ivor asked.

"Two point five million, give or take," she said. "That's what five million comes to, split two ways. I'm pinching myself."

"A tidy packet of loot," said Ivor.

Bambi-Sue looked troubled. "I can't help thinking about your other partner. The woman—what's her name?"

"Have no sisterly qualms about what we're doing to Percy Quinell," Ivor said. "At the very least, this will have taught her something that should prove valuable to her throughout the rest of her life—my legacy to her." He closed his eyes and sighed deeply. "With all the rich fools out there, it makes a great deal more sense for a beautiful woman to steal money than marry it."

Bambi-Sue sniggered. "The one day in seven he wasn't a poor dirt farmer, my beloved daddy was a Pentecostal preacher, and even he couldn't have shoveled it much thicker than *that*. But you missed the point. It wasn't sisterly qualms I was having. I was worried what would happen if she gets her hands on our money first."

"Impossible. Percy—who as it turns out has marooned herself conveniently on an island in the middle of an Adirondack lake—will be informed of our success shortly and asked to meet me at the Cayman bank tomorrow afternoon. I will fail to turn up, having concluded my Cayman financial transactions earlier in the day."

Bambi-Sue shook her head. "Leaving a lot to chance, aren't you? What if she gets down there first?"

"She can't, given the infrequent schedule of the USAir Express Adirondack service. And don't worry. I've survived in this business as long as I have because I never, absolutely never, leave things to chance. If, by some miracle, she gets there first, she will find precisely the same thing as she would if she gets there as arranged: an empty bank account."

"Even so," said Bambi-Sue impatiently, "I'm just not sure you've cut her far enough out. And with two point five million riding on it . . ." She paused and did a quick calculation. "I guess what I'm trying to say is you can never cut someone too far out, can you, Ivor?"

"Bambi-Sue, you just leave everything to me. I'll have Doris book us two seats on the next flight to Miami with connections to Grand Cayman."

Bambi-Sue flashed her little girl's smile as she reached into her handbag and took out two ticket folders. First class.

USAir flight 883 with nonstop service from La Guardia to Miami International was in the final stages of boarding when its last two first-class passengers arrived at the gate. Ivor shepherded Bambi-Sue in front of him to the agent, a trim-looking young man who had airs of an aspiring pilot. With far more efficiency and dedication than the task warranted, he collected and tore the stub off Bambi-Sue's ticket.

At precisely that point, Ivor said, "I'll just make a quick call. Promised Percy an update."

Bambi-Sue and the would-be pilot registered equal looks of shock.

"It'll only take a minute," Ivor said, getting a glare from the gate agent that suggested one minute was stretching it.

Bambi-Sue waited beside the entrance to the jetway while Ivor made his call. "You look like you should be a pilot, sugar," she said to the agent. He blushed a red identical to the US portion of the logo on his podium.

Exactly one minute and fifty-three seconds after he had left, Ivor returned looking triumphant. "She is still marooned on the island. Nothing to stop us now," he said to Bambi-Sue. "Feel any better?"

She said, "When I pocket the bank draft for my share of the five million—that's when I'll start feeling better."

31

Wondering why she was not feeling at all the way she thought a woman who had just made herself a few million dollars should feel, Percy finished talking to Ivor and replaced the cordless telephone on the arm of the Adirondack chair. She positioned the phone halfway between Ivor's Leitz binoculars and what she promised herself would be the day's first and only Stoli. On the other arm of the chair, the right one, was a chamois cloth, a tin of oil and a scrupulously cleaned Smith & Wesson .357 Magnum.

Percy treated herself to a nip of the vodka with one hand and used the other to raise the binoculars in front of her eyes. She scanned over the lake to her dock, up the path to her camp's back door, across the parking area, past the front of the main building, then back to the dock. She made two more slow circuits until she was sure that she had no uninvited visitors, at least not at present.

That hadn't been the case late Sunday afternoon when Plunkett dropped by. And a half hour after he left, Aldon.

Percy had another sip of vodka, this one to bolster her courage. She replaced both the glass and binoculars, retrieved the telephone, and tried to decide whether it made more sense to call Bo or Plunkett first. Her conclusion was that it really didn't matter. Not at this point.

Bo must have been sleeping on top of his telephone. The voice that answered halfway through the first ring was thick and dull and sounded like it came from someone who had just been hauled from the depths of sound, dreamless non-REM slumber.

She counteracted it with tones of cheerfulness and conviviality. "Bo, darling. I know you're in the city, but on the off chance that you were coming up here tonight, I thought I'd call and invite you to a small and very private gathering at my camp. Around nine. It's a celebration, of sorts."

The dull voice emitted a few barely audible *"Huh, huh, huhs."*

"I think there's a shuttle flight out of Newark at 4:15."

There were a few more *"Huh, huh, huhs"* and Bo said, "Hold reservations on it already. Can I ask what is being celebrated? So I may bring along something . . ." He paused and said, "appropriate."

"I was hoping you'd ask," Percy said merrily. "It's to celebrate my purchase of your share of Realty Associates."

Percy said she would like to speak to Trooper Plunkett and was unceremoniously put on hold for a full five minutes. During that interval she watched a young cottontail come up the trail at a very unrabbitlike walk, apparently without a care in the world. Once in the clearing, the rabbit waited until the scurrying figure of Winston topped the rise, paws scrambling for a hold in the gravel and loose earth. The rabbit then hopped across the clearing and went into a hole at the base of a cedar. Winston took up an alert posture, tipped his muzzle heavenward and began baying.

A voice that could have belonged to any state or local bureaucrat, just so long as he was a petty one, came over the receiver.

"I was hoping to reach Trooper Plunkett. Personally," said Percy.

The bureaucratic voice imparted the fact that she was speaking to

Senior Investigator Culley and that Plunkett himself was unavailable.

"Do you have a way to get a message to him? It's urgent."

Grudgingly, the voice admitted to that possibility.

"My name is Percy Quinell. Tell Trooper Plunkett that I will continue calling him at this number every hour until I reach him. Tell him I think it's high time he and I had our little visit. The official one."

Plunkett arrived in Ray Brook fifty-five minutes after Percy's call. His central nervous system was still trying to deal with the twin miseries of what felt like a combination of a major bout of influenza and the worst hangover of all time.

He was in no mood to coddle Culley, who after a month of neglect, had finally taken an interest in the bizarre events transpiring in the jurisdiction, at least insofar as those events related to the disappearance of Quentin Quinell, would-be son-in-law of Judge John Conoscenti.

"She called," said Culley, who sat in Plunkett's cubicle.

"So you said," said Plunkett, gesturing for Culley to stand. When he grudgingly obeyed, Plunkett fell into the chair and tipped his head back to take some of the pressure off his eyes.

The telephone warbled. Plunkett sat up. "Hallo," Plunkett said, leaning back again.

There was silence on the line and then that familiar one-octave deeper-than-expected voice said, "It as bad as it sounds?"

"Umph," said Plunkett, trying to concentrate.

"Anybody listening?"

Plunkett pushed the button that activated the speaker phone. "Does it matter? Message said your call was official," he said.

After a pause Percy said, "No, I don't suppose it does matter." Plunkett could hear the hollow rattle of ice cubes in a glass. "Be at my camp at eight-thirty tonight. Sharp. It is important that you come looking like a cop—but alone. Alone, understand. Park your car in the garage. Be sure to close the garage door."

"Then what?" said Plunkett.

He heard the ice cubes rattle again, this time followed by a long relieved-sounding sigh. Percy's husky voice said, "Didn't believe me, did you, when I promised you'd get your answers—all in good time?"

"Percy, I—"

"Well tonight is a good time. And, Plunk—you won't forget your gun."

After the connection was broken, Plunkett turned to Culley and said, "Any thoughts?"

Culley offered Plunkett a smile that was far too wise for its owner's years. He said, "You heard the lady."

32

Ivor led the way into the high-ceilinged lobby of the Grand Cayman's Hyatt Regency Britannia. He and Bambi-Sue marched directly to the registration desk, Ivor looking paternal and proud, Bambi-Sue wide-eyed. The solitary clerk working the desk at that hour, 7:45 P.M., was a fetchingly beautiful young Caymanian woman, her straight black hair trimmed page-boy fashion, her skin the color of fine antique mahogany. She welcomed Ivor with a sleepy smile that was filled with seductive promise.

"Two rooms," said Ivor. "Under the name of—" He turned to Bambi-Sue.

"Cline," she said.

The smile fell from the receptionist's face, which Ivor found regrettable.

She consulted her computer. "Only one room reserved under that name."

Ivor was about to voice his indignation when he noticed that the smile of seductive promise so recently on the receptionist's face had migrated across to Bambi-Sue's.

"Figgered it was time we got to know each other," she said.

-258-

★ ★ ★

Within five minutes, the receptionist had equipped them with the keys to their suite. As they turned to follow the bellman, she said, "One other thing, Mr. Rhys. A Mr. Bodden from Cayman Trustco left this at the desk earlier this evening." She extended a thick business envelope and consulted a message slip taped to it. "Said to tell you that he regrets that business will be taking him off the island temporarily. Said he thought you would understand."

Ivor's fingers leapt out and snapped away the envelope. The old Money Smile beamed. "What did I tell you?" he said to Bambi-Sue. "I suggest we go to the lounge immediately and examine the contents of this envelope."

Ivor set a course across the lobby toward the bar. Ordering on the march, he selected a table unashamedly in the center of the room and gestured for Bambi-Sue to sit across from him.

After the glasses were filled, Ivor held his aloft. "Shall we?" he said, and carefully pinched away a corner of the envelope, using his index finger as a letter opener. He parted the envelope, peered inside, and slowly withdrew two pages of Cayman Trustco letterhead held together with a paper clip. Affixed to the backside of the second sheet was a buff-colored bank draft.

"Let's see it," said Bambi-Sue, reaching out.

Ivor held the documentation aloft until Bambi-Sue put her hand back on her lap.

"Thank you," he said, withdrawing his half-glasses from the breast pocket of his new, blue, seersucker suit coat. He balanced the glasses on the end of his nose and cleared his throat. "It's from Bodden," he announced, then read, " 'Dear Mr. Rhys: Account number 500804 has been closed as you requested. Enclosed find a deposit slip showing that a full refund of my fee has been returned to your personal account. I regret that circumstances prevent me from performing the services we discussed. I hope you will keep Cayman Trustco Ltd. in mind should your future business plans require our specialized offerings. Yours truly . . .' "

Bambi-Sue made another grab, this time successfully securing a hold on the deposit slip. She turned her back on Ivor and scanned it furiously. Her first reaction was a single *"Peep."* After the *peep,* there was a sob.

Ivor seized the slip. He extended his index finger and counted off each zero. Then recounted. The Money Smile vanished. Ivor shook his head. "Ten thousand," he said.

Bambi-Sue emitted a huge sob. "Five thousand each . . ." She sobbed even louder and gestured with her tear-filled eyes toward the remaining piece of Cayman Trustco letterhead.

Ivor brightened. "I imagine this will explain everything," he said. "Probably just some minor—"

He let the hand holding the paper fall onto the table. "Oh Lord," he whispered. "It's from her. Dated July 21." Ivor closed his eyes and counted backwards. "The day we first met with young Bodden. She must have been on to me right from the outset."

"What does it say?" said Bambi-Sue.

Ivor read. When he raised his head, he said, "What it says is: 'The five million belongs to me now. I guess there is an element of truth to that old saying that no one is easier to con than a con man. A plague upon it when thieves cannot be true one to another! With all my love, Persephone.' She signed it *Persephone.*"

Bambi-Sue slammed a dainty fist on the table. "Her!" she said. "I told you, you—" She was unable to go on without inhaling five times in succession.

Ivor sighed ruefully. *"Henry IV, Part I,"* he said without expression. "I used to read that play to her as a girl. And all along, I thought she had forgotten."

"Fuckin' marvelous," snarled Bambi-Sue.

Ivor frowned at her. "You just don't understand, do you?"

"Oh, I understand all right," said Bambi-Sue. "I understand that you allowed some woman to sucker you. Sucker us. That much I understand. What I don't understand is what we do next."

Ivor treated her to a grandfatherly look of wisdom. "Things could be a whole lot worse. We have ten thousand sitting in a Cayman bank account. That should go a fair way, even around here." He swept the room with a gnarled hand. "And by the time it's spent, I'm sure you and I'll have figured out a good use for that lovely suite of offices on Wall Street. There's a great deal I could still teach you, and in the process, we could roll up a tidy fortune. Who knows, I may even be able to figure a way to get the five million back from Percy."

"Yeah, tell me about it."

Ivor shrugged and picked up his Champagne. "Bodden's father, for starters. He and I—"

"Spare me." Bambi-Sue stood.

"Where are you going?"

"What if I said I was going to make a phone call—to Bo?"

Ivor's hand trembled. "Bambi—I hardly think—" He put down the glass. "Why?"

"He might want to know that Percy Quinell has his five million."

"I hardly think that will help our situation."

Bambi-Sue smirked. "Even if it doesn't make getting our hands on the money easier, it very definitely does remove one nagging little possibility—one that might cast a shadow over our stay down here." She kept the smirk in place but it grew more tender. "Maybe even our whole future as business partners."

"And that possibility is . . . ?"

"That you and she are still in cahoots."

33

Showered, shampooed, and back in her camp bedroom, Percy put on a simple white cotton pullover dress. She thought the loose-fitting garment lent her an air of innocence—something she might have occasion to call upon before the evening ended. The wide black leather belt she always wore with it made a convenient, if only passably comfortable resting place for the .357 Magnum, which she might have occasion to call upon if innocence failed.

Her night table clock said 8:03, nearly a half hour before Plunkett was due. Percy slipped the gun beneath the belt, barrel downward. She bloused the dress over the belt, and came to the conclusion that she would reconsider her resolution to have only one drink that day.

She proceeded down the stairs, flipping on lights as she went. The kitchen switch was on the far wall, close to the back door. She navigated the familiar room in the dark and turned on the outside floodlights for the benefit of her soon-to-arrive guests.

The first thing she saw through the screen door was the muzzle of the shotgun. Behind the muzzle's perfect black circle was a length of charcoal gray barrel, then an open but slightly squinted eye. Below the eye was an ugly smile.

"Meet Mr. Mossberg," said Aldon.

Trying to act as if the shotgun were not there, Percy glanced at the clock on the stove. She wondered if there was the faintest possibility that Plunk would choose that evening to be early. Her conclusion was probably not.

"You, me, and Mr. Mossberg, we got a date," Aldon said, ending his announcement with a dull, *"Ha-ha."* He settled his cheek back into position. "A Dutch date, because you're gonna be doing the driving—in that fancy new car of yours."

"Aldon," she said. "I'm not going anywhere with you."

Aldon emitted another *"Ha-ha."* He readjusted the gun. If he pulled the trigger, the load would have been centered directly upon the up-turn at the end of her nose. "There's two ways to do this," he said. "My way and . . ." He gave her another smile, one that may have had his idea of come-hither thrown in. "And Mr. Mossberg's way," he said, and started that *"Ha-ha"* business again.

Percy did her best to return his smile, *sans* come-hither. "There might be a third way . . . Aldon," she said. "What about what I said on the dock the other day? Have you thought about it? We could strike a deal . . . you . . . and me."

Aldon shook his head slowly against the gun's stock and may have shown a trace of genuine remorse. "Shoulda got to me sooner. Deal's a deal," he said. "Besides, I did think about it. Lots. What I thought was that you ain't got nothing to bargain with. At least nothing I ain't gonna get anyways."

Percy's garage was hidden behind a rocky knoll at the end of a short spur off the driveway. According to local lore, the camp's original owner forbade internal combustion engines to approach within a hundred yards of her retreat. It was said that their racket and exhaust fumes distressed her, reminded her too much of the source of the family fortune that built the place.

To a point, Plunkett sympathized with the sentiment, especially if there were plenty of paid servants around to park cars and make the trek between garage and main building on the proprietor's behalf.

One of the three stalls in Percy's garage was already occupied by a black Trans Am, not the sort of vehicle Plunkett associated with Percy Quinell, even without the cardboard pine tree deodorizer hanging from the rearview mirror.

Wondering who else might be there, Plunkett closed the garage door and set out toward Percy's camp. The first fifty yards was made in darkness. But once he was on the driveway itself, Plunkett's way was lit by the main building, where every light seemed to be on. He mounted the back steps and raised his hand to knock. In mid-motion he stopped, considered the Trans Am, and slowly moved the hand down to unholster his pistol.

No one answered the three whacks he subsequently administered to the screen-door frame, so he repeated the action. One full minute after the second volley of knocks, Winston appeared around the corner, approaching one plodded pace at a time.

Plunkett gave another rap. It caused Winston to sit on his haunches, raise his muzzle toward the ceiling and let out a long mellow howl.

When even the howl failed to bring Percy, Plunkett checked his watch. It showed 8:37, seven minutes past the time Percy had said to be there. Plunkett opened the screen door.

Winston stopped howling. He scampered across the kitchen and started to do a surprisingly fast-footed dog dance in front of one of the cupboard doors, nudging it every third or fourth step with his snout.

"Percy?" Plunkett called. "Anyone here?"

The dog started to whine, still keeping up his dance. Plunkett bent and opened the cupboard. It contained a bag of dog kibble and two stainless-steel bowls—Winston's larder, to judge by the velocity of his tail-wagging.

"Percy," Plunkett called again.

All he got in response was another pathetic whine from Winston, pathetic enough to remind Plunkett that Percy neglecting to feed her silly old dog was completely out of character.

"Where are you taking me?" said Percy.

"Just shut the fuck up and turn off here like I told you," said Aldon.

She pulled the Porsche off Stewart Mountain Road and parked it out of sight behind a bus-sized hunk of granite.

"Now you and me get to go for a walk," said Aldon. "A nice evening stroll in the woods." He laughed.

"I think I've played along far enou—"

Percy heard a loud *crack* and felt a searing pain on her cheek.

"Don't sass me." Aldon raised his hand, held it aloft for her to see, then brought it down again. "Now get your ass in gear, or I'll do you right here. I'm gettin' sick and tired of takin—" He cut himself off with a series of hisses drawn through clenched teeth.

Percy opened her door. The interior lights glinted off the barrel of the shotgun, about six inches away from her right temple. "Nothing funny," Aldon said. He jabbed toward her ear with the gun. "Slow. Slow," he started saying, sliding toward the passenger's door, keeping the gun on her, still saying, "Slow, slow, slow."

She stood. Aldon's face appeared on the other side of the car. In a quick motion he brought the gun around so its barrel rested on the car top, aimed at her forehead.

"Here," he said, reaching behind him and coming back with a flashlight. "You get to be the leader."

Plunkett believed there was nothing faster or more efficient than a computer—when everything worked. But let in some little electronic glitch, and any self-respecting microcircuit would show that at its silicone heart it could be as stubborn as the most ill-tempered nineteenth-century pack mule.

So he had to sit there in the kitchen, holding Percy's phone in one hand and a piece of paper bearing the license number of the Trans Am in the other, watching old Winston munch and chomp and slop his dinner one kibble at a time while the computer in Ray

Brook attempted to connect the number on the Trans Am's plate to the name of a registered owner.

"Trans Am, you say," said Culley.

"Eighty-eight."

Across the phone line, Plunkett heard a furious *rat-a-tat-tatting* of keys, a sigh, and then a few widely spaced lesser *tats*. Finally there was a *"Hum,"* but Culley showed no indication of wanting to share its cause with Plunkett. "Well," he said, after two more key taps. "I have that number, but it isn't registered to any eighty-eight Trans Am. A seventy-eight LTD. Owner's name is Edna Hewitt. . . ."

Ignoring the niceties of search and seizure, Plunkett opened the driver's door of the Trans Am and scanned its interior with the rechargeable flashlight he had borrowed from Percy's kitchen. The first thing that caught his eye was the three-quarters empty bottle of Jack Daniel's under the driver's seat. He also took passing note of the dozen or so cork-filtered cigarette butts in the open ashtray.

It was the last item his light fell upon—the opened box of Remington 12-Gauge deer slugs on the passenger's seat—that got Plunkett wondering what, exactly, Percy and Aldon could be up to together.

They walked in silence, Percy trying to move as slowly as possible, putting Aldon and his gun out of mind, letting herself feel the pressure of the .357 Magnum strapped to the small of her back, tantalizingly close, if she could only find an opportunity to get at it before Aldon's shotgun took off the side of her head. Every five or ten paces, she would hear Aldon utter one of his *"Ha-has,"* but aside from that annoying tic, he comported himself like a bashful high schooler escorting his first prom date until they reached a pair of wooden doors built unto the face of a rock ledge.

"This is it," he said, and hooked open one of the doors with the toe of his work boot. When she failed to leap inside immediately, he whacked her between the shoulder blades with the butt of the gun.

Percy took three stumbled steps into what she first thought was a cave—a cave that smelled strongly of some hard-to-identify hydrocarbon. It wasn't until she stood still that she realized she was in a mine and recognized that the figure holding a hissing Coleman lantern was Bo Scullin.

Aldon came up behind her and dealt another blow to her back—this one halfway between the shoulder blades and the .357.

"Call off your goon," Percy said, taking an involuntary two steps toward Bo and his circle of light.

Apparently Bo hadn't heard. He placed his lantern on a fifty-five gallon drum—one of hundreds that lined the walls and disappeared into the gloom. He got his fingers around the knob on the lantern, turning it a notch brighter, then lowering it again, and not finding that level satisfactory, bringing it back up.

Once the lantern was burning to Bo's satisfaction, he swigged from a squat square bottle and cleared his throat. "I hope you don't object to"—he washed down a hiccough with a slug from the bottle—"object to my change of venue for tonight's little soirée."

In the background Aldon snickered.

"Given what you said on the telephone," Bo rambled on, "this just seemed so much more . . ." Bo waved the gin bottle at the drums. "Apropos?" he said, more as a question than a statement.

He pointed to the ground. There was a slick, dark puddle. Blood, was the first thing Percy thought.

"Transformer lubricant," Bo said. "Stuff's loaded with PCBs. So be careful. You might get cancer." He broke out into the most unbecoming series of giggles and squeaks Percy had ever heard.

Once recovered, Bo said, "But I'm not being a good host." He took a Styrofoam cup from on top of the barrel, looked inside it, grimaced, swished a little of his gin around in the cup and splashed it onto the floor beside the PCB puddle. Dishwashing attended to, he poured and extended the cup toward Percy. She took it, even though gin ranked second only to single malt Scotch on her personal list of liquids that made better paint-brush cleaners than beverages.

"Percy would have done this over Waterford," Bo said to

Aldon. "The High Peaks' very own little Martha Stewart would have sat me down on one of those leather sofas in that fancy camp with a flute of Dom and some of those silly little smoked salmon canapés she makes, and only then would she have told me that she was going to steal my company from me." He swigged and looked at her. "That pretty close to the way the evening was supposed to be scripted?"

Percy stuck her nose into the cup, even though she had no intention of drinking. "Pretty much," she said. "But I think I had it written in there somewhere that first I was going to ask you if you ever really, truly thought you'd get away with such a dumb scheme."

Bo gave his face a loose floppy shake that made Percy think of Winston. She hadn't fed the poor guy and wondered who would—now.

"It's no time for your little games, Percy," said Bo. "I don't mean to spoil the fun, but I know." When that failed to spark an immediate epiphany, he said, "I know everything," and eyed her. "Got a phone call about an hour ago. Heard all about you and Ivor Rhys."

Percy let out an involuntary sigh, which she immediately regretted.

Bo pressed his advantage. "I'm not stupid," he said, somewhat too proudly. "Figured there was a remote chance of getting my money back, so long as you were out of the picture." He treated himself to a swig. "Of course, had to find out a convenient way, which I must thank you for so thoughtfully providing."

"It's too late," she said. "The money's in a numbered account in the Caymans."

Bo stared at her dumbly. He gave his head a half-hearted nod and said, "So what?" When no response came, he said, "If you're not around in ten days to exercise your option, Realty Associates stays mine. It's a win-win situation—for me." He smiled a smile of sweet victory. "For you, I'm afraid it's—" He had to think for a few seconds before coming out with, "Lose-lose."

"Lose-lose," Aldon mumbled, finishing with a quiet laugh.

Bo gazed upon his little assemblage. "So I'm out five million. That's not a bad price to pay for the company." He swung the gin bottle toward the rows of barrels in the gloom. "A company that stands to make untold millions, now that your stepson and Lisa Perry are out of my way, not to mention your husband." Bo chuckled and treated himself to a private grin. "Fool came to me and actually insisted I put a stop to this." He patted the nearest fifty-five-gallon drum. "Said he'd go to the cops. Can you imagine?"

"I told him to. Said I'd turn the whole lot of you in if he didn't."

That news seemed to surprise Bo. He said, "You might just as well have signed his death warrant."

Percy allowed a moment of silence before saying, "That so."

"I mean, what choice did I have? Once we made the deal with— Well, let's just say that unless I lived up to my part of the bargain—providing a discreet disposal site—I would have wound up in the East River. As for Barron . . . well . . . it came down to self-defense, pure and simple. You, too, for that matter. They made it clear: I either play along, and they make me rich, or I don't, and I'm dead."

"Bo, are you so stupid that you don't realize that if it wasn't for me running interference, you'd have been arrested a couple of weeks ago? Only thing that's kept the local cops from putting two and two together is that I've got them wondering whether I might have murdered Barron. You should be grateful that until this afternoon you were far more used to me free than charged with premeditated murder."

Bo's smirk stayed affixed.

"Besides, the cops know about our little get-together tonight," Percy said. "In fact, I invited one along."

Instead of vanishing, as Percy had hoped, Bo's smirk grew while he slowly withdrew a small chrome-plated handgun from his front pants pocket. Looking uncertain as to what a person was expected to do with such a device, he shoved it in Percy's general direction and said, "Well then I guess we don't have much time to waste, do we, Aldon?"

Still, Bo needed seven minutes to deliver the requisite lecture, which Percy estimated a man less taken by the sound of his own voice could have summed up in eight good, functional Anglo-Saxon words: You should never have fucked with me, bitch.

Bo rambled along, detailing Lisa's brilliant plan about reinvesting the money generated by the chemical waste scheme—money that needed laundering anyway—in the Manhattan real estate market. He described the geometric profits to be reaped, which explained why there was no way Percy would have been allowed to get her hands on the company—ever.

Lecture complete, Bo turned to Aldon and said, "She's all yours," and turned to walk into the shadows.

Aldon cleared his throat in a where-are-your-manners way.

Looking almost sheepish, Bo turned and pointed the pistol at Percy. "Well for Christ's sake," he muttered to Aldon.

Aldon leaned the shotgun against one of the chemical drums and turned to face Percy, taking hard, shallow breaths. He had the fingers of both hands looped over his Mack truck belt buckle.

She was about to reach for the .357 when Aldon spread his arms and came directly toward her. Lacking the .357, Percy struck out with the Styrofoam cup. She brought it around in a half-circle, splashing Aldon's eyes with gin. He blinked, rubbed his face once with the back of his wrist, but didn't miss a step.

Aldon wrapped one arm around her and used the other to pull up her dress, moving his hand along her thigh. His fingers brushed the .357. There was a pause. Just long enough for Aldon to utter a single "Wha . . ." Then his fingers began clawing furiously for the revolver.

Percy brought her knee up abruptly between his legs. He expelled a blast of air and bent forward at the waist. She pulled the .357 away from him and at the same time managed a dancing step that put Aldon directly between her and Bo.

Bo fumbled his own little handgun into something approximating the firing position. The gun issued a pathetic crack, not much louder than a snapped piece of kindling. Aldon stiffened in his half-embrace of Percy.

She squirmed around him and leveled the .357 at Bo. Without aiming, she squeezed the trigger. The gun boomed and her arm jerked upward.

Plunkett put his truck in four-wheel-drive and, thinking to hell with it, veered off the shoulder of Stewart Mountain Road. The Dodge nosedived into a thicket of alder, came down with a hard *clunk* that caused the seatbelt to dig into Plunkett's chest. The truck then rose up, as if cresting a wave. Except it was cresting a boulder. The rear end bucked and wagged, first to the left, then the right, ripping the steering wheel out of Plunkett's hands.

A huge overhanging hemlock branch appeared in the headlights, coming directly at Plunkett's eyes. Involuntarily, he ducked, waiting for the crash of broken glass. Instead there was a dull sounding *womp,* followed by a vigorous brushing noise.

Plunkett raised his head just as the truck reared up, came back down with a *crunch* on its undercarriage, bounced once, ricocheted off the trunk of a white pine and landed in the center of Aldon's trail.

Plunkett drove as fast as he dared, given the darkness and the narrowness of the cleared area. He stopped the truck in front of the wooden doors and jumped out, not bothering to turn off the engine.

The snap of a small-caliber weapon was immediately followed by the authoritative boom of something big. Plunkett unholstered his pistol, and holding it in front of him with both hands, lunged inside.

In the whitish half-light cast by a Coleman lantern, Plunkett saw the blurry silhouette of Percy holding a revolver. Seated and using a fifty-five-gallon drum as a comfortable back support, Aldon Hewitt looked on. He would have appeared slightly bemused had he not been sitting in a pool of blood. Bo Scullin lay a few feet away on the floor. Bo rolled over and began to raise a small automatic pistol toward Plunkett.

"Police!" Plunkett hollered.

Bo's pistol kept coming.

"Drop it!" Plunkett said, aiming his own gun.

Plunkett and Bo fired simultaneously.

Bo lurched up from his semiprone position, a dime-sized red spot dead-center on his forehead. He fell facedown.

Plunkett swung his pistol to Percy. She still held her gun. "Drop it, Percy," Plunkett ordered.

Percy examined her hand. When her eyes met his, they looked mildly surprised at what they had seen down there. She shrugged. Dropping her gun, she said, "Hi, Plunk."

34

What became known as the High Peaks Murders were not closed—officially—until Friday, August 14, a clear cool day with the distinct crispness of autumn carried along on a northerly breeze, the third such day in a row.

Friday, August 14, was also the day Garwood Plunkett officially tendered his resignation as a New York State Trooper, and at noon sharp, the first client booked the services of G. Plunkett, Adirondack Guide.

Plunkett met the client on a stretch of the West Branch of the Ausable River locally known as The Islands. Less than five miles downstream from where young Duane Dockwheiller had hooked the corpse of Barron Quinell, The Islands stood at a point where the river unraveled into a series of channels separated by gravel bars. Below, the Ausable flowed in to Lake Everest. In years past, before the chemical spill, it had been Plunkett's favorite place to fish in late summer. As the water cooled, the big brown trout would begin to make their way upstream out of deep summertime hideaways in the lake. The Islands was their first stop.

Plunkett's client was there when he arrived. She had spread a red-checked tablecloth over the gravel. A basket was opened on the cloth, and beside it was a small cooler designed to hold a six-pack of cans.

The client herself was clad in full fly-fishing regalia: waders, vest, a wide-brimmed canvas hat—all brand new. A landing net wagged against her backside, and she held an eight and one-half foot graphite fly rod in her right hand. She looked good. As sexy as he had ever seen her. Plunkett told her as much.

"Yeah," said Linda. "Well you can get your mind off that right away. This is a professional relationship. I'm here to learn how to fly fish. You are here to instruct me."

"Giving up on spinning tackle and worms?"

Linda snuffed. "I'm not about to give up on anything. Not quite yet. Just thought I'd try . . ." She shrugged under the vest. "Plunk, this is the only way I figured I could get a few minutes together."

"Been a lot on my mind." Plunkett began to rig his own rod.

"I'll bet," said Linda. "You know. It wouldn't hurt to keep your friends up to date on things."

Plunkett didn't respond. He finished setting himself up and then asked to see Linda's rod. "Nice outfit," he observed.

"Your father," Linda said. "He picked it out for me." Then she added, "Can be a charming old guy, when he wants."

"So I'm told," said Plunkett.

"It was him who suggested we try here. Said the big one's would be coming back as soon as the water temperature started dropping, just like they did after the long, hot summer of thirty-six."

Plunkett fed out a little line and let his stone fly nymph drift in the current. "Read in the paper where the state biologists still claim the chemical spill killed them all off."

"You believe what you read in that paper . . ."

Plunkett shook his head. "Frankly, I don't know what to believe anymore." He made one halfhearted cast. "Rumor mill tell you what happened today?"

Linda was silent for a moment as she imitated Plunkett's feeding out line. "I believe the rumor mill even less than the papers," she said, barely audible above the swish of the river.

"Officially, it's like Percy said. Bo and Lisa had Aldon kill Barron once he got cold feet and threatened to go to the police about them offering the mob a handy toxic waste disposal site. Lisa ended up dead after Quentin persuaded her to cop a plea. Once again, Aldon did the honors. Next it was Quentin's turn. They found his body in a drum in the mine. Looks like Aldon may have killed the young hiker in the Dumpster over by Saranac Lake, but Culley—Sergeant Culley, as soon as his promotion officially kicks in—hasn't figured out how that fits yet."

"It ever cross Culley's mind that it might have been Percy that Aldon was working for all along—not Scullin?" said Linda.

"Guy named Blevins—president of Saranac Chemicals—says it was Bo and Lisa that set up the scheme. Claims they forced Percy off the board before there were the first hints of wrongdoing."

"Blevins, too," said Linda. When Plunkett looked at her quizzically she added, "Goddamn men tripping all over each other to protect her."

"Remember that fly-earring that I thought was such an incriminating piece of evidence? According to my father, she bought it the day after Barron's body was discovered."

"He remembered the exact day?"

"Said it wasn't often he got something as good-looking as Percy darkening the shop doors."

"Doesn't explain how it got down by the river?"

"Her lawyers say she went down to look at the spot where Barron was found—sentimental reasons."

"Sentimental," said Linda. "I bet. If it was me, I'd charge her with misleading a police officer—or whatever it's called."

"That was talked about, but there's no real evidence that she actively obstructed our investigation. Officially, there wasn't even an investigation to obstruct. Her lawyers'd just say it was a combination of circumstantial evidence and my overactive imagination. Besides, what did she possibly have to gain by making the police think she killed her husband?"

Linda stiffened her back. "What sort of guide are you, anyway? I'm paying good money to be taught to fly-fish. Come on."

Plunkett sloshed a few paces into the river until the water came up to his knees. He pointed the tip of his rod toward the center of the run. "Picture a clock. You start the rod at nine o'clock, bring it back to one o'clock." He did so and let the line uncoil behind him in a low, flattened loop. "Bring it forward and stop at eleven o'clock. Then let the rod drift down to nine o'clock."

Plunkett's line shot out across the run. He followed it downstream with his rod tip, mending with a series of little flicks. When it was directly downstream, he allowed the line to settle. "Not a damn thing," he muttered, and hauled back his line and repeated his cast.

"They're saying all the land that belonged to the company Percy's husband and Bo Scullin owned will get donated to the Department of Environmental Conservation to be set aside for good. Ten thousand acres—something like that," Linda said.

Plunkett watched the line's movement, his fingertips alert for bumps or tugs. "There was the potential for a huge lawsuit over the cleanup of the chemicals in that mine. Percy's lawyers turned out to be pretty shrewd politicians. They gave the Department the land in exchange for the state undertaking responsibility for the clean-up. Percy keeps the camp and two hundred acres."

"Only two hundred acres. Poor Percy," said Linda, making no effort whatsoever to hide her sarcasm.

"Quinell's and Scullin's company is bankrupt," Plunkett said. Bo cleaned out the till before he died. No trace of the money."

"Jeeze, you mean Percy might have to go out and work for a living. Have to let her know I have an opening for a dishwasher."

"Percy's out of the country. Indefinitely."

"Where?"

"No one knows. Or rather, no one's saying."

"She can do that? Just disappear."

"Not a thing anyone can do to stop her—legally."

Linda snorted and shook her head. "That figures."

"At least that's what her lawyers told me"—he paused—"when they broached the subject of me being caretaker of her camp while she's away."

-276-

"Wonderful. You working for Percy, too." Linda turned her back and uttered a sarcastic, "Caretaker . . ."

Plunkett tried another cast, with no luck.

"Maybe it's time you let your client get a cast in, guide," said Linda. She positioned herself in the river six feet upstream from Plunkett. "A clock," she said, and proceeded to perform a flailing exercise that left her line in a series of tight squiggles, the most distant of which was ten feet in front of her."

"Like this," said Plunkett, and demonstrated.

"Found a place to live yet?" Linda said.

"Got a few leads."

They were silent for a moment. Plunkett picked up his line and cast it across the river.

"I was thinking," Linda said, "about all that space I have up there above the restaurant. I could put a partition in. Rent half out to you. Say four hundred a month."

"Dunno," muttered Plunkett.

"Well, three-fifty then," said Linda.

Plunkett grinned. "Was the partition part I was questioning."

Linda brought her rod back vigorously and snapped it forward. Her line went across the river, straight and flat. She beamed. "That was easy enough." She blushed, saying, "Casting, I mean."

Her line drifted downstream.

"You get in any trouble—over shooting Bo?" she said.

"Just some routine stuff. Paperwork, really. It was pretty clear I had no choice."

"So that's it?" said Linda.

"Culley. The Troop Commander. Judge Conoscenti. They all seem satisfied."

"Percy must be satisfied, too," said Linda. "Things couldn't have worked out better for her if she had planned it that way. Plunk, it ever dawn on you that maybe Percy did? That maybe she set Barron up? She had to know what could happen, given Bo's business associates. That you were just one other little piece in Percy's grand plan—the piece that would pull the trigger on Bo for her?"

-277-

Plunkett was concentrating on Linda's line.

"What about you, Plunk? You satisfied with the way things turned out?"

He shrugged. "In a strange way, I suppose justice was done."

"But the way it was done—that doesn't bother you, as a police officer?"

"I'm a guide."

"Plunk, dammit—" She shook her head. "You knew all along, didn't you?"

Plunkett was silent.

"Right from the start, you knew, yet you—" She stopped. Swallowed.

"Maybe I ought to crack us a couple of beers," Plunkett said. "Change our luck."

He reeled in his line and made it halfway to the cooler before Linda screamed. He looked back in time to see her new rod bent until its tip touched the water, bouncing and jerking crazily in her hands, the line shooting off down river.

"Don't pull too hard on it," he called, running to her side.

"It's huge," she whispered.

Plunkett could see the steady bump, bump, bump of a big fish's tugging on her rod.

"Let him tire himself out," he said. "Lift your rod tip."

Linda did. The line began to rise. A brown trout that would have easily gone twenty-four inches burst from the water. It hung in the air just long enough to allow Plunkett and Linda a glimpse of its bronzed magnificence, then fell back. Linda's line snapped.

Neither could talk immediately. Plunkett looked at Linda's slack line in the current, happy that there was still at least one out there somewhere. But it didn't help the sick, hollow sadness deep in the gut that comes when a big one gets away. He stood there beside the river not knowing what to do next.

It was Linda who said, "You forgetting about those beers, guide?"

★ ★ ★

Coincidentally, a second, entirely different sort of fishing expedition was just about to get underway on the bone-fish flats surrounding Little Cayman.

The two Boddens, father and son, stood on a beach on the remote northeastern coast of the island. A flat-bottomed fiberglass boat was pulled up not far away with two fully-rigged, nine-foot-long, graphite fly rods resting in racks beneath the gunwales.

Young Bodden was waiting for a lift over to the airstrip for a flight to Grand Cayman. He wore a three-piece navy suit. In place of his usual gold chains, he had on a red tie held in place by a magnificent emerald-studded gold tie bar.

His father fingered the tie bar. "When did you get this?"

"Month or so ago. Gift from a friend."

"Very good friend, I should think."

Bodden senior was in a tattered pair of dress trousers that once might have been part of a banker's wardrobe, before someone crudely hacked them off just above the knees. His Oxford shirt was buttonless and its tails were knotted about his waist. Retirement had been kind to him. He was in far better physical shape and possessed far more of the family's rakish good looks than his desk-bound son, to whom he began repeating a paternal lecture.

"Never, never forget that Cayman Trustco's success rests firmly on client relations," the older Bodden said, not noticing that his son was mouthing the words as they were spoken.

Young Bodden glanced sheepishly at three puffy cumulus clouds that looked lonely and lost out over the Caribbean. The clattering of a vehicle making its way along the sandy track leading to the beach house became audible over the crunch of waves.

Young Bodden examined his tie bar. "Very well, Father," he said. "The draft for the five million is in the top bureau drawer."

His father nodded. "I was thinking of presenting it after dinner."

A faded red pickup bounced into the clearing between the beach and the scrub forest.

Young Bodden picked up his overnight bag and said, "Good luck."

A naughty twinkle came into his father's eye.

The truck stopped and the passenger door opened. The first thing that caught Young Bodden's eye was his father's fishing companion's hair. To his eye, it was the exact color of white gold. The second thing he noticed was the smile that spread across her face as she looked past him toward his father, who waited with one leg cocked on the bow of the boat. The smile was puckish, a few degrees to the right of center and bisected by a tiny gap between her front teeth.